Realisms in East Asian Performance

Realisms in East Asian Performance

Edited by
Jessica Nakamura
and
Katherine Saltzman-Li

University of Michigan Press • Ann Arbor

Copyright © 2023 by Jessica Nakamura and Katherine Saltzman-Li
Some rights reserved

This work is licensed under a Creative Commons Attribution-NonCommercial 4.0 International License. *Note to users:* A Creative Commons license is only valid when it is applied by the person or entity that holds rights to the licensed work. Works may contain components (e.g., photographs, illustrations, or quotations) to which the rightsholder in the work cannot apply the license. It is ultimately your responsibility to independently evaluate the copyright status of any work or component part of a work you use, in light of your intended use. To view a copy of this license, visit http://creativecommons.org/licenses/by-nc/4.0/

For questions or permissions, please contact um.press.perms@umich.edu

Published in the United States of America by the
University of Michigan Press
Manufactured in the United States of America
Printed on acid-free paper
First published October 2023

A CIP catalog record for this book is available from the British Library.

Library of Congress Cataloging-in-Publication data has been applied for.

ISBN 978-0-472-07642-0 (hardcover : alk. paper)
ISBN 978-0-472-05642-2 (paper : alk. paper)
ISBN 978-0-472-90384-9 (open access ebook)

DOI: https://doi.org/10.3998/mpub.12254299

The University of Michigan Press's open access publishing program is made possible thanks to additional funding from the University of Michigan Office of the Provost and the generous support of contributing libraries.

Contents

Illustrations	vii
Note on Transliteration and Names	ix
Acknowledgments	xi
Introduction: From Realism to Realisms JESSICA NAKAMURA AND KATHERINE SALTZMAN-LI	1

Part I: Revealing Realisms

1. Theatrical Realism on the Kabuki Stage:
   Methods and Theories ... 19
   KATHERINE SALTZMAN-LI

2. Stylized Reality on the *Jingju* Stage:
   Revisiting *Picking up a Jade Bracelet* as a Case Study ... 37
   XING FAN

3. Racing the Real: Korean Realism Theater and Racial
   Representation in Cha Bumseok's *Yeoldaeeo* ... 56
   SOO RYON YOON AND JI HYON (KAYLA) YUH

Part II: Real Life Onstage

4. The Subversion of Everyday Life: Neoliberal South Korea and
   the Theater of the Everyday in the Plays of Park Kunhyung ... 79
   KEE-YOON NAHM

5. From Realist Drama to Theater of the Real:
   Postsocialist Realism in Contemporary Chinese Theater ... 100
   ROSSELLA FERRARI

6. Three Kingdoms of Pain and Sorrow:
   Verisimilitude of Warfare Presented in *Pansori Jeokbyeokga*   126
   MIN-HYUNG YOO

Part III: Technologies

7. Mediated Laughter and the Limits of Realism:
   Laughing Letter and the *Kinodrama* Experiment in
   1930s Japanese Performance   143
   ARAGORN QUINN

8. Realism, the Real, and Mediated Reality:
   Hirata Oriza and Beyond   160
   M. CODY POULTON

9. Realisms in Japan's Eighteenth-Century Puppet Theater   175
   JYANA S. BROWNE

10. Costumes of the Present: Clothing and Realism
    in Traditional Chinese Theater   194
    GUOJUN WANG

Part IV: Evolving Realisms

11. Colonial Temporality, Diasporic Displacement, and Korean
    Realism in Yun Baek-nam's *Destiny*   215
    MISEONG WOO

12. The "Deep Realism" of Style: From Michel Saint-Denis
    to Huang Zuolin   233
    SIYUAN LIU

13. After the Colloquial: Legacies of Realistic Expression
    in Contemporary Japan   252
    JESSICA NAKAMURA

    Contributors   271

    Index   275

Digital materials related to this title can be found on the Fulcrum platform via the following citable URL https://doi.org/10.3998/mpub.12254299

Illustrations

1.1	Double page from the kabuki actor critique booklet *Yakusha genkindana* (1835).	28
2.1	Master performer Li Yuru as Sun Yujiao in *Picking up a Jade Bracelet*, 1956.	49
3.1	A scene from Cha Bumseok's *Yeoldaeeo* (*Tropical Fish*), 1966.	66
3.2	Various scenes from Cha Bumseok's *Yeoldaeeo*, 1966.	67
3.3	A scene from the 1971 movie adaptation of *Yeoldaeeo*.	71
4.1	*In Praise of Youth*, written and directed by Park Kunhyung, 2013 revival.	88
4.2	*Don't Be Too Surprised*, written and directed by Park Kunhyung, 2007 premiere.	93
5.1	*Thunderstorm 2.0* (*Leiyu 2.0*), directed by Wang Chong with Théâtre du Rêve Expérimental, New York City, 2018.	110
5.2	Performance of *World Factory*, a collective creation by Grass Stage directed by Zhao Chuan, Chengdu, 2016.	113
5.3	The documentary theater production *One Fine Day* (*Meihao de yitian*), directed by Li Jianjun with the New Youth Group, Beijing, 2013.	119
7.1	*The Laughing Letter* stage with screen visible stage right.	145
7.2	Stage layout of *The Laughing Letter*.	150
9.1	Tatsumatsu Hachirōbei operating a puppet in *Love Suicides at Sonezaki*, from *Mugikogashi* (1826).	181
9.2	The long rod mechanism for puppets developed by Bunzaburō, from *Shibaigakuyazue* (1800).	186
10.1	Illustration of the scene "Remaining Trace" in *Peach Blossom Fan*.	201
10.2	Photo of Mei Lanfang costumed as the female protagonist of *A Strand of Hemp*.	206
13.1	A promotional photograph from *Jiman no musuko*.	263

Note on Transliteration and Names

Studies in this volume rely on East Asian languages and their writing systems, in modern and premodern forms. Transcription and methods of romanization have been left to the discretion of individual authors based on current practice in their respective fields, and they sometimes differ between chapters. Romanized terms are given in italics, unless their usage is well established in English. All English-language translations are by individual contributors unless otherwise noted.

Throughout the volume, names have been written following the East Asian convention of family name before given name, except when referencing an author of scholarship published in English, including the contributors to this volume, or an artist whose name is customarily given in a different order.

Acknowledgments

We are fortunate to be colleagues at the same institution, where *Realisms in East Asian Performance* developed out of our mutual interest in theatrical realism and shared observations about its many manifestations in the performance forms we study. Our early conversations resulted in the conference Realisms in East Asian Performing Arts, originally scheduled for May 2020 and reorganized in an online format in October 2020. In this volume's journey from preliminary discussions to conference to book, we are grateful for the generosity of a number of parties along the way.

We first extend our gratitude to the scholars and performers who participated in the 2020 conference; their presentations and our discussions were critical in shaping the volume. We also thank the many people and UCSB campus units involved in the details of organizing and supporting the conference: East Asia Center academic coordinator Lisa McAllister and graduate student assistant Rebecca Wear for their problem-solving acumen and energy in planning and running a virtual conference and Eric Mills and Severo De La Cruz of our respective departments for coordinating finances during the lengthy process from conference through publication.

Cosponsorships for the conference came from our home departments of East Asian Languages and Cultural Studies and Theater & Dance, together with the departments of History, History of Art & Architecture, the Comparative Literature program, and the East Asia Center. Professor Abdulhamit Arvas graciously supported the project while still a colleague at UCSB. We also received conference funds from the Deans of the College of Letters and Science and a financial award and conference publicity assistance from the Interdisciplinary Humanities Center.

We are especially grateful to the Carsey-Wolf Center at UCSB, whose generous Faculty Research Support Grant aided us greatly for both the conference and the volume.

We thank the reviewers of the original volume proposal and later of the manuscript. Not only were we gratified by their recognition of the volume's potential, but their comments spurred us to further develop that potential into what we hope is a volume that will provoke ongoing discussion and research. Not knowing who those anonymous reviewers are, we express our sincere gratitude here.

The University of Michigan Press has been a dream press, and LeAnn Fields a dream editor for her expertise, enthusiasm, and ability to make a long and complicated process clear and smooth-sailing. We feel extremely fortunate to have seen this volume through under her guidance. It was a pleasure to work with editorial associates Flannery Wise and Haley Winkle as well as our project manager, Marcia LaBrenz, our meticulous copy editor, Daniel Otis, and the talented design team at the press. Profound thanks to Dr. Suzy Cincone, independent copy editor extraordinaire, who worked with us to prepare the final manuscript for publication.

The contributions of family and dear friends to a long-range project such as this one are less specific, more omnipresent. We each have those to whom we devotedly say, this wouldn't have happened without you, nor would it have been as meaningful.

Introduction

From Realism to Realisms

JESSICA NAKAMURA AND KATHERINE SALTZMAN-LI

In the Chinese *jingju* (Beijing Opera) *Picking up a Jade Bracelet*, performers replicate realistic gestures that include selecting a thread, passing it through the eye of a needle, knotting it, and embroidering a design onto a shoe. Contemporary South Korean director Park Kunhyung's *Don't Be Too Surprised* (2007) depicts the reality of the quotidian by putting the family bathroom onstage, where it becomes a site of self-violence. During the height of experiments with realistic expression after the influx of newly translated modern Western plays, the 1937 Japanese performance of *The Laughing Letter* integrated filmed and live scenes to create a hybrid form called *kinodrama*.

These examples, from the chapters in this volume, point to the many manifestations and potentialities of realism in East Asian performance. The astonishing accuracy with which the *jingju* actor reproduces delicate actions is one way that performers have long entertained through artful mirroring of familiar behavior. *Don't Be Too Surprised* showcases realism's capacity for social and political critique by staging an extreme vision of daily life to expose social inequities of the commodified everyday. *The Laughing Letter* highlights the ways in which theatrical realism is a dynamic concept: the production placed realistic expression as central to reevaluations of representation onstage with the advent of film, challenging emerging discourses of mediation.

As is apparent in the above examples, instances of theatrical realism are born out of a multitude of social and performance conditions. They illustrate the basic idea that what constitutes reality differs depending on place and time. The reality of 1930s Japan is drastically different from that of *jingju*'s nineteenth-century China, which is also radically different from South Korea in the twenty-first century. Given such diversity, we unsurprisingly find multiple representational strategies for recreating reality on stage. Accordingly, the examples presented in the chapters of this volume expose the fact that our long-established idea of realism as a nineteenth-century Western theatrical style is itself specific to a certain place and time.

Realisms in East Asian Performance offers inclusive views of realism that acknowledge the multiplicity inherent in representing reality. Contributors identify and historicize practices of realistic expression from the seventeenth century to the present to reevaluate entrenched ideas about realism's origins, occurrences, and means. Chapters demonstrate that realism appears in East Asia under different guises and to many effects, thus challenging assumptions about what it means to portray real life on stage. Some contributors also propose that realism need not be the only mode of presentation in a single piece or program, but may be interspersed with other modes of expression, including the spectacular. In making these arguments, our chapters collectively reevaluate acts of representation on stage, not just for East Asia, but for theater and performance studies more broadly.

Rethinking the History of Realism

In its focus on East Asia, *Realisms in East Asian Performance* works to upend the established history of theatrical realism, a history defined by the work of European and Russian artists, including Henrik Ibsen, Anton Chekhov, Konstantin Stanislavski, and August Strindberg, and in the work of American playwrights Eugene O'Neill and Arthur Miller and acting teachers Stella Adler and Lee Strasberg. Based on this orthodox history, theatrical realism appeared elsewhere only after Euro-Russian-American practice made its way across the globe, including into East Asia, with the importation of plays, theories, and production methods.[1]

As we assert, where scholarship in theater and performance studies is unable to disentangle itself from prevailing Western definitions of realism, our knowledge of theater suffers. The effects of this limited understanding are experienced in fundamental ways. The singular description of realism creates the false impression that the rest of the world follows the West in developing modes of representing reality. Further, the tendency of Western realism toward an all-encompassing naturalistic aesthetic reinforces lingering assumptions that many Asian performance forms are wholly spectacular and theatrical—in other words, not realistic to any degree. In East Asia, these assumptions are particularly applied to traditional performance forms, and some of our contributors aim to debunk this idea.

For studies of theater and performance more broadly, a definition of realism confined to Western origins limits our ideas of its representational force and interpretive possibilities. With postmodern reevaluations of form and narrative, theater and performance scholars have repudiated realism, exemplified by Elin Diamond's influential work from the early 1990s that criticizes the "life-like stage sign" that "reinforces the epistemology of an 'objective world.'"[2] This attitude toward realism continues in recent scholarship that avoids realism altogether even as we see an increase of verbatim and documentary theater. Studies that make clear efforts to distinguish their topics from any exploration of realism include Carol Martin's "theater of the real" about the popularity of these aforementioned forms (2012), Jacob Gallagher-Ross's "theaters of the everyday" (2018), and Lindsay Brandon Hunter's exploration of "mimetic theatricality" (2021).[3]

At the same time, in other recent theater and performance analyses, scholars have recuperated realism, highlighting its diverse applications.[4] As Roberta Barker, Kim Solga, and Cary Mazer assert in their discussion of realistic stagings of early modern drama, "though realist approaches can certainly lead to ideological traps . . . we emphasize that scholars and theater artists can acknowledge and deal with these problems *from within the multivalent idiom of realism itself.*"[5] Dorothy Chansky's *Kitchen Sink Realisms* (2015) and Sarah Bay-Cheng's "Virtual Realisms" (2015) have considered the role of realistic conventions in constructions of gender and questions of digital technology, respectively.[6] Amy Holzapfel's *Art, Vision, and Nineteenth-Century Realist Drama: Acts of Seeing* (2015) revisits nineteenth-century realistic drama to show that the aim was not conceived as simple objective depiction, but as an interweaving of subjective and affective qualities necessary to theatrical art.[7] Despite these wide-ranging directions, we nevertheless note that the touchstone of these studies remains an idea of realism that developed primarily in nineteenth-century Europe.

Scholars outside of theater and performance studies have shown that identifying realistic expression as a global phenomenon gives a clearer picture of realism's interpretive versatility. In special issues of *Modern*

Language Quarterly ("Peripheral Realisms," 2012) and *Novel* ("Worlding Realisms," 2016), scholars consider realism as a critical representational mode in areas of minor and world literature.[8] As Jed Esty explains in his article "Realism Wars" for the *Novel* special issue, realism has become a multivalent concept and interpretive framework, "vital to readers, writers, and critics of the global novel," and as his article title makes clear, a contested one.[9] Scholars in East Asian literature, art, and film have called attention to the rich instances of realism that exist in these fields. Marston Anderson troubled entrenched definitions of realism in literature in his 1990 *The Limits of Realism: Chinese Fiction in the Revolutionary Period*, and in the last five years, scholars have turned to realism as a means to investigate such topics as gender in film (Lewis), film theory (Yamamoto), remembrance (Mello), scientific illustration as a prehistory to photography (Fukuoka), and the avant-garde (Jesty).[10]

Realisms in East Asian Performance adds to this turn in scholarship in its focus on performance and in its expansive temporal scope. In contrast to most of these recent studies, which focus primarily on the modern and contemporary periods of the nineteenth and twentieth centuries, our volume's long historical inquiry, from the premodern to the contemporary, has allowed us to see longer processes of development of East Asian realisms. Prior scholarship on East Asian theater, some written by contributors to this volume, established the influence of Western realistic plays at key moments in the development of modern theater movements in China, Japan, and Korea.[11] Nineteenth-century Western realism was imported into Japan in the early twentieth century through translations of plays, and then moved into Korea and China through artistic exchange in the region, in part due to cultural transfer resulting from Japanese imperialism. While recognizing the significance of this movement of plays and ideas, our volume engages with some of the effects of the overwhelming focus on the importation of Western dramatic literature in East Asian theater histories. It allows us to work toward a corrective in analyzing the region's performance forms, and in the process, to expand how we understand theatrical realism globally. For example, in basing definitions of realism only on Western models, a significant incompatibility arises when we note that the primacy of the play script, and of the playwright and director as theater artists, is not universal. Such primacy leads to the relatively singular visions that have typically controlled the Western creative process from the late nineteenth century. Yet, as we explore in this volume, other hierarchies, troupe structures, and methods do not at all preclude realism. We have aimed at discovering the many possible conditions for realism in East Asia during and beyond this particular historical moment to consider additional factors and processes in these performance histories.

In locating case studies from an extended time frame, several key points have emerged across our volume. As mentioned earlier, some chapters discuss performance forms that mix realistic and nonrealistic conventions, showing how engagements with reality need not be sustained throughout a performance to have an impact or carry out their effects: a single production may stage particular elements based on real life, such as gesture, while other elements, such as scenery, may be abstract, imaginary, or fantastic. Other chapters draw attention to the ways in which traditional performing arts intersected, and continue to intersect, with modern theater forms that developed after the importation of Western realistic plays. We especially consider local realisms together with examples that incorporate imported forms and concepts, with some chapters adding to previous studies that have highlighted the ways in which Western realism had profound effects on emerging twentieth-century dramaturgy throughout the region, requiring artists to negotiate between multiple modes of realistic expression. Several take up the hold that socialist realism has had on manifestations of realism in modern and contemporary China, Japan, and South Korea, offering new cases and proposing new views on the topic. This work leads to another key contribution of the volume, to deepen our overall understandings of the role of realism in modernization processes and the central intellectual contribution of realism to modernity itself, not just in the West but in East Asia as well.

Many Realisms

To acknowledge the many ways in which theater portrays reality onstage and represents conceptions of "real life," "reality," and "the real," we refer to realisms in the plural. Sometimes the practices we identify remain grounded in the locality where they arose, sometimes they travel and are adopted and blended with conventions in other places, as in the case of Japanese *shingeki* in colonial Korea. The differing conceptions of reality that underlie realism's multiple forms onstage have operated under a number of terms. Volume contributors introduce vocabulary related to realistic expression, including the Japanese contemporary *kōgo* (colloquial) or simply the term *jitsu* (truth, the real) used in premodern theorizing to contrast with a paired term *kyō* (falsehood or fabrication); the

Chinese modern terms *xieshi* (realism or drawing from nature) and *xieyi* (defined by Siyuan Liu as "writing meaning"), which together are important for theorizing realism in twentieth-century Chinese spoken drama (*huaju*); and the modern Korean *sasiljuuigeuk* (realism theater) or the contemporary *ilsanggeuk* (theater of the everyday). Some of these terms are broadly applied, and others emerge in relation to a single theater form or at a specific historical moment. Investigating the applications of these terms contributes to new possibilities for theorizing theatrical realism overall and working toward definitions of realism that encompass a broad set of concepts and practices.

In expanding realisms and identifying realistic expression across sites in East Asia, our volume activates inter-Asian dialogues on theatrical production. We highlight the continuities and influences across the region, while also paying attention to local particularities. As Emily Wilcox reminds us in *Corporeal Politics: Dancing East Asia*, East Asia "does not simply refer to a collection of political units" or "a fixed or homogenous cultural community," but rather East Asia "points to a complex history of multidirectional exchanges, competing discourses and ideologies both internal and external to the region, and political struggles over East Asia—as a place, a transnational community, and a political idea."[12] As we have pointed out, such a "complex history" is apparent in the movement around East Asia of translated play scripts and theories that followed the introduction of modern Western theatrical realism. Some of our chapters further examine the ramifications of these exchanges. For instance, as Miseong Woo examines in her chapter, Korean artists adapted modern Japanese *shinpa* plays to foreground political commentary on imperialism. By examining realisms across East Asia, we acknowledge a longer history in which performance traditions have, for centuries, moved through the region and provided influences that sparked development of existing forms. We see such influence in Min-Hyung Yoo's chapter on realistic expression in the Korean storytelling performing art *pansori*, in which he examines the canonical work *Jeokbyeokga*, an adaptation of the Chinese *Romance of the Three Kingdoms*.

In bringing together research on theater throughout East Asia, and indeed from an international group of scholars offering different scholarly perspectives and methods, we hope to demonstrate the value, necessity even, of comparative intraregional studies to understand concepts in theater history. We work against what Aparna Dharwadker describes in "The Really Poor Theater" as a Western-centric historiographical tendency: "Since the mid-twentieth century European/Western figures in theatre have been linked to their non-Western counterparts mainly through the frameworks of interculturalism, Euromodernism, and Europhone cultural production."[13] Not only do we seek to counter this tendency, but given the long history of cultural exchange within the region, our volume highlights artistic influences and points of connection and contrast within East Asia, rather than between an East Asia often collectively conceived and a Western other. In other words, we elaborate on developments of realism in traditional and modern Asian performance cultures on their own terms instead of always in relationship to Western realism.

Realisms in East Asian Performance is organized by topic, and each of the volume's four parts brings together different performance forms, putting into fruitful conversation premodern, modern, and contemporary examples from across the region. Chapters in part I, "Revealing Realisms," foreground previously underrecognized occurrences of realism and their significances; chapters in part II, "Real Life Onstage," explore how realism manifests notions of the everyday and its potential for social and political commentary; chapters in part III, "Technologies," consider how developments in realism as a mode of representation have often gone hand in hand with the introduction of new technologies; and chapters in part IV, "Evolving Realisms," explore realism at moments of political, artistic, and social change to identify factors that affect developments in realistic expression.

Many of our chapters touch on more than one of the section topics. The chapters, in their variety, underscore the widespread practice of realism in East Asian theater, leading to our assertion that realism is neither a modern innovation nor an exceptional mode of presentation across the region. Our investigations show it to be pervasive, not only in the modern period, but at many points over the long theater histories of East Asia. While the chapters cover a diverse set of topics, our coverage is certainly not, nor could it ever be, exhaustive. Rather, the volume offers deep dives into practices from three areas in the region: China, Korea, and Japan. We bring together a combination of chapters that revisit forms and artists well covered in existing scholarship and chapters that introduce new topics heretofore under-discussed in English-language materials. Our choices are driven by efforts to begin to create histories of realism, a necessary step that makes possible our argument about realism's far-reaching presence. We hope that our investigations stimulate additional research, especially into areas in East Asia not covered in this volume as well as elsewhere in the world.

In what follows, we elaborate on each of the four sections and highlight the inquiries and the analytic and methodological approaches that guide them. We hope that the volume will be read not only for its specific studies of East Asian theater forms, but for the strong connections within a section and across sections that enable a deeper consideration of the workings of realism.

Revealing Realisms

Throughout the volume, we introduce new analytical inquiries to identify realisms and revisit the term to more fully empower its value in theater and performance analysis. Chapters in "Revealing Realisms" particularly ask, what can be revealed as a realistic element and what does such an identification mean? How might drawing attention to realistic practices alter how scholars write about these forms? By engaging with these questions, chapters in this section highlight a key intervention of the volume: to reevaluate theatrical forms and their histories for where we might find and analyze realistic representation, joining in Fred Robinson's call for theory to "react" to realism's "own non-linear development."[14]

To this end, two of the chapters explore what are usually called traditional performance forms, kabuki and *jingju*. Both have been considered for their high level of theatricality without due attention to their diversity of modes of presentation, including realistic conventions. In contrast, these chapters locate histories of realistic expression in these forms. Katherine Saltzman-Li examines recorded ideas and practices related to theatrical realism in kabuki, particularly exploring how actors prepared and trained for realistic portrayal during a foundational period of kabuki history (late seventeenth into the eighteenth centuries). She then proposes that realism was an important goal, not just in the early period, but throughout kabuki history, and that new engagements with realism consistently pushed significant developments in kabuki's long history as a popular performing art.

Categorizing something as "realistic" takes on methodological implications, as in Xing Fan's chapter, which seeks to move beyond the "haunting paradigm" of Western realism. In contrast to scholarship that positions *jingju* as separate from Western theatrical realism, Fan analyzes the performance text of the play *Picking up a Jade Bracelet* to reveal what she describes as "an alternative realist tradition." Like many chapters in this volume, Fan elucidates a specific performance history to make a clear break from entrenched imported definitions, calling attention to the ways in which notions of Western realism have simultaneously defined and limited ideas of *jingju*.

Soo Ryon Yoon and Ji Hyon (Kayla) Yuh similarly ask how makers of Korean realism theater (*sasiljuuigeuk*) presented aspects of their world in ways that differed from Euro-American theatrical realism. Through their analysis of Cha Bumseok's mid-twentieth-century Korean play *Yeoldaeeo* (*Tropical Fish*), they identify ways in which realism, in its process of worldmaking, shapes interrelated ideas of race, ethnicity, and nation. Like Fan, they challenge received perceptions of the controlling role played by imported Western notions of theatrical realism in understanding modern East Asian theater. Elaborating on the entangled histories of modernity, Western realism, and conflict across the region, they explore complex representations of race onstage as an effect of Japanese and American imperialisms, a topic that Miseong Woo also explores at the end of the volume.

Real Life Onstage

Chapters in "Real Life Onstage" explore enactments of everyday life and so-called ordinary people, teasing out the complex relationships between realism and conceptions of the quotidian, the ordinary, and the "common" person. More broadly, chapters in this section, as we see in the chapters in "Revealing Realisms" and across the volume, ask how realistic expression can reflect the world back to us and what strategies are used to do so. These chapters also explore connections between the everyday and realism's potential for engendering social and political commentary.

Two of the three chapters in this section investigate realism as it relates to contemporary East Asian theater to highlight how reevaluating the everyday has taken on a sense of urgency. Since the mid-twentieth century, theater artists across East Asia (and the rest of the world) have engaged with the quotidian, a focus that emerged along with influential scholarly theories of the everyday by such thinkers as Henri Lefebvre, Michel de Certeau, and, later, Lauren Berlant. In his chapter on contemporary Korean theater of the everyday (*ilsanggeuk*), Kee-Yoon Nahm applies these theories to the plays of Park Kunhyung. Nahm identifies aesthetic strategies in Park's plays, contrasting the earlier social realism of twentieth-century Korean theater with Park's contemporary theater of the everyday, in which Park highlights quotidian precarity and affective responses to ordinary life in neoliberal Korea.

Like Nahm, Rossella Ferrari explores realistic portrayals after a period of major societal change that fundamentally altered the everyday. Focused on twenty-first-century postsocialist China, Ferrari identifies the fragmentation of reality in a range of performances by Chinese artists. These works, she argues, present reality in the process of becoming, ultimately challenging the relationship between theater and reality. Underscoring a major point of the volume, Ferrari's chapter illustrates the complex, evolving, and dynamic connections between what is experienced as realistic and surrounding sociopolitical conditions. Nahm and Ferrari each distinguish contemporary representations of real life from the theatrical realism of early- and mid-twentieth-century East Asia discussed in chapters by Yoon and Yuh, Aragorn Quinn, Liu, and Woo, a distinction that Jessica Nakamura builds on in her investigation of realism in the work of contemporary Japanese artists.

Min-Hyung Yoo further diversifies relationships between realism and the everyday in his analysis of *Jeokbyeokga*, one of the five classics of *pansori*, a genre of Korean musical storytelling most likely originating in the seventeenth century. Yoo's everyday is that of men conscripted into war against their will and for reasons that had no specific bearing on their lives. An adaptation of the fourteenth-century Chinese novel *Romance of the Three Kingdoms*, *Jeokbyeokga* trades the Chinese novel's focus on heroes for the story of poor commoners forced into war. Analyzing four songs original to *Jeokbyeokga*, Yoo finds that the *pansori* makes its critique of the cruelty of warfare through its portrayal of common soldiers. Yoo's analysis contributes to a major point of the volume by highlighting how realism is entangled with its specific surroundings and how strategies of realism allow artists to comment on the world around them.

Technologies

This section focuses on the relationship between developments in realism as a mode of representation and the introduction of new technologies. While advances in technological aspects of theatrical production have been used to enhance the spectacular, our volume highlights how theater makers harness technological innovations in their portrayals of reality. As chapters in this section show, the advent of new media, such as film in the twentieth century, or significant new capabilities in existing forms, may usher in large-scale changes to representation, but smaller-scale enhancements to material conditions of theatrical production may also have large effects. In either case, this section explores how such changes can alter the ways that reality is shown and the ways in which a performance can be perceived as realistic.

Throughout modern theater history, film has been cast as a realistic and even authentic foil to the fabrication of theater. Aragorn Quinn analyzes how theater complicates ideas of accuracy and verisimilitude typically associated with film. His chapter looks at a key historical moment in early-twentieth-century Japan: the 1937 *kinodrama* (film/theater hybrid) production of Yagi Ryūichirō's *The Laughing Letter*, a landmark for its early integration of live performance and film with recorded sound. Against emerging discourses regarding the potential for accurate depiction of real life in film and other mediated technologies, Quinn argues that *The Laughing Letter* highlights the failures of such technologies, challenging the idea of filmic portrayals as more authentic. His chapter contributes to the historiographical work of many chapters in this volume, and its exploration of realism through the intersection of Japanese film and staged theater puts it in conversation with M. Cody Poulton's chapter on "mediated reality."

M. Cody Poulton shows how technological advancements in media continue to have a central role in the unfolding of realistic portrayals onstage. He investigates Hirata Oriza, a contemporary Japanese playwright who was influential in developing Japanese realistic style in the 1990s, situating Hirata's realism in relation to film, specifically with reference to the ideas of seminal film theorist Siegfried Kracauer. Poulton enriches our understanding of Hirata, a key figure in contemporary Japanese realistic expression, and moves us into the twenty-first century with discussions of later performance experiments in augmented and digital realities.

Both Jyana Browne's chapter on eighteenth-century innovations in Japanese puppetry and Guojun Wang's chapter on Chinese Ming dynasty theatrical costumes consider the physical means of representing reality. Browne writes of two kinds of realism during this heyday of Japanese puppet theater, with one developing after the other: emotional realism, found in the dramatic situations created by playwrights and the chanter's expressive delivery; and realism of the everyday, effected mostly by the movements of the puppeteer. Key to the emergence and later prominence of realism of the everyday were technical advances in puppet bodies and puppeteering. While contributing further to our understandings of the important role of the puppeteer, a role sometimes overshadowed in scholarship by playwriting and chanting, Browne's chapter illustrates how developments in theatrical technology and realistic expression are often interconnected.

Where Quinn's chapter considers ideas of representational authenticity, material authenticity is important in Guojun Wang's chapter on theatrical costumes as a technology that shapes perceptions. Wang explores the inter-relationship between the stage, sartorial styles, and society through costumes in contemporary styles, which he argues helped create a sense of realism for Ming dynasty (1368–1644) audiences. He then addresses how subsequent Qing dynasty (1644–1912) costuming disclosed new social and political realities. His exploration of changing practices in costuming across time creates bridges to the main inquiry of the next section.

Evolving Realisms

Chapters in this section further explore the relationships between realistic expression and the world offstage. While earlier chapters addressed the potential of realism for social and political commentary, contributors to this section share an interest in how realism evolves in conversation with social, political, and economic forces. These chapters identify and analyze modern and contemporary realisms at moments of major national and international change.

Miseong Woo's chapter highlights the political potential of realism against the backdrop of diaspora and colonization during the tumultuous period of 1910s Korea. She analyzes Yun Baek-nam's *Destiny* (1920), identifying it as a key production that marked Korean theater's transition from the influence of Japanese *shinpa* to the development of a Korean realism drama in the 1920s. For Woo, *Destiny* commented on current realities of the Korean peninsula, using the setting of Hawaii to put diasporic conditions in conversation with life in Korea under Japanese rule. As such, Woo's exploration of this transitional period in Korean theater history highlights the role of realism in commenting on social and political life even in the face of oppressive political conditions.

Siyuan Liu puts artistic influence at a politically and culturally critical moment in modern Chinese history at the center of his chapter. Liu examines how twentieth-century director Huang Zuolin moved away from the orthodoxy of *huaju* (modern spoken drama) based in Stanislavskian-inspired realism. He traces the impact of Huang's mid-1930s period of study in England with the antirealistic director

Michel Saint-Denis and the effect it had on Huang's *huaju* stagings. In reminding us that there were alternative non-Stanislavskian traditions of influence that also moved around the world, Liu opens up a productive reevaluation of the history of Western realism in East Asia and worldwide.

Jessica Nakamura similarly takes up the evolution of theatrical style in her chapter by examining the legacies of realistic expression in the generation of Japanese playwright-directors that followed Hirata Oriza. Examining representative productions of Iwai Hideto and Matsui Shū, artists who worked directly with Hirata, Nakamura considers their work as further developments of Hirata's *gendai kōgo engeki* (contemporary colloquial theater) realistic style. Analyzing Iwai's and Matsui's productions for new approaches to *gendai kōgo engeki* that have resulted in multiple theatrical aesthetics, she joins others in the volume in reevaluating the scope of realistic theater conventions and in considering realism's broader conceptual applications.

Over its thirteen chapters, *Realisms in East Asian Performance* highlights the richness of realism in East Asia and its range of practices, concepts, and styles. Multigenre, diachronic, and transnational, the volume explores the relations of realisms to tradition and modernity, and to the social and political embeddedness of theatrical practice. The volume demonstrates that realism is a productive lens for understanding performance cultures across the region. At the same time, by multiplying examples and analyses grounded in specific performance histories, it invites further dialogue about this key issue in theater studies overall, contributing, we hope, to a more dynamic idea of what constitutes the real and its representations onstage.

Notes

1. This thinking is in line with what Steve Tillis defines as the "Standard Western approach" to theater history in *The Challenge of World Theatre History* (Cham, Switzerland: Palgrave Macmillan, 2020).

2. Elin Diamond, "Realism and Hysteria: Toward a Feminist Mimesis," *Discourse* 13, no. 1 (1990): 61. See also Diamond's *Unmaking Mimesis: Essays on Feminism and Theater* (London: Routledge, 1997).

3. See Carol Martin, *Theatre of the Real* (London: Palgrave Macmillan, 2013); Jacob Gallagher-Ross, *Theaters of the Everyday: Aesthetic Democracy on the American Stage* (Evanston, IL: Northwestern University Press, 2018); and Lindsay Brandon Hunter, *Playing Real: Mimesis, Media, and Mischief* (Evanston, IL: Northwestern University Press, 2021).

4. Some such efforts go back a few decades: as early as 1992, Sheila Stowell

argued for "rehabilitating" realism, working against an ahistorical approach in considering dramatic styles, in "Rehabilitating Realism," *Journal of Dramatic Theory and Criticism* 6, no. 2 (1992): 81–88.

5. Roberta Barker, Kim Solga, and Cary Mazer, "'Tis Pity She's a Realist: A Conversational Case Study in Realism and Early Modern Theater Today," *Shakespeare Bulletin* 31, no. 4 (Winter 2013): 576; emphasis in original. Their introduction to *Shakespeare Bulletin*'s special issue traces the history of criticisms of realism, including that "realism's early critics saw in it a monolithic system of representation imposing a hegemonic ideology of the 'real'" (575).

6. See Dorothy Chansky, *Kitchen Sink Realisms: Domestic Labor, Dining, and Drama in American Theatre* (Iowa City: University of Iowa Press, 2015); and Sarah Bay-Cheng, "Virtual Realisms: Dramatic Forays into the Future," *Theatre Journal* 67, no. 4 (2015): 687–98.

7. Amy Holzapfel, *Art, Vision, and Nineteenth-Century Realist Drama: Acts of Seeing* (New York: Routledge, 2014).

8. Editors for these special issues explore multiple realisms "in the peripheries of the twentieth-century literary world-system" (Jed Esty and Colleen Lye, "Peripheral Realisms Now," *Modern Language Quarterly* 73, no. 3 [2012]: 269), and "across media, centuries, hemispheres, and political crises" (Lauren Goodlad, "Introduction: Worlding Realisms Now," *Novel: A Forum on Fiction* 49, no. 2 [2016]: 184). Works such as Peter Brooks's *Realist Vision* (New Haven, CT: Yale University Press, 2005) and Fredric Jameson's *The Antinomies of Realism* (London: Verso, 2013) examine European "realist novels" and painting and their legacy.

9. Jed Esty, "Realism Wars," *Novel: A Forum on Fiction* 49, no. 2 (2016): 319.

10. The topic of realism in East Asia has frequently appeared: at the center of Diane Wei Lewis's exploration of gender in film in *Powers of the Real: Cinema, Gender, and Emotion in Interwar Japan* (Cambridge, MA: Harvard University Asia Center, 2019); Naoki Yamamoto's genealogy of Japanese film theory in *Dialectics without Synthesis: Japanese Film Theory and Realism in a Global Frame* (Berkeley: University of California Press, 2020); Cecília Mello's *The Cinema of Jia Zhangke: Realism and Memory in Chinese Film* (London: I. B. Tauris, 2019); Maki Fukuoka's *The Premise of Fidelity: Science, Visuality, and Representing the Real in Nineteenth-Century Japan* (Stanford, CA: Stanford University Press, 2012); and Justin Jesty's discussion of "avant-garde realism" in *Art and Engagement in Early Postwar Japan* (Ithaca, NY: Cornell University Press, 2018).

11. See M. Cody Poulton's *A Beggar's Art: Scripting Modernity in Japanese Drama, 1900–1930* (Honolulu: University of Hawaii Press, 2010); and Siyuan Liu's *Performing Hybridity in Colonial-Modern China* (New York: Palgrave Macmillan, 2013).

12. Emily Wilcox, "Introduction: Toward a Critical East Asian Dance Studies," in *Corporeal Politics: Dancing East Asia*, ed. Katherine Mezur and Emily Wilcox (Ann Arbor: University of Michigan Press, 2020), 7. Wilcox provides an overview of critical area studies in East Asia and describes how the *Corporeal Politics* volume intersects this history.

13. Aparna Dharwadker, "The Really Poor Theatre: Postcolonial Economies of Performance," *Journal of Dramatic Theory and Criticism* 31, no. 2 (2017): 99.

See also Kuan-Hsing Chen's *Asia as Method: Toward Deimperialization* (Durham, NC: Duke University Press, 2010) for a discussion of the need for inter-Asian scholarly dialogue.

14. Fred Miller Robinson, *Rooms in Dramatic Realism* (New York: Routledge, 2016), xi. Like the other theater scholars who reevaluate realism, Robinson focuses on a particular history of Western realism, but his assertion that we should take "hold of [realism's] theatrical strangeness," referencing the language of Bertolt Brecht, is similar to our aim to cast our eyes differently on realistic expression in East Asia.

PART I | Revealing Realisms

1 | Theatrical Realism on the Kabuki Stage

Methods and Theories

KATHERINE SALTZMAN-LI

A Japanese story from a twelfth-century tale collection relates how a painter was able to draw a likeness of a missing assistant from memory with such exactitude that the man sent in search of the boy—whom he had never met—was able to find him based only on the remarkable accuracy of the portrait. Subsequently, the artist drew a rotting corpse that looked so genuine it severely frightened a man who took it for the real thing, even to the point of sensing its stench.[1] In the story, the artist's ability to convey reality to this degree is highly praised, but the results of his extraordinary technical skill also have an uncanny quality that conversely suggests something unreal, the real's other.

The near convergence in an image of the signifier and its signified is one ideal of artistic realism. Such semiotic iconicity comes to full fruition in the story of the painter. It is not, however, universally prized, and it has rarely been the goal in Japanese stage arts. While there are and have been forms of theater that fully aim to imitate reality by putting a slice of the real onstage (especially in modern and contemporary theater), kabuki's theatrical realism emerges out of the relations among a mix of presentational modes and is one performance experience among many. As such, it suggests that we might look more closely for realism wherever theater-making takes place, with the understanding that it need not be the only or even the predominant mode. And while likeness is a critical component, as Bert States wrote several decades ago, "the suspension of disbelief does not depend in the least on what we would today call a photographic likeness of the image to reality. It depends only on the power of the image to serve as a channel for what of reality is of immediate interest to the audience."[2]

In what follows, I look at contributing elements and practices of theatrical realism in kabuki, a form of popular theater in Japan's Tokugawa period 徳川時代 (1603–1868; also referred to as the Edo period 江戸時代 after its capital city Edo [modern-day Tokyo], or the early modern period). I give a historical account related to realism over kabuki's full 300-year early-modern history, but I particularly explore recorded practices and ideas from the Genroku era (a reign era from 1688 to 1704, but up to around 1740 to demarcate a flourishing cultural period). At that time, many lasting defining features of kabuki were first innovated, and it was also a foundational period for concepts of theatrical realism. I draw in particular on a wealth of Genroku-era records from those who created performances and those in the theater watching them. In the former case, I draw primarily on *geidan* 芸談, contemporary actor treatises devoted to actors' ideas on acting, including methods of preparing for roles; in the latter case, I refer mostly to the remarkable *yakusha hyōbanki* 役者評判記, the actor critique booklets published and commercially available for most of the Tokugawa period in connection with annual productions. They ranked actors and gave narrative criticism meant to reflect audience opinion.[3] I also draw on what scholars call *gekisho* 劇書, theater treatises and encyclopedias. Altogether, these sources help uncover the conditions and intentions behind theatrical realism in kabuki—especially at a critical formative period and then later at heightened moments of change—to reveal its occurrences, practices, and functions, and I argue that evolving conventions of realism were at the core of kabuki's vitality and longevity, from the earliest days into the twentieth century.[4]

Genroku Kabuki and Realism

We find realistic intention in all major forms of premodern Japanese performing arts, even the poetic and often otherworldly noh, or the fundamentally mechanistic and corporally divided bunraku puppet theater. A performing art more often noted for its spectacular elements, realistic practices go back to the earliest days of kabuki, which was founded right around 1600. In the early seventeenth century, dances and skits were performed first by women as *onna kabuki* 女歌舞伎 (women's kabuki) under the pioneering genius of a woman named Izumo no Okuni (d.

ca. 1613), and then by young men as *wakashu kabuki* 若衆歌舞伎 (young men's kabuki). One kind of skit performed in Okuni's kabuki showed encounters between lovers, mostly men meeting prostitutes. Another kind involved Okuni engaging with the spirit of a man named Nagoya Sansaburō, a man whom she had actually known before his death. The degree to which the lovers' meetings felt realistic to their audiences cannot be fully known, but these skits were based in contemporary relations in a way that was new to Japan's live theater. The encounters with Nagoya Sansaburō's spirit show noh's early influence on kabuki, yet the fact that the spirit was of a man the performers and possibly audience members had truly known may well have brought a certain frisson of the real to these skits of reunion.[5]

Concern with accurate, realistic portrayal became more conscious for actors and playwrights during the Genroku era, given particular impetus by the fact that all roles from the later seventeenth century, male and female, came to be performed by male actors only. This restriction, due to a government ban on female performers, led to two prominent features initiated in the Genroku era that are particularly significant to this study, the development of multi-act plays and the elaboration of role types. From the Genroku era, two of the three major types of kabuki plays that composed a full day's program were *jidaimono* 時代物 (period pieces) and *sewamono* 世話物 (plays depicting current life).[6] Overall, *jidaimono* are set in identifiable earlier historical periods with plots that focus on stories of political intrigue among samurai and nobles, while *sewamono* focus on characters and stories mostly out of the contemporary commoner classes. *Sewamono* are often described as relatively realistic, in contrast to the social and temporal remove of *jidaimono*. However, some acts in *jidaimono* are focused on the lower-down ramifications of the grand doings at high levels that typically frame the plot, and *sewamono* contain highly lyricized sections. Both types of plays balance stylization and aestheticization with realistic elements of situation, story, and sets.

Genroku plots frequently revolved around the transformation of characters within a play that leads to revelation of true identity, purpose, or nature.[7] These plots took different forms in the two major urban areas of the period. A disguise and revelation plot element for lead male characters was the basis of a characteristic Kamigata (Kyoto/Osaka region) genre of plays, *o-iemono* お家もの (plays focused on family conflict, usually between generations). A common plot revolved around a *yatsushi* やつし role, a young man in love with a courtesan, who needs to hide his identity when visiting his lover so that his family will not learn of the liaison.

The moment of revelation in these plays, the moment when the male character reveals his true identity, was referred to with the words *jitsu wa* 実は, meaning "in reality." Ironically, this is when he leaves behind the presentation of the intimate reality of a lovers' meeting to return to the plot, where fantastical elements might well take over.[8]

In Edo, the adoption of the wild and powerfully fierce qualities of the protector god Fudō formed the basis of the acting style of the top Edo *tachiyaku* 立役 (male-role actors) of the time, Ichikawa Danjūrō I (1660–1704; acted under the name Danjūrō I from 1675–1704) and his son Danjūrō II (1688–1758; acted as Danjūrō II from 1704–1735, then acted under the name Ichikawa Ebizō II until his death). Their characteristic acting and the roles they pioneered and performed in a style called *aragoto* 荒事 (wild acting) demand a particular physicality—intimidating appearance through an imposing stance and costuming that is typically oversized and visually arresting. The actor barely moves onstage, instead projecting his power in the manner of the frightening and menacing Fudō, statues of whom are placed in front of Buddhist temples. In other words, the actor transforms himself, becoming Fudō-like in order to take on the deity's daunting qualities and protective purpose: *aragoto* characters protect their worlds from the evil of political antagonists just as Fudō protects the dharma from evil. The principal character in the iconic play *Shibaraku* is a quintessential *aragoto* character in all respects. The play is also an example of a revelation plot, as the lead character is unknown to the other characters when he first appears onstage, later revealing himself and his purpose.[9]

Where did realism fit into such plots and styles of acting? Unable to watch performances, we can search for answers in the contemporary records: records on acting, many that were compiled by disciples (*geidan*), and the critique booklets (*yakusha hyōbanki*) from hired writers that were written to represent audience points of view. Along with theoretical statements found in treatises on kabuki (*gekisho*), inheriting in some cases pre-Tokugawa ideas, we can enter into the world of Genroku kabuki to a remarkable degree.

Theoretically, the most significant precursor to Genroku-era discussions of realism on the kabuki stage is found in the complex writings of the pioneering noh actor and playwright Zeami (1363–1443). Zeami's treatises address his guiding ideas for artistic practice, ideas that were manifold, often opaque, and that changed over time. In his early writings, he discusses *monomane* 物まね, literally "the imitation of things," which for him meant enacting certain kinds of roles according to ideas of appropriateness in depiction. For example, he argued that "the main point [of imitation] is to present a comprehensive likeness of the object portrayed," but he added that "the degree to which imitation is appropriate depends on the object of imitation."[10] He discusses the demands of imitating high-placed persons and the problems of imitating low-placed persons, all from a reception standpoint:

> [High-placed] persons are out of our ken. We should, nevertheless, make every effort to research their language and inquire into their demeanor and to seek their criticisms after they have seen our performances . . . it's not good to imitate too closely the vulgar habits of bumpkins and louts . . . don't imitate every last detail of even lower occupations. It would be unseemly to bring them before the eyes of high-ranking spectators. Presenting them with such a sight would be too vulgar and would offer nothing to draw their interest. Make sure you give this due consideration.[11]

Zeami's ideas about *monomane* changed over time to become less concrete, less concerned with the realism of appearances in character portrayal, and more focused on the externalization of interior states. Throughout he advocated balancing imitation with the two foundational arts in noh performance, dance and chant.

Given the formative importance of noh on early kabuki, it is not surprising to find the concept of *monomane* in Genroku-era records. The term was borrowed into kabuki to refer to the more fully developed, multi-act dramas that arose after the ban on *wakashu kabuki*, as contrasted with the dances and scenario-based skits that had been the main fare of earlier seventeenth-century kabuki: by the Genroku era, plays were referred to as *monomane kyōgen* 物まね狂言 or *monomane kyōgen zukushi* 物まね狂言尽, meaning "*monomane* plays."[12] Illustrations of theaters in the critique booklets of the early eighteenth century show the term written at theater entrances to describe what was then generally on offer.[13]

The elaboration of plots and the development of the characters within them in the new *monomane* dramas was aided by the addition of a new kind of troupe member, *kyōgen sakusha* 狂言作者, the men devoted to writing and mounting the multi-act dramas in collaboration with lead actors. Growing structural complexity and a new focus on dialogue and monologues led to this new need for playwrights. Actors were now judged in part on how well they delivered lines and created character through words. Thus, we might think of *monomane kyōgen* as meaning dramas at least partially centered on dialogue and its delivery.

We find comments in the critique booklets treating *monomane* as an element of the actor's art, and one taken into consideration in determining actor rankings.[14] Often the actor's ability is discussed through a comparison with another actor. For example, the 1703 critique of an actor specializing in comic roles (*dōkegata* 道外方) compares him with another comic-role actor of equal rank, saying that the actor under consideration is better at *monomane*, while the other has better timing.[15]

The term *monomane kyōgen* was eventually shortened simply to *kyōgen* or *shibai* 芝居 (plays), and *monomane* in the sense of the vocal delivery in an actor's performance changed to *kowa-iro* 声色.[16] As we have seen, *monomane* in kabuki was never used to indicate a comprehensive concept of imitation, but another term, *jigei* 地芸 (literally, "ground art"), also *jikyōgen* 地狂言 ("ground plays"), begins to appear in records of this time to refer to dialogue-driven scenes and the kind of acting they required, as opposed to music-accompanied dance plays and the skills they required. In the critique booklets, we find comments about an actor being good at *jigei* or in *jikyōgen*. Early on, for example, an *onnagata* 女方 (female role specialist) in a 1694 critique is said to be "good at lament scenes, dialogue, and *jigei*."[17] In a 1710 critique addressing the *jikyōgen* of an Osaka *wakaonnagata* 若女形 (young female role), we find "he's not young, but always seems young in his roles," certainly a compliment in terms of acting skill in *jikyōgen*.[18] A 1717 critique of an Edo *tachiyaku* begins with praise overall, and then especially praises him in *jikyōgen*.[19] The opposite also occurs, when actors are criticized as being poor in *jikyōgen*, or, less harshly, as "getting better at *jigei*."[20]

As with *monomane* references, actors are often compared. The *jikyōgen* of Yoshizawa Ayame (1673–1729) and Mizuki Tatsunosuke (1673–1745), two top contemporary Kyoto *wakaonnagata*, are compared in a 1701 critique to help make distinctions when both were given the same high rank.[21] In 1719, two actors with the same rank are compared, with "one better in *jikyōgen* though the other is more adored."[22] As late as 1732, it is said of an Osaka *wakaonnagata*, "no one compares with him in *jikyōgen*," and earlier, in a 1715 critique, the Edo *tachiyaku* Matsumoto Kōshirō is evaluated, not with respect to a contemporary actor, but with regard to former actors.[23]

These comments point to the establishment of *jigei* as a component of the new multi-act dramas and as a criterion for the success of an actor's art. Other words pointing to ideas of "reflecting" or "matching" reality can be found in the critique booklets and in other records of the time.²⁴ The combination of the various terms underscores Genroku attention to dramas that engage audiences with the reality of their world. To the extent that *jigei* points to a new realism, it also does so from being placed in a relational context: it is realistic in juxtaposition to the improvised skits and group dance pieces that had been the main fare of pre-Genroku performances, and to the evolving category of dance plays, *shosagoto* 所作事, which feature performances by star actors that highlight expression through dance movement.²⁵ It is also relational in the sense that *jigei*'s realism came from a new awareness of acting with others—less about the earlier strutting of individual stuff, relatively speaking—which led to new kinds of character interactions on stage and new expectations from audiences.

Anecdotes and teachings of famous actors have been recorded, often by disciples, into the treatises known as *geidan* 芸談 (teachings on art). *Geidan* are an invaluable source for ideas about how actors thought about and prepared for realistic portrayal in this new era of greater collaboration. As recorded in the treatise *Kengaishū* 賢外集 (*The Kengai Collection*), among the teachings from pioneering Kamigata male-role actor Sakata Tōjūrō (1647–1709) on preparing for *jigei* roles, we find "no matter the role, the actor's objective is always to reproduce [*utsusu* うつす, imitate or reproduce] reality [*shinjitsu* 正真, reality or truth]."²⁶ However, at this phase of working out just what meeting that objective entailed, he adds an echo of Zeami's exhortation that theater is a form of entertainment and that the reality of some characters will interfere with its basic purpose: for Tōjūrō, a beggar "should not be played according to reality."²⁷ The reason is because it would violate the goal to entertain and the idea that in kabuki "we want everything to be thoroughly splendid [*kabi* 花美]."²⁸

In an anecdote in the same treatise, Tōjūrō gives an example of his method of preparing roles through observation and enquiry, in this case by grounding his performance in an unexpected encounter that was similar to the one he was to play onstage:

> [S]ince I have never done such evil business, I have been very embarrassed about how to act the part. . . . I have been troubled by this night and day and came to the conclusion that unless I was fortunate enough to meet such a man and find out what his feelings were, I would not learn a thing about this seducer's role. Now my wish has been granted [due to his encounter with a woman who

attempted to seduce him, allowing him access to the feelings of an adulterer even though he fled the woman's attempt] and I have learned how to play it.²⁹

Actor Arashi San'emon I (1635–1690) went even further, actually setting up the situation he would play on stage in order to experience it. He purposely made his young lover jealous to learn how to act a lovers' quarrel. Observing the lovers' spat, Tōjūrō is recorded as saying, "It's not the moment for quarrels with boyfriends, come on, come on; rehearse, rehearse!" to which San'emon replied that that was just what he had been doing: "From the moment when I handed out the first wine-cup up to the cup of reconciliation that we have witnessed, including the jealous boy and the people who calmed him down, I have remembered it all. This is the rehearsal for the next play."³⁰ He ends the retelling of the encounter by saying, "Ask any actor and he will say that invented scenes are bad [作りたる事ハわろし], and truth [*makoto* 実] is good."³¹

For *onnagata*, some top actors insisted that offstage reality should underlie onstage realism. The practice of living like a woman at all times was most memorably recorded in the treatise *Ayamegusa* あやめぐさ (*The Teachings of Ayame*), comprising the ideas of star Genroku-era *onnagata* Yoshizawa Ayame (1673–1729):

> The *onnagata* should continue to have the feelings of an *onnagata* even when in the dressing room. When taking refreshment, too, he should turn away so that people cannot see him. To be alongside a *tachiyaku* [actor of male roles] playing the lover's part, and chew away at one's food without charm and then go straight out on the stage and play a love scene with the same man, will lead to failure on both sides, for the *tachiyaku*'s heart will not in reality be ready to fall in love.³²

In another teaching, Ayame emphasized an idea of appropriateness over spectacle. He describes a visit to a temple at plum-blossom time. Other spectators were taken with some rare flowers on display and ignored the plum blossoms, even though they were at their height of beauty. Ayame continues:

> Yet the only part that drew my interest was where there were some excellent arrangements of plum-blossoms. I was filled with admiration for the skill with which the ordinary flowers were arranged. In *onnagata* acting it is the same sort of thing—the basis of the art is not

to depart from a woman's feelings. Should he try to be out of the ordinary, or make it his first object to be unusual, or make strength the fundamental of his performance, rare though his flowers may be, it does not follow that one can ever say that they are good ones.[33]

Ayame's "woman's feelings" are better understood as an "*onnagata*'s feelings," that is, they are part of the creation of the kabuki female. Yet the necessity of offstage existence as a kabuki woman—in physicality, gestures, and feelings—proposes that realism occurs exactly through the connection between offstage and onstage behavior, situations, and appearance, no matter how constructed or idealized they may be.

Role Types and Realism

Kabuki is an art of transformation that not only manifests in plots such as the Genroku *jitsu wa* plays and later plots that hinge on revelations, but also in the body of the actor. While all acting involves degrees of transformation, kabuki acting requires actors to adapt their physicality to play certain kinds of characters on a regular basis, whether specializing in female or male roles. At least since both women and young men were banned from the stage by the mid-seventeenth century, kabuki has been a theatrical art grounded in role types. The essentializing of human characteristics into role types, a fundamental of many world theater forms, establishes conventions in characterization that function as starting points for role creation. From acting to playwriting to troupe composition, role types are central to many aspects of kabuki, a fact reflected in the critique booklets where actors and the discussions of their performances are organized according to role type (see figure 1.1).

All kabuki role types require training one's natural body into idealized gender representations purposed for the art. Dance lessons have long been the fundamental early-childhood start for all kabuki acting careers, but most subsequent training focuses on specific role types and roles, learned according to the methods of predecessors and mentors. In the process of training and performing, the actor takes on the patterns of expression that transform his natural body into a "kabuki body" meant to express itself through movement, vocalization, and gesture associated with role types.[34]

Role-type specialization is initially chosen according to family lines. However, an actor can be pushed by his father/mentor to train under a different master if it better suits his inherent qualities and capabilities.

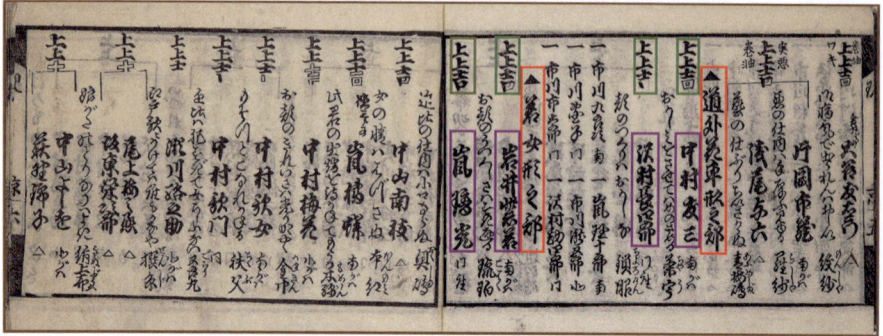

Figure 1.1: Double page from the kabuki actor critique booklet *Yakusha genkindana* 役者現銀店 (1835) showing organization by role types. Role-type names, under the solid black triangle headings, are outlined in red. Actors are listed accordingly and ranked. The names of the first two actors whose roles fell under the highlighted types are outlined in purple, and their rankings, above their names, are outlined in green. Courtesy of the C. V. Starr East Asian Library, University of California, Berkeley.

Most actors play either female or male roles; only a small number of very talented actors have made a success of performing both. Such actors are referred to as *kaneru yakusha* 兼る役者 (actors who can play many kinds of roles, especially with regard to gender division). This kind of actor has been an exception to the rule that a goal of actor training is to form a specific physicality. In *Ayamegusa*, we find, "If one who is an *onnagata* gets the idea that if he does not do so well in his chosen career he can change to a *tachiyaku*, this is an immediate indication that his art has turned to dust. A real woman must accept the fact that she cannot become a man."[35] This quote is a reminder that some *onnagata* actors idealized a practice that made a fiction of everyday life in order to generate a sense of reality for their onstage presence.[36]

The idea that role type and role choices should find some basis in an actor's own personal qualities holds for all role types, female or male. A section on role types in a 1750 treatise on kabuki addresses the issue of role-type suitability, ending with the statement, "It is dangerous in the art of acting [*yakusha michi* 役者道] for an actor to play roles not suited to his talents [*waga michi naranu michi* わが道ならぬ道]."[37] More recently, this idea is expressed with the word *nin* ニン (one's person, personal qualities). One's *nin* must match a role in some significant way. "His *nin* is right" (ニンがいい) or "his *nin* is well suited to this (kind of) role" (ニンがかなう) are phrases that acknowledge the match.[38] *Nin* encompasses physical and other attributes of the actor, which form a foundation for the kabuki body that the actor develops and presents over the course of his training and career. Where an actor's *nin* connects with role type, role choices, experience, and abilities, possibilities exist for expressing something real.

The kabuki body has been described as "not fundamentally a body that exists in real life. It is an embodied image of an illusion."[39] This statement may be true, but a kabuki body that gradually forms itself through daily practice and performance has every possibility of conveying a sense of the real to an audience immersed in the conventions of the art. Having trained and learned a role according to a predecessor's methods, an actor's own characteristics and acting strengths later mold his performances. Over time, performance *kata* 型 (forms or patterns) practiced by specific actors and acting lines develop for portraying characters associated with specific role types; in Tokugawa-period practice, these *kata* should not be seen as mitigating a sense of the real, but rather as a well-honed method for creating it.

From the Genroku era, the number and kinds of role types gradually increased, offering greater initial precision in characterization: from simple distinctions by gender, age, and good vs. bad, to greater differentiation in age/gender types (young, middle-aged, old), and then to more specific types in terms of nature, such as distinctions in male characters between evil and truly evil role types (*katakiyaku* 敵役 vs. *jitsuaku* 実悪), with subcategories such as evil aristocrats (*kugeaku* 公家悪) and sexy villains (*iroaku* 色悪). This increase continued throughout the eighteenth century and after, with the addition, for example, of wise male roles (*sabakiyaku* 捌き役) and martial women (*onna budō* 女武道). The greater type specificity led to more nuanced possibilities for playwrights and actors in depicting social realities and cultural concerns, and a nineteenth-century flurry of new genres incorporating new subtypes and staging elements demonstrated that kabuki was a performing art attuned to evolving outside circumstances.

Realism in Post-Genroku Kabuki

As we saw in the earlier discussion of Genroku kabuki, the blend and balance of fiction and reality formed the foundation of kabuki's theatrical realism. Tōjūrō wrote that "the actor's objective is always to imitate reality," but in accordance with the dictates of the art as a form of entertainment.[40] More real and less real are meant to balance and highlight each other in the creation of convincing representation. The seminal Edo-period playwright Chikamatsu Monzaemon (1653–1725) was famously reported to have said that theatrical art is where the real (*jitsu* 実) and the unreal (*kyo* 虚, falsehood) come together: "Art is created in the membrane separating the real and the unreal."⁴¹ Attention to the relationship between the real and unreal, which forms a foundation for kabuki's realism, was of theoretical and practical concern throughout kabuki history. A Kamigata treatise aimed at playwrights from the century after Chikamatsu again addresses the intersection of the real (in this case, *makoto* 誠, truth, reality) and the unreal (*uso* 嘘, falsehood):

> A teaching from long ago has the adage, "While there are fabrications [*uso*] that seem true [*makoto*], do not speak of truths that seem false." Plays clearly express a fiction, causing people to cry and to laugh, and you must create this fiction not only through persuasion, but also by considering shifts in popular taste. You must understand that the creation of realistic fiction is the hidden aim of the playwright.⁴²

There is a specific echo here of Chikamatsu's ideas: Chikamatsu had suggested that externalizing his characters' interior, normally unspoken thoughts and emotions discloses truth, an example of "fabrications [speaking words that would never be spoken aloud] that seem true [expressing a character's real feelings]." The later treatise also insists on the playwright's awareness of "shifts in popular taste," drawing attention to the importance of social and cultural contexts in the creation of onstage realism. What can read as realistic changes over time, thus the exhortation to playwrights to stay attuned to the offstage world.⁴³

In the nineteenth century, new play genres were tied to presenting new realities. *Kizewamono* 生世話物 (plays that feature characters from lower levels of society, for example thieves and other outlaws) told stories of harsh, desperate lives; such plays were increasingly prevalent in the waning Tokugawa period, and were created and performed through further refinements in role types. Edo's last traditional head playwright, Kawatake Mokuami (1816–1893), contributed plays in several evolving late-Tokugawa and early-Meiji (1868–1912) genres.⁴⁴ As a pupil of the master *kizewamono* playwright Tsuruya Nanboku IV (1755–1829), Mokuami also developed the subgenre of *shiranami mono* 白浪物 (robber plays). Moving into the Meiji period, as kabuki began to radically change, he developed two other new genres, both of which reflect greater experimentation through new engagements with the real. The first was *katsureki mono* 活歴物 ("living-history" plays), championed by Ichikawa Danjūrō

IX (1838–1903), that placed a new emphasis on historical accuracy by portraying and costuming historical figures according to the customs of their time. The second was *zangiri mono* 散切物 ("cropped-hair" plays), *zangiri* referring to the short haircuts and other Western-influenced fashions of Meiji Japan that are featured in these plays.[45] Even so, like other nineteenth-century playwrights, Mokuami employed old techniques to portray the new realities, relying on established plot structures, dialogue and narration, acting and vocal delivery, and the musical *kata* that are integral to kabuki. He was especially famous for lyricizing his plays with dialogue in poetic meter (*shichigo chō* 七五調, alternating lines of five and seven syllables) together with the frequent use of the nineteenth-century lyrical narrative musical style of *kiyomoto* 清本. He put his beautiful lines in the mouths of his commoner and robber characters, once again present the real within a kabuki framework that always demanded balance between the real and the unreal.

The new genres attempted different forms of realistic portrayal, whether in *kizewamono* with characters based on contemporary lower-level members of society, or in *katsureki mono* with the idea of historical accuracy. To an extent, these were surface changes, but it cannot go unnoticed that attempts to modernize kabuki involved engagements with depicting the real, as had been the case in the Genroku era and at subsequent points in Tokugawa kabuki's long history.[46]

The new Meiji genres had a short stage life. These experiments in reorienting kabuki through incorporating the real in ways that broke with earlier conventions, including the "living history" plays and the attempt to reintroduce women actors, pushed the boundaries of kabuki realism and marked those boundaries by their failure. The late-Tokugawa and Meiji experimentations with depicting the real could not keep pace with the new social and cultural changes, and the connections between offstage life and onstage performances that underlay kabuki's theatrical realism and fed kabuki as a popular art could not be maintained. Supporting structures (playwriting methods, management and financial systems, and playhouse arrangements, to name a few) changed drastically, and kabuki was on its way to becoming a showcase classical theater. Rather than simply new genres, such as Mokuami contributed to kabuki's evolving relationship to the real, new performing arts emerged that met the needs of this experimental time, and kabuki slowly came to reflect a world sealed off from everyday relevance. When connections to offstage life were broken, it lost much of the basis for its brand of theatrical realism.

Conclusion

Okuni's genius was to entertain for her time, whether in temporary performing venues or the most exalted social site, the imperial court where she was invited to perform. In retrospect we see this as a period when the start of a long peace after constant warfare was marked with new forms of entertainment. Okuni's group dances and skits of everyday encounters established the rudiments of a performing art that remained attuned to the artful depiction of life's realities.

Constant flux and innovation, often through opportunistic appropriation from other performing arts, are among the most consistent attributes of Tokugawa-period kabuki throughout its several centuries. I argue here not only that realism was a consistent component of the actor's art, and in general a recurring representational mode in kabuki at least since the Genroku era, but that its various manifestations over time kept kabuki relevant and popular for its full Tokugawa run. In Genroku materials, we find that some actors were very concerned to draw from personal or observed experiences to prepare their roles, even to the point of forcing those experiences on others to understand their characters' situations. We also find references to conventions that enabled the representation of real conditions. For example, in explaining that plain white garments were worn under outer garments to represent naked skin, one treatise explains that no one found it unreasonable or unnatural (*muri* 無理) "because people are accustomed to seeing what is a practice handed down from the past, that white cloth should serve for skin. So that the audience should accept it as natural [*shizen* 自然] is, I suppose, again only natural [*shizen*]."[47] As with defining characteristics of role types, conventions lead to naturalization, which in turn lead to possibilities for theatrical realism.

From the Genroku era, actors and playwrights alike carefully considered the mix of imitation and artistic license—the real or truth, and the unreal or falsehood—in theoretical statements and production choices, which led to various manifestations of realism. By freeing the discourse on theatrical realism from an all-or-nothing expectation, we clear the way for more accurate theater histories. On examination, realism played a significant role in propelling changes during kabuki's long early-modern history, where major artistic and formal developments were linked, at least in part, to new engagements with enacting the real. This observation revises the narrative of established scholarship that holds that realism in kabuki only became important with the importation in the late nineteenth and early twentieth centuries of Western realism, which resulted in the creation of wholly new types of plays, aims, and viewing experiences. By contrast, my examination has led to the recognition of realism's long-term significance in kabuki and Japanese theater history.

Scholars as diverse as Richard Schechner and Judith Butler have long since made clear that the realities of our behaviors and daily living are themselves learned and constructed; therefore, it should not be surprising that what we perceive as real onstage must also be constructed and accepted. In kabuki's history, these constructions, or conventions, convincingly and renewably engaged audiences with offstage experience and gave insight into contemporary life. Performances blending the real and the unreal, the everyday and the spectacular, brought imaginary and real worlds before the eyes of audiences, presenting real life in a world of entertainment. Early on, Sakata Tōjūrō theorized these blends and practices for kabuki actors, advocating for observation-based character portrayals while not violating the basic purpose of kabuki as an art of entertainment and beauty. Over several centuries, kabuki's theatrical realism emerged and re-emerged out of this negotiation, and a significant force driving kabuki as a popular art form over such a long period was that it never lost its connection to the realities of everyday existence or its grounding in extravagant theatricality.

Notes

1. The tale collection is *Konjaku monogatari shū*. An English translation of this tale, "Kudara no Kawanari the Painter Competes with the Craftsman of Hida," can be found in *Japanese Tales from Times Past: Stories of Fantasy and Folklore from the Konjaku Monogatari Shu*, trans. Naoshi Koriyama and Bruce Allen (Tokyo: Tuttle Publishing, 2015), 164–66.

2. Bert O. States, *Great Reckonings in Little Rooms: On the Phenomenology of Theater* (Berkeley: University of California Press, 1985), 185.

3. In most years, the booklets were published two times a year, with separate volumes for each of the three major urban centers of the period, Edo, Osaka, and Kyoto.

4. Kabuki was not uniform during any of the highlighted periods discussed in this chapter. At any given time, there were differences in practices, but also interchanges, between the major urban centers of Edo and Kamigata, in preferred play content and acting styles, play structures, play preparation and ways of composing programs, kinds of audiences, and ways of experiencing a day at the theater. In examining realism over kabuki history, I offer glimpses into a huge topic, but they are carefully chosen to introduce the salient issues.

5. The main character in many noh plays is a ghost, brought to appear

onstage through the prayers of a priest. With the aid of the priest, the ghost recounts a critical experience in its life, with the hope of release from its lingering effects in order to achieve Buddhist enlightenment. In contrast to noh's ghost characters, often of historical figures from long ago who are typically caught in spiritual torment, Nagoya Sansaburō was not only a man of the time (he seems to have died in 1603), but his appearance onstage had a secular purpose and contemporary flavor.

6. The third major type is *shosagoto* 所作事 (dance plays). *Jidaimono* are multi-act plays, usually without a close plot follow-through from one act to the next, whereas *sewamono* are typically tightly constructed three-scene plays. The ways in which these two types of plays intermixed in programs varied over place and time; they were sometimes separate, and sometimes *sewamono* were interspersed between acts of the *jidaimono*.

7. Character transformation and revelation are also important in post-Genroku plots. For example, *modori* もどり characters reveal a "return" to true allegiances, and tour-de-force acting is fully focused on transformation in *hengemono* 変化物, plays in which an actor takes on several roles, transforming from one to the other before the audience's eyes.

8. Audiences flocked to these plays to see the love scenes between the male and female characters, whose interactions were understood to depict encounters that could actually occur between customers and courtesans in courtesan houses. Few in the audience would actually have been able to set foot in a courtesan house, but social interest was high. Top actors would have the opportunity to interact with courtesans, and the observation-based role preparation discussed here could bring realistic portrayal to their performances in these plays.

9. My English translation of *Shibaraku* can be found in *Kabuki Plays on Stage: Brilliance and Bravado, 1697–1766*, ed. James Brandon and Samuel Leiter (Honolulu: University of Hawaii Press, 2002), 42–65.

10. Tom Hare, *Zeami: Performance Notes* (New York: Columbia University Press, 2008), 31.

11. Hare, *Zeami*, 31.

12. "Plays" is a translation of the word *kyōgen*, the term used to refer to plays during much of the Tokugawa period.

13. For example, see the illustration in the Edo critique booklet of 1714 in *Kabuki hyōbanki shūsei* (歌舞伎評判記集成 *Collected Kabuki Critique Booklets [First Period]*), ed. *Kabuki hyōbanki kenkyūkai* (Tokyo: Iwanami Shoten, 1974), 5: 431.

14. See *Kabuki hyōbanki shūsei*, 2: 209, regarding the high-ranked Yoshizawa Ayame. As part of his critique, we are told that "he bases [his acting] in *monomane*" (物まねをたねとして). The same words begin the critique of the not-highly-ranked Kaneya Kingorō later in the same critique booklet (2: 265), showing *monomane*'s use as a measure of evaluation, and also showing that the actor may or may not succeed in his *monomane* acting.

15. *Kabuki hyōbanki shūsei*, 3: 376.

16. The term came to refer to practices of imitating actors' voices and delivery.

17. *Kabuki hyōbanki shūsei*, 1: 580.

18. *Kabuki hyōbanki shūsei*, 4: 436.

19. *Kabuki hyōbanki shūsei*, 6: 424.

20. *Kabuki hyōbanki shūsei*, 8: 249.
21. *Kabuki hyōbanki shūsei*, 3: 38.
22. *Kabuki hyōbanki shūsei*, 7: 361.
23. *Kabuki hyōbanki shūsei*, 10: 322 and 5: 606, respectively.
24. For discussion of examples taken from the critique booklets of the terms *utsuru* (映る, 移る) and the nominalized *utsuri* (映り, 移り), see Matsuzaki Hitoshi 松崎仁, *Kabuki, jōruri, kotoba* (歌舞伎・浄瑠璃・ことば *Kabuki, Jōruri, Words*) (Tokyo: Yagi Shoten, 1994), 345–58.
25. The point is often evident in the critique booklets, as for example in one from 1712 comparing an actor's *shosagoto* with his *jigei*. *Collected Kabuki Critique Booklets*, 4: 624.
26. Charles Dunn and Torigoe Bunzō, ed. and trans., *The Actors' Analects* (Tokyo: University of Tokyo Press, 1969), 223. This book has both the original Japanese and a translation, both of which I reference in my discussions. I also compared this version with another Japanese version: Shuzui Kenji, ed., *Yakusha rongo* (役者論語 *Actor's Analects*) (Tokyo: Iwanami Bunko, 2003).
27. Dunn and Torigoe, *The Actors' Analects*, 222.
28. Shuzui, *Yakusha rongo*, 65.
29. Dunn and Torigoe, *The Actors' Analects*, 130.
30. Dunn and Torigoe, *The Actors' Analects*, 93.
31. Dunn and Torigoe, *The Actors' Analects*, 93.
32. Dunn and Torigoe, *The Actors' Analects*, 61.
33. Dunn and Torigoe, *The Actors' Analects*, 62–63.
34. Watanabe Tamotsu uses the term "kabuki body" in Watanabe Tamotsu et al., *Kabuki no shintai ron* (歌舞伎の身体論 *Theories of the Body in Kabuki*) (Tokyo: Iwanami Shoten, 1998); see 1–30.
35. Dunn and Torigoe, *The Actors' Analects*, 55.
36. See Watanabe, *Kabuki no shintai ron*, 10–16, for further discussion of this issue.
37. From the 1750 treatise *Kokon yakusha taizen* (古今役者大全 *Encyclopedia of Past and Current Actors*), in *Nihon shomin bunka shiryō shūsei* (日本庶民文化資料集成 *Collection of Materials on Japanese Popular Culture*), ed. Geinōshi Kenkyūkai (Tokyo: Sanichi Shobō, 1973), 6: 12. What I have translated as "talents" is the idea of the artistic profile the actor has developed through training and performing.
38. *Nin* ニン literally means "person" (sometimes written as 人), but more generally, "personal qualities." For further discussion of *nin*, see Watanabe Tamotsu, *Kabuki no kotoba* (歌舞伎のことば *Kabuki Words*) (Tokyo: Taishukan Shoten, 2004), 184–89.
39. Watanabe, *Kabuki no shintai ron*, 3.
40. Watanabe, *Kabuki no shintai ron*, 9.
41. My slightly altered translation based on Donald Keene, trans. and ed., *Anthology of Japanese Literature* (New York: Grove Press, 1955), 389.
42. Katherine Saltzman-Li, *Creating Kabuki Plays: Context for Kezairoku, Valuable Notes on Playwriting* (Leiden, NL: Brill, 2010), 208. The treatise is *Sakusha shikihō: Kezairoku* (作者式法・戯財録 *Valuable Notes on Playwriting: A Methodology for Playwrights*, 1801). "Realistic fiction" is literally "fabrications that seem real" 誠ら

しきうそ. The treatise is concerned with playwriting in the latter half of the eighteenth century. For further discussion of the pairing of *jitsu* and *uso*, see *Creating Kabuki Plays*, 98–104.

43. This treatise also contains more specific advice on the mix of the real and the unreal in a section devoted to plays based on recent sensational events. To create such plays, the treatise recommends combining factual accounts and gossip—the real and the unreal—to appeal to the audience's knowledge and interest in the event. See Saltzman-Li, *Creating Kabuki Plays*, 104–8.

44. "Last traditional head playwright" means that he functioned in the theater as those in his position had before him, as the top member of a hierarchy of men who wrote and helped produce plays. After Mokuami, this group system changed.

45. Mokuami also wrote in several other genres, notably for present purposes, *jitsuroku mono* 実録物, a term that refers to literary and dramatic works based on contemporary records, with the idea of transmitting truth through fictional forms. While *jitsuroku* fiction was written in the Tokugawa period, in drama it is a Meiji-period genre in which old plays were rewritten to play with the idea of truth and the real. An old play title is typically preceded by the word *jitsuroku*, as for example, the famous Edo-period play *Kanadehon Chūshingura* 仮名手本忠臣蔵, rewritten as *Jitsuroku Chūshingura*.

46. Other Meiji plays that engaged with the real and were associated with changes in kabuki were the many war plays produced at the time of the Sino-Japanese War of 1894–1895 as part of *shinpa* 新派 ("new school" kabuki, as opposed to the "old" Tokugawa kabuki).

47. Dunn and Torigoe, *The Actors' Analects*, 114.

2 | Stylized Reality on the *Jingju* Stage

Revisiting Picking up a Jade Bracelet *as a Case Study*

XING FAN

Realism has become a haunting paradigm for modern literature and art in China as a whole.[1] As Marston Anderson observes, from its beginning as a promise of cultural transformation around the turn of the twentieth century, realism "continues to have considerable rhetorical—and political—bite in China today: the literature of each major period of political thaw . . . has been applauded as a salutary return to the 'realist' tradition of preliberation fiction."[2] The trajectory of *jingju* 京剧 studies during the twentieth century echoes this obsession with realism except for one inconsistency: *jingju* was assumed to lack a preliberation realist tradition to which it could return. Rather, referred to as *jiuxi* 旧戏 (old drama) or *jiuju* 旧剧 (old theater)—sometimes as a primary example of *jiuxi* or *jiuju*—from the 1910s to the 1940s,[3] *jingju* was actually construed as a symbol of traditional China that was considered "hypocritical, conservative, passive, constrained, classicist, imitative, ugly, evil, belligerent, disorderly, lazy, and prosperous only for the few" since day one of the New Culture Movement.[4]

This interpretation explains how *jingju* studies may have developed what amounts to a paradoxical identity obsession with realism during the past century. On the one hand, changing interpretations of realism—Ibsenism as defined by Hu Shi, socialist realism imported from the USSR, revolutionary realism (in combination with revolutionary romanticism), new realism, and post-socialist realism—have been used as prescriptions for *jingju* dramatic literature. On the other hand, however, academic effort during the past century has focused on defining an independent cultural and aesthetic identity for *jingju* performance by juxtaposing it with realism. In this paper, I argue that the obsession with justifying (and demarcating) *jingju*'s independent cultural and aesthetic identity as a parallel to Western theatrical realism fails to consider that the construction is both framed and constrained by a Western conceptualization of not only theatrical realism, but of theater itself. In *jingju*, the performer—not the playwright—is centered in the creative process, and literature is one layer of a performance text. *Jingju*'s performance text, composed with carefully chosen and polished vocabularies in literature, directing, acting, music, and spectacle (costume, makeup, scenery, lighting, and special effects), embraces theatrical realism through a stylized reality onstage. I revisit *Picking up a Jade Bracelet* 拾玉镯 (*Shi yuzhuo*), a play from the *jingju* traditional repertory, as a case study to illustrate how this stylized reality is constructed in a three-dimensional way in alignment with *jingju*'s stage principles.

Beginning in the 1910s when Ibsen was introduced in China,[5] Chinese scholars searched for strategies with which to identify and articulate the differences between *xiqu* 戏曲—Chinese indigenous theater—and Western realist theater. Overall, although "realist" is not always clearly defined—and even when it is, the definitions vary—*xuni* 虚拟 (pretense) and *chengshi* 程式 (conventions) are pinpointed as the two signatures denoting *xiqu* as unrealist, antirealist, and/or nonrealist. As May Fourth intellectuals attacked China's *jiuxi* while promoting Western theatrical realism, Zhang Houzai (1895–1955) in 1918 voiced perhaps the strongest defense of *jiuxi* for its distinctive approach to acting and the stage.[6] First, employing *jiaxiang* 假像 (pretense) based on *chouxiang* 抽像 (abstraction), *jiuxi* was economical and efficient. For example, one could perform riding on a horse by simply holding a whip and raising a leg. In this way, "anything can be presented on stage, despite how substantial its quality or quantity."[7] Second, *jiuxi* had *guilü* 规律 (principles) for all actions. These principles did not restrict acting, but on the contrary offered the boundaries of a space in which performers enjoyed full freedom. And third, *jiuxi* was emotive because of its music and song. Recognizing music as a key component of *jiuxi*, Zhang emphasized the irresistible power of song in expressing sentiments. Zhang's arguments on pretense and principle highlighted two key features for defining *xiqu* performance, accentuating a disengagement from concrete objects with a concomitant freedom to independently develop principles by which to create theater.

Most likely because Zhang delivered this defense as an invited response to specific criticism of *jiuxi*, he, in his own words, "only made it to mention several of *jiuxi*'s strengths, but did not cover others."[8] It was Yu Shangyuan (1897–1970) and Zhao Taimou (1889–1968), two leading figures of the National Theatre Movement during the 1920s, who carried this theoretical task forward.[9] With the overarching vision of "producing Chinese theater by Chinese, for Chinese audiences, and with Chinese sources,"[10] the National Theatre Movement acknowledged the legitimacy of *xiqu* as an Eastern theatrical form and re-examined its conceptualization of theater and practices on stage. In 1926, Yu Shangyuan established a parallel between two pairs of arts. One pair was realist painting vs. presentational painting, which Yu called "pure fine arts";[11] the other pair was realist/*xieshi* 写实 ("writing reality") theater vs. nonrealist/*xieyi* 写意 ("writing meaning") theater. It was through this juxtaposition that Yu strongly advocated for the value of *jiuxi* as "pure art."[12] Yu's analysis concluded that, as a nonrealist/*xieyi* performing art, *jiuxi* performance clearly defined the stage as an area that both the performer and the audience remained conscious of at all times while the audience was viewing a performance; *jiuxi* acting employed symbols, such as the whip, to efficiently and effectively present actions without the limitations of real objects; and *jiuxi* performance offered a unity of music, song, and dance that appealed bodily, emotionally, and intellectually.[13] In 1927, in a nuanced discussion of the direction of theater in the future, Zhao Taimou acknowledged *jiuju*'s style as an achievement for which Western artists were longing in the context of the "expansion of the anti-realistic movement" in Western theater.[14] Zhao emphasized the significance of *chengshi*: "One characteristic of *jiuju* is *chengshihua* 程式化 (conventionalization). [For example,] to wave a whip is to ride on a horse, an arm gesture may push and open a door, tables and chairs may represent a mountain, flags are a carriage, four soldiers can represent a troop, and a circle can represent a trip of thousands of miles. . . . I argue that we should absolutely keep these."[15]

Qi Rushan (1876–1962), an important adviser of Mei Lanfang (1894–1961, one of the Four Great *Dan* master performers of *jingju* during its heyday), shared Yu's and Zhao's approach to realist/nonrealist theater categorizations. Elaborating on the essence of *guoju* 国剧 (national drama)—also a term for Chinese indigenous theater and often referring to *jingju* throughout the 1920s and 1930s—Qi approached it from an evolutionary perspective, positing "nonrealist/advanced vs. realist/primitive" categorizations within China's indigenous theatrical forms.

He theorized that *meishuhua shidai* 美术化时代 (period of aestheticization) was a phase of theater development more advanced than *xieshi de shidai* 写实的时代 (period of the realist), and identified *pihuang* 皮簧, synonymous with *jingju*, as an exemplar of the aestheticized form.[16] In aestheticized forms, in contrast to primitive forms, "much dance-acting is included in performance. All kinds of movements now have principles. Song, speech, body language, and facial expressions all have aesthetic principles. Not only are movements not allowed to be realistic but also facial expressions are not allowed to be real. In summary, there is 'no movement that is not dance, no sound that is not music.'"[17]

In the People's Republic of China since the 1940s, in the process of establishing, articulating, and defending *xiqu* performance as a unique and complete system—in the context of fostering the new China's national cultural identity in different political climates—the narrative gradually settled down to confirm *xiqu*'s *xieyi* style and highlight its *xuni* acting, use of *chengshi*, and synthesis of artistic methods.[18] For example, in 1957, Zhang Geng (1911–2003), one of the key proponents in defining *xiqu* aesthetics, identified five "formal characteristics" of *xiqu*: first, *xiqu* performance relies heavily on acting techniques and strict *chengshi*; second, *xiqu* performance requires a synthesis between acting and other artistic elements; third, based on the previous two characteristics, the rhythm of *xiqu* performance is flexible, with focal scenes elaborately presented and the rest as succinct as possible; fourth, based on the previous characteristics, *xiqu* performance transcends space and time; and fifth, *xiqu* performance features diverse methods and sources.[19] In an article in 1990 highlighting his "decades of work on *xiqu*,"[20] Zhang focused on two points while discussing the foundation and manifestations of *xiqu* aesthetics. First, as a *xieyi* theater, *xiqu* pursues *sheni* 神似 (spiritual similarity)—as opposed to formal/physical similarity—in character portrayal, which is based on a vivid and precise depiction of the character's inner world through role-type-specific acting techniques. Second, different from *huaju* 话剧 (spoken drama), and "in particular the realist *huaju* during the nineteenth century," *xiqu* transcends space and time on the stage, employing a "combination of *xu* 虚 (intangible, nonrealistic, and/or nonmaterial) and *shi* 实 (tangible, realistic, and/or material) in performance which is based on song and dance."[21] This pairing of *xu/shi* manifests in both stage properties and acting while implementing these stage properties, and as Zhang states, "the combination of *xu* and *shi* does not have fixed rules but changes according to the situation."[22] This framework has been consistent in official theorizations of *xiqu* aesthetics in the PRC.

As generations of twentieth-century scholars, all employing different strategies, teased out interpretations of the differences between *xiqu* and Western realist theater, *xiqu*'s independent cultural and aesthetic identity was proposed to be conceptually discrete yet parallel to Western realist theater: *xieyi* theater as a parallel to *xieshi* theater. Although specific strategies gradually changed from gap-spotting—focusing on sharpening distinctions between *xiqu* and Western realist theater, to problematization—with an interest in negotiating realistic elements within *xiqu* as nonrealist theater, the theorization of these "realistic elements" did not reach beyond acknowledging their existence. Furthermore, the tension between literature and stage practice, and the interrelations among those "realistic elements" in major artistic aspects—as well as the strategies to explicate them—remained vague. Most recently, Fu Jin (b. 1956), a leading scholar in *xiqu* studies, discussed the inadequacy of using *xuni, chengshi,* and *xieyi* to describe the aesthetics of *xiqu* acting, because "*xuni* and *chengshi* are frequently seen in different arts and *xieyi* is especially vague."[23] Fu proposed to approach the system of *xiqu* acting as "three interconnected layers: techniques, role types, and schools of performance."[24] Fu's proposal advocates attention to genre-specific practices; however, it does not offer a theoretical framework for approaching *xiqu*'s cultural and aesthetic identity, for two reasons. First, techniques, role types, and schools of performance are also frequently seen in many classical performing arts, as *xuni* and *chengshi* are seen; and second, *xuni, chengshi,* and *xieyi* speak to *xiqu* as a synthesis of major artistic components, including literature, directing, acting, music, and spectacle, whereas Fu's proposal is limited to acting.

Earlier, I framed this century of academic effort as part of a paradoxical identity obsession with Western ideas of theatrical realism because this effort is inherently self-contradictory. Taking *jingju* as an example, the "*jingju* is nonrealist" approach is based on a foundational belief in Western ideas of theatrical realism—at best, Western outlooks on presentational art and representational art—as the *original* premise: the exemplar to which all others must be contrasted and compared. With this approach, the realistic elements found in *jingju* performance are defined in terms of the concept of Western theatrical realism, and consequently, this definition makes it nearly impossible to explain or theorize them in a nonrealist theater, beyond acknowledging their existence. Realism in *jingju*, I argue, manifests in a different fashion from sporadic or random realistic elements. To better understand *jingju*'s independent cultural and aesthetic identity, it is imperative to acknowledge its alternative realist tradition: a stylized reality onstage that is based on *xuni* acting and represented through *chengshi* in performance text. In the following section, I use *Picking up a Jade Bracelet* (hereafter *Bracelet*) as the primary case study for analysis. This choice of case study is not meant to offer a generalized discussion of the *jingju* stage; rather, it is intended to offer a point of departure from which to decontextualize realistic elements in performing arts from Western conceptualizations of dramatic literature, dramaturgical structures, and acting techniques.

Bracelet's earliest performance record appears in *Dumen jilüe* 都门纪略 (*A Brief Introduction of the Capital*, published 1845 and reprinted 1910).[25] The earliest extant script was printed in 1912.[26] Featuring a romantic encounter between Sun Yujiao 孙玉娇 and Fu Peng 傅朋, *Bracelet* is the opening episode of *Shuang jiao qi yuan* 双娇奇缘 (*Serendipitous Encounters with Two Fine Ladies*). Today, *Bracelet* is often staged as a short, standalone production of forty to fifty minutes. In the succinct plot, Sun Yujiao helps her widowed mother run a small business raising and selling fighting roosters. Home alone one day, she feeds the roosters and sews while watching them outside the front gate of her home. Fu Peng, a young military commander who has inherited that title from his father, happens to pass by and immediately falls in love with Sun. Using the excuse of purchasing a rooster, Fu courts Sun and leaves a jade bracelet on the ground as a token of love. Shy and hesitant, Sun eventually picks up the jade bracelet and accepts it. Sun's neighbor, Aunt Liu, witnesses all of this. After Fu leaves, Liu tests Sun, who at first denies her interest but later asks Liu to be her matchmaker. Sun gives Liu an embroidered shoe as her love token for Fu. The production ends with Liu promising Sun that she will come back with Fu's response in three days.

Bracelet offers a strong case for how *xuni* is the foundation of stylized reality on the *jingju* stage. Contrary to the long-standing, dominant theory that *xuni* accentuates nonrealist theatrical aesthetics, I call close attention to the fundamental principle of *xuni* acting, which is being both accurate and true to life. On the *jingju* stage, *xuni* is always—and only—a method for pursuing the sense of "being real" onstage. In *Bracelet*, the accuracy and truthfulness to life in acting is applied in three areas: movement arrangement, space regulation, and stage properties.

The purpose of movement arrangement, often with musical accompaniment, is to give movements representing daily life a strong sense of reality. *Xuni* acting is at the core of the solo scene featuring Sun Yujiao embroidering her shoe.[27] Sitting in a chair, Sun leafs through a book in which she has previously placed colored threads between different pages. After a couple of attempts, she finds the right match for her shoe. She takes one thread out of the skein, knots the rest of the threads, and puts them back in the book. She then splits one thin thread into two thinner ones, hangs one on her left arm, and puts the other one back in the book. She takes a needle from her hair bun and pins it on her apron. She takes the thread from her arm, holds one end, bites off its tip, and gently spits the fiber out. Making sure that the fibers stay together, she takes the needle from her apron and inserts the end of the thread through the needle eye. She then pins the needle on her pants and sees that the two tails are of approximately the same length. She holds the end of the right tail between her teeth, and uses both thumbs, index fingers, and middle fingers to rub the left tail so that the thread is tight. She then takes the right tail in her right hand, fastens the end of the tightened left tail between her teeth, and uses both thumbs, index fingers, and middle fingers to rub the right tail. While working on both tails, her eyes swiftly shift focus between the two tails. When both tails are tight, she puts them together and rubs them between her palms to twist them into one firm thread. She takes the needle from her pants, holds it with her left thumb, left index finger, and left middle finger, then runs her right thumb, right index finger, and right middle finger from the top to the bottom of the firm thread three times; each of these movements is accompanied by a sound effect provided by the spike fiddle. Holding the two ends of the thread, she then gently tests its firmness with her teeth three times, each of which is accompanied by a different sound effect provided by the spike fiddle. She uses her right hand to make a knot, passes the threaded needle to the right hand, picks up her shoe upper fabric with her left hand, and begins to embroider.

For this section, the performer does not use a real needle or thread, but the movements, the order of those movements, and the body language itself are purposefully designed to look realistic. More importantly, details that support the "reality" of sewing are given meticulous attention. Master performer Xiao Cuihua (1900–1967, male) stressed that "when rubbing the right tail [after fastening the end of the left one by the teeth], the reason why the left hand should be lowered first before joining the right hand is to 'reveal' the left tail in *xuni* acting [by moving the hand around the thread that is not physically present]."[28] When Sun embroiders, Master Xiao stressed, "performers should pay attention to the length of the remaining thread, because it should be shorter stitch by stitch; only by this, will it look real. At the same time, before bringing the needle through the fabric for each stitch, she should gently straighten the remaining thread so that it will not make a knot. Through these movements, [performers] will 'truthfully' present the needle and the thread in *xuni* to the audience, and also portray the character's manner."²⁹

Stylized reality on the *jingju* stage also manifests in a meticulous regulation of space that prioritizes precision of action and movement in order to nurture the perception of onstage reality. In *Bracelet*, Sun Yujiao's solo performance includes action in three spaces: her room, the yard outside of her room, and the street outside the front gate that leads to the yard. Her room door and the front gate—and the three spaces they demarcate—are all represented through *xuni* acting on a stage with only one table and two chairs. A comparison of the performance texts of two master performers illustrates how precise positioning of the room door and the front gate plays a significant role in character portrayal.

When the production opens, we see one table and two chairs, positioned at upstage center. Master performer Xiao Cuihua's version begins with Sun Yujiao's entrance, followed by her self-introduction delivered while sitting in a chair, indicating it is in her room. Sun then goes to the yard, opens the chicken coop door to let chickens out, and feeds them in the yard. She then opens the front gate and herds the chickens out to the street for some air. Hearing someone's steps, she rushes to herd the chickens back to the coop, but then realizes that she is mistaken. She moves a chair and sewing utensils to the front gate, which is a side-by-side double door. She closes one side of the double door, leaving the other one open, sits down behind the closed panel, and begins to embroider. Master Xiao's choice of Sun's final stage position is as follows: "Here, my choice is to open one door panel and to close the other, and to have Sun put her chair behind the closed panel, approximately thirty to sixty centimeters away, so that passers-by do not see her but she can observe the street. This matches her 'shy' personality, and it conforms to [a young woman's demeanor in] a feudal society. When she meets Fu Peng, this [positioning] can also help acting."³⁰

Master performer Li Yuru's (1924–2008, female) version has the same beginning but includes two major differences in the following sections. One is that Sun directly herds the chickens out of the front gate to feed them. Master Li's reasoning is that "it is not quite clear [to feed chickens in the yard first and then herd them out of the front gate], because there are too many locations to portray in too short a period of time: chicken coop, yard, and street outside. With too much detail, [all the positions] may be vague to the performer, and become even more vague to the audience."³¹ The other major difference in Li's version is that, after feeding the chickens, Sun does not herd them back, but moves her chair just outside the front gate and begins embroidering while watching the chickens. Master Li particularly comments on the differences between her version and Master Xiao's version of this final positioning: "Master Xiao's version [of sitting behind a half-closed front gate] is truly beautiful, but [I am afraid that] it is not always clear to the audience. In addition, some say that a young woman at that time should not simply appear like this in public space. I think she sells roosters, so she needs to do business with customers, often in public. At the same time, she is also watching her chickens while sewing outside of the front gate. So I don't think it is anything abnormal."[32] Despite these different approaches, Master Li confirms the connection between these two versions: "I strictly followed what I learned from Master Xiao. To put it simply, it is the precision in *xuni* movements. For example, [during a single performance] I never change the positions for the front gate, for herding chickens, for doing sewing, and for picking up the jade bracelet; I do so to convey the sense of reality to the audience."[33]

In the above discussion of movement arrangement and space regulation, the focus of *xuni* acting is to represent actions and locations vividly regardless of the physical absence of stage properties, such as needles and thread, and stage sets, such as room doors, gate panels, and a chicken coop. Beginning with Qi Rushan's theory of "no real properties on the *jingju* stage,"[34] it has also been discussed as the signature of *xuni* acting in general. It is imperative to note and acknowledge, however, that this is not always true. The physical presence of stage properties, sometimes with costume pieces, can play a significant role in defining the intangible components of acting and generating a sense of reality. Many scholars categorize it as symbolism when explaining the employment of physical stage properties in *jingju* acting. The most famous examples are a whip symbolizing a horse and an oar standing in for a boat. Expanding on Qi's theory, the identification of stage properties as symbols would then emphasize the fact that there is no real horse or real boat on the stage. I argue that this is inaccurate, because in stage practice, a whip and an oar function only as key tools for the performer in representing the existence of a horse and water onstage. This representation necessitates an intricate performance text accomplished by both performers and musicians. In the meantime, these stage properties accomplish their task through their palpable physical presence: the whip is really on stage, as is the oar. There are rarely "no real properties on the *jingju* stage"; stage properties are simply selectively used to serve the onstage reality.

In *Bracelet*, in addition to a jade bracelet that is the central object of the production, Sun Yujiao employs three stage properties in her solo scene: a book in which she stores color-coded threads, a shoe upper fabric that she embroiders, and a small basket for the book and the fabric. These properties by themselves do not symbolize sewing, but they help the performer represent Sun's sewing. Master Li Yuru comments on these properties as "clever choices": "Our predecessors were truly clever. In order to assist our *xuni* acting to convince the audience that it is true, they selectively chose these properties. We should use them carefully."[35]

Based on the foundation of *xuni*, stylized reality on the *jingju* stage is represented through *chengshi* (conventions) in literature, acting, music, spectacle including costume and makeup, and use of onstage space. Contrary to the aforementioned theories that *chengshi* accentuate non-realist theatrical aesthetics, I call close attention to the fact that *chengshi* perform complex functions as they become the medium through which what they present becomes real and truthful to the *jingju* stage. An analysis of three versions of Sun Yujiao's entrance in *Bracelet* will illustrate how performers, based on detailed character analyses, accomplish character portrayal through thoughtful arrangement of *chengshi* of literature, acting, music, costume, and makeup.

In terms of the character's role type, Sun Yujiao belongs to the role subcategory of *huadan*: generally young, lively female roles with a comparatively lower social status. This role-type belongingness, establishing Sun's sex, age, and social status, is the foundation on which performers construct the performance text. Master Xiao identifies Sun as a lively young woman who is able to help her mother run a business but who is also shy:

> Sun Yujiao's mother is a passionate Buddhist devotee who visits the temple almost every day, leaving her daughter home alone. They run a small business raising and selling fighting roosters. When her mother is not home, Sun is the only one to deal with customers, but she is shy and a bit afraid of talking to strangers. She feels that she can handle female customers, but it is hard to deal with males. But her mother does not care too much about this, and still leaves her home alone quite often. So, Sun is often a bit worried about her situation. At the same time, as she grows up, she also has some secret thoughts about marriage, and therefore there is the line "new worries layered on old worries" in her set-the-scene poem.[36]

Based on this character analysis, Master Xiao employed choices in makeup and hairdo, percussive pattern, lyrics, and speech type to convey his nuanced understanding of the character. In his version, Sun Yujiao wears traditional *datou* for her hairdo.[37] *Datou* is frequently used for roles belonging to the *qingyi* role subcategory for loyal wives and young ladies of privileged origin. This choice of hairdo accentuates Master Xiao's interpretation that, although Sun is a young and lively girl of humble origins, she is also mature enough to run a business independently and handle her own life.

Master Xiao chose *xiaoluo maozitou* (small-gong-hat) as the percussive pattern accompanying Sun's entrance.[38] In *jingju*, "small-gong-hat" is often used to accompany a protagonist's first entrance, to introduce an aria in quadruple-beat, slow meter, and to lead to a recitation of a prelude. Usually used for characters of comparatively higher social status, "small-gong-hat" for Sun Yujiao, in Master Xiao's version, grants her a more mature character than regular *huadan* girls. Following "small-gong-hat," Sun Yujiao delivers a prelude, then a set-the-scene poem, and finally a set-the-scene speech.[39] In Master Xiao's version, Sun uses heightened speech, which is rare for *huadan* roles, most of which use colloquial speech.

[prelude]
With both eyebrows frozen with worries,
I learn sewing,
and embroidering with care.
(*Sun sits down in a chair upstage center.*)
[set-the-scene poem]
Tears fall on my sleeves,
with new worries layered on old worries;
the beauty of youth passes by so fast,
and I am shy to meet people.
[set-the-scene speech]
I am Sun Yujiao. Unfortunately, my father passed away early, leaving mother and me with a business of selling roosters. My mother is a Buddhist devotee and visits the Pudu Temple every day, leaving me alone at home. I shall let the roosters out and do some sewing.[40]

Though identifying Master Xiao's performance in *Bracelet* as most influential on her own stage art, Master Li composes her performance text for Sun Yujiao differently. During the 1950s, in preparation for international tours, Master Li gave Sun's entrance a much brighter and lighter tone by means of several major changes. She changed Sun's hairdo to *zhuaji* (see figure 2.1),[41] which is often used for young girls. Master Li also removed Sun's prelude, set-the-scene poem, and set-the-scene speech. For musical accompaniment of Sun's entrance, instead of "small-gong-hat," Li's version employs *nanbangzi dai luo* (small-gong-in-*nanbangzi*), the combination of a melodic accompaniment in the mode of *nanbangzi* and *xiaoluo chuanzi* (small-gong-link) as the percussive accompaniment.[42] The decision to replace "small-gong-hat" with "small-gong-in-*nanbangzi*" is based on the consideration that the former is for traditional loyal wives and young ladies of privileged origin, and sounds formal and somewhat heavy, whereas *nanbangzi* mode often accompanies young girls' songs, and "small-gong-link" is a conventional percussive pattern for the *nanbangzi* prelude for young girls. In this version, Sun enters while swirling the tail of her braid with her right hand and immediately begins to sing her first aria in *nanbangzi* mode. Master Li believes that "the effect of this choice is not bad, because at least international audiences understand that this is a quite lively girl. In retrospect, however, this arrangement can be used for any young girl, and it diminishes Sun Yujiao's individuality in *Picking up a Jade Bracelet*."[43]

After multiple rounds of polishing, Master Li settled on the following version. She abandoned the *zhuaji* hairdo and returned to the traditional *datou* hairdo, based on the conviction that the former "not only weakens Sun's character but is also not appropriate to the plot. Sun Yujiao should look more mature [than regular young lively girls] so that she can make decisions for her own marriage."[44] Master Li also gave up the accompaniment of "small-gong-in-*nanbangzi*" and returned to the option of percussive pattern only to accompany Sun's entrance. For the percussive pattern, she and her *gushi* (drum player), Zhang Senlin, chose *xiaoluo dashang* (small-gong-entrance), which in *jingju* often opens a moderately peaceful scene with characters from humble origins.[45] In performance, the *gushi* skillfully conveyed his own understanding of the character through his musicianship. Immediately following "small-gong-entrance," he "attracts the audience's attention with several firm beats of the single-skin-drum beater, in order to introduce the lead character. It does not sound very happy or lively, but rather reserved, therefore matching Sun Yujiao's status and situation."[46] Master Li further confirms that "with this percussive accompaniment, it is not possible to walk as quickly [as other young, lively girls on the *jingju* stage and it accentu-

Figure 2.1: Master performer Li Yuru as Sun Yujiao, wearing the *zhuaji* hairdo, in *Picking up a Jade Bracelet*, 1956. Image courtesy of Li Ruru.

ates Sun's personality]."⁴⁷ Master Li also returned to the choice of Sun delivering a prelude, a set-the-scene poem, and a set-the-scene speech, all in heightened speech, with revised lyrics to reflect her understanding that Sun is not as sentimental as in Master Xiao's version but is also fully aware of her marriageable age.

> [prelude]
> With both eyebrows frozen with worries,
> each and every day,
> I am reluctant to pick up my embroidery.
> (*Sun sits down in a chair upstage center.*)
> [set-the-scene poem]
> Weeping willows turn green in each spring,
> and my concerns grow with them;
> the beauty of youth passes by so fast,
> and I am shy to meet people.
> [set-the-scene speech]
> I am Sun Yujiao. Unfortunately, my father passed away early, leaving mother and me with a business of selling roosters. My mother is a Buddhist devotee and visits the Pudu Temple every day, leaving me alone at home. It is a fine day today. I shall let the roosters out and do some sewing at the gate.⁴⁸

Master Xiao and Master Li conceived of Sun Yujiao quite differently, and therefore they chose different lyrics, different percussive patterns, different melodic accompaniments, and different hairdos to convey their understanding. In the above discussion, I pointedly do not call attention to obvious differences in their choices of body language or vocal production, in order to emphasize that the character's portrayal springs from a performance text that includes acting but reaches beyond acting itself. The composition of these performance texts defines the character's portrayal both by acknowledging Sun's femaleness and accentuating her individuality as a unique female character, all made possible by thoughtful choices of an interactive combination of *chengshi* contributed to by all artistic aspects of a production. The focus of their creative work was to employ *chengshi* to make the Sun Yujiao of their understanding true to the *jingju* stage.

The fact that realism has been such a haunting paradigm for *jingju* studies during the past century calls for positioning theatrical realism more clearly in culturally specific performance histories. To this end, I propose that an effective discussion of *jingju*'s cultural and aesthetic identity must reach beyond a Western conceptualization of theatrical realism and of theater itself, through an examination of *jingju*'s performance text, which not only includes acting but embraces literature, directing, acting, music, and spectacle (costume, makeup, scenery, lighting, and special effects). Only such a performance text can reveal to us an alternative realist tradition. In this tradition, *xuni* acting always prioritizes the pursuit of accuracy and truthfulness to life; *jingju* practitioners conduct detailed and in-depth character analyses; they convey the understanding of their characters through thoughtful use of *chengshi*; and a significant portion of their creativity is focused on how to use those *chengshi* in different artistic areas in a seamless fashion, thus constructing the stylized reality of the *jingju* stage.

Notes

1. I thank Katherine Saltzman-Li and Jessica Nakamura for their feedback on an early version of this paper and for their guidance through this process of research and writing. I am immensely grateful to the anonymous readers for their suggestions on the broader contextualization of this discussion and on the reading of symbolism in *jingju* acting. I dedicate this paper to *jingju* practitioners whose creativity made this performing art's innovative tradition possible.

2. Marston Anderson, *The Limits of Realism: Chinese Fiction in the Revolutionary Period* (Berkeley: University of California Press, 1990), 4.

3. From the 1910s to the 1940s, *jiuxi* and *jiuju* were interchangeable terms for Chinese indigenous theater. In some discussions, they referred specifically to *jingju*. In the People's Republic of China, *jiuxi* and *jiuju* were replaced by *xiqu* 戏曲 as the umbrella term for more than three hundred indigenous regional theatrical forms in China.

4. Chen Duxiu, "New Youth Manifesto" ("Xin qingnian xuanyan"), *New Youth (Xin qingnian)* 7, no. 1 (December 1, 1919). Translation is from Anderson, *Limits of Realism*, 27. Contrary to this generalized label accentuating stagnation and backwardness, *jingju* has been an ever-changing performing art. The period from the 1890s to the 1940s was a complicated and exciting chapter in *jingju*'s history, featuring new plays and productions with daring innovations in acting, costumes, makeup, music, theater architecture, business management, and practitioner training. As Joshua Goldstein aptly describes, from the 1890s to the 1920s, "In Tianjin, Beijing, and especially Shanghai, 'new' styles were hatching daily: Civilized new drama (*wenming xin xi*), contemporary-costume new drama (*shizhuang xin xi*), ancient-costume new drama (*guzhuang xin xi*), and reformed Peking drama (*gailiang jingxi*), among others." *Drama Kings: Players and Publics in the Re-creation of Peking Opera, 1870–1937* (Berkeley: University of California Press, 2007), 89–90. During this period, which is often referred to as the Jingju Reform Movement, some practitioners experimented with more realist stage

properties, scenery, and acting. Despite wars during the 1930s and 1940s, *jingju* at Yan'an, the Chinese Communist Party's headquarters, has been credited as the beginning of the revolutionizing journey for old theater. Assessment of this chapter in *jingju*'s history is beyond the scope of this paper, but it is intriguing that, in spite of a handful of ancient-costume new dramas, rarely were any of the new creations during this phase made part of *jingju*'s permanent repertory, although these creations are often discussed as meaningful experiments. For example, see Ma Shaobo et al., eds., *History of China's Jingju (1)* (*Zhongguo jingju shi [shang]*) (Beijing: Zhongguo xiju chubanshe, 1990), 298–372. For a substantial discussion of the Jingju Reform Movement and its demise during the New Culture era, see Goldstein, *Drama Kings*, 89–171. For some leading practitioners' reflections on their experiences, see Mei Lanfang, *Forty Years Onstage* (*Wutai shenghuo sishinian*) (Beijing: Zhongguo xiju chubanshe, 1987), 211–365; and Nantongshi wenlian xiju ziliao zhengli zu, *A Pioneer of Jingju's Reform* (*Jingju gaige de xianqu*) (Nanjing: Jiangsu renmin chubanshe, 1982). For *jingju* at Yan'an, see Xing Fan, *Staging Revolution: Artistry and Aesthetics in Model Beijing Opera during the Cultural Revolution* (Hong Kong: Hong Kong University Press, 2018), 15–27.

5. One early major introduction appeared in the *New Youth* (*Xin qingnian*) June 1918 special issue on Ibsen. For Ibsen studies in China during the twentieth century, see Kwok-kan Tam, *Ibsen in China, 1908–1997: A Critical Annotated Bibliography of Criticism, Translation and Performance* (Hong Kong: Chinese University Press, 2001).

6. Zhang Houzai, "My Views on China's Old Drama" ("Wo de Zhongguo jiuxi guan"), *New Youth* (*Xin qingnian*) 5, no. 4 (October 1918). Zhang Houzai was an experienced spectator of traditional theater. His defense was a response to Hu Shi's invitation to elaborate on *jiuxi*'s strengths and the reasons why song in *jiuxi* cannot be replaced by speech. For May Fourth intellectuals' agenda on drama reform, see Goldstein, *Drama Kings*, 134–71. For a highlight of May Fourth intellectuals' harsh criticism of Chinese traditional theater from March 1917 to November 1918, see Yang Yingping's "'Layman's' Intervention with Theater: *New Youth* and China's Modern Theater Revolution" ("'Menwai han' dui xiju de ganyu—*Xin Qingnian* yu Zhongguo xiandai xiju geming"), *Theoretical Studies in Literature and Art* (*Wenyi lilun yanjiu*) 1 (2008): 85–91.

7. Zhang, "My Views on China's Old Drama."
8. Zhang, "My Views on China's Old Drama."
9. For an investigation of the National Theatre Movement's theoretical framework with special attention to Yu Shangyuan, see Siyuan Liu, "The Cross Currents of Modern Theatre and China's National Theatre Movement of 1925–1926," *Asian Theatre Journal* 33, no. 1 (2016): 1–35.
10. Yu Shangyuan, "Foreword" ("Xuyan"), in *National Theater Movement* (*Guoju yundong*), ed. Yu Shangyuan (Shanghai: Xinyue shudian, 1927), 1.
11. Yu Shangyuan, "On Old Theatre" ("Jiuxi pingjia"), in *National Theatre Movement* (*Guoju yundong*), 194–95.
12. Yu, "On Old Theatre," 194.
13. Yu, "On Old Theatre," 195–98.
14. Zhao Taimou, "National Theater" ("Guoju"), in *National Theatre Movement* (*Guoju yundong*), 10.

15. Zhao, "National Theatre," 14. Zhao used the English word "conventionalization" in the original text.

16. Qi Rushan, "The Characteristics of National Theatre" ("Guoju de tedian"), *Central Daily* (*Zhongyang ribao*), February 16, 1937; Qi Rushan, "The Characteristics of National Theatre (continued)" ("Guoju de tedian [xu]"), *Central Daily* (*Zhongyang ribao*), February 17, 1937. Examples of the aestheticized forms include *kunqu* 昆曲, *pihuang* 皮簧 (*jingju*), and *bangzi* 梆子. Joshua Goldstein uses "aestheticism" in discussing Qi's theory in *Drama Kings*.

17. Qi, "The Characteristics of National Theatre (continued)."

18. The entanglement of *xiqu* and Western theatrical realism in the theoretical construction for *xiqu* performance in the PRC, manifested in different fashions in different movements and debates, is beyond the scope of this paper. For example, under the dominant influence of Stanislavsky amid the Theatre Reform Movement during the 1950s, realism in *xiqu* was a focus of discussion. A Jia (1907–1994), a veteran *jingju* performer and director, advocated for life experience instead of inheriting conventions as the foundation of realism in *xiqu* acting, and criticized the formalist tendency in *xiqu* performance. See A Jia's discussion in "On the Realism in *Xiqu* Performing Art in Our Country" ("Tan woguo xiqu biaoyan yishu li de xianshizhuyi"), *People's Daily* (*Renmin ribao*), November 16, 1952. For a comprehensive examination of the Theatre Reform Movement and its profound influence on *xiqu*, see Siyuan Liu's *Transforming Tradition: The Reform of Chinese Theater in the 1950s and Early 1960s* (Ann Arbor: University of Michigan Press, 2021). Also, in the "dramatic outlook" (*xijuguan*) debates of the 1980s, Huang Zuolin's "*xieyi* dramatic outlook" was a key focus of discussion. In 1962, Huang discussed Stanislavsky, Brecht, and Mei Lanfang to illustrate different conceptualizations of theater and the stage, encouraging *huaju* creations to break through the dominance of Stanislavsky. In the midst of a crisis in *huaju* creation in the 1980s, the "dramatic outlook" debates revisited Huang's theory. The focus of debate was *huaju*; topics included the conceptualization of theater, the relationship between theater and politics, and the suppositionality of the stage, among others. Although *xiqu* was not the focus of debate, Huang's interpretation of Mei Lanfang's theatrical approach is generally accepted as an important reference for *xieyi* theater. For Huang's "*xieyi* dramatic outlook," see "A Random Discussion of 'Dramatic Outlook'" ("Mantan 'xijuguan'"), *Theater Journal* (*Xiju bao*) 3 (1962): 1–7. For publications during the "dramatic outlook" debates of the 1980s, see Du Qingyuan's *A Collection of Different Opinions on Dramatic Outlook (1)* (*Xijuguan zhengming ji [yi]*) (Beijing: Zhongguo xiju chubanshe, 1986); and Zhongguo xiju chubanshe bianjibu, *A Collection of Different Opinions on Dramatic Outlook (2)* (*Xijuguan zhengming ji [er]*) (Beijing: Zhongguo xiju chubanshe, 1988).

19. Zhang Geng, "An Initial Discussion of the Artistic Principles in *Xiqu*" ("Shi lun xiqu de yishu guilü"), in *Zhang Geng's Self-selected Essays* (*Zhang Geng zixuan ji*), ed. Zhang Geng (Beijing: Zhongguo xiju chubanshe, 2004), 218–25.

20. Zhang Geng, "On Three Themes of *Xiqu* Aesthetics" ("Xiqu meixue san ti"), *Studies of Literature and Art* (*Wenyi yanjiu*) 1 (1990): 26.

21. Zhang, "On Three Themes of *Xiqu* Aesthetics," 19–20.

22. Zhang, "On Three Themes of *Xiqu* Aesthetics," 20.

23. Fu Jin, "An Initial Discussion of a Theoretical Framework for *Xiqu* Acting" ("Xiqu biaoyan lilun tixi chuyi"), *Chinese Theater* (*Zhongguo xiju*) 8 (2013): 55.

24. Fu, "An Initial Discussion," 56.

25. Li Dongdong, "A Study of *Picking up a Jade Bracelet*, a *Jingdiao* Episode Script from the End of Qing and the Beginning of Republican China and Collected by the Shuanghong Hall at Tokyo University" ("Dong Da Shuanghongtang cang Qing mo Min chu jingdiao zhezi *Shi yuzhuo* yanjiu"), *Theater Literature* (*Xiju wenxue*) 8 (2013): 132.

26. Li Dongdong, "A Study of *Picking up a Jade Bracelet*," 131. Li examines two early versions: one was printed in 1912, and the other is likely to be from the same period, though its print year is unknown.

27. The following description of movement arrangement in this solo scene is based on the *yinpeixiang* (sound matched with images) version of Master Li Yuru's (1924–2008, female) performance: https://tv.cctv.com/2010/07/30/VIDE1355604161882761.shtml. In this video, the audio recording of Master Li's performance (year unknown) is matched with the video recording of Chen Chaohong's performance. Chen was Li's disciple, and therefore her acting is most likely very close to Li's version. Depending on the performer's acting training and understanding of the character, actual movement arrangement in this scene may vary.

28. Yu Lianquan, *Picking up a Jade Bracelet* (*Shi yuzhuo*), in *Yu Lianquan's Art of Performing Huadan Roles* (*Yu Lianquan huadan biaoyan yishu*), ed. He Baotang and Li Xiaoqin (Beijing: Zhongguo xiju chubanshe, 2016), 103. Xiao Cuihua is Yu Lianquan's stage name.

29. Yu, *Picking up a Jade Bracelet*, 104–5.

30. Yu, *Picking up a Jade Bracelet*, 102.

31. Li Yuru, "On the Art of Performing *Huadan* Roles" ("Lun huadan biaoyan yishu"), in *Li Yuru on Theater Art* (*Li Yuru tan xi shuo yi*), ed. Li Ruru (Shanghai: Shanghai wenyi chubanshe, 2008), 25.

32. Li Yuru, "On the Art of Performing *Huadan* Roles," 26.

33. Li Yuru, "On the Art of Performing *Huadan* Roles," 19.

34. Qi, "The Characteristics of National Theater (continued)."

35. Li Yuru, "On the Art of Performing *Huadan* Roles," 19.

36. Yu, *Picking up a Jade Bracelet*, 95.

37. In the aforementioned *yinpeixiang* version (see note 27), Sun Yujiao's hairdo is traditional *datou*. For more information on hairdo, costumes, makeup, and wardrobe practices, see Alexandra B. Bonds, *Beijing Opera Costumes: The Visual Communication of Character and Culture* (New York: Routledge, Taylor & Francis Group, 2019). For a manual with illustrations for makeup and hairdo for female roles in *jingju*, see Ma Jing, *Techniques for the Makeup and Hairdo for Female Roles in Traditional Jingju* (*Chuantong jingju danjue huazhuang jifa*) (Beijing: Zhongguo xiju chubanshe, 2009).

38. *Xiaoluo maozitou* (small-gong-hat):(支) | 台 台 | 台 台大 | 台大 台 | 台(多罗 0)||.

39. In *jingju*, prelude, set-the-scene poem, and set-the-scene speech are *chengshi* for major characters' self-introductions on their first entrance. This self-introduction often includes the character's name and a brief background of the

story onstage; sometimes, it offers a plot synopsis. These three *chengshi* are often used together and in this order, but it is not unusual to use a set-the-scene speech only for the self-introduction.

40. Yu, *Picking up a Jade Bracelet*, 96.

41. I thank Dr. Ruru Li for granting me permission to use this production photo. This chapter is published in 2023, which marks the fifteenth-year anniversary of Master Li Yuru's passing. One of the first-generation professional *jingju* female performers, Master Li, with her fellow actresses, significantly contributed to *jingju*'s stage art. The complex entanglement of realism, gender portrayal, and the performer's sex encourages us to continue examining their legacy.

42. *Xiaoluo chuanzi* (small-gong-link): | 衣大　大大大 ‖: 台台 :‖ 台大 | 衣 | 台 ‖.

43. Li Yuru, "On the Art of Performing *Huadan* Roles," 23. I could not find the video of this version of Master Li's performance during the 1950s, but master performer Liu Xiurong's (1935–2021) performance, shot in 1990, uses a similar entrance. See video here: https://www.bilibili.com/video/av26712725/

44. Li Yuru, "On the Art of Performing *Huadan* Roles," 21.

45. *Xiaoluo dashang* (small-gong-entrance): | 多罗 衣 | 台. 大 | 台 0 ‖: 台大 台 :‖ 台大 台大 | 台 台 | 台 另 ‖: 台— :‖ 台— | 台另 台 ‖.

46. Li Yuru, "On the Art of Performing *Huadan* Roles," 21.

47. Li Yuru, "On the Art of Performing *Huadan* Roles," 21. Zhang Senlin is the *gushi* in the aforementioned *yinpeixiang* version of Master Li's performance.

48. Li Yuru, "On the Art of Performing *Huadan* Roles," 23–24. In the *yinpeixiang* version (see note 27), Master Li recites a different prelude and a different set-the-scene poem. The prelude is: "Young girls do not understand life concerns; I become shy as I embroider mandarin ducks." In Chinese literature and art, paired mandarin ducks are a popular trope for life partners, romance, and love. The set-the-scene poem is: "Doing embroidery alone, I feel that my sorrow is deepened by the spring. Gentlemen are everywhere, but no one pursues a fine lady." According to Master Li's narrative of the revision process for this production, the performance in this audio recording is most likely an earlier version, taking place before the version quoted in her "On the Art of Performing *Huadan* Roles."

3 | Racing the Real

Korean Realism Theater and Racial Representation in Cha Bumseok's Yeoldaeeo[1]

SOO RYON YOON AND JI HYON (KAYLA) YUH

Introduction

South Korean playwright Cha Bumseok, whose post–Korean War oeuvre became widely known for its realist aesthetics, once stated, "An author must delve deeper into the consciousness [of people]; and with that, artistic subjects must be open [to] reflecting on the reality where we are fearful of our proximity to the truth."[2] Cha, whose 1966 play *Yeoldaeeo* (*Tropical Fish*) figures centrally in this chapter, directs our attention to his broader worldview, in which artists must confront truths, however fearmongering they may be. In their everyday aesthetic practices, which often create dissonances with reality, artists must fight the urge to look the other way during difficult political conflicts. What Cha saw was the need for theater to lay bare this fearful truth, and expose a new reality where class, gender, and ethno-racial identities were highly contested as post–Korean War South Korea began to undergo rapid sociopolitical changes.

This chapter focuses on the interiority of the "truth" of Cha's worldview, and its racialized reality in what is commonly termed "realism theater" (*sasiljuuigeuk* 사실주의극) in Korean theater history. Our argument is twofold. First, worldmaking on the modern Korean theatrical stage was an inherently racialized process. Second, the process was simultaneously connected to representational experiments that appropriated elements of Euro-American theatrical realism, among other "foreign" influences. We discuss how the establishment of realism theater was intimately tied to the development of theater makers' understanding of national and racial identities. In the process, we contend, their "racing" of the real in Korean realism theater assigns racialized and nationalized dispositions and qualities to stage elements, which assists the narrative development and articulation of political ideology on stage. By "racing," we point to American civil-rights legal scholar john a. powell's concept of "race," which he uses as a verb. Powell asserts that race is not a quantifiable "objective truth," but something that functions depending on one's perception, thereby constructing a reality in which objects, environments, and identities are always already assigned a particular racial designation.³ While powell's concept is deeply rooted in America-specific racial politics, we argue that "race" as a verb can also apply to a broader cultural context outside the US, and to the schemes applied to the realization of a world on stage.

Focusing on the formations of ethnic and racial subjectivity in the worldmaking process, we ask, how did theater makers envision the new world on stage as they were increasingly exposed to various cultural influences? How did their imagined world manifest "realism theater" that diverged from Euro-American theatrical realism? How did realism shape and frame representations of race, ethnicity, and "nationness"? To address these questions, this chapter examines the original Korean play *Yeoldaeeo*, written by playwright Cha Bumseok and performed by his theater troupe Sanha (산하) in 1966.

As will be discussed, ideas and conventions of theatrical realism were introduced much earlier, and *Yeoldaeeo* was certainly not the first instance in which Korean audiences saw racial "others" on stage. Theater makers in the early twentieth century had already been familiar with realist techniques, ideas, and plays, representing what they imagined was an ideal world not yet available to colonized Koreans in the 1920s and 1930s. *Yeoldaeeo*, on the other hand, shows how dramatists of the 1960s became increasingly aware of their responsibility to materialize the world they believed should unfold in the emerging postcolonial nation-state, thereby revealing how a unique historical context shaped the practices and craft of realism in worldmaking.

Even as theater makers employed Euro-American imports of theatrical realism, their appropriative uses of these conventions can be seen as a direct outcome of their reckoning with major historical shifts, formations of colonial subjectivity, and emerging national identities in a rapidly changing sociocultural environment. Therefore, a closer look at how theater makers adopted Euro-American theatrical realism to make sense of their worldmaking onstage and off allows us to complicate the taken-for-granted notion that theatrical realism and its Korean iteration, "realism theater," are simply outcomes of Western modernity. In so doing, we critically reexamine the assertion that Korean and Asian theatrical realism are transplanted from Euro-American conventions, and reconsider the idea that Asian theater is a passive receptacle for Western theatrical realism.[4]

In what follows, we outline the specific historical and cultural context of realism theater in Korea, highlighting some traits of early realism theater on the Korean stage, such as the production of Gogol's *Revizor* (*Geomchalgwan* 검찰관, *Government Inspector*) in 1932, which shows how realism theater served colonial Koreans in the 1930s.[5] Much of this chapter is devoted to discussing *Yeoldaeeo*, and how theater makers addressed racial politics and new ethno-racial and national consciousness in their changing society as Koreans wrestled with the changes brewing during the first half of the twentieth century and into the 1960s. In closing, we consider the film adaptation of *Yeoldaeeo* and how the introduction of film in the 1960s began to hypervisualize racialized subjects to represent the world more "realistically," only to intensify the "racing" of the world that theater makers had conceptualized on the theater stage.

Korean Realism Theater: A Brief History

The term "realism theater" is a direct translation of *sasiljuuigeuk*, which is often translated as "Korean realism" and "theatrical realism" in Western scholarship. Our use of the term "realism theater" in this chapter designates a form rooted in a specific cultural framework related to, but ultimately divergent from, the nineteenth-century European realism movement, recuperating its experimental and ideological nature.[6]

Realism theater was both a movement and a new genre, first shaped under Japanese colonial rule between the 1920s and 1930s. Its styles were introduced as part of the *singeuk* movement (新劇, New Drama), which dramatists mobilized to resist the dominance of *sinpageuk* (新派劇, New Wave Drama),[7] an early-twentieth-century popular commercial genre.[8] Realism theater was born as a composite genre out of the need to address sociopolitical issues, and first emerged in formalistic adaptations of early-twentieth-century Euro-American naturalist and realist theatrical imports. During the postcolonial 1950s and later, following the US occupation, it was reshaped by American theater conventions. By its nature, then, Korean realism theater has been a political and ideological articulation.

More specifically, realism theater denotes a new genre emerging from an amalgamation of several formalistic styles to embody sociopolitical and cultural changes in Korea, whereas Euro-American realism points to a theater movement within the specific historical moment of modernity. For instance, early Korean theater makers did not strictly distinguish realism from naturalism, in part because of their specific need for the political instrumentality of realism theater. Artists actively absorbed and referenced various aspects of realism, naturalism, expressionism, socialism, and structuralism to make the most effective representation of what they saw as reality, which was different from Western reality.[9] This viewpoint helps us recognize realism theater as a new genre, rather than an assimilation into the international theater movement, complicating the assumed temporal synchronicity of formalist realism in Euro-America and elsewhere.

Furthermore, realism theater was an ideological movement mobilized to mirror and raise awareness of contemporary social issues in Korea. The dramatists' adaptations of 1920s Russian theater, for instance, were not simply derivative of European realism, but a strategic study of methods for staging Koreans' state of despair. Moreover, their adaptations of Russian and other Euro-American realism plays played a significant role as an allegorical reflection of the global racial order that was organized around European Whiteness. Practitioners of Korean realism theater saw Russian plays such as *Revizor* as bearing semblance to the harsh social conditions of Koreans, but in a way that romanticized Russian Whiteness as idyllic, untamed, and premodern, qualities that the practitioners likewise associated with Koreans.

As an example of the theatrical practices, expectations, and conventions of Korean theater in the 1930s, the 1932 production of *Geomchalgwan* (the Korean adaptation of *Revizor*) merits a closer look. *Revizor*, Nikolai Gogol's satirical play from 1836, depicts a corrupt small-town mayor and his cronies anxiously awaiting the arrival of a government inspector from Saint Petersburg, only to be swindled by a con man who takes advantage of the situation. The performance of *Geomchalgwan* drew mixed opinions. On one hand, it was critically acclaimed, noted especially for its "unique set and acting."[10] On the other, critics found the production too removed and elitist; the Silheommudae's (실험무대, Experimental Stage) adaptation was expected to be a social commentary about colonial Korea's rampant political corruption under Japanese rule, much like the corruption and incompetence of government officials in imperial Russia.

The performance was first translated and staged by the small theater collective Silheommudae, working under the Geukyesulyeonguhoe (극예술연구회, Theatre Research Group, abbreviated as Geukyeon 극연) in 1932. This production was directed by Hong Hae-seong, whose working experiences in Tokyo's Tsukiji Little Theater (a Japanese theater company founded in 1924) influenced his stage direction and designs. The stage design included a long dinner table toward stage left, wallpaper with distinctive spade patterns, and five portraits of Russian figures as a backdrop, which is similar to the design of Tsukiji Little Theater's production of *Revizor*.[11]

Nevertheless, this connection does not mean that Korean realism theater was derivative of Japanese practices. On the contrary, as theater historian Kim Hyeon-cheol argues, Hong's adoption of European theater mediated by his experience at Tsukiji was the fastest way to cultivate artistically rich "soil for the growth of modern Korean theater."[12] According to Kim, it most likely did not matter to Hong whether the source was "Ibsen, Goethe, Chekhov, Bernard Shaw, Greek, or Shakespearean drama as long as it stimulated and inspired [experimental] efforts for the future theater" of Korea.[13] In other words, the early adoption of Tsukiji Little Theater's theatrical realism and aesthetics was how theater makers like Hong attempted to take a shortcut to Western drama, specifically in hopes of finding pathways for staging the Korean reality on stage.

This is akin to a strategic appropriation of Western hegemonic culture: Hong's aesthetics reflected the reality of a Korea where Chinese, Japanese, and Western hegemonic forces were racing to make claims to the peninsula. In a way, the polysemous nature of his work inflected through Western and Japanese theater practices was figurative of the political reality of colonial Korea. Therefore, Hong's deployment of Tsukiji Little Theater's mise-en-scène to his own production was his idea of expediting the progress of Korean modern theater, a concern of Hong's own professional career and a source of the anxiety around the growth of Korean modern theater, an anxiety shared by many theater makers in colonial Korea.

In comparison, the realism theater style of the postliberation 1950s mirrored the postcolonial, post–Korean War reality influenced by the US occupation. Theater historian Lee Seung-hyun notes that post–Korean War realism theater should be understood in the context of the "radical reconfiguration of the [post–World War II] 'Western-centric world order' into which South Korea was suddenly inserted by American hegemony,"[14] which was both political and deeply cultural.[15] Therefore, the plays written and performed during this time brought different versions of reality onto the stage. Our analysis of *Yeoldaeeo* demonstrates how realism theater captured the historical shifts and challenges of defining national identity.

In short, realism theater has been an ideological articulation of racial, ethnic, and national consciousness relating to nascent, often contested, ideas of Koreanness; it goes beyond a formalist theater movement. This calls for a critical review of realism theater in the context of racial and national identity-building, and more specifically how it has prescribed racial and ethnic dispositions to characters and objects as part of staged reality in order to make sense of the changing world.

Racing the Real on Stage

Critically reexamining Korean realism theater that required assigning racial identities to stage elements recalls what Ric Knowles describes as "material-culture methodologies of theatre."[16] In this framework, things—props, costumes, makeup, and masks—as well as general "theatrical thingness" activate the space of realism.[17] Through this activation, different, often conflicting ideological effects and forms of sociality embodying the inner truths of our reality are enlivened and materialized. The qualities and nature of things, however, are neither neutral nor universal. They are highly racialized, and in turn, they also racialize the world on stage, where things direct and engage with the actions of the performers. As Dorinne Kondo argues, theater is a site where we see how "worlds are made . . . in collaboration with objects and technologies that are themselves replete with possibility," often in a way that transforms racial desires but also reenacts racial stereotypes.[18] For instance, the dramatic contrast between Western and traditional Korean rooms in Cha Bumseok's *Yeoldaeeo* illustrates how things and the world around them are assigned racial dispositions. The term "racing" is useful in efforts to understand how a worldview is reenacted on stage through using racial designations for characters, props, and stage settings. Realism theater as a process of racing draws from john a. powell's suggestion that racing involves "both assigning and depriving groups of racial identity."[19] Powell notes that "to race" is to engage in a top-down process that "operates as a verb before it assumes significance as a noun."[20]

This top-down process of assigning is rooted in historical specificity. Realism theater showcases a wide range of experiments informed by the emergence of racial thinking as well as the desire for a new subjectivity that challenges racial hierarchies. It is this context that shapes authentic representations of Whiteness in early realism plays from the 1930s and the articulation of the racial dispositions of the characters in *Yeoldaeeo*. For instance, the reality presented in *Geomchalgwan* is of romanticized Whiteness rooted in the Korean viewers' aspiration to Russian socialist ideals, whereas the reality in *Yeoldaeeo* is of racial and ethnic anxiety emerging from defining and rebuilding what constitutes Koreanness amid the postwar reconstruction of South Korea.

Racing of the real in *Yeoldaeeo* reflects the consolidation of Koreanness in the postcolonial, postwar nation-building project. Assigning racial dispositions to rooms and objects in *Yeoldaeeo*, for instance, is in dialogue with postwar anxiety around multiracial war children as well as the state-led campaign of the "one ethnicity one nation" ideology (*ilgukilminjuui* 일국일민주의). In *Yeoldaeeo*, there is a distinct separation of space; the bifurcation between a Western-style living room and traditional Korean rooms conditions the intergenerational and interracial tensions that shape each character's racialized worldview differently. One of the objects, a tropical fish, is also racialized and likened to the Chinese African American woman character who is already out of place.

The thematics, mise-en-scène, and props in *Yeoldaeeo* acted as indirect gestures to and allegories of the raced world-in-making parallel to the changing social reality. In short, the artists actively pursued the use of the stage as a mediated space in which to digest, experiment, and materialize what they thought was a new world unfolding with the ripples of the unfamiliar, yet operative, concept of race.

The Reality of Koreanness: Racing Heterogeneity in *Yeoldaeeo*

Cha Bumseok's play *Yeoldaeeo* presents a world in which the issues of Koreanness, Blackness, and multiraciality are explicitly contested. Cha, often hailed as a contemporary pioneer in Korean realism theater, wrote about a tropical fish in *Yeoldaeeo*, a living object that symbolizes the out-of-placeness of a multiracial Chinese Black woman living in postwar Korea. By imbuing mundane objects and household items with racial qualities—in other words, racing the elements of a domestic setting—Cha's worldmaking envisions a space where the clash between conflicting values and identities becomes palpable.

Set in a residential area in Seoul between spring and autumn, the play follows an interracial international marriage between Yang Jinwoo, an upper-middle-class doctor from South Korea who studied in the US, and Gloria, a Chinese African American law student from the American South whose mother was "technically born from a Portuguese and a negro [transliterated as *nigeuro*]."[21] The play begins with the couple returning to Seoul after getting married in the US without permission from Jinwoo's parents. The play ends with the family broken up due to conflicts arising from Gloria's presence. Each of the family members represents certain aspects of conservative norms as well as changing social values. Lee Maria, Jinwoo's mother and the play's main antagonist, becomes the most vocal opponent. She frequently refers to Gloria as a "darkie" (*kkamdungi*) and "that woman." Both Maria's younger son Jingyu, a philosophy student at college who often cites Nietzsche to mock his mother's Christian zeal, and her youngest daughter Jinju, a mischievous figure who later befriends Gloria, symbolize the changing modern values that become a source of conflict for their parents' generation. Through their story, *Yeoldaeeo* reflects ethno-racial anxiety around the politics of Koreanness and multiraciality in the process of defining what Koreanness meant during the period of postwar reconstruction.

Yeoldaeeo was produced by Cha Bumseok's theater troupe, Sanha, and staged as a four-act performance in 1965. It was later presented to a larger audience between April 6 and April 10, 1966, at the National Theatre of Korea. It was the fifth repertoire for Sanha, a relatively young theater troupe Cha founded in 1963. The production was directed by thirty-year-old Pyo Jae-soon, who had started his career as a founding member of Sanha and assistant director of the troupe's productions. Following Cha's specification of set designs in the script, award-winning stage designer Jeong Woo-taek used "real" objects (this emphasis on real objects was noted by theater critics) as props,[22] and divided several sections of the stage to demarcate boundaries between different, often contrasting rooms in both Korean and Western styles. While some critics noted that these spatial arrangements seemed "unnecessary" and "disjointed," Cha purposefully specified the imbalance between these different rooms to highlight cultural, racial, gendered, and intergenerational differences.[23] *Yeoldaeeo* received critical acclaim and prestigious awards, including the Korean Drama and Film Awards (currently the Baeksang Arts Awards) and Dong-a Drama Awards; it was a rare case of a commercially successful production that also addressed the difficult subjects of racial politics and stereotypes. Cha's unusual casting choices also made the performance noteworthy. Alongside popular actors such as Jeon Woon, Baek Seong-hee, Lee Sun-jae, and Gang Bu-ja, Cha cast Kang Hyo-sil, one of the actresses in his theater company Sanha, to play the role of Gloria. Kang Hyo-sil, who Cha thought was "exotic" and "Western-looking," was praised for her "passionate" acting.[24]

Cha Bumseok has stated that he wrote the play specifically to cast Kang Hyo-sil.[25] However, whether Kang's features were visually convincing as a representation of Blackness was not a priority for Cha's staged reality. Cha's realism is not based on visual mimicry, not to mention that the hypervisual rendering of Blackness is always already an imagined optic. While Cha's play at times resorts to colorism and close descriptions of Gloria's racialized features, her multiracial Blackness is described as somewhat "grayish and brownish, not really black" as a gesture to her ethno-racially ambiguous appearance.[26] At the same time, Gloria's Asianness shapes her innate longing for Asian cultures, complicating the conviction that the actor portraying Gloria should display a distinctive racial appearance. Gloria confesses, "I wanted to come [to Korea] one day. I've always missed and longed for it ever since I was a child. . . . My father's country was China, and so the Asian blood runs through my body, and perhaps that blood makes me aspire to Asia."[27] Through Gloria, Cha highlights both the Korean family's anxiety about Gloria's Blackness, and Gloria's Asian affinity with the Korean family as a multiracial woman. The character description of Gloria states, for example, that Gloria has "East Asian habits and disposition."[28]

Gloria's multiraciality as well as her Asianness and Blackness illustrate the centrality of racial politics as the focal point of the performance. Jinwoo and Gloria's marriage is not a tangential matter emerging from Jinwoo's rebellion against his conservative mother, as much as a device for narrative development that clarifies a racialized trope contrasted against the Koreanness of Jinwoo's family. For instance, Gloria first meets Jinwoo when he intervenes in a racially charged assault to save Gloria from White men on campus. Following a blackout, the scene transitions to the past in the American South of the 1960s, where the audience can hear "a long duration of people shouting and police sirens evoking a riot somewhere." The sky is "redder than blood." Gloria is harassed by several White boys who, on Jinwoo's intervention, "walk away while whistling and jeering."[29] Gloria confides in Jinwoo and explains that she studies law because "powerless people need power to defend themselves." Gloria and Jinwoo make sense of a Black-Korean affinity, based on their shared experiences of oppression. Jinwoo refers to Koreans having had "experiences similar to those of Black people" in the past, when "Japanese people politically brutalized Koreans."[30]

While this Black-Korean affinity is formulated on a "common victims of history" ideology, cultural practices shared by both Koreans and African Americans serve as a reminder of the slippage between affinity and incommensurability. Gloria and Maria are both devout Christians, yet Maria's Christian ideology does not align with Gloria's, especially in the way that Cha depicts how Christianity works to support each character's personal dispositions. Having Christian beliefs and praying with her fellow church members in a room she takes time to decorate in an American style resembling "a first-class hotel room," Maria trusts that her God will give her all the wealth and happiness she deserves, a trust betrayed by the introduction of Gloria to her family.[31] Gloria's belief, on the other hand, is modest. Gloria is depicted with an oppressed, "God's child"–like image. She mostly resigns to the couple's bedroom upstairs, cordoned off by other more visible rooms downstairs.

Indeed, one of the key features in the realist representations of the world of Jinwoo and his family appears in the play's unique spatial configuration (see figures 3.1 and 3.2). Cha specified in the script the details of the set designs and spatial arrangements, which were materialized by director Pyo Jae-soon and art director Jeong Woo-taek.[32] The descriptions of the set design reflect the contradictory and tension-inducing domestic space. The stage directions consistently invoke the division between Western and traditional rooms, which converge in the common area of the living room. Parts of the script, for instance, specify the exaggerated enlargement of the Western-style chamber, which appears to "occupy most of the space on stage," indicating the centrality of the Yang family's materialistic aspiration to a Western lifestyle.[33] Lighting and interior design also differ in the traditional room and the Western-style room; the latter has, according to the script, "a more modern taste and contemporary charms, providing a good contrasting effect."[34]

However, Cha's representation of cultural and ethnic heterogeneity in domestic reality was criticized by major media outlets as "distracting" and "delimiting [the broad range] of 'acting areas,'" particularly due to the frequent transitions between different rooms and the characters' movement across these spaces.[35] Nevertheless, Cha's stage design and directions are ultimately effective for indicating the daily clashes that arise from cultural and generational differences. The spatial arrangements and domestic items also embody the overlapping layers of unre-

Figure 3.1: A scene from Cha Bumseok's *Yeoldaeeo* (*Tropical Fish*), 1966. Its stage design highlighted contrasting relationships between the Western-style room seen here and a traditional Korean-style room, alluding to the domestic and ethno-racial tension between Gloria and the family members. Sanha Theatre Company, *Dong-a ilbo*, April 16, 1966.

solved tension between the family members' deep-seated biases toward Korean culture or Western culture, the latter being violently imported and transplanted to the domestic space through Gloria's "foreign" body.

Cha's meticulous care in arranging different elements of a domestic space showed his interest in approximating a real-life domestic setting on stage, which he saw as a way to cater to the real concerns of ordinary people, veering away from creating a stage reserved for elite theater's parochial concerns and overemphasis on theatricality. One of Cha's methods to that end was to move away from the abstract experimental rendering of reality and the overemotional treatment of social issues. Time and again, Cha's use of "things" attests to his aesthetic proximity to the people's reality, not to the cultural elites or select few to whom the elite theater is afforded.

In this domestic setting, mundane objects such as tropical fish are not only metaphors for the characters' subjectivity but also reflect changing South Korean society. Korean households began to raise imported tropical fish sometime between the late 1950s and the early 1960s, replacing the common goldfish. Judith Hamera, discussing the habits of caretaking

Figure 3.2: Various scenes from Cha Bumseok's *Yeoldaeeo*, 1966. The play's stage design emphasized the contrast between a Western-style room and the traditional Korean-style room seen here, alluding to ethno-racial tensions between characters in the play. Sanha Theatre Company, *10 Years of Sanha Theatre Company* (1966), Arko Arts Archive.

aquariums in American households, writes that the aquarium not only served as "a pedagogical entertainment," it was symbolic of the mobility and leisure of middle-class family vacations, during which the family would collect souvenirs for their aquarium.[36] An aquarium filled with exotic imports in upper-middle-class Korean households functioned as a display of both family wealth and a Westernized cultural life. Uncannily titled "Tropical Fish Enjoys Her First Spring as a New Bride," a 1959 Korean news article explained that Korean households began to "host new guests" from the tropics in the summer of 1958 when Korea started importing tropical fish for display purposes.[37] However, imported tropical fish died when the temperature dropped during winter, to the point that the government conducted research on the "impossibility of breeding tropical fish in the Korean climate."[38] Critics also condemned the excessive consumerism of the nouveaux riche as exemplified by tropical fish shopping, which "many of the regular citizens trying to survive the postwar poverty" considered "an enemy."[39] In this way, the simulated tropical environment created to accommodate tropical fish inside an aquarium alludes to a decorated fantastical world contained within a domestic setting, where latent tensions erupt into a more visible social experience and discourse.

According to Cha's worldview, the performance of newfound middle-class stability and wealth in postwar Korea is interrupted by Gloria's insertion of her otherness, which is metonymized by the tropical fish. Tropical fish, the key object of the entire play, do not appear very often, except when Gloria engages with them from time to time. Gloria's ordeal as a diasporic multiracial woman who attempts to make sense of her place in a new cultural environment is symbolized by the tropical fish in the Yang family's living-room aquarium. In the beginning, Gloria is comforted by her new sister-in-law, Jinju; Gloria talks with her about how tropical fish do not belong in the Korean climate, but that they will eventually adapt to the new environment, hinting at her own displacement and difficulties of adapting. In the end, however, Gloria becomes distressed and is confined to her room, family members having drugged her with antidepressants without her knowledge. She comes out to aggressively insert herself to the living room—the space reserved for the rest of the family—and smashes the aquarium, protesting that she is not crazy and that she wants to get out of the aquarium.

The process of racing in *Yeoldaeeo* uses objects and the design of a domestic setting to reflect the creation of postwar Korean middle-class identity. On the one hand, objects in *Yeoldaeeo* are adornments representing the desire to catch up with Western (and White European-American) cultural consumption. On the other hand, they are the prelude to racialized and gendered tensions within the household, suggesting more significant social concerns about homogenous Koreanness and postwar multiraciality in South Korea. Cha Bumseok's choice to cast Kang Hyo-sil was also intended to veer away from highlighting the play's obvious racial overtones. However, Kang's ambiguously exotic features also served as a device for emphasizing both Gloria's Blackness and her innate affinity with Asianness, which mobilized the audience's patronizing sympathy for an innocent oppressed Black subject. This complex alterity is reduced to a difference signified by Blackness in the movie adaptation of *Yeoldaeeo*, which cast an African American actress to play Gloria.

Visual Excess in the Film Adaptation of *Yeoldaeeo* and "Racing" in Post-1960s Drama

The film adaptation of *Yeoldaeeo* features a hypervisualization of Blackness, created through the use of color film introduced after the 1960s. The prominence of color film may partially explain how post-1960s theatrical realism in Korea began to rely on actors' visual mimicry as the authentic version of reality. Film director Kim Sa-gyeom created a movie adaptation of *Yeoldaeeo* featuring an African American actress, Susan Jackson, a casting choice that nullified the more complicated multiraciality Cha had formulated. While this chapter focuses more on the theater stage as a space of racing through worldmaking and considers the film adaptation as a byproduct, examining the heightened colorism in the film adaptation illuminates a pathway through which realist representations of race and racialized worlds on stage become much more reliant on hypervisuality of race, especially Blackness.

The film adaptation was originally titled *Geomeunsaeassi* (*The Black Bride*), and later retitled to *Geudae gaseume dasi hanbeon* (*I Want to Be in Your Arms Again*). The original title put emphasis on colorism, highlighting the Blackness of Gloria. While director Kim Sa-gyeom worked with Cha Bumseok to adapt the script from the staged version, its cinematic iteration represented race issues in the context of visual excess and the unfitness of Blackness within a Korean household, a household similarly hypervisualized through an overemphasis on Orientalist cultural tropes. Despite the film's effort to retain the original play's commentary on racial politics, its visualization of body images complicates its purported critical engagement. Shot in 35 mm Technicolor film with CinemaScope, the newest introduction of American technology to the Korean film industry, the movie's credit titles begin with a close-up shot of a black tropical fish, which approaches the camera lens until the credit titles transition to a view of the "French-style two-story house" of the Yang family.[40] While some of the descriptions of Gloria are reproduced from the original play, the movie script puts additional effort into emphasizing Gloria's Blackness as well as Asianness, which is explained as evidence for her affinity with Korean culture through her performing in accord with everyday cultural norms.

This is projected onto the body of actor Susan Jackson, whose Gloria becomes a more pronounced visual signifier of race in the cinematic representation than she was on stage and in the play's script, where Kang Hyo-sil's "raced" disposition remained ambiguous.[41] The movie script explains that the *hanbok*, a traditional article of Korean attire, looks good on Gloria thanks to her "tall and slender figure."[42] In another scene, sitting with Jinwoo's younger sister Jinju in the living room where "her Black skin shines under the sunlight," Gloria reluctantly refuses the coffee Jinju offers, because she "is not in America and so drinking scorched Korean rice tea instead is enough."[43] Susan Jackson, the actor, was also expected to align with these visual significations and the performance of cultural norms. Jackson, who was a twenty-three-year-old stationed at the Busan American military base headquarters at the time, was noted by news reporters for her rich emotional reactions and her petite stature, which were a "very good fit" with Koreans, echoing the film's anticipation that Gloria should "fit" with Korean social norms.

In this instance, Ju Yon Kim's discussion of the mundane is instructive. Kim asks us to pay attention to "which [mundane] traits lend a reality to the performance and which ones exceed the designated role, thereby disappearing into insignificance, challenging the 'truth' of the performance, or extending the scope of the [role.]"[44] In the case of the film adaptation of *Yeoldaeeo*, the "mundane," which Kim defines as "everyday enactments" attached to the body in racial formation, evinces Gloria's efforts to assimilate despite her Blackness: tensions around Blackness are diffused by the normative quotidian actions of wearing *hanbok*, making kimchi, and drinking tea instead of coffee.[45]

However, Gloria's efforts to assimilate into traditional middle-class Korean customs, supported by her reticence and modesty, are doomed to fail. In the movie, her fragile body and soul are often contrasted with the scientific and rational side of the Yang patriarch and his sons. Their beliefs in both Western science and Christian enlightenment are deeply

Figure 3.3: A scene from the movie adaptation (1971) of Cha Bumseok's *Yeoldaeeo*. Gloria (performed by Susan Jackson) is seen wearing *hanbok*, the traditional Korean attire. Image © 1971 (주)합동영화사 / Hapdong Film Co.

entrenched. At the same time, Maria, as a woman in the patriarchal Korean culture, "sympathizes [with Gloria] for her willingness to come all the way to a foreign land only relying on Jinwoo." Ultimately, however, Maria cannot accept the fact that a respected family's daughter-in-law becomes "a spectacle" whenever she steps out of the house.[46] Maria internalizes racial hatred and simply relinquishes the opportunity to revise her own racist views, because she "alone can't solve the problem [of racism] when America hasn't even figured out how to solve it."[47] The anxiety around Gloria's race directly references national anxiety around multiracial children in postwar South Korea, when Jinwoo's mother and friends urge Jinwoo to reconsider having babies in the future.[48] According to Maria and Jinwoo's friends, America's structural problems cannot be tackled in a private, domestic sphere at an individual level elsewhere. This belief is undergirded visually by crosscuts to several flashback scenes showing Gloria's experiences with anti-Black racism in American cities.

Gloria's precarious body laboring to carry out quotidian norms ultimately becomes the central site of the family's quick suturing of the deep social wound. In the final scene, Gloria cuts herself while smashing the aquarium and shows her bloody hand to the family, crying, "My blood is red, just like yours!"[49] Confronted with this harrowing sight, Jinwoo's father Byeong-seob treats her injury and warmly embraces her as a legitimate member of the family. Gloria calls out to Byeong-seob, "Father!" while he carries her to the bedroom. Gloria, Byeong-seob, and Jinwoo pick up and return the fish to the shattered aquarium, where the fish becomes alive and active again. The film moves to further accentuate the colors of the (raced) flesh and blood—black and red—as a device illustrating both the inclusion and exclusion of Gloria's Blackness. Only by displaying the visual excess of red, symbolic of the sacrificial violation of her body, is Gloria finally accepted into the family as its rightful daughter-in-law. This is in stark contrast with the original theater performance, which ends inconclusively with Gloria smashing the aquarium in defiance, on which the younger son of the family, Jingyu, murmurs a Nietzschean sentence, "God is dead, we killed the god with our knife."[50]

In the end, technological advancement in cinematic representation reshaped the appearance of racialized identities on-screen. This has partly affected post-1960s stage conventions that began to include blackface makeup among other devices that used visual excess as a means to approximate reality, elements that the previous generation of realism theater makers had not used. For instance, the 1978 Korean adaptation of *The Island* (1973) by South African playwrights Athol Fugard, John Kani, and Winston Ntshona about two apartheid-era inmates featured two Korean actors with heavy blackface makeup. The efforts of the actors in painting their entire faces and bodies were praised by the media for their "theatrical ingenuity"; one of the actors explained that he wished to "*live* truthfully in [his] everyday life, and *realize* the truth on stage."[51] The visual mimicry based on hypervisual Blackness in this case was thought to be a way to approximate what the theater company considered "real" in their worldview about oppressed South African freedom fighters. The case of *The Island* illustrates that theatrical realism previously based on raced mundane objects, which signified a worldview in the making, became a more rigid, surface-level materialization of the racialized other. While the earlier theatrical experimentations on stage opened possibilities for exploring various issues of politics and national-racial identities (albeit ambiguously), the late 1960s introduction of color films contributed to changing methods of "racing" toward more obvious depictions of Blackness through colorism on screen.

Conclusion

The discussion of early-twentieth-century racial consciousness and the case studies of *Yeoldaeeo* explored in this chapter demonstrate how early- to mid-century realism theater in Korea presented visions of the real, rife with the emerging issues of nationalism, ethno-racial heterogeneity, colonialism, and Western hegemony. This chapter sought to both historicize and theorize how practices of Korean realism theater used casting choices, props, stage designs, lighting, and costumes—which are conceptualized "things" that activate reality on stage—to explore changing national and racial consciousness in the broader sociocultural context. The elements of Korean realism theater are "raced"—in other words, assigned racialized and nationalized dispositions and qualities—to assist the narrative development and articulation of political ideology on stage.

However, "racing" also became an act of hypervisible racialization of characters and spaces in later theater productions where "realism" was equated with racial mimicry. Problematic uses of blackface makeup and woolly wigs, for instance, were introduced as a way to approximate Blackness in post-1960s theater productions that emphasized colorism and racial hypervisuality. Nevertheless, the early examples discussed in this chapter show how the formative years of realism theater used the racing of objects to articulate sociopolitical anxieties, from which we understand that Asian performing arts have engaged critically and imaginatively with precarious "realisms" in manifold forms.

Notes

1. The authors would like to thank Jeong Min Joo and Gu Ji-yun for their research assistance. Research for this chapter was partially funded by Lingnan University Research Seed Fund. All *hangul* words in this chapter are romanized using the RR (Revised Romanization) system.

2. Cha Bumseok, "Rejecting Indiscriminate Imports of Foreign Styles . . . 'Reality Where We Fear Proximity to Truth' . . . Should Be Open to More Topics for Artists" (외래 풍조의 무비판도입 배격 . . . '진실에 접근하기 두려운 현실' . . . 연예인에 소재개방하라), *Dong-a ilbo* (동아일보), November 24, 1971.

3. john a. powell, "The Racing of American Society: Race Functioning as a Verb before Signifying as a Noun," *Law & Inequality: A Journal of Theory and Practice* 15, no. 1 (1997): 103.

4. See Meewon Lee, "The Modernization of Korean Theatre Through the Reception of Western Realism," in *Modernization of Asian Theatres: Process and Tradition*, ed. Yasushi Nagata and Ravi Chaturvedi (Singapore: Springer, 2019), 23–39.

5. Throughout this chapter, we mention both *Revizor* in reference to the original play by Gogol and *Geomchalgwan* in reference to the Korean adaptation by Silheommudae.

6. For general discussions on Korean realism theater, see Jae-beom Hong and Seong-kwan Cho, "The Method of Action Analysis and the North Korean Realism Theatre in the 1960s," *Asian Theatre Journal* 35, no. 2 (2018): 378–94; Yun-Cheol Kim, "An Introduction to Contemporary Korean Theatre," *Critical Stages/Scènes Critiques* 6 (2012); https://www.critical-stages.org/6/an-introduction-to-contemporary-korean-theatre/

7. Japanese *sinpa* is the origin for the term *sinpageuk*, but the Korean style eventually came to mean various commercial forms distinct from traditional performance. See Lee Seung Hee 이승희, "Formation of Sinpageuk and Original Plays" (신파극의 형성과 창작희곡), in *100 Years of Contemporary Theater in Korea* (한국 현대연극 100년), ed. National Theatre Association of Korea (Seoul: Yeongeukgwa ingan, 2008), 69–98.

8. Lee Eun Kyeong 이은경, "Development of Geundaegeuk [Modern Theatre] and Seeking New Changes" (근대극의 등장과 새로운 변화의 모색), in *100 Years of Contemporary Theater in Korea* (한국 현대연극 100년), 131–99.

9. This is also partly due to the training of artists and intellectuals in Japan, China, and the US in the colonial and postcolonial periods. For example, similarly syncretic practices in the Japanese *shingeki* movement influenced Geukyeon's productions. Lee Chin-A 이진아, "The Formation of Korean Modern Theater Aesthetics as Modern Views of the Art—Focus on the Relationship between 'Theater Art' and 'Reality'" (근대적 예술관으로서의 한국연극미학의 형성—'연극예술'과 '실재(현실)'의 관계를 중심으로), *Journal of Drama (DR)* (드라마연구) 34 (2011): 350–91.

10. "Unique Stage Set and Acting in Silheommudae Performance" (빗다른 장치와 연기로 실험무대공연), *Dong-a ilbo* (동아일보), June 22, 1932.

11. Nam-Seok Kim 김남석, "A Study on *Revizor* as the Founding Performance of Geugyesuryeonguhoe" (극예술연구회의 창단 공연작 <검찰관>에 관한 연구: 실험무대 출범 정황과 창립 공연 무대 사진을 중심으로), *Research of Performance Art and Culture* (공연문화연구) 39 (2019): 167–96.

12. Kim Hyeon-cheol 김현철, "Study of Interconnectivity between Hong Hae-seong's Drama Theory and His Experiences at Tsukiji Little Theater" (축지소극장의 체험과 홍해성 연극론의 상관성 연구), *Journal of Korean Drama and Theater* (한국극예술연구) 26 (2007): 86.

13. Kim Hyeon-cheol, "Study of Interconnectivity," 86.

14. Lee Seung-hyun 이승현, "Post-War Realism Theater and Forms of Its Fissures: On Yim Hee-jae's Drama" (전후 사실주의 희곡과 그 균열의 양상: 임희재 희곡을 중심으로), *Journal of Korean Drama and Theater* (한국극예술연구) 41 (2013): 82.

15. See Christina Klein, "The AFKN Nexus: US Military Broadcasting and New Korean Cinema," *Transnational Cinemas* 3, no. 1 (2012): 19–39.

16. Ric Knowles, "Editorial Comment: Theatre and Material Culture," *Theatre Journal* 64, no. 3 (2012): 1.

17. Knowles, "Editorial Comment," 3.

18. Dorinne Kondo, *Worldmaking: Race, Performance, and the Work of Creativity* (Durham, NC: Duke University Press, 2018), 27, 30.

19. Powell, "The Racing," 113. Shannon Steen also uses "race" as a verb to illustrate how Asia is "figured" as a racialized site in modern American theater. See Shannon Steen, "Racing American Modernity: Black Atlantic Negotiations of Asia and the 'Swing' Mikados," in *AfroAsian Encounters: Culture, History, Politics*, ed. Heike Raphael-Hernandez and Shannon Steen (New York: New York University Press, 2006), 167–87.

20. Powell, "The Racing," 104.

21. Cha Bumseok 차범석, *Yeoldaeeo* (열대어), in *Complete Works of Cha Bumseok*, vol. 3 (차범석 전집 3), ed. Min-young Yoo 유민영 and Seong-hee Jeon 전성희 (Seoul: Taehaksa, 1965), 205.

22. Im Yeong-woong 임영웅, "Unusual Topic, Common Tragedy" (이색적인 소재, 상식적인 비극), *Kyunghyang shinmun*, April 13, 1966.

23. Im Yeong-woong, "Unusual Topic."

24. Im Yeong-woong, "Unusual Topic."

25. Lee Tae-ju 이태주, "Words from a Master Artist: Playwright Cha Bumseok" (원로 예술인에게 듣는다: 극작가 차범석), *Arts Council Korea Culture and the Arts Monthly* (월간 문화예술), December 2000.

26. Cha, *Yeoldaeeo*, 205.

27. Cha, *Yeoldaeeo*, 215.

28. Cha, *Yeoldaeeo*, 188.

29. Cha, *Yeoldaeeo*, 216–17.

30. Cha, *Yeoldaeeo*, 220.

31. Cha, *Yeoldaeeo*, 193.

32. "The Third Dong-a Theater Award" (제3회 동아연극상), *Dong-a ilbo* (동아일보), March 31, 1966.

33. Cha, *Yeoldaeeo*, 189.
34. Cha, *Yeoldaeeo*, 189.
35. "Theater Company Sanha's *Yeoldaeeo*" (<산하>의 열대어), *Joongang ilbo* (중앙일보), April 9, 1966.
36. Judith Hamera, *Parlor Ponds: The Cultural Work of the American Home Aquarium, 1850–1970* (Ann Arbor: University of Michigan Press, 2012), 41.
37. "Tropical Fish Enjoys the First Spring as a New Bride" (시집온 열대어의 첫 봄맞이), *Dong-a ilbo* (동아일보), March 8, 1959.
38. "Impossible to Breed Tropical Fish Due to Climate Control" (열대어 사육 불가능 기후관계로), *Chosun ilbo* (조선일보), October 23, 1959.
39. "Enemy of the Poor, 'Luxury for Eyes'" (빈자의 적 '눈의 사치'), *Dong-a ilbo* (동아일보), September 12, 1959.
40. *I Want to Be in Your Arms Again* (열대어 영화 오리지널 대본), film script, Korean Film Archive, Seoul, 2.
41. "Susan, the New Black Bride Who Arrived in Korean Film Scene" (한국영화에 시집 온 검은 새아씨 스잔), *Kyunghyang shinmun* (경향신문), July 6, 1968.
42. *I Want to Be in Your Arms Again*, 7, Scene #15.
43. *I Want to Be in Your Arms Again*, 16–17, Scene #37.
44. Ju Yon Kim, *The Racial Mundane: Asian American Performance and the Embodied Everyday* (New York: New York University Press, 2015), 8–9.
45. Kim, *The Racial Mundane*, 3.
46. *I Want to Be in Your Arms Again*, 32, Scene #71.
47. *I Want to Be in Your Arms Again*, 16, Scene #36.
48. *I Want to Be in Your Arms Again*, 46, Scene #104.
49. *I Want to Be in Your Arms Again*, 52, Scene #130.
50. Cha, *Yeoldaeeo*, 277.
51. "Interview: Lee Seung-ho and Seo In-seok in Silheomgeukjang's *Island* 'Toiling Away in Bare Feet in the Middle of a Winter'" (인터뷰: '한겨울에 맨발로 뛰어야 하는 고역' 실험극장 [아일랜드]의 이승호, 서인석), *Dong-a ilbo* (동아일보), February 17, 1978. Emphasis added.

PART II | Real Life Onstage

4 | The Subversion of Everyday Life

Neoliberal South Korea and the Theater of the Everyday in the Plays of Park Kunhyung

KEE-YOON NAHM

In 2007, the theater of the everyday (*ilsanggeuk*) became a focal point for critics and scholars charting new trends in South Korean theater. Featuring familiar settings, colloquial language, uneventful plots, and loose dramatic structures, new playwriting captured the small details and concerns of daily life in twenty-first-century South Korea. In the context of modern Korean theater history, this trend could be interpreted as a swing of the pendulum back to realism after decades of theatricalist experimentation; *madanggeuk* in the 1970s and 1980s merged Korea's rich tradition of oral and masked performance with Brechtian political theater, while the 1990s saw a surge in postmodernist abstraction. Yet most critics also noted that the contemporary theater of the everyday was distinct from early- and mid-twentieth-century social realism despite the common investment in verisimilitude and lived experience.[1]

How exactly is the theater of the everyday different from realism? Korean critics grapple with this question, debating whether this new aesthetic pushes the boundaries of traditional realism or falls short of its ethos of social engagement and critique. This essay surveys the critical discourse (little of which has been introduced outside of South Korea), observing how the theater of the everyday raises broader questions about the aesthetic and political implications of representing the everyday in theater. Following this overview, I turn to the work of playwright and director Park Kunhyung, whose plays about the lives and perspectives of the socially marginalized both exemplify and challenge the premises underlying the theater of the everyday. Furthermore, I situate Park's work in the context of social upheaval at the start of the new millennium, as South Korea dove headfirst into the arms of global capitalism.

As a sociological concept developed by theorists such as Henri Lefevre and Michel de Certeau, the everyday has long been embedded in capitalist structures. More recently, Lauren Berlant and others have pointed out the ways in which late capitalism disrupts our sense of—and aspiration toward—the ordinary as much as it organizes it, calling attention to affective responses that arise when we realize that personal and social crises are not exceptions from everyday life, but rather are the new normal.[2] Later in this essay, I draw parallels between neoliberalism's impact on both theories of the everyday and theatrical realism in order to reconsider earlier models of understanding and depicting ordinary life. I then argue that the neoliberal turn in Korean society after the 1997 financial crisis motivates the formal and aesthetic strategies of Park's plays, distinguishing this new "affective realism" (to borrow Berlant's term) from twentieth-century social realism. This theoretical foundation informs my readings of Park's plays *In Praise of Youth* (1999) and *Don't Be Too Surprised* (2007), where the everyday is recast into a scene of ongoing, normalized precarity.

The Everyday in Post-IMF South Korean Theater

The theater of the everyday was first explored in the Summer 2007 issue of *Korean Theatre Journal*, which featured a special section titled "Theatricality and the Everyday." It should be noted that the playwrights mentioned there were not part of a self-defined theater movement, nor were they responding to a conscious call to depict the everyday in theater.[3] Instead, the label was proposed by theater critics to assess the ways in which Korean theater was converging on a common set of interests and techniques. Two articles—Kim Sung-hee's "The Aesthetics and Reasoning of the Everyday" and Jang Sung-hee's "Is the Everyday a Blessing or Curse for Korean Theater?: Several Categories for Considering the Everyday"—both observed that new Korean playwriting had become preoccupied with unfiltered depictions of the everyday, presented through mundane scenarios and casual dialogue. However, Kim and Jang's views diverge beyond this point, setting the terms for robust debate over the next several years. Kim highlighted aesthetic innovations in these unassuming plays, laying the groundwork for in-depth studies of this trend in subsequent scholarly articles and her book *Korean Theater and the Aesthetics of the Everyday* (2009), which I discuss more later.

Jang, on the other hand, expressed concern that most new work seemed to pander to mainstream tastes for the familiar while being aesthetically uninspired and politically defeatist. In her essay, Jang asked rhetorically whether "theatre isn't merely copying the conservatism of popular aesthetics"—an assessment echoed later by critics such as Lee Eun-kyung, Roh Ee-jung, and Lee Kyung-mi.[4] In their view, this new "fad" had largely replaced all other theatrical forms in the twenty-first century, homogenizing the Korean theater scene. Jang argues that work by young playwrights uncritically adopts the clichéd, colloquial writing style of mainstream film and television: "The grammar of the everyday marks the decline of theater where it can no longer produce discourse, nor serve as a critical voice and aesthetic provocation."[5] Evoking Jean Baudrillard's postmodernist concept of hyperreality, Lee Kyung-mi similarly observes that "the everyday depicted onstage is yet another derivative reality, a critical misunderstanding of [authentic] reality."[6] Viewing this trend as symptomatic of a broader generational shift, Roh bemoans that "many young theatre artists in the twenty-first century completely lack the desire for self-expression. They have simply become producers of goods who gauge the audience's demands and adjust themselves accordingly."[7]

Overall, the critical discourse skewed negatively, although even the detractors commended strong work when it was offered—most notably Park Kunhyung's new plays since the late 1990s. Reading through essays and reviews during this period, I find that these critics make two interrelated assumptions about the institution of South Korean theater. First, there is an ethical imperative that theater should resist the demands of capitalism by setting itself apart from commercialism and mainstream media. Second, the theater should strive for authenticity and deeper meaning by "cracking the surface" (a commonly used metaphor) of everyday reality. Such assessments, I maintain, are rooted in the dramaturgy of twentieth-century social realism. This is explicitly the case in Roh's essay, which bears the striking subtitle, "Has the Everyday Reached Realism?" She defines realism as a politically engaged movement that intentionally jostles the audience to shed light on social issues. According to Roh, twenty-first-century Korean theater has regressed past the rise of social realism back to a state comparable to "premodern" melodrama and the star-vehicle shows in the nineteenth century.[8] As hyperbolic as it sounds, this statement echoes sentiments that run through many other arguments against the theater of the everyday, objecting to this theater's apparent lack of "critical revelations" (Jang Sung-hee), "authenticity" (Lee Kyung-mi), and "the political" (Lee Eun-kyung).[9] Thus, the standards of social realism are often operating in the background when critics note flaws and deficiencies in these new plays.

To be fair, these critics have good reason to base their assessments on this premise, because to an extent the theater of the everyday inherits the concerns and tendencies of realism. For example, many of the plays discussed by these critics focus on the struggling working class and the socially marginalized, relying on "lower-depths" narratives to illustrate how poverty, exploitation, and discrimination figure into daily life for many Koreans. To list some examples that appear frequently in the critical literature, Kim Nak-hyung's *All the Nights on Earth* (2006) is about a group of female sex workers hiding during a police sweep and passing the time with conversations about their lives. Ko Jae-gwee's *Tranquility* (2006) focuses on two characters with disabilities: a blind massage therapist and a tattoo artist with postpolio syndrome. Kim Han-gil's *Rental Apartment* (2006) is set in two identical low-income housing units inhabited by unemployed youths who aspire to becoming artists.

However, it should be noted that examinations of social inequality and precarity took on new meaning during this time as global capital and neoliberal government policies took hold of South Korea. As the country underwent fundamental restructuring after the foreign currency crisis of 1997 and bailout by the International Monetary Fund, Koreans had to renegotiate their sense of the everyday not only in the workplace but at home, where unemployment, debt, and inflation stymied long-term plans. Thus, the daily lives that these plays render in microscopic detail exist in a post-IMF context. Neoliberalism's splintering of traditional class structures and insistence on individual responsibility make the dramaturgy of social realism less viable in this environment. As a result, the struggling characters in these plays are generally isolated from broader sociopolitical contexts, rather than evolving into working-class archetypes. In other words, Korean theater had not become apolitical in the twenty-first century. Rather, the political was being restructured in these plays about neoliberal everydayness.

For this reason, I believe it is more productive to examine the Korean theater of the everyday through South Korea's socioeconomic context and debates among Korean critics, rather than compare it to similarly named theater movements in other countries. Granted, some Korean scholars noted parallels with post-1968 theater in Europe that expressed political disillusionment after a period of revolutionary fervor—especially the plays of Franz Xaver Kroetz in Germany and Michel Vinaver in France (a major figure of the *théâtre du quotidien* movement).[10] Others connected new Korean playwriting to Japan's quiet theater movement of the 1990s, which may have had some influence due to their temporal and geographic proximity; Hirata Oriza, whose plays have been staged in Korea numerous times, wrote in 1997 that "most life has nothing whatever to do with what theatre in the past has enjoyed portraying, but is grounded instead in quiet and uneventful moments."[11] Despite the similarities, however, I argue that the theater of the everyday is not another "foreign import" like many twentieth-century Korean theater movements, the international wave of Ibsenite social realism being a prime example. Rather, it is in essence a domestic response to a different kind of global current: neoliberalism as it expanded in developed Western nations toward the end of the twentieth century. If modern everyday life is regulated (though not entirely determined) by capitalism, what unites these disparate plays and playwrights is not a manifesto or foundational theory, but rather a shared sense that the conditions of work, leisure, and consumption were changing at an alarming pace. Competition, instability, and precarity were becoming new norms that permeated the Korean everyday, even as society compelled individuals to pursue an increasingly untenable, middle-class ideal of "ordinary" life.

Aside from the theater of the everyday, critics also proposed terms such as "small theater" (*jageun yeongeuk*) and "micronarrative theater" (*misijeok seosayeongeuk*) to describe the dramaturgical emphasis on vignettes and casual dramatic situations over tightly knit plots and momentous events. For example, Yoon Young-sun's *Travel* (2005) depicts five middle-aged men as they take an overnight trip to their hometown to attend their childhood schoolmate's funeral. Kim Jae-yeop's *Whatever Happened to Today's Book?* (2006) is set in a used bookstore, also about a group of friends who reminisce about their college years when they were political activists. ("Today's Book" refers to an actual bookstore that was a well-known meeting place for student intellectuals and activists, adding another layer of authenticity to the play.) Jang Sung-hee is skeptical of this "downsizing" trend in Korean theater, arguing that competition from commercial media and the financial straits that many small theater companies faced led to a general dearth of political and creative energy—an involuntary "poor theater."[12] However, Kim Sung-hee asserts that the theater of the everyday is infused with a postmodernist worldview despite presenting a recognizable social reality: "While their predecessors dug deeply into grand narratives such as Society, History, or Humanity through realist dramaturgy and traditional Korean theater forms, these young playwrights were baptized by postmodernism's lean towards micro-discourses."[13] From a postmodernist perspective, to insist that theater must somehow break through surface reality to reveal some "authentic" truth about the world turns out to be a fantasy. In that regard, the unambitious scope and lax dramaturgy of these plays could be interpreted as deliberate choices that harbor dissatisfaction with past forms—especially realism. Kim refutes the argument that the theater of the everyday is apolitical or politically ineffective, endorsing its potential to "critique and reflect on the everyday in modern society through new aesthetic and formal experiments."[14] Rather than simply rendering the everyday in fine detail, she argues that this new theater subverts common perceptions of the everyday by exposing its neoliberal base.

In *Cruel Optimism* (2011), Lauren Berlant calls for a posttraumatic approach to analyzing artistic representations of the everyday, pointing out that catastrophe, upheaval, and violence are already embedded in daily life. Under neoliberalism, normalcy and states of exception have melded into what she calls a state of "crisis ordinariness."[15] Crisis is something that we learn to live with, rather than endure and overcome. This was indeed the case with the IMF crisis. Bolstered by nationalist sentiment, South Koreans mobilized to fight off the threat of financial collapse, most evident in the widespread gold-collecting campaign of 1998, an attempt to pay off foreign debt through collective sacrifice. Yet it became apparent over the next decade that the IMF crisis was not a single event, but rather a turning point in the normalization of uncertainty and instability: a dramatic structure in which the denouement never arrives. While the national economy and megaconglomerates bounced back within a few years, many Koreans continued to flounder as job insecurity, extreme competition, and economic inequality became common, even expected, experiences. Berlant's notion of the impasse describes one pervasive affective structure that shapes the neoliberal everyday: "The impasse is a space of time lived without a narrative genre. Adaptation to it usually involves a gesture or undramatic action that points to and revises an unresolved situation. . . . An impasse is a holding station that doesn't hold securely but opens out into anxiety, that dogpaddling around a space whose contours remain obscure."[16] Berlant's discussion offers an alternative to postmodernist fragmentation for explaining the shift away from traditional dramatic structures. Realist plays in the past generally relied on a dramaturgy of crisis to reveal some "hidden truth" about society. And this dramaturgy made it possible for audiences to imagine an endpoint to that *extra*-ordinary event even if it is not a part of the plot. By treating crisis as a state of exception, a shared notion of normalcy is preserved. Thus, the consolation that, say, Willy Loman's death can offer us is that we can see ourselves avoiding his missteps to hopefully live normal lives. The impasse, on the other hand, undermines such distinctions as crisis and everydayness blur into one another, flattening out traditional dramatic arcs. The theater of the everyday, I argue, reflects South Korea's gradual adaptation to this profoundly undramatic yet affectively charged field.

To explore this idea further, I now turn to the work of Park Kunhyung, a major figure in the theater of the everyday whose plays are frequently revived, and one who is lauded even by critics who are pessimistic about the trend. My two main case studies will be *In Praise of Youth* (1999), which is generally viewed as the starting point of the theater of the everyday, and *Don't Be Too Surprised* (2007), which premiered the same year that critics such as Kim and Jang first proposed the label. Through my readings of these plays, I argue that Park is both an exemplar of the theater of the everyday and one of its greatest innovators, pushing depictions of daily life far beyond the confines of realist dramaturgy in order to highlight the widening fissures in post-IMF South Korea.

In Praise of Youth: Making the Familiar Unfamiliar

Born in 1963, Park Kunhyung started working in the theater in the mid-1980s, first as an actor at Theatre Company 76, best known for its long-running production of Peter Handke's *Offending the Audience*. Like many in the Korean theater scene, Park was both a playwright and director, writing scripts that he intended to stage himself. After several early works that went unnoticed, his breakthrough came in 1999 with the sensational success of *In Praise of Youth*, which Kim Sung-hee calls "the origin of the Korean theater of the everyday and the fuse that ignited the fad that came after."[17] The play won a slew of awards that year, establishing Park as a rising star. Park founded his own company in 2001—Theatre Company Golmokgil, meaning "alleyway"—which still serves as the artistic home of Park's original works. The company name reflects a running theme in his plays: stories of the socially marginalized who inhabit the underbelly of Korean society. *Golmokgil* evokes the urban geography of postindustrial Seoul, where the winding alleys and hillside slums of the last century are obscured by facades of high-rise apartments and office complexes. In 2006, Park won almost every major theater award, including the prestigious Donga Theatre Award and the Daesan Literature Award, for his postwar family drama *Kyung-sook, Kyung-sook's Father*. He remains a prolific artist to this day, consistently premiering a new work every few years, in addition to frequent remounts of past plays.

Although this essay focuses on Park as an important playwright in twenty-first-century South Korean theater, his practice blurs the boundaries between playwriting and directing. Many features of his writing style, such as hyper-colloquial dialogue and loose structure with frequent scene changes, can also be attributed to the way that he works with actors or makes use of small black-box spaces. Following his success, Park has taken on large-scale directing projects for state-subsidized theaters, including highly publicized productions of *Hamlet*, *Marat/Sade*, and a stage adaptation of Albert Camus's *The Plague*. The most infamous of these side projects was his 2013 adaptation of Aristophanes' *The Frogs* at the National Theatre Company of Korea, which made satirical references to several former Korean presidents. Outrage from conservatives led to him eventually being blacklisted from government funding, which factored into the 2016 mass demonstrations that precipitated the ouster of former President Park Geun-hye (the daughter of one of the lampooned political figures).[18] However, it is important to note that even as he became a major figure in Korean theater, Park consistently wrote new plays similar in style to his early pieces, and staged them in small theaters. Park's range of work suggests that his bare-bones aesthetic is an intentional choice, not a compromise due to financial limitations.

Writing in 2000, on the heels of *In Praise of Youth*'s success, theater critic Baek Hyun-mi notes what sets Park's work apart from his predecessors in Korean theater: "His theatre doesn't contain any of the trends we are familiar with. His theatre lacks the weight of history, the energy of modern society, new formal experimentation, and the passion to expose abject reality. All we see are bizarre relationships among a strange family, a few dirty and worn props, and actors who seem to be expressing trivial emotions that they lost long ago. That is why his theatre is uncomfortable and surprising."[19] Although Baek concluded that "Park does not seem concerned with establishing his own style," his theater aesthetic ironically became a hallmark of twenty-first-century Korean theater.[20] Kim Sung-hee notes: "Through Park's influence, there is a strong current in contemporary Korean playwriting that focuses on the bland and unimportant, forgoing dramatic heroes for incapable nobodies."[21] While Park was part of a gradual shift toward micronarratives in the 1990s by playwrights such as Lee Hyun-hwa and Ui Sung-shin, later artists sought to emulate the distinct style he pioneered in *In Praise of Youth*: unembellished dialogue, indistinct dramatic structures, and familiar everyday settings punctuated by sardonic humor, fantasy, and the grotesque.

The play centers on a teenage boy simply called the Youth, who has flunked his second year of high school twice. Spending his days loitering and drinking alcohol, the protagonist bears traces of the urban wanderer, a figure that has influenced conceptualizations of the modern everyday from Walter Benjamin to the Situationists and Lefebvre. Yet the Youth's aimless drifting doesn't grant him the privilege of "urban 'free association' that is designed to reveal the hidden secrets of the urban everyday."[22] Instead, the everyday, as seen through the Youth's eyes, is inhospitable and unknowable, placing him squarely within Berlant's condition of the impasse. Traditional values and institutions have crumbled away, reflected in the Youth's relationship with two failed paternal figures. One is his unemployed father; in the play's famous first scene, the Youth berates his father for not looking for a job as they drink soju together. The Father daydreams about emigrating to Japan or working on a tuna-fishing vessel, suggesting that there is no place for him in Korea. The other figure is his history teacher, who at first tries to get the Youth to graduate but eventually gives up. Aware that the Youth has many questions about the pitiful state of the world, the Teacher can only remark: "History has no power. It didn't used to be like that."[23] The Teacher is part of the "386 generation," a term coined in the late 1990s to describe the central force behind South Korea's achievement of full democracy. But the Western Enlightenment values and leftist politics that shaped his worldview have become obsolete in the age of global capitalism.[24] Just as the Youth's father is unable to fulfill the traditionally respected role of breadwinner, the Teacher fails to acclimate to the domination of capitalist ideology. Through these lethargic adult figures, *In Praise of Youth* captures the quiet disintegration of social norms in post-IMF Korea, especially those rooted in Confucian patriarchy and the ideology of the family.

As a result, the kids are left on their own. The play draws on familiar media images of juvenile delinquents indulging in alcohol, violence, and sex. As if they were gang members, the Youth's sidekick Yong-pil openly smokes cigarettes in class, and a girl nicknamed Viper threatens to torture a classmate by pulling out his fingernails. We learn some details about these young characters: that Yong-pil's father is in prison (contrary to rumors that he works for the yakuza in Japan) and that the

Figure 4.1: *In Praise of Youth*, written and directed by Park Kunhyung, 2013 revival. Image courtesy of Theatre Company Golmokgil.

Youth's parents got divorced after his father splashed bleach on his wife's face during a fight, blinding her. But the play doesn't dwell long enough on these past misfortunes for the audience to gain access to these characters' inner lives. Park portrays these teenagers' everyday with a light touch, leaving their frustrations and anxieties unresolved. This is apparent in the way that Park writes, relying heavily on his actors' improvisation based on a handful of biographical facts and personality traits. Even the published versions of his plays, collected in three volumes so far, refer to some of the characters by the name of the actor who played the role in the premiere.

Despite the lack of dramatic closure, critics read social criticism into these fragmented representations of South Korea at the close of the twentieth century. Shim Jae-min employs Bakhtin's theory of the grotesque to examine the play's inversion of social and ethical norms, writing that "Park Kunhyung uses stories of people who live in a society with inverted values to emphasize the fact that they have already accepted a distorted and inverted way of life without any resistance."[25] Kim Sung-hee makes a similar case when she writes that *In Praise of Youth* "seems to represent the everyday lives of marginalized characters, but it is founded on a critique of capitalist colonization that alienates and subjugates the everyday."[26] However, Park's plays never feel didactic. As suggested in Baek's quotation above, *In Praise of Youth* is shockingly bare-bones, eschewing any frame that would sublimate its theatrical representations into clear political messages.

Park favors irony over empathy; the romantic sentiment conjured by the play's title rings hollow against what we actually see onstage. Take, for example, the character Epilepsy, a woman in her early twenties who suffers from a neurological disorder. She works as a server at a run-down coffeehouse, sleeping in a mold-encrusted back room. She laments that she will have to find a new place to live soon because the other workers find her repulsive. Most scholarship on the play mentions the physicality of the actor playing Epilepsy (Go Su-hee in the premiere, who went on to become a successful stage and film actor) as a locus of social critique. Calling attention to the references to obesity, menstruation, and defecation in her dialogue, Kim Jeong-suk asserts that Epilepsy's stigmatized body becomes "an image of social ostracization and alienation."[27] Shim Jae-min focuses on these same corporeal elements as an example of Park utilizing the grotesque as a performative strategy for stimulating the audience's critical awareness.[28]

However, Epilepsy's misfortune is rendered inconsequential by the dramatic structure. She and the Youth become an unlikely couple when Epilepsy suggests she may be pregnant. The Youth brings her home to live with him, which angers his father. Agitated by the two bickering men, she has a prolonged seizure onstage—an apparent crisis that threatens to shatter any pretension to ordinariness that the play may have previously offered. But this disturbing scene is undercut by Yong-pil's first line in the next scene: "Fuck, I fell asleep completely. This play has no comedy! What's a movie or a play supposed to be? Entertaining, right? Action and spectacle!"[29] It turns out that Yong-pil is talking about an imaginary production of *The Cherry Orchard* that he wandered into to kill time. Considering Chekhov's impact on the modern theater, the line could be read as a knock at stuffy realist plays that can no longer meet the demands of capitalist consumerism. But on another, meta-theatrical level, Yong-pil's complaint loops back to the previous scene, deflating the emotional and symbolic weight of Epilepsy's seizure. As a result, the audience is denied the space to empathize with Epilepsy or turn her into a symbol of social alienation. Instead, they become detached voyeurs of her suffering. This distancing effect is reinforced in the play's finale: an extended, silent moment in which the Youth stares back at the audience, smoking a cigarette and holding a copy of the program for *In Praise of Youth*.[30]

Park approaches the everyday not with a magnifying glass and fine brush, but rather with Brechtian devices that disrupt "true-to-life" depictions of the socially marginalized. Unable to treat these characters as objects of empathy or embodied symbols of oppression, the audience must look past their assumptions about modern everyday life to make sense of the play. Such a strategy counters the ways in which economies of representation under neoliberal capitalism establish and circulate narratives about the working class by claiming authenticity. Katie Beswick convincingly argues that "authenticity becomes, within mainstream realist depictions, a totalizing mechanism that operates within a structure of 'capitalist realism.'"[31] Beswick goes on to note that the dramaturgy of twentieth-century social realism—for example, the kitchen-sink dramas of mid-twentieth-century Britain—has been co-opted by this new neoliberal mode where the plight of the working class becomes their destiny. Park seems to be aware of these pitfalls when he prevents spectators from fully understanding Epilepsy's hard life or the Youth's aimlessness. Furthermore, he relies on ironic juxtapositions to highlight the discrepancy between, on one hand, middle-class ideas of the modern everyday based in cycles of work and leisure, consumerism, and the entertainment industry, and on the other hand, those whose daily lives are conditioned by violence, exclusion, and precarity. By subverting our expectations of the everyday through techniques that produce "a feeling of unfamiliar familiarity" as Kim Sung-hee describes, Park exposes our very apprehension of "ordinary" life as a marker of socioeconomic privilege.[32]

Kim Sung-hee's dialectic between the familiar and the unfamiliar evokes and complicates Brecht's estrangement effect, emphasizing how recognizability and identification still figure into the audience's apprehension of social reality despite being exposed to its ideological foundations. Feelings still hold sway over the theatrical experience even as audiences are asked to engage critically with the representations onstage. Yet what kinds of feelings, and to what end? In her attempt to advocate for the efficacy of the theater of the everyday, partly in response to criticism raised by others in previous years, Kim suggests that this affective response can be sublimated into a form of critical consciousness:

> The theatre of the everyday is an "audience's theatre" that allows the audience to fill the gaps in meaning and construct the meaning of the text according to their world consciousness—in other words, guide

the audience towards proactive interpretation—by presenting ordinary, banal everyday life rather than grand narratives such as ideology or history. The value of the theatre of the everyday lies in its methods of playwriting and performance, which exceed representations of the everyday to show the cracks and gaps within it, exposing that which is obscured by everydayness: the contradictions of capitalism, the multifaceted and polysemous nature of history and the world, and the abnormal within the normal.[33]

In other words, the theater of the everyday relies precisely on dramaturgical elements that some critics may deem sloppy writing—loose structures, underdeveloped characters, and abrupt shifts—in order to activate the audience, turning them into what Jacques Rancière calls emancipated spectators who can see through the familiar, smooth surface of everydayness under neoliberalism. While I agree that *In Praise of Youth* exposes normal life as an unattainable fantasy, I am wary of views that might give the neoliberal everyday a back door to come back in. Park's work rejects the idea that his characters have been regrettably denied an everyday that they deserve, that all the Youth truly wants is to be a normal teenage boy in a normal family. Rather, the Youth lives in a perpetual impasse. The play seeks to loosen the audience's attachment to an idealized everyday so that they may recognize the absence of dramatic closure itself as the quintessential neoliberal condition. Normalcy loses its privileged status as the master signifier of socially engaged theater, the destination point of realist dramatic structure. In its place, the neoliberal everyday emerges as an empty signifier around which affective states coalesce.

In the decade following *In Praise of Youth*, Park continued to question what the everyday means in contemporary Korean society, combining theatrical verisimilitude with Brechtian techniques and grotesque imagery to disrupt the audience's tendency to revert to familiar notions of normal life. These ongoing experiments lead to, in my view, his most stunning meditation on the neoliberal everyday: *Don't Be Too Surprised*, a play about a dysfunctional family on its last legs that pushes theatrical depictions of daily life to horrific extremes.

Don't Be Too Surprised: Subverting the Everyday

In 2007, the same year that the theater of the everyday was proposed as a label for new Korean playwriting, Park premiered *Don't Be Too Surprised* at the historic Sanwoolim Theatre in Seoul. Like many of his previous plays, *Don't Be Too Surprised* highlights the daily lives of idle fathers, delinquent youth, and others who have slipped through the cracks of society. The elderly Father spends his days fishing at a nearby reservoir after he lost his *baduk* parlor because of his runaway wife's gambling debts. His First Son is an unsuccessful filmmaker, away on shoots for months at a time without contributing to the household income. His wife, named Daughter-in-Law in the script, is the only one in the family who makes money, as a *noraebang doumi*, or "karaoke assistant": women hired to provide company and, in some cases, sexual service to customers at karaoke bars. Incidentally, all the characters work or have worked in the entertainment and leisure industries. Yet they themselves lack access to the regenerative amusement that they provide for others in this economy. Physically exhausted and emotionally drained, there is no hope that their situation will get better.

The final family member is the agoraphobic Second Son, who has not stepped out of the house in years—an added burden to the family's financial struggles. The scrawny young man only eats imitation crab meat, and thus suffers from chronic constipation; in almost every scene, he squats over the toilet in the house's closet-sized bathroom. This bathroom becomes the most important space in the play after the Father hangs himself there at the end of the first scene. In the premiere, the actor was suspended in midair with a harness throughout the entire play, visible to the audience every time someone (usually Second Son) opened the bathroom door. None of the other family members have the time or capability to take care of the decomposing corpse, so it must remain in the coffin-like bathroom. Although we learn later that the Father was heartbroken to discover that his estranged wife was living with someone else, the recurring image of the elderly man dangling by his neck calls to mind South Korea's exceedingly high suicide rate, especially among senior citizens.[34]

So far in my summary, the play seems invested in authentic depictions of the most vulnerable in South Korean society, evoking the grind of daily life. However, as Kim Young-hak notes, Park balances this realist approach with sudden turns toward the grotesque as a defamiliarization tactic.[35] After the suicide, the next scene begins with the Second Son squatting over the toilet next to his Father's corpse, still trying to relieve himself. As if that weren't outrageous enough, the Father suddenly opens his eyes and begins complaining to Second Son: "Can't you hear me? Let me down! I'm tired!"[36] The Second Son recoils in disgust,

Figure 4.2: *Don't Be Too Surprised*, written and directed by Park Kunhyung, 2007 premiere. Image courtesy of Theatre Company Golmokgil.

even putting duct tape over Father's eyes to avoid his supernatural gaze. But his stomach pains give him no choice but to sit on the toilet next to the dead body.

This highly theatrical conceit seems to clash with the small, mundane scenes characteristic of the theater of the everyday. Yet in performance, these approaches meld together in strange harmony. None of the characters acknowledge the fact that the corpse speaks. They just treat the dead body as a nuisance. The play derives morbid humor from the juxtaposition of utter abjection against the familiar routines of daily life. The grotesque tableau of Second Son and the Father—bodily functions and dead matter—squeezed together in the tiny bathroom constitutes what Giorgio Agamben calls a state of exception, "an extratemporal and extraterritorial threshold in which the human body is separated from its normal political status and abandoned . . . to the most extreme misfortunes."[37] At first glance, this description best fits the Father, who was incapacitated in life and is denied respite even in death because his children lack the means to give him a proper burial. But I argue that Second Son is the play's emblem for those whose everyday existence is reduced to Agamben's bare life. While the Father begs the family to let him out,

Second Son repeatedly returns to the bathroom as if he is a denizen of that bizarre space. Even his physiology resembles the abject space; Second Son complains about the broken ventilation fan that locks in the unbearable stench, just as his own bowels are perpetually backed up.

Bong Joon-ho's film *Parasite* (2019) memorably used body odor as a symbol for economic inequality and class immobility in contemporary South Korea. But Park had pushed that potent image to a grotesque extreme in *Don't Be Too Surprised* over a decade earlier. Playwright and theater critic Kim Myung-hwa asserts that the smell is actually the main character of the play, giving her phantom sensations of the suffocating stench during the performance.[38] But the noxious smells don't come only from the Father's corpse. Before his suicide, the Father asks Second Son whether he can smell death in the house. Second Son makes a peculiar retort: "My rotting body smells worse than yours. You think I'm stupid? That I can't smell my own flesh rotting?"[39] The line suggests that Second Son is living yet somehow already dead, his everyday life devoid of purpose or agency.

With that idea in mind, I'd like to go back to Second Son's debilitating agoraphobia. We learn that he stopped going outside after his mother, a gambling addict, ran away one night with all their savings. But setting this backstory aside, Second Son's "uselessness" around the house, as Daughter-in-Law bemoans, evokes the widespread twenty-first-century syndrome known best by its Japanese name, *hikikomori*, in which young adults living with their parents suddenly stop going outside. Also known as acute social withdrawal, these individuals choose self-isolation over the stress of coping with social instability and prolonged unemployment—an effect of neoliberal restructuring not only in East Asia but throughout the world. In South Korea's case, mental health experts began raising awareness of "reclusive loners" (the official Korean term) in the first decade of the twenty-first century, counting the IMF crisis as a contributing factor to their increase. Second Son's abject status captures the existential dread of being unproductive in a society that doesn't tolerate wastefulness, shared by a generation of unemployed and underemployed youths who grew up during the recession. The bathroom that entraps him becomes a symbolic repository for human waste, both in the sense of bodily excrement and people deemed worthless by capitalism. In *Liquid Times: Living in an Age of Uncertainty* (2006), Zygmunt Bauman writes, "The volume of humans made redundant by capitalism's global triumph grows unstoppably and comes close now to exceeding the managerial capacity of the planet; there is a plausible prospect of capitalist modernity (or modern capitalism) *choking on its own waste products* which it can neither reassimilate or annihilate, nor detoxify."[40] If the theater of the everyday draws attention to small, personal spaces to observe everyday life, Park extends this most private of locations into a metonym for neoliberalism's own failing sewage system, where shit (i.e., redundant humans) has nowhere else to go.

Meanwhile, Second Son's indifferent attitude toward this nightmarish situation reflects the affective dimensions of everyday life for South Korean youth. Unlike the restless protagonist of *In Praise of Youth*, Second Son is a willing prisoner of his miserable environment, having convinced himself that he can't do anything useful—whether it is burying his father or fixing the broken ventilator. Second Son's learned helplessness leads to passive acceptance of the extraordinary events in the play. He is the recipient of the title's ironic directive: don't be too surprised. Second Son relays this phrase to his brother as the Father's last words, although the Father was actually describing the circumstances of his friend's suicide. Yet the title also captures the cool apathy of late capitalism, as Fredric Jameson postulated in his writings on postmodernism. In *Capitalist Realism: Is There No Alternative?* (2009), Mark Fisher expands on Jameson's theory to argue that global capitalism now "seamlessly occupies the horizons of the thinkable"—so omnipresent it becomes *the* realism of our times.[41] Having internalized this worldview, Second Son is nonchalant toward the abject horror around him, fully convinced there is no other way for his family to live but as human waste.

Don't Be Too Surprised marks a notable departure from previous examples of the Korean theater of the everyday, relying on theatrical effects such as the cramped bathroom and hanging body to create incisive images of social collapse in neoliberal South Korea. However, this doesn't mean that Park has lost interest in the project of examining the everyday onstage. Rather, the play shifts the terms of representing the everyday from quotidian realism to carnivalesque fantasy. Throughout the play, we encounter commodified spaces that offer momentary diversion and relief from reality. For example, when Daughter-in-Law comes in drunk after a long night, she pulls a microphone out of her purse and begins singing one of her favorite songs. In the premiere that Park directed, a moving light ball turns on, transforming the drab living room into a singing booth. In another scene, an actor jumps out of the shoe cabinet to dance wildly onstage when Daughter-in-Law describes the kinds of customers she meets at work. The First Son also can't help but bring his "work" home with him. When his brother asks about his latest project,

First Son launches into a narrated enactment of "The Third Vagabond," his science fiction B-movie about a wandering hero leading a popular uprising against an evil empire. A sci-fi prophet in full costume barges onstage to summarize the plot over an epic soundtrack. Interestingly, First Son's film turns a narrative of political revolution into commodified entertainment, indicative of "the pre-emptive formatting and shaping of desires, aspirations and hopes by capitalist culture."[42] First Son wagers his career on the belief that audiences crave this kind of escapism and excitement, while Daughter-in-Law understands that her customers at the karaoke bar need emotional release and intimacy to stay afloat in this harsh society. In other words, these fantastical sequences expose leisure, an essential facet of the modern everyday, as part of the capitalist machine.

At the same time, growing social precarity means that even this commodified everyday is out of reach for many Koreans. Park utilizes the theater of the everyday's fragmented dramaturgy to make this point. Many of these flamboyant sequences are directed toward Second Son, whose agoraphobia bars him from firsthand experience of "the outside world"—i.e., neoliberal society. But once the lights and music fade, the house reverts to its usual bleakness, with Father's corpse still hanging in the bathroom, of course. The contrast between commercial exuberance and Second Son's bare life shows that the everyday is constructed by glossing over capitalism's side-products: inequality, precarity, and humans rendered into waste.

In *The Practice of Everyday Life* (1980), Michel de Certeau asserts that actual lived experience has always managed to slip past totalizing systems, creating small moments of agency and resistance that cannot be suppressed because they are ever-changing. In the case of modern capitalist societies, the everyday is filled with instances of tactical consumption, "a subtle art of 'renters' who know how to insinuate their countless differences into the dominant text."[43] Yet de Certeau's belief that the everyday could be politicized may seem hopelessly naïve in the age of capitalist realism, where consumer culture has infiltrated every aspect of daily life, down to our most private spaces. (Would Second Son's fate have been different if he had a smartphone with him on the toilet?) Critics who panned the theater of the everyday in the first decade of the twenty-first century were concerned that theater was replicating comfortably familiar images of the everyday in the media without offering this potential for resistance and difference. Many of them called for a full return to traditional realism, although scholars such as Kim Sung-hee argued that the theater of the everyday entailed aesthetic and formal experimentation. In *Don't Be Too Surprised*, Park questions whether a return to realism is possible when representations of the everyday are utterly co-opted by capitalist media.

Meanwhile, South Korean theater would find a renewed political consciousness in the next decade, prompted by the Sewol Ferry disaster in 2014, the blacklist scandal and mass antigovernment demonstrations in 2016, and the #MeToo movement in 2018. Meditations on the everyday may seem futile when Korean society is besieged by one extraordinary crisis after another. But the everyday continues to function as a site for Korean theater to gauge the effects of capitalism on human life, not to mention the viability of theatrical realism in the age of reality television and online live streaming. Among his contemporaries, Park Kunhyung has most successfully employed the full range of tools that theater has to offer—from abrupt shifts in dramatic structure to comic and grotesque imagery—to expose the idealized notion of uneventful daily life as a seductive commodity that neoliberalism propagates.

Notes

1. Realism was a major influence in the development of modern Korean drama in the early twentieth century, as was the nation-building project of postwar South Korea. Major realist playwrights in Korean theater history include Yoo Chi-jin, Lim Seun-kyu, Ham Se-duk, and Cha Bum-seok.

2. Lauren Berlant, *Cruel Optimism* (Durham, NC: Duke University Press), 8–11.

3. Other playwrights associated with the theater of the everyday include Kim Myung-hwa, Jang Woo-jae, Choi Zina, Kim Duk-soo, Choi Chang-geun, Sung Ki-woong, and Jung Young-wook, among others. Another play often discussed in this critical context is Lee Hae-je's *Daripong Modern Girl* (2007), a collection of vignettes about the introduction of the telephone to Korean society at the end of the nineteenth century. Although this work doesn't depict modern everyday life as do the other examples above, it reflects new interest in microhistories of the late Joseon and Japanese occupation periods, moving away from the ethno-nationalist ideology that dominated Korean scholarship in previous decades. Kim Sung-hee notes that this shift in historiography coincides with the turn toward the everyday in theater. See the chapter "The Everyday in Colonial Modernity and Theatrical Representation" (식민지 근대의 일상과 연극적 재현), in *Korean Theater and the Aesthetics of the Everyday* (한국 연극과 일상의 미학) (Seoul: Yeongeukgwa Ingan, 2009); as well as Lee Sang-woo, "Microhistory, the Modern Everyday, and Korean Theater" (미시사, 근대적 일상, 그리고 한국연극), *Korean Theatre Journal* 52 (2009).

4. Jang Sung-hee, "Is the Everyday a Blessing or Curse for Korean Theater?:

Several Categories for Considering the Everyday" (일상성, 한국연극의 약인가 독인가—'일상성'을 다루는 몇 가지 범주), *Korean Theatre Journal* 45 (2007): 83. All translations of Korean sources in this essay are mine.

5. Jang, "Is the Everyday a Blessing or Curse?," 83.

6. Lee Kyung-mi, "Reconsidering the Authenticity of South Korean Theater at the Start of 2008: Cracking the Surface of the Everyday" (2008년 첫머리에서 다시 생각하는 한국 연극의 진정성—일상의 외피에 균열내기), *Korean Theatre Journal* 48 (2008): 37.

7. Roh Ee-jung, "Korean Theater in the Twenty-First Century: Has the Everyday Reached Realism?" (21세기 한국의 연극: 일상적이다, 하지만 리얼리즘에 도달했는가?), *Korean Theatre Journal* 48 (2008): 31.

8. Roh Ee-jung, "Korean Theater in the Twenty-First Century," 32.

9. Lee Eun-kyung, "A Resurrection of 'the Political' beyond the Everyday" (일상성에서 벗어나 부활한 '정치적인 것'), *Korean Theatre Journal* 60 (2011).

10. Annie Sparks, Annie Stephenson, and David Bradby, *Mise en Scène: French Theatre Now* (London: Bloomsbury, 2014), 65.

11. Quoted in Jonathan Salz, ed., *A History of Japanese Theatre* (Cambridge, UK: Cambridge University Press, 2016), 336.

12. Jang, "Is the Everyday a Blessing or Curse?," 85.

13. Kim Sung-hee, *Korean Theater and the Aesthetics of the Everyday*, 17.

14. Kim Sung-hee, "The Manner of Writing and Performance for Korean Everyday Drama" (한국 일상극의 글쓰기와 공연방식), *Drama Research* 31 (2009): 36.

15. Berlant, *Cruel Optimism*, 81.

16. Berlant, *Cruel Optimism*, 199.

17. Kim Sung-hee, "The Manner of Writing," 38.

18. For a summary of Korean theater's central role in the antigovernment demonstrations, see my article "Rebuilding the Public Theatre: The Black Tent Project in Gwanghwamun Square" in the *Theatre Times*, February 12, 2017. https://thetheatretimes.com/rebuilding-public-theatre-black-tent-project-gwanghwamun-square/

19. Baek Hyun-mi, "Quotidian yet Unorthodox, Seditious yet Cunning: A Short Reading of Park Kunhyung's Theater" (일상적이되 일탈적인, 불온하되 의뭉스러운: 박근형의 연극에 대한 짧은 독해), *Korean Theatre Journal* 21 (2000): 154.

20. Baek Hyun-mi, "Quotidian yet Unorthodox," 145.

21. Kim Sung-hee, *Korean Theater and the Aesthetics of the Everyday*, 46.

22. Ben Highmore, *Everyday Life and Cultural Theory* (London: Routledge, 2001), 139.

23. Park Kunhyung, *Park Kunhyung Play Anthology 1* (박근형 희곡집 1) (Seoul: Yeongeukgwa Ingan, 2007), 40. All translations of Park's plays are mine.

24. "386 generation" refers to Koreans in their thirties who attended college in the 1980s and were born in the 1960s. It is generally associated with student activism demanding full democracy during the military dictatorship (1980–1988) of Chun Doo-hwan.

25. Shim Jae-min, "The Function of Social Criticism in the Dramaturgy of Park Kunhyung's Plays: Centered on His Work in the Late 1990s" (박근형 연극의

드라마투르기에 나타난 사회비판적 기능—90년대 말 작품들을 중심으로), *Drama Research* 33 (2010): 228.

26. Kim Sung-hee, "The Manner of Writing," 55.

27. Kim Jeong-suk, "Corporeality, Spatiality, and Subjectivity in Park Kunhyung's Theatre: Focused on *In Praise of Youth, Kyungsook, Kyungsook's Father,* and *Don't Be Too Surprised*" (박근형의 연극의 몸성, 공간성, 그리고 주체: <청춘예찬>, <경숙이 경숙아버지>, <너무 놀라지마라>를 중심으로), *Korean Theatre Studies* 43 (2011): 49–50.

28. Shim Jae-min, "The Function of Social Criticism," 215.

29. Park Kunhyung, *Park Kunhyung Play Anthology* 1, 35.

30. Park Kunhyung, *Park Kunhyung Play Anthology* 1, 42–43.

31. Katie Beswick, "Capitalist Realism: Glimmers, Working-class Authenticity and Andrea Dunbar in the Twenty-First Century," *International Journal of Media & Cultural Politics* 16, no. 1 (2020): 80.

32. Kim Sung-hee, *Korean Theater and the Aesthetics of the Everyday*, 28.

33. Kim Sung-hee, "The Manner of Writing," 65.

34. Seo Ji-min, "The Shame of 'Highest Suicide Rate in OECD' . . . On Average 38 Deaths a Day" (부끄러운 '자살률 OECD 1위' . . . 하루 평균 38명 목숨 끊어), *Sisa Journal*, September 22, 2020. https://www.sisajournal.com/news/articleView.html?idxno=205522

35. Kim Young-hak, "A Study on the Grotesque Presented in Park Kunhyung's Theater: Focusing on *At Baekmudong, Don't Be Too Surprised*" (박근형 연극에 나타난 그로테스크 연구: <백무동에서> <너무 놀라지 마라>를 중심으로), *Drama Research* 32 (2010): 217.

36. Park Kunhyung, *Don't Be Too Surprised* (너무 놀라지 마라) (Seoul: Applizm Publishing, 2009), 94.

37. Giorgio Agamben, *Homo Sacer: Sovereign Power and Bare Life*, trans. Daniel Heller-Roazen (Stanford, CA: Stanford University Press, 1998), 159.

38. Kim Myung-hwa, "Review: *Don't Be Too Surprised*" ([리뷰] 연극 <너무 놀라지 마라>), *The Hankyoreh*, January 20, 2009. https://www.hani.co.kr/arti/culture/music/334353.html

39. Park Kunhyung, *Don't Be Too Surprised*, 88.

40. Zygmunt Bauman, *Liquid Times: Living in an Age of Uncertainty* (Cambridge, UK: Polity Press, 2007), 28–29. Emphasis in original.

41. Mark Fisher, *Capitalist Realism: Is There No Alternative?* (Ropley, Hampshire, UK: Zero Books, 2009), 14.

42. Fisher, *Capitalist Realism*, 14.

43. Michel de Certeau, *The Practice of Everyday Life*, trans. Steven F. Rendall (Berkeley: University of California Press, 1984), xxii.

5 | From Realist Drama to Theater of the Real

Postsocialist Realism in Contemporary Chinese Theater

ROSSELLA FERRARI

Introduction: Postsocialist Realities and Realisms

The scene is a police station. Three policemen who have just killed a suspect during an interrogation summon a convicted artiste, known as the Madman, to help them produce a realistic story to cover up the murder. The Madman asks whether the iron hoop that the Police Chief is holding in his hand should be used as a prop for their theatrical reconstruction of the event and, if so, how: As a noose? An enclosure? An instrument of torture? The Chief replies: "Don't always think of yourself as a convict; now you are a theater director. This hoop represents a window." A window? The Madman retorts, with contempt: "So, you want to do experimental theater? I never liked those avant-gardists; they throw a bunch of TVs and broken boxes on the stage, as if it were a junk dealer or a dumping ground, and now they have even built a pool. The truth is that they are not good enough for realist theater." The Chief explains that whether the scene should be approached realistically or symbolically depends on the Madman's artistic inclinations. "I see what you are saying. But this is someone who jumps from a building to his death. Whether you do it a bit more avant-garde and jump through this hoop or a bit more realistic and jump through that window over there, that's entirely up to you."[1]

In this scene from the 1998 Chinese production of Dario Fo's *Accidental Death of an Anarchist* (*Yi ge wuzhengfuzhuyizhe de yiwai siwang*), adapted by Huang Jisu and directed by Meng Jinghui, the latter references episodes from his career to launch a mordant attack on the orthodoxy of dramatic realism that prevailed in China at the time.[2] Despite the Madman's mock-critique of experimental theater, this character is, in fact, constructed self-reflexively as a histrionic saboteur who attempts repeatedly to hijack the policemen's realist dramaturgy with his penchant for absurdism. Meng, who is today one of China's most influential theater personalities, belongs to the generation of experimentalists who were born in the mid-1960s and came onto the scene in the early 1990s, just as the socioeconomic reforms that have since shaped China's postsocialist condition were gaining momentum.[3]

For the purposes of this study, postsocialism denotes the defining cultural order and structure of feeling in China since the end of the Mao era (post-1976), and particularly since the 1990s. After years of ideological radicalism and social disruption during the Cultural Revolution (1966–1976), the market-oriented reforms launched by the Chinese Communist Party (CCP) in the late 1970s inaugurated a new phase of modernization and socioeconomic transformation under Deng Xiaoping's leadership. The reform era ushered in unprecedented economic development, urbanization, and internal migration, which dramatically altered the structure of Chinese society. The rapid transition from a planned economy to a form of state capitalism, or socialist market economy, has generated prosperity and opportunities but also considerable wealth inequality, a widening rural-urban divide, the marketization of the cultural sphere, and rampant commoditization of every aspect of life. Furthermore, the violent suppression of the democracy movement at Tiananmen Square in June 1989 elicited feelings of disillusionment and dystopia. Yet more than three decades later, the CCP's one-party rule is still firmly in place.

In 1989, Arif Dirlik described postsocialism as "a response to the experience of capitalism" in contexts where "socialism has lost its coherence as a metatheory of politics."[4] Some scholars of Chinese culture already detect the early symptoms of the postsocialist disbelief in the grand narratives of Chinese modernity in the literary and artistic expressions of the late 1970s and 1980s. These revealed fundamental skepticism toward the project of socialist modernity and—frequently, in the new experimental arts—a disavowal of the modern tradition of realism-naturalism in all its modes and manifestations.[5] However, I concur with those who identify the 1989 political crisis (the Tiananmen Square crackdown and its aftermath) and the subsequent intensification of economic reforms, since 1992, as catalysts for the emergence of a new phase of "postsocialist [post]modernity"[6] and of postsocialism as the underlying affective regime of Chinese society.

Sheldon Lu describes postsocialism as a distinctive "cultural logic" arising in the post-1989 era from the interpenetration of divergent ideological formations, social structures, and economic systems. Lu highlights the coexistence of "capitalist modes and relations of production" in a "nominally socialist" nation-state and the turning point of China's 2001 accession to "the global capitalist regime of the World Trade Organization (WTO)" alongside the CCP's continued commitment to socialist values. Thus, the postsocialist zeitgeist is marked by disjunctions, ambiguities, and contradictions, as artists, cultural producers, and common citizens attempt to negotiate the philosophical paradoxes and practical incongruities of an enduring state of transition.[7]

The turn to postsocialism has generated a fragmented social landscape cohabited by conflicting regimes of reality. Artistically, this state of fragmentation translates into performances of a fragmented reality. These regimes interact at various levels—socioeconomic, political, ideological, and affective—as synchronous dimensions of the real. Accordingly, the modalities of theatrical engagement with the question of the real examined in this chapter, which I categorize collectively as a theater of postsocialist realism, renounce the representational totality and totalizing metanarratives that are characteristic of Chinese modernity to produce multiple renditions of reality as fragmented and conflictual.

Postsocialism is widely discussed in academic discourse on Chinese culture and society, but its implications for the study of China's performance cultures have yet to be appraised. Likewise, scholars of Chinese cinema have coined the phrase "postsocialist realism" to examine the destabilization of the tenets of Mao-era socialist realism in post-1980s filmmaking practices.[8] Yet no study to date has investigated the nexus of postsocialism and realism in the performing arts. Hence, this chapter seeks to explore the performative dimensions of China's postsocialist condition and to conceptualize postsocialist realism in contemporary Chinese theater as a paradigmatic shift from "realist drama" to "theater of the real." The analysis retraces the critical discourse on and aesthetic engagement with the conventions of twentieth-century realism in its various pre- and postrevolutionary manifestations (i.e., prior and subsequent to the Maoist revolution) to pinpoint a fundamental renegotiation of the normative modes of mimetic, representational, and psychological realism that prevailed before the reform era in favor of stylization, deconstruction, and performativity at the turn of the twenty-first century. Furthermore, the postsocialist critique of realism as constitutive of modern Chinese drama entails a broader theoretical reconsideration of notions of "drama" and "theater," along with a shift from the dramatic to the postdramatic in the realm of practice.

The chapter outlines emergent modes of *mediated, embodied,* and *documentary realism* in light of current debates surrounding the relationship between theater and reality to elucidate the praxis I describe as China's postsocialist theater of the real. These modes of realism reflect the conflicting regimes of reality that typify China's postsocialist society, in that they present reality as tensional and multiperspectival and document fragments of life's narrative as it unfolds. Rather than *represented* in an immanent state of being—finite, stable, consistent, coherent—reality is *presented* on a processual course of becoming. Becoming real, rather than being real, implies that the theatrical enactment of postsocialist realities is not the reproduction of an a priori real that can be frozen in an unchanging form of dramatic representation. It is, rather, the presentation of contingent phenomena that take shape and *become* real in the course of performance. The chapter concludes with a tentative reflection on the limits of reality-based performance vis-à-vis the regulatory capacity of the Chinese party-state. Governmental institutions constitute yet another regime of postsocialist reality, in both the literal sense of a regime as a political authority and as a system that operates within society. In postsocialist China, conflicting regimes of truth struggle to participate in the construction of reality, complicating the relationship between theater and the real.

Rejecting Realism

For the purposes of this analysis, the postsocialist redefinition of dramatic realism is assessed in the context of the experimental theater scene that has developed in China's major urban centers (mainly Beijing and Shanghai) since the 1990s. This critique is examined in relation to concomitant developments in independent film discourse—wherein the debate on postsocialism has been prominent—and to the post-1989 cultural field more broadly. Following in the footsteps of the first post-Maoist experimental wave of the late 1970s–early 1980s, the postsocialist avant-garde of the 1990s, represented by Meng Jinghui's cohort, strived to affirm alternative approaches that questioned the institution of realism as the dominant theatrical convention since the early twentieth century.

The supremacy of realism on China's modern stages originates in the spoken drama (*huaju*) fashioned after the European models that were introduced in the 1910s and 1920s, including Henrik Ibsen's social problem plays and the precepts of naturalistic acting and mise-en-scène. Although the realist convention has taken different forms and denominations over time as a result of shifting ideological priorities, it has broadly been premised on the authority of the written text (the dramatic script) and mimetic representation. To frame the analysis that follows, it is beneficial to briefly trace some key shifts in the vocabulary that has been used historically to categorize the realist paradigm in Chinese literary and art theory, for these terminological shifts reflect important conceptual shifts in the definition of realism as a mode of portraying reality.

Film scholar Jason McGrath notes that, since the early twentieth century, the term *xianshizhuyi* has designated a mimetic conception of realism that manifests (*xian*) the real (*shi*).[9] Identified by Chinese intellectuals "as the mode of modernity and nationhood," *xianshizhuyi* differs from "*xieshi* (a traditional term for realism) or *zhenshi* (the real)"—as Chris Berry and Mary Farquhar further indicate—for these notions "relate to aesthetic practices and are subordinate to *xianshizhuyi* as ideology."[10] Notably, literary reformist and *huaju* pioneer Hu Shi (1891–1962) chose *xieshi* to define the essence of Ibsenism as a dramaturgical mode that describes (*xie*, literally, writes or inscribes) the real (*shi*). Hu adopted this term in an eponymous essay ("Ibsenism") published in the New Culture Movement's flagship magazine *New Youth* (*Xin qingnian*) in 1918, which triggered a veritable Ibsen fever in modern China. The founding of the People's Republic of China (PRC) in 1949 consolidated the ascendancy of realism as literary and artistic orthodoxy. Under the CCP, modern notions of realism were remolded into what McGrath terms the "*prescriptive* realism" of the socialist era.[11] In the early 1950s, Soviet socialist realism (*shehuizhuyi xianshizhuyi*) was institutionalized as the official mode of literary and artistic creation, while a dogmatic exegesis of Stanislavskian psychological realism—emphasizing emotional and ideological identification—was endorsed as the sanctioned training and performance method in the nation's state-run theater companies and academies.

As the self-appointed standard-bearer of Chinese avant-garde theater, director Meng Jinghui took particular aim at the most revered of these institutions, Beijing People's Art Theatre (Beijing renmin yishu juyuan; BPAT), at the outset of his career in the early 1990s. BPAT is generally regarded as the depository of the twentieth-century *huaju* tradition of Chinese-style realism that developed from the dramas of Cao Yu (1910–1996), Lao She (1899–1976), Tian Han (1898–1968), and Guo Moruo (1892–1978), among others. After 1949, these playwrights took up key positions in leading theatrical organizations such as the Central Academy of Drama in Beijing and BPAT itself. Still today, their classic works are part of the BPAT repertoire. Moreover, since the 1950s, BPAT played a key role in the consolidation and creative development of the Stanislavsky system in China, thanks to the efforts of director Jiao Juyin (1905–1975) and his successors.

BPAT is also the institution where, in the first half of the 1980s, experimentalists such as director Lin Zhaohua and dramatist Gao Xingjian (winner of the 2000 Nobel Prize for Literature) took the first steps toward dismantling the entrenched monopoly of realism; the "Brechtian" director Huang Zuolin (1906–1994) at Shanghai People's Art Theatre (Shanghai renmin yishu juyuan) had pursued the same goal since the 1950s. But it was the more radical post-1989 avant-gardes that gave full shape to the critique against the institutionalization and progressive ossification of the realist norm. The praxis of directors such as Meng and Mou Sen and of new independent ensembles that emerged in the last decade of the twentieth century revealed a paradigm-shifting disconnection with the representational mode of theater-making grounded in the illusion of reality. As Gao writes of his early-1980s collaboration with Lin at BPAT, "Lin Zhaohua and I planned to break away from the established Stanislavsky patterns of realist theatre—in terms of both actor performance and the form of the production—but we kept this to ourselves and did not publicize it."[12] In contrast, the 1990s avant-gardists announced their rebellion against normative realism loudly and polemically in creative statements and manifestos that testified to their antagonistic disposition toward the orthodoxy. The postsocialist avant-garde launched a two-pronged attack against the institution of realism by disallowing both the Western-based *huaju* tradition and the prescriptive mode of realism imposed on the arts during the Mao era.

On January 28, 1989, Frog Experimental Drama Troupe (Wa shiyan jutuan) issued an address to the audience, written by Mou Sen, on the premiere of Eugene O'Neill's *The Great God Brown* in Beijing. In this manifesto-like statement, printed in the program notes to the production, Frog portray themselves as "a new theater group" that "belongs to the new century" and whose iconoclastic actions echo their resolve to alter the course of theater in China: "We are well aware that we are making history."[13] Frog was China's first independent ensemble since

1949. Its members included emergent 1960s-born artists, such as Mou and Meng, who would soon become leading figures in the experimental theater scene of the next decade. Frog's address proclaimed the inevitability of a generational and aesthetic rejuvenation at the turn of the millennium by introducing their O'Neill production as the herald of an epochal change, which was signaled by a departure from the canon of twentieth-century realism. While the premiere of *The Great God Brown* was taking place, "the old artists of BPAT" were completing a run of performances of Lao She's realist classic, *Teahouse* (*Chaguan*, 1957): "Just as *Teahouse* buried an old era, *The Great God Brown* breeds a great dream"— one of spiritual regeneration and artistic renewal.[14] As it turned out, Frog did not survive long. But Mou, Meng, and other members moved on to found new collectives and experiment with nonrealistic forms of dramaturgy that rejected accepted norms of playwriting, directing, acting, and stage design.

Meng explored the European theater of the absurd extensively in the early 1990s. His 1993 production of Jean Genet's *The Balcony* (*Yangtai*) embraced "stylization" and "formalism" as antidotes against the "superficial ostentation" and "artificial affectation" of the "rusty traditions" that sustain "the exquisite illusions of naturalism," as stated in his director's notes.[15] Inspired by Vsevolod Meyerhold, Peter Brook, and the Dadaists, Meng and his associates reacted against the realist convention represented by BPAT and other state-run establishments that "always use the same old formulae, old methods, old jokes, and old effects."[16] In a clear nod to Brook, in several mid- to late-1990s writings Meng dismisses China's mainstream theater as "brainless," "deadly theater," and repeatedly associates realism with formal obsolescence, psychological shallowness, and affective insincerity.[17]

In a series of columns appearing in *Theater and Film News* (*Xiju dianying bao*) in 1996–1997, Meng elaborates on the equation "realist theater = brainless theater." He maintains that the theater that truly is close to life does not attempt to merely "imitate life" (*mofang shenghuo*), "fabricate feelings" (*zhizao qinggan*), or "replicate reality" (*chongxian xianshi*).[18] The target of his criticism, Meng explains, is not the mode of realism that foregrounds social life but the regime of "false realism" (*wei xianshizhuyi*) that has been institutionalized as the sole conceivable mode of theater-making in China. Chinese mainstream realism has betrayed what he views as Stanislavsky's original spirit of experiment and has become stifling, regressive, and mediocre.[19] The hyperbolic rhetoric and hostility toward dramatic orthodoxy that transpires from the above statements reveals the premillennial experimentalists' deeply nihilistic position of almost-ontological antagonism toward the canon and conventions of realism.

The avant-garde's attack on realism culminates at the turn of the century with its own self-dramatization in the caustic satire of Academy-style training and the BPAT realist tradition featured in Meng's adaptation of Fo's *Anarchist*. The protagonist introduces himself as an alumnus of the (Central) Academy of Drama, where he has been trained in accordance to the tenets of Ibsenian drama, socialist realism, and Stanislavskian acting. The Madman asserts the superiority of realism and maintains that nonrealistic methods only serve to camouflage the experimentalists' incompetence. The passage quoted in the opening of this chapter hints self-reflexively at criticism Meng received at the start of his career and alludes to the nonrealistic design of pioneering 1990s experimental productions by Lin Zhaohua, Mou Sen, and Meng himself.[20] Elsewhere in the performance, the cast delivers a riotous parody of a scene from *Teahouse*, a canonical text of Chinese realism and a classic of the BPAT repertoire.[21]

Furthermore, the 1990s witnessed a nascent propensity for the postdramatic—namely, a growing commitment to "the emancipation of the performance from the literary text" and mimetic representation.[22] Marvin Carlson notes that "all the post terms"—such as postdramatic and, indeed, postsocialism—share "a sense of rejecting certain key elements of an established tradition. There is often the added suggestion that the tradition being moved beyond had a fairly settled and monolithic character, which an important part of the post movement seeks to destabilize."[23] Shanghai-based dramatist Zhang Xian was possibly the first of the premillennial experimentalists to mention "post-drama," or "post-spoken drama" (*hou huaju*), to differentiate the twentieth-century convention of script-centered realist drama from the post-1990s director- and performer-centered avant-garde theater, which values process and embodiment over textual detail and representational accuracy. The 1990s work of Mou Sen's Garage Theatre (Xiju chejian), Wen Hui and Wu Wenguang's Living Dance Studio (Shenghuo wudao gongzuoshi), and Tian Gebing's Paper Tiger Theatre Studio (Zhi laohu xiju gongzuoshi) signaled a further move away from the representational mode of text-based *huaju* in favor of performativity. As a general tendency, however, the withdrawal from the realist norm was articulated predominantly in terms of "anti-" (*fan*; e.g., antitheater, antiplot, antitext, antidrama) rather than "post-" (*hou*) in late-twentieth-century discourse; that is, in terms of a clean break with the past, rather than a temporal progression from it. In other words, the premillennial innovators positioned themselves in stark opposition to the institution of realism, hence embodying the paradigmatic "spirit of the anti" that typifies the discourse of the avant-garde as one of ontological antagonism and radical rupture with tradition.[24]

Redefining Realism

A new wave of experimental theater-makers has come onto the scene in the twenty-first century, and with them come new perceptions of the concept and legacy of realism. The postmillennial cohort, a majority of whom are independent practitioners who work primarily "outside the (state) system" (*tizhi wai*), has on the one hand taken the redefinition of the realist paradigm a step further, by embracing new aesthetics and vocabularies (such as *juchang*, detailed below) to describe their creative practice. On the other hand, however, and in contrast to their predecessors, they have also recuperated the modern canon of realist drama by means of postmodernist and postdramatic modes.

The approach of director Wang Chong with Théâtre du Rêve Expérimental (Xinchuan shiyan jutuan, est. 2008) illustrates the transition from the late-twentieth-century radical dismissal of the realist norm to its early-twenty-first-century recuperative deconstruction. Wang's trademark 2.0 series of multimedia stage productions reimagines and updates the realist canon for the digital age by recasting foundational texts of European realism, modern Chinese *huaju*, and Mao-era revolutionary realism within a postdramatic transmedia framework. The series includes *Ghosts 2.0* (*Qungui 2.0*, 2014), based on Ibsen; *Thunderstorm 2.0* (*Leiyu 2.0*, 2012), after Cao Yu's 1934 play; *The Warfare of Landmine 2.0* (*Dilei zhan 2.0*, 2013), after the eponymous 1962 socialist film classic; and *Revolutionary Model Play 2.0* (*Yangbanxi 2.0*, 2015) on the theater of the Cultural Revolution, among other works. In 2017, moreover, Wang devised *Teahouse 2.0*, based on Lao She's classic, with a cast of Beijing high school students. While actively engaging the realist dramatic canon, this body of work concomitantly departs from realist production conventions through procedures of remediation, mediatization, and versioning of reality. Wang's recourse to the language of software versioning in the 2.0 series articulates a mode of *mediated realism* that functions at different levels: in the dramaturgical process of editing and adaptation of realist texts; in the implementation and display of an array of media and mediating technologies to the production and performance of these texts; and, at the semantic level, in the self-referential reproduction of the simulated and mediatized screen-based realities of our contemporary world.

In Wang's "stage cinema" (*wutai dianying*), as he has described his style,[25] the deployment of video recording devices, CCTV cameras, loudspeakers, live filming, real-time editing, and live-feed projections disrupts the illusion of dramatic unity and the logical coherence of conventional realism. The theatrical mediation of reality by such devices generates an effect of "doubling" and discontinuity that mirrors "a simultaneous and multi-perspectival form of perceiving" China's postsocialist reality.[26] Mediated realism in the postdramatic mode—as practiced by Wang, Sun Xiaoxing,[27] and other postmillennial independents who have worked in transmedia and digital theater—engenders a new disjointed sensitivity toward the real that supersedes both "the linear-successive" pattern of realist-naturalist modernity and the teleological determinism of Mao-era socialist realism.[28]

In an essay on the creative process of *Thunderstorm 2.0*, published in 2013, Wang references *Thunderstorm* and *Teahouse* as aesthetic and political high points in the national tradition of realist drama, whose production conventions, set by BPAT during the socialist era, are deconstructed in the 2.0 mediated mode.[29] Wang's postdramatic versions subvert the canonical BPAT productions at the level of both text and performance. *Thunderstorm 2.0* retains only a fraction of Cao Yu's text. In its highly fragmented, yet internally coherent script, disparate lines from the play are recombined and reassigned to only three roles from the original large cast. Formally, it rejects the realist dramaturgy, melodramatic acting, and naturalistic design of BPAT's classic staging to expose the constructed and mediated quality of the production process through the introduction of body doubles, live camera operators, and on-the-spot shooting, cutting, and screening of the filmed material. The theater stage becomes a dynamic and multi-sited cinematic set where changes in location, costume, or makeup are made entirely visible to the audience during the live performance. The spectating process and perceptual experience of the viewer are thereby also fragmented, multifaceted, and ultimately irreproducible.[30]

Similarly, *Teahouse 2.0* overthrows Lao She's meticulous reproduction of the momentous transformations of a Beijing teahouse in the first half of the twentieth century and sets the action on a twenty-first-century Chinese campus. Performances took place in a real high-school classroom in Beijing and the majority of the cast were actual pupils from the

Figure 5.1: *Thunderstorm 2.0* (*Leiyu 2.0*), directed by Wang Chong with Théâtre du Rêve Expérimental in New York City, 2018. Image courtesy of Théâtre du Rêve Expérimental.

school. In a "reversal of the theater as propaganda machine,"[31] forty-four actors played to only eleven spectators at each performance. The 2.0 version retained Lao She's script, yet shifted its original focus on Beijing life and history to current educational issues in order to critique the reality and challenges of high-school life in postsocialist China.

Additionally, Wang's "New Wave Theatre Manifesto," issued in 2012, announced that the innovations surging from the Théâtre du Rêve Expérimental's performance mediascapes will "wash out the dust and dirt of the old theater."[32] To some extent, the tone of both writings echoes Frog's 1989 statement quoted above. Nonetheless, rather than simply rejecting the old orthodoxy in the manner of his precursors, Wang's deconstructionist interventions repurpose the realist norm to articulate a postsocialist ontology of disjuncture and fragmentation. The mediated approach to critically revisiting the past epitomized by the 2.0 treatment of the realist legacy attests to the postmillennial theater's engagement with what Lu describes as the "backward glance" and the "forward-looking . . . technological head" of Chinese postsocialism.[33] Hence, this work provides a performative reflection of the multiple temporalities and overlapping socio-ideological formations that characterize postsocialist China's conflicting regimes of reality, discussed previously.

Other twenty-first-century theater-makers have addressed the socio-affective ecologies of Chinese postsocialism through modes of *embodied* and *documentary realism*. Works in these categories tend to reveal conditions of existential uncertainty, spiritual dispossession, and economic precarity. They resonate with a definition of theater that, in the words of Carol Martin, "claim[s] specific relationships with events in the real world" and "enacts social and personal actualities by recycling reality for the stage"—namely, a theater of the real.[34]

Evidence of such performative recycling is the practice of the Shanghai-based collective Grass Stage (Caotaiban), which typifies the trend I designate as embodied, or physical, realism. The theater of Grass Stage foregrounds reality as constituted and brought to life by the movement of the untrained and unrestrained "real" bodies of "real" people, as opposed to the theatrical bodies of professionally trained performers. Since the group's inaugural production of *38th Parallel Still Play* (*Sanbaxian youxi*) in 2005, Grass Stage founder Zhao Chuan has deliberately shunned professional actors, whose bodies he perceives as either too conditioned by the institutionalized education administered in the state-run academies or too compromised by the profit-making mindset of the performing arts industries. By engaging professional actors, Zhao feared that the realities their performance sought to convey would "come off as unauthentic,"[35] whereas the Grass Stage method of "discussion through the body"[36] pursues an immediate, unmediated, and unbeautified relationship with reality (*xianshixing*).[37] This embodied pursuit of the real wants to question reality, rather than represent or recreate it. It is contingent on actual incidents in life, history, and society rather than on a theatricalized or aestheticized sense of the real. Grass Stage devised *38th Parallel Still Play* and the follow-on project *38th Parallel in Taipei* (*Taibei 38 duxian*, 2005) with partners from Taiwan, Hong Kong, and South Korea to address the effects of the Cold War on the contemporary realities of the Korean Peninsula and China-Taiwan relations. The productions incorporated biographical anecdotes and self-reflexive accounts of incidents that occurred during the rehearsal process alongside reflections on historical events.

Grass Stage has since developed a distinctive training method and performance style centered on corporeal expression, which highlights the signifying power of the collective social body of the ensemble—still today comprised mostly of nonprofessionals. Grass Stage defies script-centric dramaturgy and theatrical role-playing; their performances resist both the formalized kinesthetics of conventional naturalistic acting and "the commoditisation of the human body" that pervades Chinese commercial theater and postsocialist society at large.[38] Often taking place in nontheatrical spaces and followed by extended postperformance exchanges between actors and audiences, their itinerant shows have dealt with themes of migration, social stratification, class discrimination, the capitalist exploitation of labor, and the struggle for daily survival of the urban precariat. Such works as *Little Society* (*Xiao shehui*, 2009–2011) and *World Factory* (*Shijie gongchang*, 2014) illustrate the group's distinctive brand of social praxis that confronts the crude and uncomfortable aspects of reality. Beggars, rag pickers, sex workers, and other precarious subjects take center stage in *Little Society* to uncover the ugly face of postsocialist modernization and provide an outlet for the minor life stories of those who have been excluded from the race for prosperity of China's capitalist transition. Scholar Li Yinan suggests that Grass Stage's "true-to-life" portrayal of real, laboring bodies engenders an "overwhelming sense" of realism that genuinely captures the essence of "Realistic Drama."[39]

Such an approach to presenting reality resonates equally with the mode I designate as documentary realism. The creative ethos of twenty-first-century performance documentarians such as Li Ning, Wang Mengfan, and Li Jianjun is committed to recording the social conditions of present-day China and bearing witness to the "nameless mankind" (*wuming de ren*), as Li Jianjun describes the aesthetic pursuit of the real beyond reproducible theatricality.[40] Dramaturgical material is extracted from private chronicles, intimate accounts, mundane anecdotes, and the often-overlooked histories of ordinary citizens caught in the whirlwind of urbanization, and adrift in the transition between a socialist and a semicapitalist social order. Many works in this growing corpus of postsocialist performances of the real cast into relief the self-narratives of nonprofessional actors/participants who share personal memories and real-life stories. Others draw attention to conditions of subalternity, urban alienation, and geopathic displacement. They strive to give voice to the experiences of economic precarity and systemic discrimination of the large communities of rural migrants who toil on the margins of China's swelling metropolises, in stark contrast to the romanticized portrayals of the laboring masses in socialist-era theater.

A fundamental trait of the postmillennial redefinition of realism is that the twentieth-century assertion of ideological authenticity and the

Figure 5.2: A performance of *World Factory* (*Shijie gongchang*), a collective creation by Grass Stage directed by Zhao Chuan, in Chengdu, 2016. Image courtesy of Grass Stage.

quest for an objective and totalizing recreation of reality are superseded by the intention "to complicate notions of authenticity with a more nuanced and challenging evocation of the 'real,'" as Alison Forsyth and Chris Megson write of the global genre of documentary theater.[41] In the Chinese context, McGrath identifies a comparable renunciation of claims to "an ideological truth that underlies apparent reality" in postsocialist realist cinema, which strives instead "to reveal a raw, underlying reality by stripping away the ideological representations that distort it."[42] Intent on capturing reality uncut, with all its disjunctures and contradictions, and, frequently, by direct testimony, the reconfigured realist mode of China's new independent theater may be viewed as a performative recasting of the contemporary discourse of postsocialist realism—or, in other words, a postsocialist theater of the real.

Redefining Theater

In addition to historical shifts in the concept and critical vocabulary of realism, as outlined above, the contemporary redefinition of realism from the modern tradition of realist drama to the postsocialist theater of the real has entailed reassessing the concept and vocabulary of theater itself. Evidence of this critique is the terminological and theoretical transition, between the twentieth and the twenty-first century, from *huaju* to *xiju* to *juchang*. In the late twentieth century, *xiju* was used to differentiate the new avant-garde forms from the spoken-drama convention of *huaju*. In contrast, the postmillennial discourse is characterized by an additional reconsideration of the meaning of *xiju* and increased critical circulation of the term *juchang* to denote forms of theater—or, better still, a distinct attitude toward theater-making—that foreground place, process, interaction, multi-perspectival perception, and "the spatial and social aspect[s]" of performance.[43]

The principal theorist of the contemporary *juchang* turn is Li Yinan. Li describes *juchang* as a participative modality that values the interplay of actors and audiences as equal partakers in an event occurring in a specific place or location (*chang*), which may or may not be a conventional performance space. As such, *juchang* is both an artistic practice and a "social event."[44] Li juxtaposes *juchang* not only to "'realist' *huaju*"—with its emphasis on text, plot, narrative, and lifelike characterization—but also to *xiju*.[45] This distinction stems from her translation of Hans-Thies Lehmann's *Postdramatic Theatre* (*Postdramatisches Theater*, 1999), wherein she renders "drama" as *xiju* (or *xiju juchang*) and "theater" as *juchang*, hence "postdramatic theater" as *houxiju juchang*.[46]

The disparities in form and function that Li Yinan perceives between *xiju* and *juchang* reflect divergent perceptions of the relationship between theater and the real. While Li defines *xiju* as "the written text by a single author,"[47] *juchang* implies a dynamic and multi-angled observation of reality from the perspective of both the author and the participants (performers, spectators). Li's conceptual differentiation echoes Carlson's view that—notwithstanding the conventional demarcation between "drama" as the literary script and "theater" as its enactment on the stage—the latter remains "primarily a visual realization of a pre-existing written text."[48]

The reality that *juchang* strives to capture is neither static nor unbroken but contingent on the unique circumstances of the performance event—and often unscripted. *Juchang* denotes creative praxes that emphasize "performativity," "presence," "locality," and "a non-referential use of the body."[49] Accordingly, the postsocialist realism of China's theater of the real marks a departure from the aesthetic norm of representational "theatricality" (*xijuxing*) based on "reproduction" (*zaixian*)—to quote director Li Jianjun—and a methodological turn toward *juchang*.[50] As Li Yinan has repeatedly emphasized, *juchang* and postdramatic theater are distinct concepts. Nonetheless, in terms of their relationship to the real, one can identify a shared intention to destabilize "the traditional concept of mimesis" and a notion "of the theatre world as a fictional construct distinctly separated from everyday life and its surroundings."[51]

Many independent theater-makers have expressed their predilection for *juchang* as an accurate descriptor of their practice. Among others, Li Yinan brings the examples of Li Ning's site-specific performances in found spaces, such as derelict buildings and car cemeteries, and Wang Mengfan's dance theater with nonprofessionals. Li Ning is a theater and dance artist, filmmaker, curator, and founder of the independent ensemble J-Town Physical Guerrillas (Lingyunyan jiti youjidui) in Jinan, Shandong. Li Ning has named his method of channeling reality through the body as "physical sketching" (*jiti xiesheng*): "I use the term 'sketching,' in the sense that you are looking at the world around you from your own point of view. 'Sketching' involves study: it's inseparable from nature and life and not something that can be copied."[52]

An increased focus on corporeal presence rather than a predetermined script is equally evident in Wang's practice, whose work to date has consistently foregrounded the ordinary beauty of real, moving bodies—irrespective of age and ability. The Beijing-based director-choreographer has explored the expressive potential of the untrained bodies of young children in *The Divine Sewing Machine* (*Shensheng fengrenji*, 2017) and of the mature bodies of aging dance professionals in *When My Cue Comes, Call Me, and I Will Answer* (*Gai wo shangchang de shihou, jiao wo, wo hui huida*, 2019), in which she cast two retired ballet dancers aged fifty-eight and eighty-one. In *50/60—Dance Theater with Dama* (*50/60—Ayimen de wudao juchang*, 2015), Wang worked with six women in their fifties and sixties who were ardent practitioners of square dancing (*guangchang wu*), a wildly popular form of amateur dance carried out in public spaces. The choreography featured a repertoire of corporeal expressions ranging from different forms of dance to the performance of daily routines that, together, embodied the lived experience of a generation of Chinese women.

The connection between postsocialist realism and *juchang* is further evinced by the prominence of the notion of *chang* in the theorization of both concepts. As mentioned, *chang* means location, (gathering) place, or field. It brings to the fore the site of the performance event, and the event itself occurring in the "here and now" of that site. It is thus premised on an interactive relationship between space, action, and the bodies that witness an action in a given space. For example, in *25.3 km Fairy Tale* (*25.3 km tonghua*), directed by Li Jianjun, semi-structured interactions between performers and passengers on a rented public bus shaped the reality of the event as it unfolded within the dynamic *chang* constituted by the Beijing cityscape and the bus traveling through it on the night of 31 December 2013.

In addition to valorizing observational or documentary realism over representational or text-based realism, a characteristic of these performances is that they draw attention to liveness, contingency, and immediacy as phenomenological components of the dramaturgical process unfolding within *chang*. China's postsocialist theater of the real foregrounds the material (physical) and immaterial (affective, psychological, energetic, auratic) qualities of *chang* as the locus of a processual reality in a state of becoming, which arises contingently from the execution and exchange of actions in a shared time-space.

Zhao Chuan has written of the role of *chang* in Grass Stage's *juchang* praxis. The purpose of the group's creative method is to interrogate, rather than imitate, reality, and to intervene in social praxis; or, better still, to become social praxis by establishing a direct connection between the theater and the experiential realities of the public sphere.[53]

Experimentalists of the premillennial cohort such as Wen Hui, Zhang Xian, and Tian Gebing have also designated their practice as *juchang*. Meng Jinghui, albeit working predominantly within the category of *xiju*, has emphasized the role of *xianchang gan* (a sense of presence while being "on the scene") in avant-garde theater,[54] thus echoing the centrality of "the logic of *xianchang*" in the postsocialist realist cinema of his contemporaries.[55]

Xianchang has been discussed widely as a defining feature of post-1990s Chinese independent cinema and in connection with the style of documentary realism known as *jishizhuyi* (on-the-spot realism). Conceptualized by documentary filmmaker Wu Wenguang as "being present on the scene," *xianchang* "constitutes a particular social and epistemic space in which orality, performativity, and an irreducible specificity of personal and social experience are acknowledged, recorded, and given aesthetic expression."[56] Scholar Dai Jinhua describes *xianchang* as "an intervention in the real," tracing its origins to 1990s avant-garde performance.[57] In fact, the latter was closely linked to the independent film scene, as evidenced by numerous collaborations between Mou Sen, Wen Hui, and documentarians Jiang Yue and Wu Wenguang. Elements of performativity in Wu's documentary practice have also been acknowledged.[58] Despite such manifest connections, the nexus between *juchang*, *xianchang*, and the documentary impulse of postmillennial independent theater has hitherto been overlooked. Nonetheless, the principle of bearing witness to reality in the present continuous is central to China's postsocialist theater of the real.

Performing the Real

The practice of Li Jianjun with the New Youth Group (Xin qingnian jutuan; NYG hereafter) is an emblematic case. The group's name summons the primal scene of Chinese realism, namely, the early-twentieth-century literary magazine *New Youth*. The script (by Zhuang Jiayun) of their inaugural production of *A Madman's Diary* (*Kuangren riji*, 2011) was based on the eponymous novella by Lu Xun published in *New Youth* in 1918. However, the NYG's creative process unsettles the premises of the modern realist convention of "reproducible theater"[59] with a Deleuzian interpretation of the real as an unceasing process of becoming. Becoming real, rather than being real, indicates a condition that can neither be reproduced or fixed in a script nor represented reflexively. The distinction between being and becoming real is central to the shift from realist drama to postsocialist theater of the real because it sets a static relationship to reality rooted in mimetic representation against a reality that one "creates" and "perceives" agentively in its specific and unique circumstances, and that continually renews itself.[60] If postsocialism marks the coming into being of a fragmented reality cohabited by disparate socio-affective regimes, then the postsocialist theater of the real frames this reality not as immanence but as process—as a draft that ceaselessly rewrites itself into multiple fragmented versions, none of which can ever be regarded as final.

Another defining trait that the theater of the real shares with postsocialist art and film is the aestheticization of the ruin—of the material remains of wrecked environments and discarded spaces—as "a metaphor for the real world."[61] Li Ning's performances in abandoned locations illustrate this tendency, and so does the stage design of the NYG's early productions. The performance space of *A Madman's Diary* was filled with dilapidated construction materials retrieved from a suburban building site. The purpose was to foreground the pervasiveness of the ruin as a dominant visual cypher in the urban landscapes of demolition of postsocialist China. The fragmented rendition of Lu Xun's text within a setting of authentic "ruinscapes"[62]—itself a signifier of disjointedness and fragmentation—echoed the "poetics of vanishing" that are equally prominent in postsocialist cinematic articulations such as the films of

Jia Zhangke.⁶³ The perception of reality as a ruin conveys the ontological disjunction and heterochronicity of postsocialism, for the crumbling "remnants of time"⁶⁴ excavated from the vestiges of postsocialist China's swiftly morphing urbanscapes resurface and reconstitute themselves in the present as both mnemonic residues of the past and dormant future possibilities. Consistent with Li Jianjun's view of reality as becoming—proceeding continually from the here and now of (*xian*) *chang*—the ruin is an intrinsically postsocialist "dimension of time."⁶⁵

The postsocialist realist accent on immediacy and contingency corresponds to a thematic emphasis on mundanity in lieu of the typicality of classic realism, and on subalternity in place of the sublimity of socialist realism. The focus turns to common citizens, nonprofessional actors, and the prosaic minutiae of the quotidian. Again, this aspect resonates with the twenty-first-century transition "from public to private" and investment in "the ordinary, and more often, the socially and geographically marginalised subjects" that have been noted in independent documentary filmmaking.⁶⁶ Equally, the NYG's documentary style, which Li Jianjun describes as the "theater of the ordinary" (*fanren juchang*),⁶⁷ spotlights amateur participants who enact their own self-narratives in pursuit of a relatable "feeling of the real" (*zhenshi gan*).⁶⁸ The NYG's postsocialist poetics of ordinariness documents not only the minor histories of ordinary people but also the mundane theatricality of ordinary spaces, material objects, and daily-life scenes in an attempt to capture a polyphonic testimony of what constitutes the real in contemporary China.

The headphone theater production of *One Fine Day* (*Meihao de yitian*) can be regarded as the initiator and, arguably, most emblematic illustration of the NYG's documentary practice of theater of the ordinary. Between 2013, when it premiered in Beijing, and 2022, *One Fine Day* was staged several times in various cities (Hangzhou, Shanghai, Shenzhen, and Hong Kong) with different nonprofessional casts recruited locally through workshops and interviews. In each performance, an ensemble of nineteen individuals sits in a line facing the audience for almost the entire duration of the stage proceedings, each relating personal life episodes in nineteen distinct monologues. Participants have included homemakers, professionals, businessmen, manual laborers, and army veterans, and ages range from sixteen to ninety-one. On the one hand, the public presentation of private experience by a cross-section of Chinese society seeks to give voice and presence to common urban citizens who have been engulfed in the ebb and flow of postsocialist ruination and reconstruction of the past few decades. On the other hand, these oral

Figure 5.3: The documentary theater production *One Fine Day* (*Meihao de yitian*), directed by Li Jianjun with the New Youth Group in Beijing, 2013. Image courtesy of the New Youth Group.

histories strive to capture the fleeting sights of the fast-evolving psychophysical scenery of the twenty-first-century Chinese city.

Compositional principles of chance, choice, "repetition," and "overlaying"[69] enhance the reality-effect of the performance event in *One Fine Day*. Each actor wears an audio transmitter assigned to an individual radio frequency, and audiences can tune in via headphone sets. Since all actors deliver their monologues simultaneously, audiences must choose to either listen to one single narrative for the entire duration of the performance or to switch between channels to catch segments of several narratives. Or they can decide to immerse themselves in the cacophony of collective murmuring present on the scene at any given moment. Actors and audiences partake in an individualized experience of clashing, intersecting, and ultimately incomplete realities. Li Jianjun has described the inner conflict arising from the audience's act of decision-making and the experience of a nonlinear and nonhierarchical process of performing life—with people themselves becoming, instead of representing, a performance script—as "an affront to the aesthetics of socialist realism."[70] Indeed, the technical impossibility of listening to all narrative streams in their entirety within a single performance event implies an ontological renouncement of representational totality, and a recognition of the inevitable incompleteness of whatever one might regard as authentic or true. There are only fragments of truth, and the revelation of each truth conceals the possibility of another: "The repetition makes it impossible to see an end point; there is only steady becoming."[71]

Conclusion: Limits of the Real

China's postsocialist realism undermines the distinction between artistic representation and lived experience and unsettles notions of objectivity, authenticity, and truth on a phenomenological and ontological level. It does so by foregrounding the presence of disparate and contingent renditions of reality that are mediated, embodied, and documented through performance in a state of continuous becoming. Notwithstanding the potential for diversity and social inclusion of this approach, there are limits to the postsocialist realist theater's engagement with the real. The scope of this chapter does not permit an exhaustive assessment of the limits of the theatrical real vis-à-vis the actual sociopolitical realities of postsocialist China. Nonetheless, by way of conclusion, it is worth noting how factors specific to the Chinese regime of governmentality may add an extra dimension to the theoretical and ethical complexities that have been observed regarding the theater of the real as a mode of performance-making. Critical points in the scholarly debate have concerned boundaries between authenticity and artifice in reality-based artistic practice, skepticism about its transformative capacity and actual social efficacy, and ethical considerations surrounding the voyeuristic commodification of potentially vulnerable subjects and the public disclosure of sensitive material.

In China, the limits of the real can be an ontological or methodological question, as the contrasting approaches to realism and reality-based performance surveyed above demonstrate. But in a society where regimes of truth are sanctioned, regulated, and carefully monitored by the political superstructure, they can also be a question of articulatory boundaries. At the most basic level, noncompliance with institutional protocols and ideological restrictions can seriously jeopardize access to funding, venues, and licensing for public performance, among other matters. In such circumstances, the limits of the real are found not only in the interstices between the performed real and the "really real,"[72] but in the liminal zone between what can or cannot be presented as real, or those aspects of the "really real" that can or cannot be brought into the public sphere accompanied by a veritable claim to truth. On the one hand, the turn to *juchang* may be remedial to a theatrical system that still tends to primarily censor scripts. On the other hand, since the onset of the Xi Jinping era in 2013, demands on the arts have been rising to conform to harmonized reality narratives and "self-disciplining measures" dictated by the state.[73]

The multiple regulatory regimes embedded in China's ideological, social, and cultural governance and the resulting regulation of reality narratives and performances of the real in the public sphere open up a number of questions: How does the production of reality-based performance under conditions of reality regimentation affect the articulation of the real? To what extent does governmental scrutiny, and, especially, the awareness of such scrutiny, defy the theoretical premises of reality-based performance? Does it encourage self-regulatory behavior (of artists, actors, and audiences) that may itself be framed as a performative response to the real? Does the method of selective listening to individualized fragments of truth noted in the account of the NYG's headphone theater also imply practices of selective speaking—that is, of deliberate silencing and excluding certain aspects of reality from public discourse?

This kind of question should be asked to avoid drawing overly triumphant conclusions regarding the capacity for independent expression and the potential for democratic participation in China's theater of the real. However, the impact of institutional monitoring and individual self-regulation will require closer inspection in future research to apprehend the complex workings of the conflicting regimes of reality that distinguish the Chinese postsocialist condition. As postsocialist realism defies the conventions of realist drama, it also pushes the boundaries of the real, for it demarcates multiple dimensions of "performing reality" that both enhance and complicate the definition of theater of the real in contemporary China.

Notes

1. Huang Jisu, *Accidental Death of an Anarchist* (*Yi ge wuzhengfuzhuyizhe de yiwai siwang*), in *Avant-Garde Theater Archive* (*Xianfeng xiju dang'an*), ed. Meng Jinghui (Beijing: Zuojia chubanshe, 2000), 247.

2. Huang Jisu is a playwright, translator, and retired sociologist from the Chinese Academy of Social Sciences. His most influential theater work is *Che Guevara* (*Qie Gewala*, 2000), coauthored with Shen Lin and Zhang Guangtian.

3. Meng is an internationally renowned director and dramatist based in Beijing. He is the founder and artistic director of the Beijing Fringe Festival and the cofounder of the Wuzhen Theatre Festival.

4. Arif Dirlik, "Postsocialism? Reflections on 'Socialism with Chinese Characteristics,'" *Bulletin of Concerned Asian Scholars* 21, no. 1 (1989): 34.

5. See, for instance, Chris Berry, *Postsocialist Cinema in Post-Mao China: The Cultural Revolution after the Cultural Revolution* (London: Routledge, 2004); and Paul G. Pickowicz, "Huang Jianxin and the Notion of Postsocialism," in *New Chinese Cinemas: Forms, Identities, Politics*, ed. Nick Browne, Paul G. Pickowicz, Vivian Sobchack, and Esther Yau (Cambridge, UK: Cambridge University Press, 1994), 57–87.

6. Sheldon H. Lu, *Chinese Modernity and Global Biopolitics: Studies in Literature and Visual Culture* (Honolulu: University of Hawaii Press, 2007), 1; 207.

7. Lu, *Chinese Modernity*, 208.

8. Jason McGrath, "The Independent Cinema of Jia Zhangke: From Postsocialist Realism to a Transnational Aesthetic," in *The Urban Generation: Chinese Cinema and Society at the Turn of the Twenty-First Century*, ed. Zhang Zhen (Durham, NC: Duke University Press, 2007), 81–114.

9. Jason McGrath, "Realism," *Journal of Chinese Cinemas* 10, no. 1 (2016): 20.

10. Chris Berry and Mary Farquhar, *China on Screen: Cinema and Nation* (New York: Columbia University Press, 2006), 74; 78.

11. McGrath, "Realism," 22.

12. Gao Xingjian, *The Case for Literature*, trans. Mabel Lee (New Haven, CT: Yale University Press, 2007), 141.

13. Mou Sen, "Address to the Audience by Frog Experimental Drama Troupe" ("Wa shiyan jutuan zhi guanzhong"), in *Avant-Garde Theater Archive* (*Xianfeng xiju dang'an*), ed. Meng Jinghui (Beijing: Zuojia chubanshe, 2000), 6.

14. Mou, "Address to the Audience," 3.

15. Meng Jinghui, "Words from the Director" ("Daoyan de hua"), in *Avant-Garde Theater Archive*, 94–95.

16. Meng Jinghui, "No Doubt Theater Needs Brains" ("Xiju dangran xuyao naozi"), in *Avant-Garde Theater Archive*, 374.

17. Meng, "No Doubt Theater Needs Brains," 374.

18. Meng, "No Doubt Theater Needs Brains," 373.

19. Meng Jinghui, "Critique of Realism" ("Xianshizhuyi pipan"), in *Avant-Garde Theater Archive*, 362.

20. See Rossella Ferrari, *Pop Goes the Avant-Garde: Experimental Theatre in Contemporary China* (London: Seagull Books, 2012), 143–44; 248–50.

21. Meng also directed a radically deconstructed and wildly debated full version of *Teahouse* in 2018.

22. Marvin Carlson, "Postdramatic Theatre and Postdramatic Performance," *Revista Brasileira de Estudos da Presença* 5, no. 3 (2015): 579.

23. Carlson, "Postdramatic Theatre," 578.

24. Paul Mann, *The Theory-Death of the Avant-Garde* (Bloomington: Indiana University Press, 1991), 80.

25. Wang Chong, "From *Thunderstorm* to *Thunderstorm 2.0*" ("Cong 'Leiyu' dao 'Leiyu 2.0'"), *Yinke wenxue shenghuo zhi* 7 (2013): 76–79.

26. Tarryn Li-Min Chun, "Spoken Drama and Its Doubles: *Thunderstorm 2.0* by Wang Chong and Théâtre du Rêve Expérimental," *TDR: The Drama Review* 63, no. 3 (2019): 158; Hans-Thies Lehmann, *Postdramatic Theatre*, trans. Karen Jürs-Munby (London: Routledge, 2006), 16.

27. Sun has created cyber theater and transmedia stage works that deal with virtual reality, youth subcultures, and social media culture. An example of Sun's mediated deconstruction of the realist canon is the 2019 video performance *A Doll's House Episode I: Tik Tok Doll*.

28. Lehmann, *Postdramatic Theatre*, 16.

29. Wang, "From *Thunderstorm* to *Thunderstorm 2.0*."

30. *Thunderstorm 2.0* premiered in Beijing in 2012 and was staged in Taipei in 2013. A new updated version toured Jerusalem in 2016 and New York City in 2018. For detailed analysis, see Chun, "Spoken Drama and Its Doubles."

31. Tian Mansha and Torsten Jost, "In Conversation with Wang Chong" ("Im Gespräch mit Wang Chong"), in *The Art of Directing Today: Voices and Positions from China* (*Regiekunst heute: Stimmen und Positionen aus China*), ed. Tian Mansha and Torsten Jost (Berlin: Alexander Verlag, 2018), 313.

32. Wang Chong, "New Wave Theater Manifesto" ("Xin langchao xiju xuanyan"), in *Re-Theater: The Independent Theater Cities Map* (*Zai juchang: Duli xiju de chengshi ditu*), ed. Sun Xiaoxing (Tianjin: Baihua wenyi chubanshe, 2013), 42. For a discussion of the manifesto and Wang's approach see Yizhou Huang, "Performing Lost Politics: *Yijing yisheng Yibusheng* (Ibsen in One Take) (2012) and Wang Chong's Double-Coded New Wave Theatre," *Asian Theatre Journal* 37, no. 2 (2020): 398–425.

33. Lu, *Chinese Modernity*, 208–9.

34. Carol Martin, *Theatre of the Real* (Basingstoke, UK: Palgrave Macmillan, 2013), 4.

35. Zhao Chuan, "Physical Odyssey," in *The Body at Stake: Experiments in Chinese Contemporary Art and Theatre*, ed. Jörg Huber and Zhao Chuan (Bielefeld, DE: transcript Verlag, 2013), 104.

36. Zhao Chuan, "Why the Body?" ("Shenti weihe?"), *The Blog of Grass Stage* (*Caotaiban de boke*) (blog), February 25, 2011, http://blog.sina.com.cn/s/blog_5c5194ec0100ovlm.html

37. Tao Qingmei, "'Grass Stage' and *38th Parallel*—Interview with Zhao Chuan" ("'Caotaiban' yu 'sanbaxian'—Zhao Chuan fangtan"), *Jintian* 1 (2006), http://www.jintian.net/106/taoqingmei.html

38. Li Yinan, "The Physical Body on the Grass Stage," in *The Body at Stake: Experiments in Chinese Contemporary Art and Theatre*, ed. Jörg Huber and Zhao Chuan (Bielefeld, DE: transcript Verlag, 2013), 116.

39. Li Yinan, "The Physical Body," 119–20.

40. Li Jianjun, "Questions and Answers on the 'Nameless Mankind'" ("Fragen und Antworten zum 'namenlosen Menschen'"), in *The Art of Directing Today: Voices and Positions from China* (*Regiekunst heute: Stimmen und Positionen aus China*), ed. Tian Mansha and Torsten Jost (Berlin: Alexander Verlag, 2018), 259.

41. Alison Forsyth and Chris Megson, "Introduction," in *Get Real: Documentary Theatre Past and Present*, ed. Alison Forsyth and Chris Megson (Basingstoke, UK: Palgrave Macmillan, 2009), 2.

42. McGrath, "The Independent Cinema of Jia Zhangke," 84.
43. Li Yinan and Huang Yiping, "*Juchang*: Contemporary Theatre Performance in Germany and in China" (webinar from Centre for Modern East Asian Studies, University of Göttingen, December 9, 2020).
44. Li and Huang, "*Juchang*."
45. Li Yinan, "Lehmann's Postdramatic Theater and Chinese *Juchang*" ("Leiman de houxiju yu Zhongguo de juchang"), *Xiju* 4 (2019): 52.
46. Hans-Thies Lehmann (Hansi Disi Leiman), *Postdramatic Theater* (*Houxiju juchang*), trans. Li Yinan (Beijing: Beijing daxue chubanshe, 2010).
47. Li and Huang, "*Juchang*."
48. Carlson, "Postdramatic Theatre," 578.
49. Li Yinan, "Lehmann's Postdramatic Theater," 49, 51, 54.
50. Cited in Li Yinan, "Lehmann's Postdramatic Theater," 52.
51. Carlson, "Postdramatic Theatre," 577.
52. Li Ning, "Physical Rebels," in *The Body at Stake: Experiments in Chinese Contemporary Art and Theatre*, ed. Jörg Huber and Zhao Chuan (Bielefeld, DE: transcript Verlag, 2013), 126.
53. Zhao Chuan, "Interrogating Theater" ("Biwen juchang"), *Dushu* 4 (2006): 68. See also Rossella Ferrari, *Transnational Chinese Theatres: Intercultural Performance Networks in East Asia* (Basingstoke, UK: Palgrave Macmillan, 2020), 173–74.
54. Ferrari, *Pop Goes the Avant-Garde*, 240.
55. Luke Robinson, "From 'Public' to 'Private': Chinese Documentary and the Logic of *Xianchang*," in *The New Chinese Documentary Film Movement: For the Public Record*, ed. Chris Berry, Lu Xinyu, and Lisa Rofel (Hong Kong: Hong Kong University Press, 2010), 177–94.
56. Zhang Zhen, "Introduction: Bearing Witness—Chinese Urban Cinema in the Era of 'Transformation' (*Zhuanxing*)," in *The Urban Generation: Chinese Cinema and Society at the Turn of the Twenty-First Century*, ed. Zhang Zhen (Durham, NC: Duke University Press, 2007), 20.
57. Cited in Zhang Zhen, "Introduction: Bearing Witness," 43. See also Dai Jinhua, "Immediacy, Parody, and Image in the Mirror: Is There a Postmodern Scene in Beijing?" in *Multiple Modernities: Cinemas and Popular Media in Transcultural East Asia*, ed. Jenny Kwok Wah Lau (Philadelphia, PA: Temple University Press, 2003), 151–66.
58. Qi Wang, "Performing Documentation: Wu Wenguang and the Performative Turn of New Chinese Documentary," in *A Companion to Chinese Cinema*, ed. Zhang Yingjin (Malden, MA: Wiley-Blackwell, 2012), 299–317.
59. Li Jianjun, "Questions and Answers on the 'Nameless Mankind,'" 256.
60. Li Jianjun, "Questions and Answers on the 'Nameless Mankind,'" 258–59.
61. Li Jianjun, "Auf Ruinen Drachen steigen lassen: Die Theatertruppe Neue Jugend und ich/Flying a Kite on Ruins: The New Youth Troupe and I," *Theater der Zeit* 12 (2015): 22.
62. Corey Kai Nelson Schultz, "Ruin in the Films of Jia Zhangke," *Visual Communication* 15, no. 4 (2016): 440.
63. Zhang Xudong, "Poetics of Vanishing: The Films of Jia Zhangke," *New Left Review* 63 (2010): 71–88.

64. Li Jianjun, "Auf Ruinen," 22.
65. Li Jianjun, "Auf Ruinen," 22.
66. Robinson, "From 'Public' to 'Private'"; Kiki Tianqi Yu, *"My" Self on Camera: First Person Documentary Practice in an Individualising China* (Edinburgh: Edinburgh University Press, 2019), 14.
67. This is my translation of Li Jianjun's descriptor for the NYG's documentary practice with "common" or "ordinary" people (*pingfan ren*). *Fan* also has a connotation of "mundane," "worldly," or pertaining to the mortal and material world.
68. Tian Mansha and Torsten Jost, "In Conversation with Li Jianjun" ("Im Gespräch mit Li Jianjun"), in *The Art of Directing Today: Voices and Positions from China (Regiekunst heute: Stimmen und Positionen aus China)*, ed. Tian Mansha and Torsten Jost (Berlin: Alexander Verlag, 2018), 268.
69. Li Jianjun, "Questions and Answers on the 'Nameless Mankind,'" 263.
70. Tian and Jost, "In Conversation with Li Jianjun," 269.
71. Li Jianjun, "Questions and Answers on the 'Nameless Mankind,'" 263.
72. Martin, *Theatre of the Real*, 15.
73. China Association of Performing Arts (Zhongguo yanchu hangye xiehui), "Self-Disciplining Measures for Entertainers in the Performing Arts Industry" ("Yanchu hangye yanyi renyuan congye zilü guanli banfa"), *Zhongguo yanchu hangye xiehui*, February 5, 2021, http://www.capa.com.cn/news/showDetail?id=170365. The China Association of Performing Arts issued a set of guidelines for performing arts professionals in February 2021 to provide official directives on matters of social morality, respect for national laws and industry regulations, and patriotic behavior.

6 | Three Kingdoms of Pain and Sorrow

Verisimilitude of Warfare Presented in Pansori Jeokbyeokga

MIN-HYUNG YOO

Introduction

This chapter concerns *Jeokbyeokga*, one of the five classics of the *pansori* storytelling tradition, and how it approached the realities of warfare during the mid to late Joseon period.[1] The plot of *Jeokbyeokga* is adapted from the fourteenth-century Chinese novel *The Romance of the Three Kingdoms* with which it shares its story and characters. However, instead of glorifying war as great battles of good versus evil like the novel does, the *pansori* shows the cruel and tragic aspect of warfare where conscripted foot soldiers are separated from their families, mutilated, and constantly under threat of death. *Jeokbyeokga* emerges from the perspective of commoners and is grounded in their experiences.

Pansori is a unique genre of Korean musical storytelling, a one-person musical theater.[2] The term *pansori* is derived from the Korean words *pan*, "a place where people gather," and *sori*, "songs." *Pansori* is performed by a singer and a drummer, and it lasts up to eight hours. It is believed to have originated in the late seventeenth century, and is still performed today. *Pansori* satisfied the artistic demands of common people during the late Joseon dynasty.[3] The protagonists and point of view are usually of the common people, and the language the performers use is vernacular in nature. *Pansori* remained an oral tradition among commoners until the late nineteenth century, by which time it had acquired a more sophisticated literary content and enjoyed considerable popularity among the *yangban* aristocratic elite.[4]

The current *pansori* canon consists of only five stories, which are called the Five Classics. They are *Chunhyangga*, a love story about the son of a nobleman and the daughter of a courtesan; *Simcheongga*, in which a blind man's daughter sacrifices herself so that she can open her father's eyes; *Sugungga*, a battle of wits between a rabbit and a turtle; *Heungbuga*, the story of a good yet poor younger brother and an evil and rich elder brother; and *Jeokbyeokga*, a retelling of the Battle of the Red Cliffs, a great historical battle narrated in *The Romance of the Three Kingdoms*. All five of these *pansori* depict, to different degrees, social issues of their time. *Chunhyangga* talks about the absurdity of the social caste system. *Simcheongga* and *Heungbuga* address the problem of poverty. *Sugungga*'s primary theme is the struggle between the community and the individual. *Jeokbyeokga* also depicts the struggle between the individual and the collective, and it is the most explicit in terms of how its realist themes are structured into its narrative and delivery. *Pansori* such as *Chunhyangga* and *Simcheongga* focus on the story of a main character's fate consistently and panoramically, but the narrative structure of the *pansori Jeokbyeokga* is not designed around a personal account. *Jeokbyeokga* shows many examples of similar characters, and this multiplicity of characters cements its message.

The Romance of the Three Kingdoms is a Chinese classical novel from the most popular historical period in Chinese literature, the Three Kingdoms era, which lasted from 180 to 280 CE. During that period, three competing warlords fought for dominance in China, and the story of the battles fought by the warlords and hundreds of other characters was novelized in the fourteenth century by Luo Guanzhong, after the story had gained popularity as oral literature. Acclaimed as one of the Four Classic Novels of Chinese literature, it presents the warlords of the Three Kingdoms with clear attributes: Liu Bei, the protagonist and Confucian archetype of virtue and benevolence; Cao Cao, a villain and antihero known for ruthlessness and charisma; and Sun Quan, a pragmatist and a wild card who sometimes helps and sometimes hinders Liu Bei. In the novel, the characteristics of the protagonists and antagonists have been accentuated to make the story more entertaining and the themes more pronounced.

The novel focuses on the warlords; they are the main characters. When it was made into *pansori*, the most crucial change was the emergence of commoners as characters. The original narrative of *The Romance of the Three Kingdoms* is a heroic story told from at least three perspectives. Different from *The Romance of the Three Kingdoms*, *Jeokbyeokga* focuses on Cao Cao's soldiers, who are the direct victims of warfare, and by focusing on them the *pansori* actively and effectively criticizes war for its harm to individuals and society. It is noteworthy that the collective commoner soldiers of *Jeokbyeokga* are all under the command of the villain Cao Cao; the soldiers of Liu Bei and Sun Quan, the "heroes," are not present in the narrative. Characters such as Liu Bei and his strategist Zhuge Liang are still the heroes of the story, though not at the center of the narrative stage when the soldiers take over. Significantly, Cao Cao's soldiers do not feel hatred toward Liu Bei's forces, despite being nominal enemies. One of them even sells his horse to Zhuge Liang. Cao Cao's soldiers are themselves critical of Cao Cao while feeling friendly toward Liu Bei's side, which shows that they conceive of the latter as "good."

In the following, I analyze four songs in *Jeokbyeokga*, called "Soldiers' Lament" (Gunsaseorumtaryeong, 군사설움타령), "Death Song" (Jukgotaryeong, 죽고타령), "Song of the Ghost Birds" (Wonjotaryeong, 원조타령), and "Roll Call" (Gunsajeomgo, 군사점고), to illustrate the differences between the novel and the *pansori*, and to show that the latter highlights the realities of warfare. In these four songs, which are original to *Jeokbyeokga* and not present in *The Romance of the Three Kingdoms*, the perspectives given are those of ordinary people, not heroes, to show in full detail that conscription breaks families apart, that battles hurt and kill people with absolute brutality, and that there can be no just cause for warfare. Through the soldiers' voices and the realistic expression of their perspectives on war, *Jeokbyeokga* conveys that war itself should be subjected to criticism. It is characteristic of *pansori* in general to talk about the lives of commoners, and in the case of *Jeokbyeokga*, this tendency is more extreme. Heroes do exist in *Jeokbyeokga*, but from about halfway through the *pansori*, the focus shifts from those heroes to the faceless soldiers. In the transition from *The Romance of the Three Kingdoms* to *Jeokbyeokga*, these changes reflect how this *pansori* takes on a realistic quality by portraying the lives of everyday people.[5]

The Romance of the Three Kingdoms vs. *Jeokbyeokga*

The Romance of the Three Kingdoms arrived in Korea during the fifteenth century. It was considered one of the most famous works of literature, and it influenced many different novels, stories, and even folk religions. The *pansori Jeokbyeokga* is one of the chief examples. Of the five classics of *pansori*, it is the only one that takes place in China. However, while it is a retelling of the Battle of the Red Cliffs—the most significant naval combat in *The Romance of the Three Kingdoms*, where Liu Bei soundly defeats Cao Cao's navy—the *pansori* itself reflects life on the Korean peninsula in the Joseon period.

The structure of *Jeokbyeokga* is important in understanding the text itself. It can be divided into two distinct parts. Wars in *The Romance of the Three Kingdoms* are depicted as a series of battles in which the most important aspect of combat is the courage and prowess of heroes. The soldiers are nothing but plot elements in the heroic novel, expendables who exist to make the heroes stand out. The first part of *Jeokbyeokga* is more akin to the narrative of *The Romance of the Three Kingdoms*. It introduces the characters and the events leading up to the battle, which are as follows: a prologue in which Liu Bei, Guan Yu, and Zhang Fei become sworn brothers; Liu Bei with his brothers visits Zhuge Liang three times to invite him to become Liu Bei's advisor; Zhuge Liang uses his wits to thwart Cao Cao's invasion; and Zhuge Liang goes to Sun Quan's camp to forge alliances.

The second part of *Jeokbyeokga*, the primary focus of this chapter and the section where the representation of common soldiers really takes center stage, reveals the *pansori*'s realism. This part expands on its source material to convey the message that wars cause pain and suffering, and that it is wrong for rulers to drag people into warfare in pursuit of their own ambitions.[6] This part features the battle itself, where Cao Cao is defeated and pursued by Liu Bei's forces. The events and the placement of the songs are as follows: Cao Cao prepares for naval warfare and throws a feast, and "Soldiers' Lament" is sung by the common soldiers who are not enjoying the feast. Allied forces defeat Cao Cao's navy by setting the ships on fire, and the "Death Song" is sung by the dying troops. Cao Cao retreats, and "Song of the Ghost Birds" is sung by the ghosts of soldiers, who reprimand Cao Cao. "Roll Call" is sung by his few remaining foot soldiers; Guan Yu lets Cao Cao and his defeated men go.

While *The Romance of the Three Kingdoms* centers on characters' heroic aspects, *Jeokbyeokga* adopts a unique strategy for describing war and the recruitment of soldiers. It is a fundamental trait of *Jeokbyeokga*, contrasted with other works of literature of the time that dealt with war: in its adaptation of *The Romance of the Three Kingdoms*, *Jeokbyeokga* introduces the life, death, torment, agony, and distress of common, nameless recruited soldiers, who are grouped as the dominant focus and who collectively form a commoner archetype. As noted, it is especially novel that they are the ordinary soldiers under Cao Cao, the antagonist in the story. It is likewise essential to note that Cao Cao is not the charming, proficient villain that *The Romance of the Three Kingdoms* depicts, but rather, a pathetic, violent brute who cannot deal with his power and authority. He is ignorant, incompetent, full of bravado and hypocrisy. He symbolizes an inept tyrant who drives the people into unjust wars. Cao Cao becomes a target of criticism by the commoner conscripted soldiers, and the latter half of *Jeokbyeokga* is outlined as an internal struggle between Cao Cao and his soldiers.

These changes from *The Romance of the Three Kingdoms* are the foundation for the *pansori*'s realism: the world is not full of heroes and antiheroes, but instead of selfish and incompetent despots, whom the commoners resent and struggle against. The common soldiers in *Jeokbyeokga* are both individual and universal. The experiences they go through are personal yet common, represented by the individual soldiers repeatedly chanting about their forced departure from their families and happiness. These sorrows are caused by the loss of the most basic elements of their lives: living with their old parents, getting married, and raising children. The soldiers, along with other protagonists of the *pansori*, lack the basic factors that make happiness possible, and they fight to acquire them, showing that such struggles are a universal experience of the time. They are relatable beings who are recognizable from daily life. Lacking any special talents or powers, they appear repeatedly to convey empathy.

The Four Songs

Cao Cao's character represents rulers who are clumsy, selfish, and egotistical, and the soldiers who reprimand him represent the *pansori*'s audience. This change from the novel to the *pansori* has been the primary subject of scholarly discussion concerning the *pansori Jeokbyeokga*. The voices and perspectives of the commoners become the focal point of the latter part of the *pansori*, as pointed out by scholars such as Kim Gee-Hyong and Seo Jong-Moon.[7] Seo further points out how the attitude of the soldiers toward Cao Cao reflects the commoners' attitude toward the ruling elite of the time. However, neither Kim nor Seo links the narrative of *Jeokbyeokga* to realism. The four songs in the voice of the common soldiers—"Soldiers' Lament," "Death Song," "Song of the Ghost Birds," and "Roll Call"—are unique to *Jeokbyeokga* and take up a considerable part of its latter half. Each of the four songs carries an antiwar message while conveying four distinctive core sentiments: sorrow, torment, resentment, and rage. The four sentiments progressively escalate in intensity, just as real emotions might escalate with time and experience.

The four songs are sung in vernacular Korean, with stylistic elements that emphasize the emotions of the common soldiers. *Gyemyeonjo*, one of the two tones used to express sadness in *pansori*, is prominent in these songs. The other style, *ujo*, with a strong uplifting tone, is used in the first half of *Jeokbyeokga*, where there are also many classical Chinese words, Chinese being the language of *The Romance of the Three Kingdoms*. In the second part of *Jeokbyeokga*, however, the vernacular is heavily used. Thus, we see that the first half of *Jeokbyeokga* is more akin to *The Romance of the Three Kingdoms* in its themes, language, and style that emphasizes heroism, while in the latter half, the language and style reflect the expression of the common people. The vernacular language reflects the actual language commoners spoke, and the *gyemyeonjo* style used for sadness reflects their everyday hardships. The most prominent example comes from "Soldiers' Lament," in which one soldier is compelled to tearfully leave his wife behind and is "forced to move around the endless seas and all directions, like a tiger in a trap or fish caught in a net. When he looks in the direction of home, all that is seen are clouds in the sky. Whenever will he go back home, hold his wife's hands, and resolve all his yearning?"[8] These lines are in vernacular Korean, with no classical Chinese expressions, and they are delivered in a singing style that closely resembles weeping.

"Soldiers' Lament" is sung to enhance the confidence and morale of Cao Cao's soldiers the night before the naval combat at Red Cliffs. While Cao Cao throws a great feast for the soldiers, they remain distressed and sorrowful, having been conscripted and separated from their families. Showing the division between a ruler's aims and those of his subjects, Cao Cao's intention to rally the soldiers fails, and most of the soldiers sing about the families they left behind. The stories of separation are as varied as the faces of the soldiers. For instance, one of the soldiers was separated from his old parents, who cannot live without him. Another was separated from his newly formed family, being recently married after living alone for a long time. Another soldier just had a child after waiting for years; he laments that this is the only son in his line for many generations, and that he wedded late and did all that he could to have a child; "the baby was his solitary delight, only thing to love, and he was living with that love when the war happened, dragging the people of Wei to the Red Cliffs to fight; he could not escape, and could only say goodbye to his wife, saying 'Oh, my wife, I am being taken away to the battlefield, please take good care of our baby.' So when would he see his family again?"[9]

One soldier was simply a young boy forced to abandon a pet bird that he had befriended at home, and another was a newlywed who was hauled from his wedding-night bed into war. While there are hints of humor sprinkled throughout, it is without doubt a lament, the main sentiment being sorrow, and the theme one of separation from family due to a war that lacks a justifiable purpose. The soldier who at almost fifty years old had just had a child after years of yearning and praying, had only his newborn baby as a reason to live, but he was torn away from him, conscripted, without anyone telling him what the war was for.[10] Nameless soldiers repeat similar personal tragedies, in which they are taken from their parents, spouses, and children because of their social status. Well-deserved tranquility with family is shattered when the war takes them away. The song closes with one old soldier telling the others that they, the common soldiers, will probably pass away regardless of winning or losing the war. It depicts the sentiment among them that the misfortune has already occurred, and the result of the battle is not even pertinent to them.

"Death Song" occurs during and after Liu Bei sets fire to Cao Cao's ships. While "Soldiers' Lament" is about distress and separation from loved ones, "Death Song" expresses the excruciating pain that war brings to the soldiers through defeat and countless deaths. It lists many different kinds of death suffered by Cao Cao's soldiers, which are sung in succession in a short span of time and with a fast rhythm:

> Those poor millions can't run away, can't fly away, can't move at all, and they suffocate, they are shot by arrows, they are stabbed by spears, they die standing, die sitting, die laughing, die crying, die trampled, die beaten, die worrying, die angry, die drowned, die shattered, die broken, die torn, die scared, die with their eyes torn out, die with their backs blasted, they meet their untimely death, sudden death and death in masses, they die trying out dying, die thoughtlessly, die rolling and falling, die thumping their own chest, die pitifully, die dreaming, one dies eating one big rice cake, one takes out a big bag, reaches in, brings out poison, bites into it, and falls into the water, another climbs to the top of the sail, prays to the heavens to save him, because he is the only son in three generations, and also falls into the water, another laments that he dies accomplishing nothing, and another dies citing poetry.[11]

Each of these descriptions of death takes about one phrase in the song. Other soldiers are said to climb to the highest point of a pole and hop off. Lamenting death and isolation from family, their dead bodies "uncurled in bloody water like noodles in the broth."[12]

There is a lot of dark humor, but the song's all-encompassing feelings reflect torment and helplessness. The soldiers who are dragged toward death remain hopeless, sorrowful, and full of anguish and desperation. When a soldier who takes his own life by jumping into the river cries that he will never see his family again, the song is delivered in a quick yet sorrowful tone.

The Battle of the Red Cliffs is perhaps the greatest triumph in *The Romance of the Three Kingdoms*. In the novel, the death of the soldiers is not described in detail. However, in *Jeokbyeokga*, the song tells of these horrifying moments of merciless death and slaughter. The *pansori* recognizes that Liu Bei's triumph and Cao Cao's loss are great events. Nonetheless, by focusing on the common soldier, *Jeokbyeokga* shows that war and the death brought about by war are horrendous, arguing against war and the use of war to resolve disagreements.

As Cao Cao, with his modest number of remaining troops, flees in defeat, the souls of dead soldiers in the form of ghostly birds return and speak of their resentment toward him. "Song of the Ghost Birds" is a pun-filled song, in which the sounds of different birds are associated with various situations of defeat. For example, a ghost crow caws "gorigak gaok," making a sound that is homonymous in Korean with "retreat to the other side,"[13] indicating to the remaining soldiers that they should run to the path that Cao Cao did *not* choose. A cuckoo blames Cao Cao for conscripting him and taking him far from home. A lark despises Cao Cao's arrogance, pride, and ignorance, which resulted in their downfall and death. An oriole blames Cao Cao for utilizing his intelligence in such a way that he alone survives. A kingfisher questions why there were not enough arrows for them to shoot. "Song of the Ghost Birds" explores each element at some length. The ghost birds blame their demise on Cao Cao's decisions to go to war, and further decisions during the war. The primary sentiment in this third song in which grudges are expressed is resigned resentment toward their leader.

The following song, "Roll Call," is the most satirical of all the pieces in *Jeokbyeokga*. The soldiers' first three songs express helplessness and sadness, but the core sentiments of "Roll Call" are rage and defiance, and the soldiers express more hostility toward Cao Cao. The characters in the first three songs are soldiers without names; their only characteristics are the results of their situations. Here, however, nicknames are given to the soldiers, all referring to physical or mental disabilities, such as "Tumors in bones," "No-neck," and "Sloppy." These people do not conform to martial archetypes, and they should never have entered the battlefield. This song expresses the soldiers' utmost rage toward Cao Cao, who recruited even vulnerable and disabled men to join a purposeless war, only to die for no logical reason.

Almost all of the soldiers in "Roll Call" were severely injured in battle, and all resent Cao Cao for their condition. One soldier cries in agony and sorrow. His arms are broken and his legs are shot, and he cannot even bow to his commander. He asks his commander to kill him to end his misery and free his soul to join his family. The aforementioned "Tumor-in-bones" is so wholly disabled and harmed that he cannot walk straight. He was stabbed in one arm by a spear, in the other arm by an arrow; he can barely walk, and is so deformed that he is "half-alive and half-dead" and "rich with disability."[14] He is hunchbacked and crippled, one-eared and one-armed, and when Cao Cao sees him he is appalled but jokingly asks to boil him so that the rest of the troop could have some soup.

The three songs that are sung before "Roll Call" talk about how "normal" families were destroyed. The conscripted soldiers are dying, and they resent their deaths. In *Jeokbyeokga*'s realistic portrayal of war, "Roll Call" shows the actual destroyed lives, depicting the ugly realities and grotesque deformities and injuries. "Roll Call" shows how the war has so clouded Cao Cao's judgment that he cannot even distinguish physically disabled individuals from the physically able, and he wrongfully punishes the innocent.

Another soldier, however, remains uninjured because he limited his participation in the war. He tells Cao Cao that the dead and injured have met their fates only because of their own poor judgment. He tells how, as soon as a battle started, he would run off at a distance, sit down, watch the war, and only return for meals. He sold his weapon to buy food and drink for himself and needles for his wife. This is a stark declaration that the war is not his, but Cao Cao's. In a song with a comparatively humorous tone, the soldier says that he feels no guilt or remorse for running away or selling his weapon; he deems it a natural, rational thing to do, going so far as to say that not running away is irrational: "the other soldiers are dumb to die or be injured. When the fight is going, it is best to escape the battlefield, climb to the mountaintop, and watch the fight, only coming back for meals."[15] The individual feels no responsibility toward the community. Cao Cao's kingdom did nothing for the individual, instead taking everything away in the name of war, so this individual made a rational choice by giving up on the community. Another warrior, a horseman, answers the roll call with only his horsewhip in hand, having sold his horse to Zhuge Liang. In these two cases, the message is that the war is Cao Cao's business alone.

The outcome of the war is not shown through the eyes of the victor. The brilliant victory on Liu Bei's side is not depicted in any way. Instead, what are told are stories of Cao Cao's soldiers and the horrendous outcomes of the defeat. These men are not just passive losers, however; they all actively defy authority. Not only are they vocally defiant, even openly ridiculing their ruler Cao Cao, they are actively defiant as well, selling war items and horses to his enemy. The identity that bound the soldiers as belonging to one community was already weak, but it disintegrated completely with their disappointment in its leader. The defeat was theirs, but the choice was not their own. Their hostility is not toward their enemies on the battlefield, but toward their leader, Cao Cao.

"Soldiers' Lament" reflects the uncertainty about the future, isolation from families, and not knowing when one can return home. It expresses sorrow in its rawest form, and the emotions expressed in the many stories of personal loss and pointless sacrifice build a realistic portrayal of war's effects. Most stories in "Soldiers' Lament" are told by common soldiers missing their families, whether that be an old parent, a spouse, a child, a newlywed wife, a sibling, or even a pet bird. Although the soldiers are in the war zone, their minds are full of dread about losing friends and family. The song shows that war destroys hard-earned personal happiness, as in the case of the man late to fatherhood torn from mother and child, or the orphan who had spent his life's earnings to marry, only to be dragged out to war on his wedding night, his marriage not even consummated. Even children are not exempt from forced recruitment, as shown when an innocent child is separated from his pet bird. Cao Cao exercised his authority to force all males into the war against their will regardless of age or physical ability. In each case, the personal is obliterated by a war that cannot be justified by those who fight it on the ground. In its themes and style, "Soldiers' Lament" expresses all that the soldiers felt and experienced, and it engages listeners with the realities of life for those without power.

The soldiers in *Jeokbyeokga* are both individual and universal, forming a collective commoner archetype. *Jeokbyeokga* establishes this archetype by depicting a group of soldiers who share similar stories. *Jeokbyeokga* conveys inclusiveness by repeating stories that any member of society could experience. In both "Soldiers' Lament" and "Roll Call," characters with similar characteristics repeat almost the same stories. In "Soldiers' Lament," before the great battle at Red Cliffs, each fighter is examined distinctly as "a soldier," but after the war, they are mentioned using their positions. In "Roll Call," the soldiers are named according to either their positions or their physical disabilities, portraying them less as particular individuals and more as common soldiers, men who are not professional warriors, but commoners forcefully recruited into Cao Cao's army.

In "Soldiers' Lament," the young man who was conscripted during his wedding night does not have any urge to fight and even thinks of deserting his troops: "I tried my best to escape, but I was surrounded in all four directions, so I could not. I am a tiger in a trap, a fish in a net. When could I go back home? Would I not die and become a stack of bones? I want to go back home, hold the hands of my beloved."[16] He thinks of himself as a fish caught in the net of Cao Cao's army. The sentiment is widespread, and among those who share his opinion, wanting to win and return victorious is nothing but a vain idea.

The community itself is also meaningless. During the "Roll Call," one soldier on cook's duty tells his story of how he tried to disguise himself as a pilgrim carrying a pot when Liu Bei's troops attacked. Unfortunately for him, the pot had Cao Cao's signature Wei symbol, and because of that, he could not pass as a pilgrim. Cao Cao's soldier is not thinking about fighting for his community and his leader; the cause becomes nothing but a hindrance for him, and he curses the person who drew the Wei symbol on the pot he was carrying. Moreover, the reason he took the pot was not to cook for Cao Cao and his generals but to cook for himself after returning home when the war was over.

The soldiers' circumstances make it challenging for them to escape the destiny of committing their lives to a war that lacks legitimacy. Requesting to be executed so that one's spirit can return home to meet his family, showing one's disability to Cao Cao to make him comprehend why one must be rebellious, and selling weapons for one's own benefit— all show that the soldiers have no respect for or loyalty to their leader. The Battle of the Red Cliffs is a brilliant military success for the ones who planned the strategy and for Liu Bei and Sun Quan's soldiers, but for Cao Cao's soldiers, it is nothing but a cataclysm. In the "Death Song," their deaths are described in detail not because their deaths were justified from the heroes' side, but because the *pansori* explicitly expresses what a disaster it is for people forcefully taken to war.

In *Hwayongdo* (화용도, Huorong Pass), the closing episode of *Jeokbyeokga*, the remaining soldiers, isolated from their families during recruitment and suffering through violent warfare that killed or injured nearly all of them, repeatedly express loss and misfortune. In all four songs being discussed, soldiers are crying. For example, "Soldiers' Lament" begins with a crying soldier; "Death Song" shows soldiers who cry as they are dying; "Song of the Ghost Birds" reveals the soldiers' ghosts turning into screaming birds; and "Roll Call" includes numerous soldiers crying about their injuries. The emotional narration of many stories of individual experiences of loss and misery contributes to the realism of *Jeokbyeokga*, and the weeping that accompanies the soldiers' stories conveys the reality of the characters' feelings.

Nonetheless, *Jeokbyeokga* ends, not on a note of distress, but with a degree of hope that there can indeed be an understanding between the ruler and commoners. While toward the start of the *pansori* Cao Cao is pitiless and incompetent, he gradually learns to feel the soldiers' torment. The first instance where Cao Cao notes the plight of soldiers comes at the end of "Song of the Ghost Birds." After listening to this song, he attempts to comfort them: "Do not cry, do not cry. You are all my people who have wrongfully become ghosts. Please stop crying."[17] Moreover, the resistance that appeared during "Roll Call" really affected Cao Cao. He takes pity on the previously mentioned soldier who asks Cao Cao to kill him so his spirit can return home to his family, saying, "Your parents are my parents, and your family is my family. Let us all survive together and go home together,"[18] and Cao Cao releases him. "Roll Call" closes with Cao Cao feeling sorry for every injured soldier and calling them "my children." Through experiencing the emotions and cries of people in the community, Cao Cao, the classic villain, can arguably be said to have at long last gained some level of compassion toward his subjects.

Conclusion

The second half of *Jeokbyeokga* distinguishes itself from *The Romance of the Three Kingdoms* by portraying ordinary conscripted soldiers' reactions to war. "Soldiers' Lament" talks about the sorrow of separation. "Death Song" deals with pain and death, and "Song of the Ghost Birds" sings about resentment. "Roll Call" is a song of defiance and the collapse of group identity. Each song tells of similar tragic incidents, with nameless soldiers singing their individual stories of pain and sorrow. These stories create a realistic image of the lives of conscripted soldiers. The dichotomy of values between the individual and authority widens as the songs progress, and the emotions intensify from sorrow to rage. By the last song, "Roll Call," the soldiers, who only weep passively at the beginning of "Soldiers' Lament," express rage and openly criticize Cao Cao. The emotional progression from sorrow to rage structures *Jeokbyeokga* and underlies its realism.

This expression of rage leads to a change in Cao Cao's character, from selfish to caring. By the end of the four songs, Cao Cao seems to truly sympathize with the soldiers, going so far as to call them his own family. This results in changes in the soldiers' attitudes. At the end of *Jeokbyeokga*, Guan Yu, a lieutenant general of Liu Bei and a paragon of virtue, finally pursues and catches Cao Cao and his men. Right before Guan Yu decides to kill Cao Cao, something unexpected happens. Cao Cao's soldiers, until this point bent on criticizing, defying, and making fun of Cao Cao, suddenly bow before Guan Yu and beg for his life. Cao Cao says that his death would not be as tragic as the deaths of his soldiers and begs for his men to be let go, even at the cost of his own life.

Guan Yu lets them all go out of pity. Cao Cao, at that point, sympathizes with his soldiers enough that he has become one of them. He is no longer an incompetent leader, but just one of the defeated soldiers.[19] By being ridiculed and criticized, he has lost whatever authority he had before. In return, he gains a sort of solidarity with his soldiers and becomes a different kind of ruler, and as a result, he is spared death. I argue that the main characters of *Jeokbyeokga* are Cao Cao and his men, and that the focus on commoner soldiers and Cao Cao's changed perspective, so different from *The Romance of the Three Kingdoms*, make *Jeokbyeokga* unique.

Unlike *The Romance of the Three Kingdoms*, the narrative follows Cao Cao's side in their defeat, and the satirizing of Cao Cao and sympathy toward the soldiers are linked to the central message of *Jeokbyeokga* itself. Seen through the perspectives of common soldiers, this message is that there can be no just cause for warfare. The unique sections of *Jeokbyeokga* contradict any notion of the justification of war, by portraying the severe repercussions of conflict on both the individual and the collective. After being in a vulnerable state, even Cao Cao realizes the negative consequences of war and its severe impact on his ordinary soldiers' mental states and social relationships. Through soldiers' voices, *Jeokbyeokga* conveys the message that war devastates lives, and that the only worthwhile ruler is one who can sympathize with his subjects.

Notes

1. All translations are by the author.
2. *Pansori* is currently a Korean National Intangible Cultural Property, to protect the genre from being endangered by cultural Westernization. See Marshall R. Pihl, *The Korean Singer of Tales* (Cambridge, MA: Harvard University Asia Center, 1994) for an overview and history of *pansori*.
3. See Kim Jong-cheol's article discussing *pansori*'s popularity among the common people: "A Study on the Reception of Pansori in the Nineteenth and Twentieth Centuries" ("19segi-20segicho Pansori Suyong Yangsang Yeongu"), *Pansori Research (Pansori Yeongu)* (1996) : 141–205.
4. While this is common knowledge about the history of *pansori*, Shin Dong-heun addresses it in detail in "How the Themes of 'Chunhyangga' Changed Over History" ("Chunhyangjeon Juje Uisik eui Yeoksajeok Byeonmo Yangsang"), *Pansori Research (Pansori Yeongu)* 8 (1997): 161–218.
5. Chung Byung-heon makes similar arguments regarding *pansori* and realism, in "The Acceptance of 'Samgukjiyeoneui' in *Jeokbyeokga* ("Pansori Jeokbyeokga Ui Samgukji Yeonyi Suyong Yangsang"), *Hanjung Inmunhak Yeongu* 16 (2005): 25–48.
6. Kim Jongcheol talks about how *Jeokbyeokga* expands and creates the torment for each of the soldiers on Cao Cao's side, "closing up" on each of them. Kim Jongcheol, "Sanguozhi Yanyi and *Jeokbyeokga*" ("Samgukji Yeonyi wa Jeokbyeokga"), *Hanjung Inmunhak Yeongu* 8 (2002): 140.
7. Kim Gee-Hyong, "The Formation and Transfiguration of *Jeokbyeokga*" ("*Jeokbyeokga* Ui Hyeongseong Gwa Byeonmo"), *Hanguk Minsokhak* 25 (1993): 112; Seo Jong-Moon, "The Meaning and Significance of 'Gunsajeomgo' of *Jeokbyeokga*" ("*Jeokbyeokga* E Natanan 'Gunsajeomgodaemok' ui Jonje Yangsangwa Geu Uimi"), *Journal of Pansori* (1997): 33–35.
8. "Im Bang-wool's tradition of *Jeokbyeokga*," in *Compilation of Pansori Jeokbyeokga* (적벽가 전집 *Jeokbyeokga Jeonjip*), ed. Kim Jinyoung et al. (Seoul: Parkeejeong, 1998), 1: 84.
9. "Jeong Gwon-jin's tradition of *Jeokbyeokga*," in *Compilation of Pansori Jeokbyeokga*, 1: 299.
10. "Park Bong-sul's tradition of *Jeokbyeokga*," in *Compilation of Pansori Jeokbyeokga*, 1: 463.
11. "Park Bong-sul's Tradition of *Jeokbyeokga*," 1: 478.
12. "Park Bong-sul's Tradition of *Jeokbyeokga*," 1: 374.
13. "Park Bong-sul's Tradition of *Jeokbyeokga*," 1: 481.
14. "Jeong Gwang-soo's Tradition of *Jeokbyeokga*," in *Compilation of Pansori Jeokbyeokga*, 1: 158.
15. "Jeong Gwon-jin's Tradition of *Jeokbyeokga*," 1: 322.
16. "Jeong Gwon-jin's Tradition of *Jeokbyeokga*," 1: 300.
17. "Park Bong-sul's Tradition of *Jeokbyeokga*," 1: 481.
18. "Song Sun-seop's Tradition of *Jeokbyeokga*," in *Compilation of Pansori Jeokbyeokga*, 1: 434.
19. Kim Sang-Hoon is the only scholar who makes a similar argument in his work, in which he argues that save for one version of *Jeokbyeokga*, Cao Cao

eventually makes peace with his soldiers. While he acknowledges that Cao Cao and his men eventually reconcile, the center of Kim's argument is the one version where they do not, so the reconciliation itself is not discussed fully. Kim Sang-Hoon, "A Study of Shinjaehyo Version Jeokbyeokga's 'Jojo Who Didn't Make Harmony with His Forces Until the End'" ("Ggeutggaji Gunsadeulgwa Hwahaphaji Mot'han 'ShinJaehyoBon *Jeokbyeokga*' Ui Jojo"), *Hangukhak Yeongu* 56 (2020): 173–74.

PART III | Technologies

7 | Mediated Laughter and the Limits of Realism

Laughing Letter *and the* Kinodrama *Experiment in 1930s Japanese Performance*

ARAGORN QUINN

In October 1937, the Shin Tsukiji Theater premiered *The Laughing Letter* (嗤う手紙), a show remarkable for its integration of live performance and film with recorded sound. Written by Yagi Ryūichirō (1906–1965), directed by Kinogusa Teinosuke (1896–1982) (film) and Senda Koreya (1904–1994) (stage), this first-of-its-kind performance was billed as a *kinodrama*. While both the production and its genre have since been forgotten in the contemporary theater world and have been relegated to short asides in scholarship of theater and film history, *Letter* attracted keen interest from audiences and critics at the time of its debut. With the explosion in access to revolutionary new technologies of mediation in the 1920s and 1930s, including photography, phonographs, telephones, radio, and cinema, the discourse around new modes of mediation was often infused with the hope of new possibilities of representation. By contrast, *Letter* questioned the rapidly increasing role of these technologies and questioned the promise mediation offered in entertainment, business, and daily life in early-twentieth-century Japan.

New modes of mediation, enabling and enabled by a specific kind of relationship between the original and its copy, challenged "nonmodern" modes of performance and codified a certain kind of technological reproduction as closer to reality than modes developed before the advent of modernity. The team behind *Letter* utilized the novel form of the *kinodrama* to question this rapidly emerging ideology in perfor-

143

mance, which placed the reproduction of the body as equal to, or even more real than, the real performative body itself.

In this chapter, I resist the common scholarly representation of the *kinodrama* (and by extension, similar popular film/theater hybrid modes such as the *rensageki* and *benshi* performer) as an early-twentieth-century transitional performance mode that served as a placeholder until film developed certain technological advancements. This does not mean that theories of representation did not evolve—a central tenet of this chapter is that they do—but my stance is that the *kinodrama* is not simply a practical and formal manifestation of that theoretical evolution. It is true that many contemporary observers saw live and mediated performance as having complementary attributes: film was seen as exhibiting greater control over time and space, while live performance had color and sound. Yet the discourse prompted by the *kinodrama* touched on more profound questions for the present and future of performance, and the *kinodrama* was not seen at the time as filling in while awaiting future technological advances. I examine *Letter* for its intervention in discussions that questioned the relationship of the live and mediated body with its audience; the uncertain potential for mediation to render an ostensibly faithful copy of an original human body and voice; and, ultimately, the place of the live human body as the generative origin of performance.

The script for *Laughing Letter* was based on the play *Side by Side* (*Nebeneinander*, 1923) by German Expressionist playwright Georg Kaiser and adapted from Kubo Sakae's (1900–1958) translation titled *In Parallel* (平行, published 1934). The drama plays out in three independent stories on both the live stage and on three screens stationed around the central acting space: one centers around the owner of a Ginza pharmacy, another on a pair of executives at a recording company called Sunrise Records, and the last on a family on a farm outside of Tokyo. The otherwise unconnected plots are brought together through the eponymous letter, which was written by a philandering executive at Sunrise Records to his jilted lover on the farm, but was misdirected to the pharmacy in Ginza.

Part of the appeal of *Letter* is rooted in the dramatic irony of the original text (and Kubo Sakae's translation) as the characters become aware of the other story lines that the audience has seen play out. However, few contemporary reviewers mention the plot in any great detail. The primary appeal of *Letter*, the aspect that provoked an outsized critical conversation about the production (and that, incidentally, was not part of its German original), was the integration of live performance and film with recorded sound through the use of the three screens on stage. Yet

Figure 7.1: *The Laughing Letter* stage with a screen visible stage right. Image from a pamphlet in the author's collection.

despite featuring the flashy new technology of recorded sound in film, *Letter* actually highlights the failure of technological mediation in all facets of the show. In its very status as a translation, which alters the source material in fundamental ways, it undermines the expectation of fidelity between source and target texts, not unlike assumptions in other modes of reproduction. Within the diegetic frame of the play itself, communication technology repeatedly fails to represent the messages they purport to convey. And most obviously, the production makes metatheatrical use of the screens and live stage to layer filmed mediation and staged liveness on stage in ways that question the hierarchy of liveness over mediation in performance.

Baudrillard talks about mediation in ways that help clarify the relationship of film and liveness in *Letter*. Baudrillard sees the sign/signified relationship between the mediated object and its representation as part of a moving trajectory that tracks the development of modernity. Early in this timeline, the original is clearly different from and hierarchically above the copy. There is, he argues, a "wager on representation: that a sign could refer to the depth of meaning, that a sign could *exchange* for meaning."[1] Yet even at this nascent stage, Baudrillard sees a drive, motivated by a very specific kind of realism prized by modernists, to eliminate the gap between the sign and the referent. The sign and referent are understood as different, but the thinking goes that if the representation could be realistic enough, it could potentially eliminate the sign/signified gap and give its audience access to that prized original. Perhaps, posits Baudrillard, the map could actually *be* the territory. Or more accurately, it becomes "a simulacrum, never again exchanging for what is real."[2] The logic of mediation then works to destabilize any remaining space between the sign and signified, and ultimately to obviate the sign entirely. All that remains at the end of Baudrillard's timeline are endlessly replicable copies without any original. At the premiere of *Letter* in 1937, these trends had been in motion both on screen and on stage for decades in Japanese performance, and in this sense, we can say that *Letter* prefigures Baudrillard's trajectory by pointing to the collapse of the space between sign and signified in both stage and film.

The realism that allows for the collapse of the signified into the sign requires that any artifice be invisible and read transparently by its audience. Performative modernity in post-Meiji Japan, as per the commonly accepted story, centered in large part on reconfiguring the relationship of the stage, body, and script, connecting to its real-world referents in these new modes. Major theatrical artistic developments centered around creating tighter bonds between sign and signified than were understood to exist in premodern theater (and, for that matter, in contemporary popular theater). In other words, the copy was meant to be, as closely as possible, the original of which it was a duplicate. This played out in many facets of the stage performance.

Shingeki (New Theater) as a movement was at the fore of this trend that eschewed overtly theatrical practices in pursuit of greater verisimilitude and closer access to an unmediated truth through the stage. As Osanai Kaoru (1881–1928) would write at the founding of his Tsukiji Little Theater in 1924, the Tsukiji planned to utilize nonprofessional actors (素人を役者にする) and to amateurize professional actors (役者を素人にする). The goal was acting that was not steeped in (kabuki) training built around what was seen as the artifice of traditional theater.[3] Foremost among these practices, *shingeki* practitioners sought to do away with *kata*, an outside-in model of character development that defined the operative method of kabuki acting. Instead, *shingeki* training followed the inside-out Stanislavskian model of character development, which purportedly represented a more authentic self. Ayako Kano describes this shift away from *kata* in terms of "direct action" versus "indirect action," or internally motivated movement as opposed to externally dictated movement.[4]

The same logic that worked to close the gap between "real" and "represented" character motivations also pushed back against the disconnect between the genders of characters and the actors who played them, such as the kabuki female role specialist *onnagata*, commonly seen in many modes of Japanese performance. Characters' genders continued (and still continue) to diverge from the bodies of their actors in Japanese performance—*onnagata* appeared on film for decades after Matsui Sumako's (1886–1919) seminal performance in 1911 of Nora in *A Doll's House*—but roles from the 1910s on saw an increasing shift toward matching genders between roles and the bodies acting them. Lastly, and perhaps most central to *shingeki* ideals, the heightened classical Japanese language of traditional kabuki theater gave way to a more "natural," vernacular language. Indra Levy demonstrates how these three shifts intersected to create a closer connection between the bodies on the stage and the roles they represent. This naturalism worked to shed the masklike *kumadori* makeup of kabuki actors with a move toward a "vernacular body language" of the stage.[5] In other words, acting methodology on all fronts worked to close the gap between the character/actor and sign/signified.

Likewise, much of the popular and critical fascination with film in the early decades of the twentieth century revolved around its ability to represent the world "accurately." This superiority included an assumed greater control of space and time and far more photorealistic representation than theatrical scenic designs, confined as they were to the fixed size and location within the proscenium arch. A key appeal of early film for critics and audiences was the promise of the elision of a perceived mediation. Early accounts said of film that it allowed the audience to "see things as they really are," and that it actually allowed the medium to disappear, leaving the viewer with a sense of liveness (現実感). Reports on cinema in the early days centered on its ability to "give the feeling of touching the real thing."[6] This promise, that film and new media can transcend their very ontology as media, has been and continues to be the elusive yet tantalizing allure motivating the popularity of these genres. Philip Auslander offers poignant examples of mediation replacing liveness as the "authentic" experience, such as when concert-goers were presented with headphones to improve upon the live experience.[7]

Indeed, just as live performances enjoyed through headphones allow for a very specific kind of authentic, unfiltered experience (one unsullied by, for example, aural distractions within the live environment such as the noise of fellow audience members), film offered the promise of a certain kind of verisimilitude that earlier technology, and a live theater experience, could not reproduce. The promise was of an unmediated experience, obviously still through a lens but as if the lens were not there. Successive technological advancements renewed that promise. Kerim Yasar, for example, points out that the critical response to the advent of recorded sound in film touted the resulting "naturalness" of the combination of photorealism with auditory realism.[8] Responses were similar at the advent of color film, and more recently with the various attempts at 3D technology and the race for ever-higher levels of definition on television. Each development offers the elusive possibility of a barely-there mediation—a mediated experience in which the mediation is as nearly imperceptible as possible. The logic of this mode of realism that idealizes a film-viewing experience in which we cannot perceive the fact of mediation suggests that each step on this progression toward an always-elusive-yet-always-pursued obviation of mediation is an even more authentic experience with each succeeding technological advancement. As scholars have noted, this techno-aesthetic ideal also describes the same logic of the *genbun-itchi* movement for vernacular language that prized the elimination of artifice in theater.[9] In both theater and film, a broad swath of discourse on representation centered around the elimination of the lacuna between sign and signified.

Even where this ideal very clearly broke down, the logic of naturalism required that the sign equal the signified. Neither stage nor film can offer actual unmediated access to the object of representation. Despite Osanai Kaoru's conscious turn away from the artifice of kabuki, the Tsukiji Little Theater relied almost exclusively on the mediation of translated scripts from European modernist theater. These translations inherently created distance between viewer and actor. Yet even here, the audiences chose to believe there was no gap. Indra Levy demonstrates that *shingeki*'s goal of a more authentic theater experience paradoxically involved a willingness to suspend many layers of disbelief to commune with an exotic script.[10] In other words, the play was experienced as authentic and real *even in light of* the fundamental disconnect between an attempted natural vernacular body language and an exotic, foreignizing vernacular spoken language. Rather than a willing suspension of disbelief, the audience engaged in a disbelief that there was any suspension at all.

Producing these foreign plays with foreign characters inevitably resulted in theory failing to play out in practice. Japanese actors embodying foreign characters could by definition not be motivated, for example, to pick up a utensil in an internally motivated way that was *also* culturally specific to a context of which none of the acting troupe had any firsthand, internalized knowledge. Thus, while everything about Matsui Sumako's Nora was made up of exotic and opaque language and character motivations, her acting was received as a transparent lens into an original foreign text. The play was widely praised not despite its opacity, but rather *because* of its opacity, as Levy demonstrates. Yet even in the face of a clear and decisive disconnect between the sign and the signified, viewers of the performance speak of feeling the experience of having direct access to an unadulterated original.

Despite these prominent trends in popular and critical discourse around greater naturalism in theater and film, the obvious must be stated here: the prewar performance world did not uniformly and universally embrace this goal of a kind of realism that advocated a transparent medium ostensibly free of artifice. In terms of formal properties, while pockets of modernists (among whom Kinogusa can perhaps be grouped) embraced an ideology of transparent, photo-real representation, many or most did not. Georg Kaiser typically (although not in *Nebeneinander*) worked in expressionist modes. While Kubo Sakae typically worked in a realistic mode with plays such as *Land of Volcanic Ash*, leading members of the Japanese leftist theater world had strong affinities to dramaturgies that highlighted artifice rather than transparency. For instance, Senda Koreya, director of *Laughing Letter*, worked with Bertolt Brecht while in Germany, and Murayama Tomoyoshi helped bring European avant-garde ideals into Japanese theater. Still, it is notable that neither of *Letter*'s directors, Kinogusa and Senda Koreya, saw the production's aims as attempting to obscure the fact or effect of the film or stage medium as signs with no discernible distance from their signifieds.

As a *kinodrama, Laughing Letter* ostensibly built on the tradition of the stage/silent film hybrid form of the *rensageki*, a form popular as far back as the first decade of the 1900s in which film and staged scenes alternated in the telling of a single narrative. The creators of the *kinodrama*, however, aspired to more than just adding sound to the silent *rensageki* film.[11] Kinogusa speaks of employing the neologism *kinodrama*, rather than using the existing word *rensageki*, because Kinogusa and Senda attempted to employ liveness and mediation in a more complicated way than the *rensageki* did. In contrast to *rensageki*'s live/film alternating format, *Laughing Letter*'s juxtaposition of liveness and mediation appears at multiple levels of the production simultaneously, as a deliberate interplay of the two.[12] At the most obvious level, this manifests in the stage design, which incorporates three screens that surround the live performance space in the center of the stage.

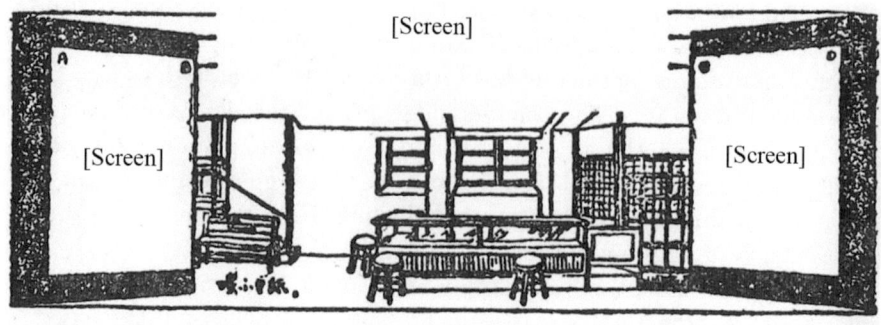

Figure 7.2: Stage layout of *The Laughing Letter*. Image from a pamphlet in the author's collection.

Figure 7.2 shows a sketch of the stage, with a screen stage left of the proscenium that depicted the farm storyline; a screen stage right of the proscenium for the record-company storyline; and a screen above the acting space attached to the theater's fly system so it could be raised and lowered in front of the main curtain for use in depicting the passage of time during transitions. The novelty and key appeal of this new form for many critics was not the adoption of recorded sound in film (which after all had existed in Japan for years by the time of *Laughing Letter*), but how the film and live stories took place in parallel, and how the live and filmed components of the production commented on one another. Through this contrast of live scenes and filmed scenes, *Letter* foregrounds the artifice of *both* mediation and liveness.

By integrating film and liveness into the narrative, *Letter* probes the ability of the live stage to represent via immediacy and copresence as much as it tests film's ability to represent reality through photorealism and aural realism. *Letter* makes no pretense of film serving as a medium that effaces the act of mediation. Kinogusa is most famous now for his film *A Page of Madness*, a film notable for its inscrutable expressionism. While Aaron Gerow makes the convincing argument that *Madness* was read in a more fluent way by its contemporary audiences, it is also unquestionably true that the film does not represent time and space in a naturalistic way. Gerow points out that critic Iwasaki Akira praises the film exactly because it embraces the rhetorical possibilities specific to cinema.[13] Kinogusa took this expressionistic approach to filmmaking, an approach that values cinema for the possibilities inherent in the medium rather than for its supposed ability to supersede its own mediation, into his approach toward the new genre of the *kinodrama*. Writing about *Laughing Letter*, Kinogusa argued that the use of film in a stage production was not simply a way to expand the possibilities of the stage. Such a view, he argued, would assume a position for theater below film as an art form. As the show's film director, Kinogusa saw the juxtaposition of live theater and film as not based in an assumed superior capacity of film to represent reality. Rather, his interest in the use of both modes was based on the representative potentialities of the liveness (直接表現) of the theatrical experience as well as the mediated nature (間接的な影) of film.[14]

Letter questions the limits of representation on several levels of the production. As a translation that exhibits only a passing resemblance to its source text, *Letter* at its most fundamental level defies expectations that a translated text will transparently represent its source. Within the confines of the performance, *Letter* probes the failure of mediation in the interplay of stage and screen, and within the narrative in repeated examples of the essential functions of communication technologies breaking down.

Technological Failure

Within the performance itself, *Laughing Letter* repeatedly highlights the failure of media to represent the message they purport to convey. Throughout the production, messages in both old and new technologies fail at critical junctures in their fundamental function of communication. The eponymous letter sets the entire plot in motion when a man forgets to post it and mistakenly leaves it in a tuxedo. The play begins when that letter winds up in a pharmacy in Ginza. Before the proprietor can return the letter, he spills ink on the address, making it unreadable and forcing him to open the letter to try to determine the identity of the sender. It turns out to be a breakup letter written by a man telling his ex-lover that she should not be so worked up about the demise of their relationship. Reading this letter sets off a string of events that ends with the pharmacist's arrest, the loss of his store, and the death of his daughter. Until the bitter end, the belief that finding the intended recipient of this letter will save her life drives him and his daughter Nami toward a fixation on correcting the failure of this letter to perform its primary function.

It turns out that the sender of the letter, a man named Noma, is a prominent figure in the Japanese music industry—and a flagrant womanizer—

who quickly forgets both the woman and the letter. He is focused on a new project with a company called Sunrise Records, where he has discovered a beautiful young new singer whom he believes he can turn into a star. The minor hurdle in this project is that she cannot sing. Her name is Hatoko, and she is the daughter of the president of Sunrise Records, and also a famous, glamourous competitive glider pilot who was involved in a dramatic crash that made news all across the country. Thus, she has the looks and personal story to become a star. To get over the minor problem of her terrible voice, Noma hires a beggar street singer to record the vocals for the song he is passing off as Hatoko's hit, called "Somewhere Somebody Is Laughing." When, after much travail, the intended recipient of Noma's letter is located by Nami and her father, it turns out that Noma has forgotten the letter entirely and the addressee has long ago overcome the distress that prompted the letter in the first place. In short, the letter that unites the three disparate threads of this narrative has failed in its role as a technology for conveying a message across time and space.

Newer, more dazzling communication technology fails in the story as well. This is particularly evident in Noma's attempt to call in a press release of his new story to the society section of the paper. He begins his conversation with:

> NOMA: [*talking into the phone*] Society section. Right. I'll tell them the reason for my call myself when you put me through. [*says this in a tentative voice and then with greater confidence when the phone answers*] Society Section? I am Yamada from the Glider Association. G—LI—DER. The thing that flies in the sky; a flying glider. I have a news story that I want to let you know about. The widely praised lone woman of flying, Kariyama Hatoko who was in the Spring Glider Competition . . . what? The "kari" in "Kariyama" is the "kari" in "hunter." The character "to protect" with the animal radical, "yama" is "yama," and the "hato" in Hatoko is the "hato" like a dove, coo-coo . . .
>
> HATOKO: What do you think? I was great, wasn't I? [*Pulls Kaneko*]
>
> NOMA: Have you forgotten? She was the woman in that famous crash. Yes, yes. Well, [Hatoko] is doing something different now. No, not airplanes. Records. Records. No, she didn't set a record, a record for a record player. The ones for music. . . . The crash did something to her vocal cords. Huh? Vocal cords, you know, in your throat, the things that make sound vibrate. [*getting irritated*] Hey, can you put someone on the line who

can understand? Hello, hello? That moron hung up on me!!! [*hangs up*]¹⁵

This tool, the telephone, which ostensibly facilitates communication in stunning new ways, instead obfuscates the message through mediation. In this short conversation, Noma impersonates someone he is not; he is unable to even share a common vocabulary of gliders and records, and he cannot communicate the characters of Hatoko's name (which incidentally would be easy to do on his hand if he were there unmediated and in person). Thus, *Letter* features recurring examples of failure of mediation: an undelivered letter, a fraudulently represented singer on the radio and phonograph, and a telephone that impedes rather than aids communication.

Modality Failure

The performative modality also highlighted a concern with a loss of the original. Prominent avant-garde thespian and artist Murayama Tomoyoshi, in writing about his viewing of *Letter*, downplayed the difference in naturalistic representation between film and stage, particularly as it appeared in *rensageki*. While film offered some modes of expression that stage did not, he saw these advantages as being grounded in the way it overtly mediates: the use of double exposure, controlling the movement of time, and transitions such as fade-outs and fade-ins. Like Kinogusa, Murayama saw the stage as offering something that film inherently cannot: liveness, spontaneous interaction with the audience (舞台の上と観客席との生理的交渉), immediacy, the irreproducible nature of live theater. Moreover, unlike many critics who were wowed by the quickly developing technologies that made film an increasingly impressive spectacle, Murayama focused on what film could still not do, such as representing color. He went out of his way to praise the *Laughing Letter* production because its costume design employed muted earth tones that helped to mask the fact that film would not have been able to reproduce a colorful design palate of the characters on stage. Further, as impressive as the use of recorded sound with film was, it used technology with a low fidelity that Murayama found it difficult to hear. These new film techniques may have been *more* naturalistic than what had come before, but Murayama did not see film as being remotely close to live theater in terms of qualities we typically think of as realistic. Rather, he saw film and theater as complementing each other.¹⁶

These features of the performance, which called into question the limits of the expressive ability of mediation, or—to put it more judgmentally—as the failure of mediation to convey reality, sparked critical conversations about the limits of performative naturalism itself. Critics tended to agree with Murayama that theater offered a liveness and unmediated reality that film could not replicate. Yet the striking thing about these arguments is that critics saw the new talkie/theater hybrid as highlighting the fact that unmediated reality could still not be real *enough*. Even with seeming immediate access to the senses, an expressive value that should (or at least could) be filled through mediation was still lacking. Kinogusa noted that by juxtaposing actors projected on screen with their live bodies, theater had new possibilities for expressing rising emotion and psychological states than it had with the live body alone. Extended monologues, he argued, can be represented as true dialogs with oneself if they are expressed in tandem with one's filmed image on a screen.[17] This scenario plays out to striking effect in *Letter* during a key moment in the production when Nami (played by Yamamoto Yasue [1902–1993]), suffering from the shame of being a hunchback and saddled with the burden of finding the intended recipient of Noma's letter, appears on screen and on stage at the same time.

On stage, as if in a trance Nami walks to the medicine box stage left. At that moment, Nami also appears on screen, holding the letter and watching Nami on Stage. On stage, Nami reaches the medicine box.

NAMI ON SCREEN: You are going to kill yourself?

On stage, Nami opens the medicine box.

NAMI ON SCREEN: It's because your happiness has become intertwined with the happiness of the girl in the letter.

Nami on Stage puts the poison to her lips.

NAMI ON SCREEN: I can see it now in the papers. "Ugly Girl with a Beautiful Heart Dies Clutching Letter."

In one swallow, Nami on Stage downs the poison.

NAMI ON SCREEN: And what about the beautiful girl in the letter?
NAMI ON STAGE: [*calling out*] She will clap and laugh at me!
NAMI ON SCREEN: Come now, Nami-chan.

NAMI ON STAGE: And that man's little mustache will twist into a sneer! Everyone in the world—you can all laugh!
NAMI ON SCREEN: What are you talking about, Nami-chan?
NAMI ON STAGE: You can all laugh at the ugly girl with the hunchback who sunk the family business. The hunchbacked girl who turned her father over to the police! The girl who destroyed her life because of a dirty, smudged letter!

Nami on Screen holds the letter as if it were a precious object and retreats.

NAMI ON STAGE: Hand me . . . give me the letter.

Reaching out towards the screen, she takes the letter from the stand. Nami on Screen backs away, watching nervously.

NAMI ON STAGE: It's all because of this letter . . . this letter . . .

Clutching the letter, she collapses to the floor, despondent. Nami on Screen's face approaches nervously.

NAMI ON STAGE: [*painfully getting up*] But I won't die for this letter! I will rip it up. Rip it up . . .
NAMI ON SCREEN: Nami-chan!
NAMI ON STAGE: [*As she reaches her right hand toward the letter, her arm stiffens . . .*] Curse it. Is this really something to die for? I'll rip it up and scatter the pieces across the room. Across the world. Curse it! Curse it!
NAMI ON SCREEN: Nami-chan! Nami-chan!

Unable to muster the strength to tear the letter, Nami on Stage falls down dead. As Nami on Stage gasps her last breath, Nami on Screen disappears. The words from the letter scatter, rising over the stage. Like water droplets, they float across the screen—music plays—the drops of water are drawn towards the window and disappear as the music fades.[18]

As spectacle, the performance makes flashy use of its technology: a talking image in communication with the original of which it is a copy makes for mesmerizing theater. It is a far more complicated use of film technology than that of earlier *rensageki* in which film and stage simply alternated live and filmed scenes to tell a single story. Placing live and filmed scenes on stage simultaneously implicitly raises doubts about the promises of mediation and reproduction. It is unclear, for example, which Nami has the agency to act, especially when they seem to be at odds.

They seem to die at the same time, but the initiative to act seems to shift between the two before that point. The filmed Nami even has to ask for an explanation of Nami's intentions, as if she does not have access to her own inner thoughts. This dynamic of playing multiple Namis off of each other, especially off of the ostensibly "original" body of the Nami on stage, is qualitatively different from seeing an actor in a typical film. We can think of a normal film recording as the actor's work in the same way that another artist might present a sculpture or a musical composition to an audience. The difference here is that we have an assumption of some degree of "continuous personhood" (to use Michael Lambek's term) across the live/mediated rupture.[19] Yet that continuity no longer holds when both the real and the copy coexist simultaneously and interact with each other. Thus, *Letter* plays out Baudrillard's notion of a simulation in a very deliberate way. That is, the referent is no longer in a hierarchical position over the sign. To the extent that the simulation itself, highlighted by having both live and copy on stage together, is in actuality the real subject of this scene, we can say that the simulation becomes its own sign in the circular process of erasure of the original.

Thus, despite the technological flair of the production, the directors Senda and Kinogusa, and Murayama from the perspective of an audience member, see *Letter* as a comment on the limits of that technology, impressive though it may have been. As an actor, Yamamoto Yasue also found the representative power of stage and film to be at disconcerting odds with each other. Yamamoto herself spoke in her own article about her experience in *Laughing Letter* from the perspective of the one who was mediated. While she saw the skill set of stage actor and screen actor as having a great deal of crossover, she nonetheless hesitated to even attempt to act for the camera. *Laughing Letter* was her first experience of film acting, and she described the process as a curious loss of agency. She speaks, not of having the camera capture her acting, but of having to match her acting to the medium of the camera. Because the film would be shown on stage in dialog with her own live performance, when she prerecorded her filmed role she had to be cognizant of looking in the direction where her future self would be in relation to the screen. Without carefully modulating her voice, movement, and other aspects of her performance for the camera, her stage and film performance would not match—it would risk "poking out" from behind the filmed performance (演技がはみ出したり).[20] In addition to being restricted by the location of her own future self, she also noted that since most of her filmed scenes were closeups, her movement was constrained in the present by the camera as well. She then noted that when she got on stage, her acting for the live audience was determined by her filmed performance from some time in the past, which was in turn constrained by the demands of the camera in that past and by her own movements in the future. When the live and filmed Nami enter into dialog on screen, then, the source text in this translation from body to screen and back becomes unclear. It recalls Theseus' pair of ships, one maintained from its original state and one rebuilt from original parts. The original/reproduction relationship breaks down.

The question of the degree of continuity that exists between a source and its reproduction is central to the statement that *Laughing Letter* is making. A letter fails to arrive at its destination, and ultimately does not truly mean what it purports to communicate; a telephone interferes with conversation rather than facilitating communication; and the singer of a hit song on the radio is not the glamorous personality she is presented as being. Most significantly, a woman has a dialogue with her mediated self in real time on stage. The sense that a reproduced self is uncomfortably connected to, yet not actually, oneself is familiar to anyone who has spent extended time staring at oneself on video chats, and it was particularly unnerving at the beginning of film history in Japan. Eric Cazdyn recounts the anecdote about the filming of the oldest extant Japanese film, a recording of a stage production of *Momijigari* starring Ichikawa Danjūrō (1838–1903) and Onoe Kikugorō (1844–1903). Danjūrō is reported to have said that seeing himself was "terribly strange," and that he did not want the film screened during his lifetime.[21] Danjūrō was among the first to experience his own simulation in this brand-new medium. The likeness was at once a striking visual representation of his performance but also disconcertingly unlike his performance. It is strange in the same way that Nami's filmed role is strange, because despite its photorealism, it is ultimately only a flattened version of the overdetermined live performance. Even if, as was the case here, the sign is a deceptively convincing representation of the referent, it still lacks the depth of the referent. *Letter* is then a very early engagement with the imbrication of film/video and live performance that has accelerated exponentially in recent decades, and even more quickly in recent years.[22] *Letter* confronts the crisis of media's erasure of the original, a tendency that Baudrillard saw in these early days of new media as the beginning of a progression of representation within the context of an increasingly mediatized world.

Notes

1. Jean Baudrillard, *Simulations* (New York: Semiotext[e], 1983), 10–11.
2. Baudrillard, *Simulations*, 11.
3. Osanai Kaoru 小山内薫, "The Plan for the Jiyū Theater" (自由劇の計画 "Jiyūgeki no keikaku"), in *Osanai Kaoru engekiron zenshū* 小山内薫演劇論全集 (Tokyo: Miraisha, 1964), 102.
4. Ayako Kano, *Acting Like a Woman in Modern Japan: Theater, Gender, and Nationalism* (New York: Palgrave, 2001), 66–70.
5. See chapter 7 in Indra Levy, *Sirens of the Western Shore: The Westernesque Femme Fatale, Translation, and Vernacular Style in Modern Japanese Literature* (New York: Columbia University Press, 2006).
6. Aaron Andrew Gerow, *Visions of Japanese Modernity: Articulations of Cinema, Nation, and Spectatorship, 1895–1925* (Berkeley: University of California Press, 2010), 42–44.
7. Auslander notes, "The people watching *Yes* with headphones clapped on their ears are trying to achieve a kind of aural intimacy that can be obtained only from the reproduction of sound." Philip Auslander, *Liveness: Performance in a Mediatized Culture* (London: Routledge, 1999), 35.
8. Kerim Yasar, *Electrified Voices: How the Telephone, Phonograph, and Radio Shaped Modern Japan, 1868–1945* (New York: Columbia University Press, 2018), 203–7.
9. Iwamoto Kenji 岩本憲児, *From the Silents to the Talkies: The People and Culture Who Founded Japanese Film* (サイレントからトーキーへ：日本映画形成期の人と文化 *Sairento kara tōkī he: Nihon eiga kaiseiki no hito to bunka*) (Tokyo: Shinwasha, 2007).
10. Levy, *Sirens of the Western Shore*, 214.
11. See Iwamoto, *From the Silents to the Talkies*.
12. Murayama Tomoyoshi 村山知義, "Viewing a *Kinodrama*" (キノドラマを見る "Kinodrama wo miru"), *Nihon Eiga* 日本映画 10 (October, 1937): 36.
13. Aaron Andrew Gerow, *A Page of Madness: Cinema and Modernity in 1920s Japan* (Ann Arbor: University of Michigan Press, 2008), 56.
14. Kinogusa Teinosuke 衣笠貞之助, "A Conversation about *Kinodrama*" (キノドラマを語る "Kinodrama wo kataru"), *Nihon Eiga* 日本映画 9 (September, 1937): 15.
15. Yagi Ryūichirō 八木隆一郎, *The Laughing Letter* (嗤う手紙 *Warau tegami*), *Nihon Eiga* 日本映画 9 (September, 1937): 145.
16. Murayama, "Viewing a *Kinodrama*," 36.
17. Kinogusa Teinosuke 衣笠貞之助, "What Is a *Kinodrama*?" (キノドラマとはどんなものか "Kinodorama to ha donna mono ka"), in *Shin Tsukiji Gekidan* 新築地劇団 6 (July 1937): 5.
18. Yagi, *The Laughing Letter*, 173–74.

19. Michael Lambek, "The Continuous and Discontinuous Person: Two Dimensions of Ethical Life," *Journal of the Royal Anthropological Institute* 19 (2013): 837–58.

20. Yamamoto Yasue 山本安江, "Performing in the *Kinodrama The Laughing Letter*" (キノドラマ嗤う手紙に出演して "Kinodrama *Warau tegami* ni shutsuen shite"), *Nihon Eiga* 日本映画 9 (September, 1937): 60–61.

21. Eric Cazdyn, *The Flash of Capital: Film and Geopolitics in Japan* (Durham, NC: Duke University Press, 2002), 15.

22. One poignant example of this trend even in the staid context of traditional Japanese theater can be seen in the recent kabuki production of *Yoshitsune and the Thousand Cherry Trees* run at Kabukiza in Tokyo and Minamiza in Kyoto, featuring Ebizo, the preeminent actor of the kabuki stage, and a hologram of Hatsune Miku, the digitally generated singer developed by the Sapporo-based company Crypton Future Media.

8 | Realism, the Real, and Mediated Reality

Hirata Oriza and Beyond

M. CODY POULTON

Preface

Contemporary Japanese playwright and director Hirata Oriza (b. 1962) has been instrumental in creating a new style of realism on the Japanese stage. His so-called "quiet theater" has, I contend, marked a restitution of representational techniques from the film and television screen back into the three-dimensionality of the stage. This essay will argue that technological advances such as photography and film and, today, digital online media have profoundly influenced how each generation understands and articulates realism. The COVID-19 pandemic has at the same time been a major hurdle, yet a potential opportunity, to those practicing live performance regardless of its style. In essence, technological advances change our sense of reality.

Film as the Definitive Realist Art Form

In the final pages of *A Hundred Years of Japanese Film*, Donald Richie describes what he regards as a fundamental antagonism in Japanese culture toward realism as an expressive mode:

> Despite the many exceptions, a general apathy to realism as a style is one explanation for the enormous popularity of manga and anime. Another is that the attractions of "virtual" reality are to be seen more

strongly in Japan than in most other countries, perhaps because "reality" itself is regarded in so tenuous a fashion. One of the comforts of virtual reality is that, even when it concerns itself with gunmen and monsters, it is not dangerous. Reality itself, on the other hand, is traditionally perceived as perilous. . . . Virtual reality is also enormously tractable. One can control a virtual landscape or a virtual person more easily than one can the real thing.

Japan is historically very familiar with this. It early perfected, for example, a classical garden style that is virtual in that it is entirely "programmed." The differences between the seventeenth century garden of Katsura Rikyū Imperial Villa in Kyoto and the computer game *Dragonball* are manifest, but their similarities should not be overlooked. Three of these are the taming of nature, the idealizing of the environment, and the making of everything into what it ought to be rather than what it is.

Such a will to dominate nature might then explain Japan's perhaps otherwise puzzling lack of interest in realism as a style, and its corresponding lack of respect—if that is the term—for reality itself.[1]

Richie's line of reasoning here presents a number of problems—for one, any form of artistic representation, whether we are speaking of gardening or film, is a framing and taming of reality, an act of control over it. What we hear most of all in Richie's musings is an old man's lament over the passing of the art of live-action drama and the rise of other modes of representation, some of them interactive, that flaunt their artificiality.

I am sympathetic to his nostalgia for the realism of cinema. Teaching Japanese film to my students recently, one of the first things I learned was that, although everyone was familiar with anime directors like Miyazaki Hayao or Kon Satoshi, virtually no one had seen a live-action Japanese film before, unless it happened to be *Godzilla*. New digital technologies have superseded older ones, undermining our confidence in reality itself.

It is my argument here that new media very much determine how ideas of realism (and reality) are articulated. For the twentieth century, the realist art form par excellence was cinema, as Siegfried Kracauer demonstrated so eloquently in his 1960 book, *Theory of Film: The Redemption of Physical Reality*. Drawing on philosophy, art history, and literature, Kracauer argues that the relatively new medium of cinema brought audiences in direct contact with their physical surroundings, the materiality of their daily lives, in a way like no other art form that had preceded it, and for radically different purposes:

To the extent that painting, literature, theatre, etc., involve nature at all, they do not really represent it. Rather, they use it as raw material from which to build works which lay claim to autonomy. In the world of art, nothing remains of the raw material itself, or, to be precise, all that remains of it is so molded that it implements the intentions conveyed through it. In a sense, the real-life material disappears in the artistic intentions.[2]

Referencing art historian Erwin Panovsky, Kracauer claims that all other art forms proceed from an ideal toward physical reality, from "top to bottom," as it were, whereas "the camera is materialistically minded; it proceeds from below to above.... Guided by film, then, we approach, if at all, ideas no longer as highways leading through the void but on paths that wind through the thicket of things."[3]

The earliest films were completely nonnarrative. It was enough to show to audiences recordings of their own lives, scenes of traffic in the street, or departing locomotives. Yet this is not simply an inevitable result of the invention of the camera, especially for taking moving pictures, as revolutionary as this technology was to the course of other art forms like painting and theater. Kracauer argues, in a way that at first glance seems paradoxical, that it was in fact an ideological revolution that foregrounded cinema as the representative art form of the twentieth century. Following on empirical philosophers such as John Dewey and Alfred North Whitehead, he asserts that cinematic realism demonstrated a decline of faith in ideology; this includes not only religion, but totalizing political philosophies such as Marxism and fascism, too. "The remedy for abstractness . . . is the experience of things in their concreteness," he writes.[4] Realism, Kracauer claims, stems from a fundamental disenchantment with ideas and ideologies. When ideology fails us, we are redeemed by a direct plunge into the "thicket of things."

Hirata Oriza, Film, and Realist Theater in Japan

In the standard history of realism on the modern Japanese stage, social, political, technological, and cultural factors have determined how realism has been understood and manifested theatrically since at least the efforts made by Tsubouchi Shōyō (1859–1935) and others to reform kabuki in the 1880s. I have discussed this issue elsewhere,[5] but here I address more recent trends in realist theater in Japan. Since the mid-1990s Japanese theater has been marked by a "return of the real" ushered in by theater artists like Hirata that is quite different from what Hirata himself describes as the ideologically inflected realism of *shingeki*, Japan's modern drama, which since the 1920s was motivated largely by a leftist worldview.

Reality returned with a vengeance to Japan in the late twentieth century with such sobering events as Chernobyl (1986), the fall of the Soviet Union (1991), the bursting of the economic bubble in Japan (a fall of one kind of capitalism) at around the same time, and in 1995, the Hanshin Earthquake and the Sarin gas attack on Tokyo subways by the cult Aum Shinrikyō. This trend also brought about fundamental changes in theatrical expression, akin in some respects to the "theatre of the real" discussed by Carol Martin.[6] In fact, it is from the 1990s that the term *riaru*, a transliteration of "real," comes to supersede other terms in the Japanese language such as *genjitsusei* or *shajitsusei*, or even *riarizumu* (*shingeki*'s version of realism). *Riaru* describes the quality of realism, not only of an artistic product, but of anything that approaches the real thing in its appearance or effect on a person. It is semantically closer to "reality" than to "realism." This renewed sense of the real arose not only because contemporary events shook the complacency of the Japanese, but because the public was bombarded with new media, even more sophisticated technologies of mimicking and even undermining one's sense of physical reality. Currently, the word *riaru* is also being used to distinguish live theater from remote, online recordings.

Hirata's style of realism was very much inspired by what Kracauer maintained, since for Hirata realism was the redemption of physical reality after the failure of ideology. As Kracauer demonstrated, cinema was the twentieth century's quintessential realist art form. In a similar manner, the *riaru* of Hirata and his contemporaries has taken its cue, not from earlier theatrical or artistic models, but largely from cinema and television. (By the same token, many contemporary playwrights make their living writing TV drama.) Miles Orvell argues in *The Real Thing* (1989) that innovation in the nineteenth and twentieth centuries, especially in the technologies of sight and sound reproduction, arose in "an effort to get beyond mere imitation, beyond the manufacturing of illusions, to the creation of more 'authentic' works that were themselves real things."[7] It was not the painting but the photograph—especially the *katsudō shashin* (moving photographs, an early term for film)—that was the prototype for realism. Walter Benjamin's "work of art in the age of mechanical reproduction" is, like the photograph, a "copy of truth" (a literal translation of *shashin*), something that can infinitely duplicate reality. In the performance arts, a copy of the real is paradoxically cited to maintain a work's authenticity. What is striking about Hirata's best theater is that it is capable of manifesting the aura of an original work of art through his attention to reproducing onstage the realia of banal, everyday reality.

While Aristotle's theory of mimesis is the *locus classicus* for many, if not most, models of realism in theater and its sister arts, it is not the only one, nor does it readily account for cinematic realism. In *Mimesis and Alterity: A Particular History of the Senses*, Michael Taussig describes another kind of realism, unrelated to Aristotle's theory of mimesis but more common to shamanistic cultures, one in which copying is achieved through contact or identification with the thing, person, or event that one wishes to represent or emulate.[8] Certainly, many versions of realism in traditional Japanese theater can be traced to shamanistic rituals, but this is not restricted to either traditional or Japanese theater. More recently, works like the Wooster Group's *The B-Side*, to name just one, which uses audio recordings of songs sung by African American prison inmates, achieves an eerie aura of the real through an almost shamanistic citation of the original songs, with the actors onstage seeming to channel the voices of the original singers. Hirata's work similarly achieves comparable effects through an eminently rational, rather than mystical, methodology of copying reality. I see Hirata's aura of the real as having to do especially with the unique temporality of his performances, as I will explain later. Suffice it to say here that it is a temporality that is more cinematic than theatrical.

Hirata's signature and most enduring work, the one for which he won the Kishida Kunio Award for Japan's best drama of 1994, was *Tokyo Notes*, a manifesto of his new realism.[9] Set always in the near future whenever it is produced, the play presents a family reunion in the lobby of a suburban art museum in Tokyo, where almost the entire extant collection of paintings by the Dutch master Jan Vermeer is being exhibited, having been evacuated from a war-torn Europe. Vermeer was a realist painter par excellence, and much is made in the play about the act of observation and the technologies, particularly the invention of the lens, applied to sight and representation among the artists and philosophers of early modern Holland. (Vermeer most likely used a camera lucida, a draftsman's device that used a lens to project an image of a scene onto a two-dimensional surface so it could be traced.)

Tokyo Notes was also clearly an homage to what is arguably one of the greatest films in the history of cinema, *Tokyo Story* (*Tokyo monogatari*,

1953), and surely one of the greatest films of its director Ozu Yasujirō (1903–1963). The film is about an elderly couple who travel from a small town to the capital to stay with their children. The film is an understated but devastating anatomy of the decline of the family system in Japan, and an excoriating portrait of the indifference of children to their elderly parents. Hirata has said that he tried to imagine how such a story would play out in his own generation. In his drama it is a daughter looking after her aged parents who comes to the big city, only to discover that her siblings and their partners are indifferent to one another. It is a family slowly disintegrating into its individual parts, solipsistic shells.

Like that of Ozu, who disliked plot because it used characters, and to use characters was to misuse them,[10] Hirata's dramaturgy is antidramatic. "Most life has nothing to do with what theater in the past has liked to portray, but is grounded instead in quiet and uneventful moments," Hirata wrote in an early manifesto of his style.[11] His early theoretical writings stress that art's true mission should be to capture things "as they are" (*ari no mama*), without editorial statements on what it all means. Hirata learned much about dramaturgy from the way Ozu made his films. The avoidance of plot for its own sake, the tendency to linger on moments of silence, gaps in conversation, pauses in action, a focus on subtle, apparently minor details, and an aversion to melodrama or exposition—these are all features of both Ozu's and Hirata's styles.

The playwright has written that, under the influence of Western drama, modern Japanese drama was driven by the character's struggle with his or her social circumstances. Like his aversion to plot, another revolutionary aspect of Hirata's dramaturgy was his focus not on subjectivity or character, but on setting as the chief determinant of what a character does. Influenced by psychologist J. J. Gibson's theory of affordances, Hirata's dramaturgy typically began with a search not for a theme, or a hero or heroine, but a space, an environment that could let something happen, a situation if you will. For *Tokyo Notes*, it was the lobby of an art gallery, a place where family, friends, coworkers, and strangers could intermingle. The playwright's mother is a clinical psychologist and was undoubtedly as important an influence on his thinking as his father, who wrote scenarios for film and television, but it is significant that it is not personal psychology so much as social dynamics that drive the plots, such as they are, for many of his plays.

Hirata's use of language is undoubtedly the most revolutionary aspect of his dramaturgy. It is so inimitably "Japanese" (or at least, in its standard, Tokyo variety) that my colleagues and I have used *Tokyo Notes* as textbook material to teach the language.[12] In this respect we can start to agree with Hirata's assertion that his stage dialogue represents the consummation of the Meiji project to bring the spoken and written languages together in a way that *shingeki* dialogue may never have been able to do.[13] Hirata himself calls his style "contemporary colloquial theater" (*gendai kōgo engeki*).[14] It is, all said, startlingly natural. Yet on the surface, his dialogue often seems banal, a succession of empty *aisatsu*, or greetings, small talk. This is a style perfected by novelists such as Satomi Ton, on whose work Ozu and his scenario writer Noda Kōgo based *Equinox Flower* (*Higan-bana*, 1958) and the last film they made together, *Late Autumn* (1960). Satomi was a writer whose stories seemed to amble genially from "hello" to "goodbye." Ordinary greetings such as "the weather's nice today" are ridiculed as empty rhetoric by the ingenuous boys in Ozu's *Good Morning* (*Ohayō*, 1959), but the film makes it clear that much of human—that is, especially Japanese—discourse is predicated on such empty, conventional phrases. It is the space around such language that writers and directors like Hirata and Ozu settle into and explore: it's all in the nuance, the pause, the ellipse, the context.

Hirata has said that Japanese is a "high context" language, reflective of a close-knit homogeneous society that requires little explanation for things. Japanese has conversation (*kaiwa*), but dialogue (*taiwa*) is virtually unknown, he writes. The playwright has described conversation as pleasant speech among people who all know one another well. Dialogue, on the other hand, exists to convey information among people unfamiliar to one another, and this form of discourse is hardly known to the Japanese. "Reading the air" (*kūki o yomu*)—trying to discern another's implicit message or intent—is a major preoccupation for the Japanese. This helps to explain the almost Pinteresque importance of the pause, of what is left unsaid, in a Hirata play. Much of Hirata's extra-theatrical career, on which much of his public profile has been staked, has been devoted to teaching a wide range of Japanese—from students to doctors and even politicians—to improve their communication skills, especially with others outside their small and circumscribed social networks.

Hirata's directorial method also resembles Ozu's in his indifference to psychological motivation. It is the antithesis of the so-called Method devised by American disciples of Konstantin Stanislavski such as Lee Strasberg, Stella Adler, and Elia Kazan. As in much traditional theater, truth here is attained through a devotion to form—*kata*—by learning how to inhabit the character from the outside in. Hirata drills his actors over and over again to repeat certain actions, certain speeches, now slower, now faster, until they attain the right rhythm. Gesture, speech, and action are the indicators of character. If there is a psychological method to Hirata's theater, it would be behaviorist. The playwright has written unapologetically that he moves his actors around the stage like chess pieces to achieve his particular effect.

Since 2008 Hirata has collaborated on a number of projects at Osaka University, where he is on the faculty in the School of Communication Design, with the roboticist Ishiguro Hiroshi, famous for his geminoids—copies of real people, like himself, his daughter, the trans TV personality Matsuko Deluxe, and even the early-twentieth-century novelist Natsume Sōseki. Their first collaboration was on a short twenty-minute play called *I, Worker* (*Hataraku watakushi*) featuring two human actors playing husband and wife and their two servants, played by Wakamaru robots built by Mitsubishi Heavy Industries. (Other robots have since been employed.) One notable challenge of writing plays with robots and androids has been a matter of programming them to recite their lines in time to the human actors, since improvisation and extemporizing are still next to impossible for these machines. Yet in the process, both playwright and engineer made an interesting discovery: directing was not so different from programming. (Indeed, Hirata has become quite proficient at programming his mechanical actors.) Reflecting on their collaboration on *I, Worker*, Hirata wrote: "Most human communication is not empathic but rather based on learned patterns of response to stimuli. My actors were shocked to learn this, but what makes it so congenial to work with Ishiguro is that I used precisely the same vocabulary with Ishiguro's robots as I do to direct my actors."[15] Speaking of this play and a number of other subsequent collaborations with Ishiguro, the most celebrated being *Sayonara*, his 2010–2012 two-hander with American actor Bryerly Long and Ishiguro's Geminoid F, Hirata has remarked that an important aim of their research was not so much to amaze people with what robots and androids could do—the "wow factor" that seems to be so much the point of engineers' demonstrations of their pet projects—but to move his audiences in a way that only works of art can do. He has claimed that his robots and androids have moved people without resorting to Stanislavskian methods. No interiority whatsoever is required for emotional effect. We don't need empathic agents to move us; acting need not be emotional by nature to elicit emotions. Our very human tendency to personify our devices is enough to achieve this. Long herself has said that, to imbue a sense of greater liveness to the android she was interacting with, she had to dial down her own movements and emotions.

The "real" of Hirata's dramaturgy and directorial method derives from attention to the unfolding of *real time*—through nuance, pace, voice, volume, timbre, and action—that is precisely calculated. As the audience assembles, some actors are already onstage, speaking quietly to one another, as if the play has already begun. There are typically no scene changes, but an almost classical evocation of the Three Unities of time, place, and action. The plot, such as it is, unfolds in a series of meandering encounters and desultory conversations about ordinary things. As in an Ozu film, the denouement is subtle, stealthy, undramatic, but powerful.

Hirata's direction of his works is exacting. The running time of his plays varies by less than a minute from one performance to the next, so carefully calibrated is the timing of the dialogue, including the many pauses that are as much a hallmark of his style as of Pinter's. So precise is Hirata's style of directing that critic Nakanishi Osamu has called it "digital."[16] Like so much contemporary media-inflected realism, Hirata's work possesses the structured, split-second duration of cinema, and now, due to his work with robots and androids, performance times are even measured in milliseconds.

Signs of the Future

In a late interview, David Bowie remarked that "it seems impossible to talk about reality today without putting the word 'virtual' before it or 'TV' after it."[17] What is the nature of reality in a digital world? And how do digital media affect theories and practices of mimesis? Can we talk about representation in a world where, à la Baudrillard, original forms seem to have vanished, leaving only simulacra, copies of other copies?

Theater is leaving the analogue behind even without what Peter Eckersall and others have called the "new media dramaturgy" of groundbreaking performance groups such as dumb type.[18] I would like to outline what might be the future of a Hirataesque digital dramaturgy. It is already happening in Japan in a variety of genres, platforms, and formats, from video gaming to the immersive projection mapping of productions by the pop group Perfume or the digital art collective Team Lab. The performances of so-called "2.5 dimensional" culture and Vocaloid artists also exhibit this trend. In many of these cases, the quest for simulation has resulted in the creation of "real presences" on stage that are neither real nor human but are appreciated by adoring audiences all the more for their artificiality. In contrast, the 2.5

dimensional performances that have become immensely popular, like the musical *Tenisu no ōjisama* (*Prince of Tennis*) or the stage version of the popular anime *King of Prism by Pretty Rhythm*, flatten their human performers to the superficiality of manga and anime characters. This "flat dramaturgy" is one feature it shares with Hirata's studiously understated, now somewhat manneristic style.[19]

More box office has been drawn by 2.5 dimensional productions than any other kind of theater in recent times. At the same time, the hugely popular "ultra-kabuki" (*chō-kabuki*) show *Hanakurabe Senbonzakura*, starring Nakamura Shidō and Vocaloid idol Hatsune Miku, was attended in April 2016 by up to 13,000 spectators in the Makuhari Messe in Chiba, with thousands more attending the show remotely on their screens at home and feverishly registering their approval in real time on Nikoniko Dōga, which was simultaneously projected on a screen beside the main stage as the show went on. Since even before the COVID-19 pandemic, productions like this discovered the potential for live streaming to accommodate audiences of a capacity unthinkable in the limited physical world of three-dimensional, live performance. For a variety of reasons, not least economic but also epidemiological, conventional stage performance is being superseded by a plethora of online, digital forms, more remote than "real."

The pandemic has made it very difficult to produce, perform, or see live theater; most of us have had to content ourselves, or at least try to, by watching it online. In 2021, three festivals of the performing arts were held in Japan: Kyoto Experiment, and in the Tokyo area, Theatre Commons and Tokyo Performing Arts Meeting (TPAM).[20] Much of the content is available online, but not all. At Theatre Commons in February 2021, I attended a virtual reality film directed by the Taiwanese director Tsai Ming-Liang, *The Deserted*; an earlier 4K version premiered at the Venice Biennale in 2017. It was also one of the very few non-Japanese productions available at a festival known for introducing international work to Japanese audiences. A small group of people were seated, masked and subject to the usual precautions taken for social distancing required at the time, in a room in an art gallery in Roppongi. The experience was, as might be expected from VR, immersive, but each spectator engaged with it separately and uniquely, depending on how they viewed the film, because the mere act of turning one's head would make a new scene emerge. Under the goggles, I suddenly found myself in a room with walls that seemed to grow out of bare rock; there was a kitchen and living area and a small balcony looking out on dense green tropical vegetation; the air was loud with the sounds of insects and birds. An older woman was preparing some food while a man sat slumped on a sofa, using an electrical massager to activate his back and shoulder muscles. He was evidently very ill.

And where was the spectator seeing this? Somewhere suspended in the air in the corner. I could view all around me, but not see myself. I was a disembodied ghost—where my feet and hands should have been there was nothing, only the ground underneath. Images in the foreground were distorted, as if a deep hole had opened beneath me, as if my presence had created a bubble in space-time, bending floor, walls, ceiling, and sometimes even bodies into circles where straight lines should be. Had I risen from my chair I'd have fallen flat on my face. Only by being rooted in my seat could I avoid vertigo.

The film lasted for about an hour and unfolded in a series of scenes devoid of dialogue or much action. Tsai's work is reminiscent of Ozu's and Hirata's slow, anti-narrative dramaturgy. Occasionally the scene shifted to a jungly garden, or to the road outside the abandoned apartment building we had just been inside, or into other rooms. Besides the sick man and the older woman, who may have been his mother, there were two other women, about the same age as the man. Everyone seemed trapped in their own interior worlds; one of the women was even shown trapped in a room without doors or windows. Something like a climax came when the other young woman was shown embracing the sick man in a large bathtub. Were they having sex, or was she drowning him as an act of mercy? No, the embrace seemed to aid in his recuperation. We too felt the longing for physical contact, because we the spectators had become disembodied voyeurs. Later, the couple lie on a dirty mattress, sharing laughs. In the final scene the man appeared in the kitchen preparing dumplings, then sitting down to eat them, the first solid food he had taken. The film replicated in many ways the kind of experience many of us have gone through during the pandemic, one of sickness and isolation, with an eventual promise of recovery and togetherness.

The essence of the VR experience accentuates the ghostliness of what one experiences under the goggles and earphones. One is engulfed in what one sees and hears, but one is physically absent and the people in the film are entirely unaware of your presence. Are they ghosts and only you are real? Or is the opposite the case? Or is everyone a ghost? Yet one feels the sick man's infirmity, his pain, even his fleeting pleasure. Tsai Ming-Liang's film was both disembodied and visceral, which is what made the experience so paradoxical and mysterious, so dreamlike. The absence of any dialogue between the characters only accentuated this feeling.

Marshall McLuhan identified a tendency in Western culture, born of Cartesian dualism, to aspire to a transcendence of the corporeal, to become pure spirit; this he called *angelism*. This tendency is no longer, or not necessarily, a syndrome unique to offspring of the European philosophical tradition. As Karl Marx wrote of modernity, "all that is solid melts into air." Our technological devices today have more than ever made this feeling a reality. The digital world has enabled us to maintain connections online, but can we leave our bodies behind, or do we become trapped inside our flesh as we sit glued to our screens? Technology and the pandemic have turned us all into *hikikomori*, shut-ins fearful of the real world, its viruses, germs, and strangers.

As a student of live performance in Japan, I am concerned about the future of this art form in a world where bodies are latched to screens and prevented from gathering in public spaces. Still, for quite some time already the performing arts have been waging what seems forever like a losing war with other media (photography, film, radio, television, video, and now a plethora of digital modalities). With the introduction of every new technology, theater, music, dance, and other forms of live performance have had to adapt, redefine themselves, rediscover what is unique about their art and the resources that only they can exploit. That said, it seems to me that the essence of live performance is *immediacy*—corporeal existence in the here and now, with an engagement of all senses and not only sight and sound. The sensorium of live performance is something impossible in a world on screen.

Nevertheless, we need to remind ourselves that all art, all representation, is mediated. Baudrillard has summed up the paradox of representation (and thus also, *pace* Diderot, the paradox of the actor) in a neat maxim: "To dissimulate is to pretend not to have what you have; to simulate is to pretend to have what you do not have."[21] The more we attempt to represent some version of reality, the more we have recourse to artifice.

In crises like the pandemic, our sense of reality, as well as our notions of truth, are nevertheless being tested. Playwright Okada Toshiki (b. 1973), a member of the current generation of theater artists whose vernacular style has been profoundly affected by Hirata's work, recently noted that, due to the COVID pandemic, our current reality seems stranger than fiction:

I think, always, reality and fiction are juxtaposed. Of course, now things are much clearer as to how reality seems to be stranger than fiction. The virus is invisible. So if we are afraid of the virus, it means that we have some fictional imagination. Otherwise, you can't see any virus around you. We have to manage the balance between reality and fiction. In other words, we have to have some imagination and we have to care how and what is taking our imagination. We have to care, we have to manage our way of using our imagination in a different way than in fear. Otherwise, my imagination is taken only by fear. We need to find alternative ways of engaging our own imaginations. I believe fiction is a very strong option. . . . For me, fiction can be an alternative reality, or fiction can be something that enables tension within reality. Fiction can work in a way that can illuminate reality.[22]

Okada's quest for the truth underscores the importance of the imagination and the power of fiction. Fiction and reality are therefore not antithetical; the former informs our understanding of the latter.

In another recent essay, Okada elaborates on what the pandemic may be doing to change how we do theater in the future. In an article he has given the tongue-in-cheek title "Sounding like a Typical Post-Corona Theory of Theatre," Okada focuses on how COVID has impacted two important features of live performance: locality (*basho*) and mobility (*idō*).[23] The pandemic has stolen the place where one can perform, usually the theater building itself, as well as the artist's ability to stage works and encounter other artists and audiences in different places. For the past couple of years, the online environment has become the new locality, a place that is everywhere and nowhere, and our mobility as artists or audiences remains only in the realm of the imagination. In investigating his own artistic process since the pandemic, Okada has discovered that in fact he has been grappling with problems he first encountered after the Great East Japan Earthquake and Tsunami a decade ago, an event that fundamentally changed his theatrical style.

In short, what he realized then, and is reminded of now, is that humanity is attempting to understand and deal with events that are way beyond the scale of human understanding, events humans cannot control or even adequately represent. Faced with a succession of environmental crises, we are like the proverbial blind man trying to identify an elephant. In his recent performance and installation collaborations with the visual artist Kaneuji Teppei, Okada has been exploring a space in which the human is decentered, even overwhelmed, by the physical scale and reality of the natural and artificial worlds, with productions that reference the massive earthworks carried out in Rikuzentakata after the tsunami, or the plethora of appliances that we accumulate. Aristotle called mimesis at root an exclusively human activity, but in works like Okada's *Eraser* series, we encounter an artistic landscape of realia that is both posthuman and postdramatic.[24] It seems like no coincidence, then, that Okada's *Eraser Mountain* was one of the last shows to be staged at the Skirball Center at NYU before the pandemic shut down the city's theater in March, 2020. Even as digital devices tend to disembody us, varieties of performance now that luxuriate in physical reality, such as Okada's, present a world that is very much becoming "a world without us."

Notes

1. Donald Richie, *A Hundred Years of Japanese Film* (Tokyo: Kodansha International, 2001), 252–53.
2. Siegfried Kracauer, *Theory of Film: The Redemption of Physical Reality* (Oxford, UK: Oxford University Press, 1960), 300.
3. Kracauer, *Theory of Film*, 309.
4. Kracauer, *Theory of Film*, 296.
5. See M. Cody Poulton, "The Rhetoric of the Real," in *Modern Japanese Theatre and Performance*, ed. David Jortner, Keiko McDonald, and Kevin Wetmore (Lanham, MD: Lexington Books, 2006), 17–31; M. Cody Poulton, *A Beggar's Art: Scripting Modernity in Japanese Drama, 1900–1930* (Honolulu: University of Hawaii Press, 2010).
6. Carol Martin, *Theatre of the Real* (London: Palgrave McMillan, 2013).
7. As quoted in Martin, *Theatre of the Real*, xv.
8. Michael Taussig, *Mimesis and Alterity: A Particular History of the Senses* (New York: Routledge, 1993).
9. See Hirata Oriza and M. Cody Poulton, "*Tokyo Notes* by Hirata Oriza," *Asian Theatre Journal* 19, no. 1 (Spring 2002): 1–120; Hirata Oriza and M. Cody Poulton, *Citizens of Tokyo: Six Plays* (New York: Seagull Books, 2019); M. Cody Poulton, "World History and Modern Japanese Drama: The Case of Hirata Oriza's Plays," in *Historical Consciousness, Historiography, and Modern Japanese Values*, ed. James C. Baxter (Kyoto: International Research Center for Japanese Studies, 2006), 263–73.
10. As noted in Richie, *A Hundred Years*, 120.
11. Hirata Oriza, *Cities Do Not Need Festivities* (*Toshi ni shukusai wa iranai*) (Tokyo: Benseisha, 1997), 182.
12. See Denton Hewgill, Noro Hiroko, and M. Cody Poulton, "Exploring Drama and Theatre in Teaching Japanese: Hirata Oriza's Play, *Tokyo Notes*, in an Advanced Japanese Conversation Course," *Sekai no Nihongo* 14 (September 2004): 227–52; Denton Hewgill, Noro Hiroko, and M. Cody Poulton, *Real Japanese, Using Oriza Hirata's Play, "Tokyo Notes"* [CD-ROM] (Tokyo: Kinokuniya Shoten, 2007).

13. See M. Cody Poulton, "Hirata Oriza on the Rise and Fall of Japanese Literature . . . and Theatre Too," *Asian Theatre Journal* 38, no. 1 (Spring 2021): 35–53.

14. See Hirata Oriza, *For the Purposes of Contemporary Colloquial Theater* (*Gendai kōgo engeki no tame ni*) (Tokyo: Banseisha, 1995).

15. Hirata Oriza and Ishiguro Hiroshi, *Robot Theatre* (*Robotto engeki*) (Osaka: Osaka University Communication Design Center, 2010), 18.

16. Nakanishi Osamu, "Hirata Oriza/Hatsune Miku/Robot Theatre" ("Hirata Oriza/Hatsune Miku/Robotto Engeki"), *Theater Arts* 55 (2013): 15–22.

17. Paul Du Noyer, "David Bowie: The 2003 Interview," *Paul Du Noyer* (website), https://www.pauldunoyer.com/david-bowie-interview-2003/

18. The company's name is typically not capitalized, as with Okada Toshiki's company chelfitch.

19. Hirata's directorial style is evident in spades in Hamaguchi Ryūsuke's award-winning 2021 film, *Drive My Car*, which features a number of actors from his Seinendan company. This is arguably a case where a theatrical style has imprinted itself on cinema, an exception that proves the rule.

20. TPAM changed its name, along with its organizational structure, to YPAM (Yokohama Performing Arts Meeting), in December 2021.

21. As quoted in Matthew Potolsky, *Mimesis (The New Critical Idiom)* (Basingstoke, UK: Routledge, 2006), 154.

22. Benjamin Gillespie, Sarah Lucie, and Jennifer Joan Thompson, "Global Voices in the Time of Coronavirus," *Performing Arts Journal* 126 (2020): 5, https://doi.org/10.1162/pajj_a_00532

23. Okada Toshiki, "Sounding Like a Typical Post-Corona Theory of Theatre" ("Ika ni mo posuto-korona na engekiron"), trans. M. Cody Poulton, in *Okada Toshiki and Contemporary Japanese Theatre*, ed. Peter Eckersall, Barbara Geilhorn, Andreas Regelsberger, and M. Cody Poulton (Aberystwyth, UK: Performance Research Books, 2021). Okada's essay was originally published in *Viewpoint* 93 (The Saison Foundation Newsletter), March 31, 2021.

24. See Okada Toshiki, *chelfitch x Kaneuji Teppei Eraser stone* (*chelfitch x Kaneuji Teppei keshigomu ishi*) (Kanazawa: 21st Century Museum of Contemporary Art, 2020).

9 | Realisms in Japan's Eighteenth-Century Puppet Theater

JYANA S. BROWNE

The eighteenth century was a time of enormous artistic and technical innovation in the Japanese puppet theater (*ningyō jōruri*, later known as bunraku). The form, which grew out of two competing styles of chanted storytelling, included four main artists: the chanter (*tayū*), who performed all the narrative passages, the dialogue for the various characters, and any songs; the shamisen player, who provided melodic and rhythmic accompaniment; the puppeteers, who operated the puppets; and the playwright, who crafted the script and oversaw its realization. Early puppet theater performances took place in temporary theaters at festivals and shrines and along riverbeds. By the eighteenth century, Osaka had developed a licensed theater district, Dōtonbori, which was the hub of artistic exchange and theatrical innovation for the city.

Dōtonbori hosted approximately eight theaters, including four kabuki theaters and four puppet theaters.[1] The leading puppet theaters were the Takemoto Theater and the Toyotake Theater, which specialized in dramatic storytelling by a chanter accompanied by the shamisen and puppets. Each had a distinctive chanting style and identity. The two additional puppet theaters specialized in mechanical dolls and trick puppets (*karakuri ningyō*). Their performances emphasized spectacle, the dexterity of the puppeteer, and puppets that could transform or move due to hidden gears and strings. The geographic proximity of these different forms of theater enabled extensive borrowing among them. The major puppet theaters used *karakuri* mechanisms to develop more complex

175

puppets and the kabuki and puppet theaters shared repertoire, performance techniques, and staging practices.

Playwright Chikamatsu Monzaemon (1653–1725) and chanter Takemoto Gidayū (1651–1714) at the Takemoto Theater pioneered realism on the puppet stage in the early eighteenth century through carefully crafted dramatic situations and a depth of emotional expressivity in the chanter's voice. During the height of their fame, puppeteer Yoshida Bunzaburō (d. 1760) came of age. He debuted at the Takemoto Theater in Osaka using single-operator puppets in 1717 for Chikamatsu's *The Battles of Coxinga in Later Days* (*Kokusen'ya gonichi kassen*) and became the lead puppeteer for the theater in 1725. In collaboration with Takeda Izumo I (d. 1747), who took over the theater's management from Gidayū in 1705, Bunzaburō developed and oversaw the innovative implementation of new mechanisms for the articulation of the puppet body and the transition from single-operator puppets to the elaborate three-operator puppets still in use today. While single-operator puppets remained in use throughout the eighteenth century, their purpose shifted from being the sole type of puppet in use to being deployed for specialized moments that showcased the dexterity and virtuosity of the puppeteer. Increasingly, the three-operator puppet came to be favored as it could articulate elements of the face and hands with precision and strike complex poses that conveyed character with specificity. Bunzaburō was critical in developing a number of the new techniques that enabled the minute articulation of the puppet body, particularly the mechanism for the left hand. Due to his skill as a puppeteer and these innovations, Bunzaburō pioneered a new form of realism that focused on the faithful representation of everyday life in which the puppet's body moved with greater resemblance to the human body. By the 1740s, with Bunzaburō's most famous roles, the puppeteer's importance to the theater was solidified. Unlike the early-eighteenth-century puppet theater, which located realism in dramatic situations and the expression of feeling, particularly through the playwright's craft and the chanter's recitation, as the form developed and increasingly came into competition with kabuki, puppeteers emerged as the key architects of the "real" on stage. Through Bunzaburō's innovations, ideas of the real moved from the voice to the body with movement as the animating factor.

Emotional Realism

At the start of the eighteenth century, the puppet theater cultivated an emotional realism that represented the inner thoughts and feelings of characters that lay beyond the boundaries of what could be expressed in everyday life. This realism drew from contemporary life but was meant to reveal a deeper truth that could only be articulated in performance. In these early years in the development of the puppet theater, the playwright and the chanter were the key artists shaping the form, and thus the pursuit of the real and its mode of expression.

Chikamatsu, the leading playwright of the period, emphasized that conjuring a real feeling on stage did not mean a transparent reflection of reality. For Chikamatsu, the puppet theater's approach of representing an internal reality was a significant difference in the form's approach compared to kabuki, which pursued a faithful depiction of external reality. In *Souvenirs of Naniwa* (*Naniwa miyage*, 1738), the record of Chikamatsu's theoretical approach to his art as documented by his friend Hozumi Ikan, Chikamatsu stressed that the trend to consider kabuki actors "skillful to the degree that their acting resembles reality" missed the real role of art. In addition to the fact that such extreme fidelity to reality would be impractical, he claimed that "art is something which lies in the slender margin between the real and the unreal."[2] He tells a story of a woman in the court who had an image of her lover carved into wood. The craftsman faithfully reproduced the man in every detail of the doll, including the pores of his skin. Rather than pleasing the court lady, the doll left her chilled and caused her feelings toward her lover to cool. Through this example, Chikamatsu demonstrated that art needs to move beyond verisimilitude and requires a degree of stylization to please its audience.

Furthermore, by inhabiting the "slender margin between the real and the unreal," Chikamatsu claimed that art can provide access to the inner life of characters, particularly female characters, that would not be able to be expressed in everyday life due to social constraints. He explained, "In recent plays many things have been said by female characters which real women could not utter. Such things fall under the heading of art; it is because they say what could not come from a real woman's lips that their true emotions are disclosed. If in such cases the author were to model his character on the ways of a real woman and conceal her feelings, such realism, far from being admired, would permit no pleasure in the work."[3] The real, for Chikamatsu, resists an exact true-to-life representation and simultaneously enables expression beyond the confines of the everyday.

Chikamatsu realized the emotional realism he sought in part through his crafting of dramatic situations. In his playwriting, Chikamatsu carefully constructed the dramatic circumstances facing the characters to convey the emotional core of a scene by drawing from everyday life situations. Initially, he learned how to structure a scene to bring out an emotional realism from kabuki actor Sakata Tōjūrō (1647–1709), and when he transitioned back to writing exclusively for the puppet theater he applied these techniques across entire plays for his contemporary life plays (*sewamono*) based on recent love suicides and murders.[4]

The emotional realism of Chikamatsu's scripts could not have been brought to life in performance without the work of his close collaborator, chanter Takemoto Gidayū. Gidayū was the preeminent performer at the Takemoto Theater, and his attention to the emotional flow of the performances drew audiences and imitators. Gidayū emphasized this depth of feeling in his treatises on the art of the chanter, theoretical writings which were often published as the prefaces to printed editions of plays. In his famous preface which appeared in *The 1687 Gidayū Collection of Jōruri Scenes* (*Jōkyō yonen Gidayū danmonoshū*), he advised, "When one chants the love scenes tenderly, the audience will be charmed. The *serifu*, speech, parts are like the shallow rapids of a river; the *fushi*, melody, passages are like quiet pools. . . . When chanting scenes of grief and sorrow, one must not disregard reality."[5] The notation of these *serifu* and *fushi* sections were published in the print version of the plays, whether the texts were intended for readers or amateur performers, which speaks to their important role and how the musicality of the play was an integral component even in the printed texts.[6] The chanter's performance brought audiences to the puppet theaters, and kabuki theaters capitalized on the popularity of the chanters' versions of the plays to lure audiences to their adaptations. After the success of Chikamatsu's *Yosaku from Tanba* (*Tanba Yosaku matsuyo no komurobushi*, 1707) at the Takemoto Theater, Osaka's Iwai Theater, a kabuki theater, advertised their performance of the same play with the slogan, "According to the authorized text by Takemoto Gidayū."[7]

Chikamatsu and Gidayū's collaborations include multiple examples of the pairing of a dramatic situation from everyday life with the vocal nuances of the chanter's art to achieve an emotional realism that enables an expression of the inner emotions of the character. A poignant example appears in *Love Suicides in the Women's Temple* (*Shinjū mannensō*, 1710), a contemporary life play that tells the story of Oume, the daughter of a merchant who lives near Mount Koya, who chooses to die by suicide with her lover rather than marry the man selected by her father. In the second act, Oume hides upstairs in her bedroom with her lover, Kumenosuke, while her parents try to convince the groom to go through with the marriage despite the rumors that their daughter has been seeing another man. Oume's mother suspects that Oume might consider suicide, so she gives an impassioned plea to her daughter in the guise of speaking to the groom. Musically, the speech, a *kudoki* or "impassioned display of love and grief" which takes place at a critical moment in the play and is its musical climax, is the highlight of this scene.[8] The mother tells the groom that if he refuses the marriage her daughter would likely commit suicide due the shame and suffering the groom's refusal would bring to the family. She says,

> Supposing I tried to dissuade them, saying something like, "Don't kill yourselves, you mustn't kill yourselves, this is no time to die. You'd make your parents unhappy and expose yourselves to the worst criticism. Consider it's your duty to your parents. Please don't kill yourselves." It's almost unthinkable, I know, that they'd go through with it anyway, but, in the simple-minded way of young people, they might worry only about the disgrace to themselves. And how tragic it would be if they died!

Here the narrator interjects, "Each word she utters travels in two directions, upstairs and downstairs. Kumenosuke, hearing her words, returns his dagger to its sheath; they cannot kill themselves now. Silently embracing, they weep."[9] By the end of the speech, the mother has coaxed Oume downstairs and convinced the groom to go through with the marriage. The mother's entreaties achieve their emotional resonance due to the delicate position she is placed in by the scene. She must appeal to her daughter and Kumenosuke without the groom realizing he is not the main intended audience for her words. Additionally, the audience would have been able to see that upstairs Kumenosuke already had his dagger drawn, which increases the stakes for her pleas. As the *kudoki* of the scene, Gidayū would have been charged with ensuring the speech had the full emotional impact in performance.

The collaboration between playwright and chanter to achieve emotional realism also materialized in less climactic moments. One such example is the scene in which the protagonists of *Love Suicides at Sonezaki* (*Sonezaki shinjū*, 1703), Ohatsu and Tokubei, escape the brothel. Ohatsu extinguishes the light in the brothel and flees in the darkness to find Tokubei in the garden. The lovers can hear the maid inside trying to relight the lamp. As Tokubei and Ohatsu face the brothel entrance, the narrator recites, "They unfasten the latch, but the hinges creak, and frightened by the noise, they hesitate. Just then the maid begins to strike the flints; they time their actions to the rasping sound, and with each rasp open the door further until, huddled together and their sleeves twisted round them, they pass through the door one after the other, feeling as though they tread on a tiger's tail."[10] The everyday-life situation in this scene makes it easy for the audience to identify with the characters' emotions as they try to control their nerves and time their escape. The text incorporates a number of onomatopoetic sounds which give the chanter the opportunity to embellish the sonic dimension of the scene. With the addition of the onomatopoetic sounds, the text reads, "The maid strikes the flint with a *futt futt* and the lovers use the sound to cover the sound of the door. When she strikes the flint hard—*kwap*, they open it slightly *ssssht*. When she strikes the flint with a *kuchh kuchh* the lovers open the gate *ssssht sssssht*."[11] In this scene, the everyday dramatic situation, combined with the chanter's aural representation of the sounds of the door and the flint, draw the audience into the emotions of the characters as they escape.

In the *Sonezaki* escape scene described above, the puppets' movements in performance likely underscored the aural repetition through the timed visual repetition of the two actions, the maid striking the flint and the lovers opening the door, and therefore added to the emotional realism of the scene. But puppetry was not always used to augment the everyday. In the early eighteenth century, the most memorable moments for the puppets were often highly spectacular moments in the performances. Referencing the performance of *Sonezaki*, *Jōruri's Intertwined Branches* (*Jōruri renri maru*, 1704) stated that the Takemoto Theater's production was "exceptional in music, writing, and puppetry."[12] The puppetry moment in *Sonezaki* that generated the greatest stir was a transformation of the puppet for Ohatsu from a woman into the bodhisattva Kannon.[13] The puppeteer, Tatsumatsu Hachirōbei (d. 1734), was well known for his integration of trick puppetry elements from the mechanical puppets that were used in performances in a nearby theater in Dōtonbori. The whole opening scene of *Sonezaki* provided an opportunity for Tatsumatsu to show off his skill with the single-operator puppet and culminated in the transformation of the puppet into a shining, golden bodhisattva before the audience's eyes. This spectacular use of the puppet is unlike the more modulated emotional realism in the *Sonezaki* escape scene or the mother's speech from *Women's Temple*. While puppetry could support the emotional realism of these scenes, it was often deployed for more theatrical effects.

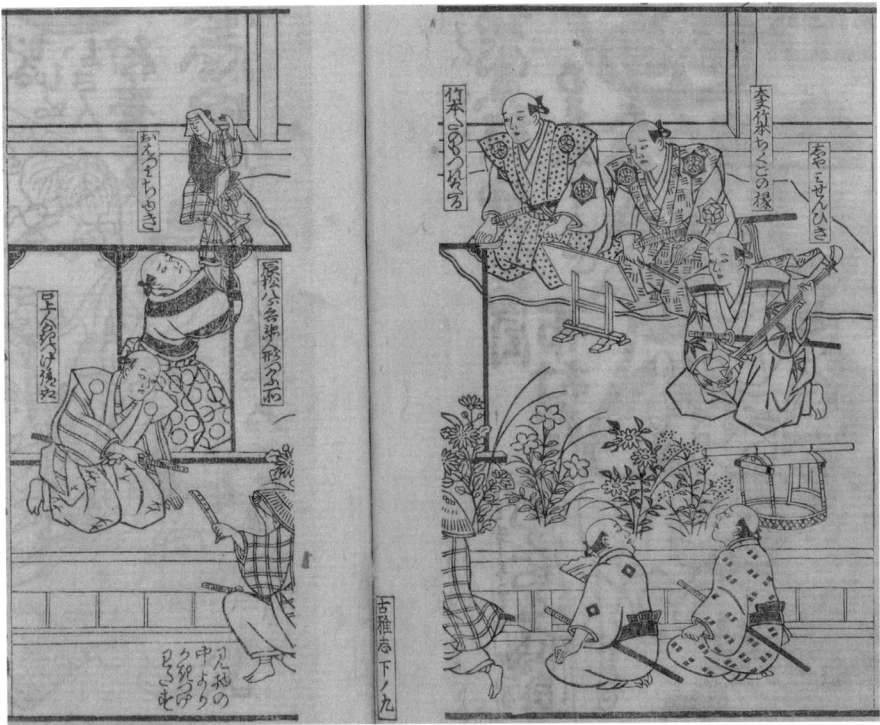

Figure 9.1: Tatsumatsu Hachirōbei operating the puppet Ohatsu in the opening scene of *Love Suicides at Sonezaki*. From *Mugikogashi* (1826). Image courtesy of the National Diet Library, Japan.

During the early eighteenth century, the playwright and chanter captured the emotional core of the story by combining dramatic situations from everyday life with musical scoring that highlighted emotional pinnacles and reinforced the sense of the everyday. While puppetry contributed to this emotional realism in some scenes, it was predominantly used for theatrical spectacle. As puppeteers continued to innovate, the puppets became increasingly suited for enhancing fantastical rather than realistic aspects of the plays.

Puppetry Innovation

While Chikamatsu and Gidayū's emotional realism was the hallmark of the Takemoto Theater in Osaka, puppeteers in the city centers of Edo and Osaka were continuously experimenting with ways to increase the articulation of the puppet for both realistic and spectacular ends. Edo and Osaka puppeteers diverged in the techniques they developed, but to more fully articulate the puppet body, each focused on increasing the number of puppeteers operating the puppets. In Edo in the late seventeenth century, puppeteers developed a method that enabled the manipulation of the puppet by multiple puppeteers. The puppet was placed on a rod that was fixed in place on the stage. One operator manipulated the arms, another the legs, and a third supported the torso of the puppet and the rod. This apparatus increased the expressivity of the puppet, but decreased the dynamism in staging, since the puppet could not move fluidly on stage. While this was the first instance of three puppeteers manipulating the puppet, the practice did not spread beyond Edo and fell out of use.[14] In contrast, the Osaka method integrated the mechanisms in mechanical dolls and the techniques used for the single-operator puppet, which enabled a greater range of movement and a seamless transfer of skills, while maintaining the full use of the stage space. Bunzaburō and the Takemoto Theater were the center of these advances, which came to be adopted by all puppeteers working in the tradition. While the Edo and Osaka experiments simultaneously increased the expressivity of the puppet through its ability to articulate smaller units of the body, the Osaka method combined coordinated minute movements with the ability to move in space and realize stage pictures, and thus more closely resemble not just the movement of a human body but also its movement in space. Ultimately, the greater range and detail of movement would enable Bunzaburō to develop his signature puppetry style of a realism based in fidelity to human movement in everyday life.

In Osaka, the first innovations involved manipulating smaller aspects of the puppets using mechanisms developed from mechanical dolls. The puppeteers held the puppet from the back to operate strings connected to the puppet's head. By 1725 the eyes and mouths of the puppets could open and close, and the heads gained increased range of motion. As the puppets became more expressive, the chanter and shamisen player were moved to an adjacent performance space, which gave the puppets additional stage space and allowed for more complex scenery. In 1733, puppeteers developed the mechanism for articulating the fingers on the hands.

A crucial leap forward came the following year in 1734, when a three-operator puppet was first used in *The Courtly Mirror of Ashiya Dōman* (*Ashiya Dōman ōuchi kagami*) at the Takemoto Theater. The production primarily used the usual one-operator puppets, but a key moment called for a vivid display of the full puppet body with limbs extended, so the puppeteers created two three-operator puppets to realize the spectacular tableau and two extraordinary bodies. In this scene of *The Courtly Mirror*, a play set in the Heian period (794–1185), two porters, Yokanbei and Yakanbei, are charged with the safe transport of Princess Kuzunoha and the child Abe Dōshi. Villains attack, a fight ensues, and the porters emerge victorious. They raise the palanquin that contains the princess and the boy high on their shoulders and strike a pose of triumph before transporting the palanquin to safety. As the porters move into the tableau, the narrator describes how they bare their chests as they pick up the palanquin and take one huge breath.[15] The evidence from written and visual sources indicates that the moment was realized on stage as described in the text. For instance, a history of puppet theater from the late 1790s, *Jōrurifu*, recounts, "The puppetry was excellent. Yokanbei and Yakanbei had separate operators for the left hand and for the feet, and the belly (*hara*) of the puppets moved." The *Gendainenkan* (1757) differed slightly by recounting that Yokanbei's belly expanded rather than moved.[16] The emphasis on the movement or expansion of the puppet's abdomen probably described the big breath taken by the characters before posing with the carriage. As for the tableau, an illustration in the program (*bansuke*) from a revival in 1748 shows the porters flanking the palanquin at its front and back. The door of the palanquin is open to reveal the princess and the child, and the porters are on either side holding the palanquin with both arms raised. This stance would have required a puppeteer for each arm to hold it up, support the palanquin, and expand the puppet's abdomen.[17] The puppetry innovations for *The Courtly Mirror* made possible a stylized, theatrical tableau featuring the extraordinary bodies of the two porters. Yokanbei and Yakanbei, stripped to the waist with their arms raised, embodied strength and bravery. The audience could marvel as their abdomens expanded with their breath to create a more robust puppet body.

The available evidence does not allow us to determine which of the Takemoto Theater puppeteers pioneered this role. Scholars have proposed Yoshida Bunzaburō and Yoshida Saburobei as candidates, but the puppeteer's identity remains unknown.[18] While it is undecided whether Bunzaburō operated the three-operator puppet in *The Courtly Mirror*, a decade later he made this technology thoroughly his own by moving away from the extraordinary and spearheading the manipulation of the three-operator puppet to summon everyday life on the puppet theater stage.

Realism of the Everyday

Bunzaburō's signature style of realism of the everyday came to fruition in the 1740s with the productions *Summer Festival: A Mirror of Osaka* (*Natsu matsuri Naniwa kagami*, 1745), *Sugawara and the Secrets of Calligraphy* (*Sugawara denju tenarai kagami*, 1746), and *Yoshitsune and the Thousand Cherry Trees* (*Yoshitsune senbon zakura*, 1747) at the Takemoto Theater. While productions of the early eighteenth century highlighted an emotional realism that captured the inner feelings of characters that would not have been expressed in everyday life, Bunzaburō used the innovations in puppetry that expanded the articulation of the puppet body to develop a realism of the everyday in which the puppet's movements became more humanlike. The crafting of the dramatic situation and the vocal art of the chanter, which were so integral to drawing out the character's feelings in earlier plays, continued to play an important role in creating this new style of realism on stage, but Bunzaburō's skills increasingly made the puppet the center of artistic expression for the puppet theater.

The first production in which Bunzaburō presented the puppet body in a startling new way was *Summer Festival*, a contemporary-life play that drew its inspiration from a late-seventeenth-century incident in Osaka. *Summer Festival* tells the story of Danshichi Kurobei, a fishmonger, who ends up murdering his father-in-law. Despite Danshichi's strong character, the cruelty and greed of others drives him to accidentally wound his father-in-law and then kill him. In *Summer Festival*, the world of contemporary Osaka is rife with villains, violence, and danger that overwhelms the goodness in the heroes and heroines of the story.

Bunzaburō brought out the grittiness in the murder scene with a strong focus on the bodies of the characters and the interactions between these bodies and the environment. First, he radically shifted the costuming of the puppet body. Conventionally, costumes were padded and bulky to create the illusion of a body underneath the garment. For *Summer Festival*, however, Bunzaburō costumed Danshichi in a summer-weight cotton kimono with brown stripes. The thin material enabled the audience to glimpse the movement of the limbs and trunk of the puppet through the fabric.[19] With this costume choice, Bunzaburō could not rely on the shaping provided by the costume to create the illusion of the body and instead had to use the movement of the body to create the illusion of bones and muscle. In addition to drawing the spectators' attention to the movement of the puppet's body, he introduced staging that would have the puppet body collide with real substances by incorporating actual mud and water into the action, so the puppets became covered in mud and then doused with water.[20] Both the lightweight, brown-striped kimono (which came to be called "Danshichi stripes") and the use of water and mud were rated as highly effective in performance.[21] The chronology of puppet theater, *Jōrurifu*, recounts, "This was the first time a puppet was dressed in a single-layer kimono. It was Yoshida Bunzaburō who conceived of using real mud and splashing water. His way of manipulating the puppet was particularly humanlike [*hito no gotoku*]."[22]

The emphasis on the garment, the mud and water flung onto the puppet, and the movement demonstrates a desire to simulate everyday reality on the puppet stage through the body of the puppet. The kimono, mud, and water are all materials from everyday life, and in addition to bringing a "realness" onto the stage, each is used to highlight the puppet body and how it moves. The kimono reveals the articulations of the more mobile and expressive three-operator puppet. The mud and water are brought on stage to coat and then clean the body. The staging even includes Danshichi drawing the water from the well, which was an opportunity for Bunzaburō to showcase the puppet engaged in an everyday, human sequence of movements. The realism Bunzaburō achieved in this scene moves away from the emotion that had been so central to concepts of the real in the early eighteenth century. Bunzaburō's realism is located in the body, particularly in the movement of the body and the body's interactions with the materials it touches.

The shift toward a realism of the everyday in puppetry was mirrored in developments in playwriting and chanting. Unlike the realism grounded in the dramatic situation and emotional expressivity achieved by the playwright and the art of the chanter at the beginning of the century through lyrical, narrative passages, playwriting incorporated significantly more dialogue with sparser narration. Through the influence of kabuki, the dialogue reproduced everyday speech, and playwrights used expressions and verbal variation to depict each character with greater specificity. The lines of dialogue became shorter than the lengthy speeches in earlier plays, and generally the textual component of the production was minimized. Chanters responded to these changes by developing new techniques of recitation that captured everyday speech and the particularities of character.[23] While the chanter's ability to convey the emotions of the characters did not disappear, the expression of character and the accurate representation of everyday speech became critical vehicles for creating the real on stage.

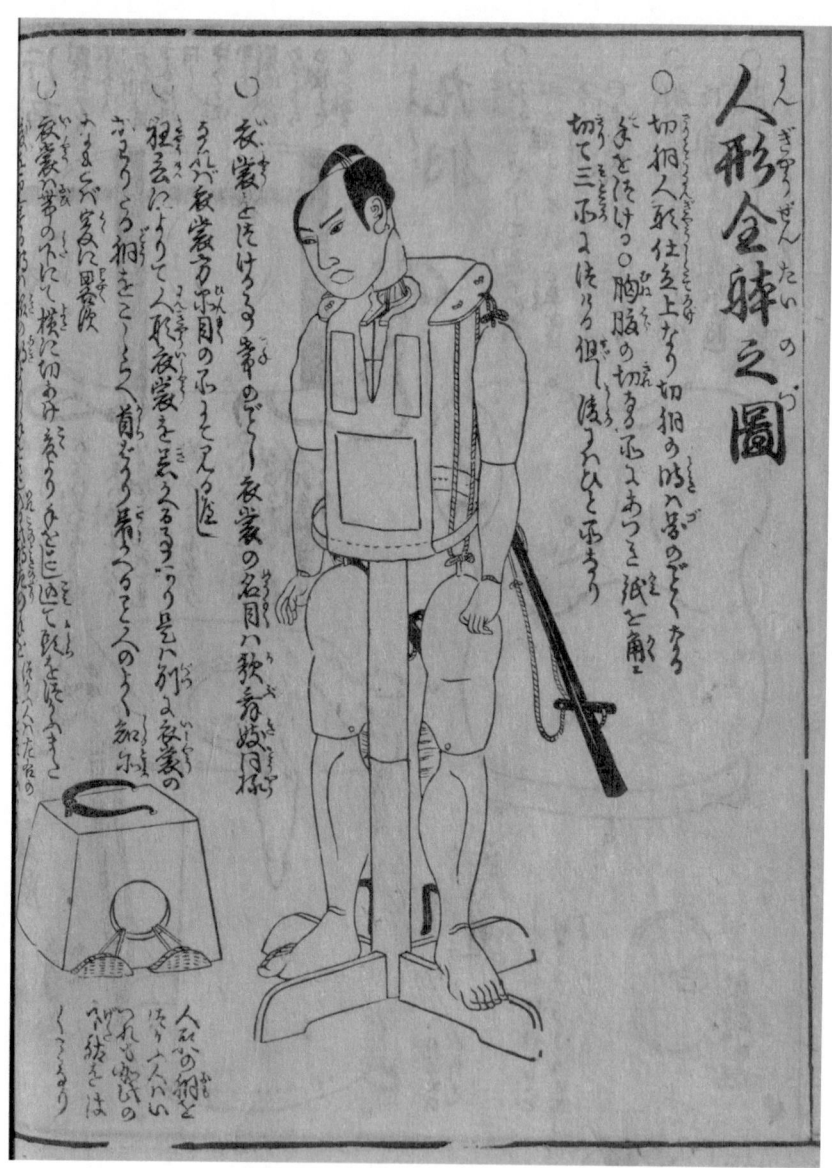

Figure 9.2: The long rod mechanism (*nagai sashigane*) developed by Bunzaburō. From *Shibaigakuyazue* (1800). Image courtesy of the National Diet Library, Japan.

After the success of *Summer Festival*, Bunzaburō continued to refine the puppet to increase its expressive potential. While the ability to articulate the fingers of the right hand had existed since 1733, the left hand used in the initial three-operator puppets did not have the same dexterity. To enable the full articulation of the left hand, Bunzaburō invented the long rod mechanism (*nagai sashigane*), which used strings to control the subtle movements of the hands and fingers. Most likely the long rod was first used for female characters, such as the prostitute Ume in *Hiragana seisuiki* (1739) and Chiyo, Matsuōmaru's wife, in *Sugawara* seven years later.[24] It is thought to have been used first for a male character in *Yoshitsune* the following year, when Bunzaburō puppeteered the role of the loyal fox, and had the left hand operator use the long rod to fully realize the character.[25] In *Yoshitsune*, Bunzaburō extended the techniques for minute articulation of puppets from human characters to animals as well by developing a new technique to enable the ears of the fox puppet to move. The innovations of the left hand mechanism and the fox ears demonstrate the importance Bunzaburō placed on the range of expression through movement for the puppet, whether in human or animal form.

Many sources point to new designs for hairstyles and kimonos Bunzaburō developed for these plays, which demonstrate his continued attention to the body of the puppet and how it conveys character. He chose a crest that interwove plum and young pine for the kimono of Sugawara Michizane, to remind audiences of the famous poem written after his exile about his longing for plum and pine trees from his home in Kyoto, and of the triplets named for these elements who serve as his protectors in the play.[26] For the triplets, he designed kimonos of yellow silk with red at the cuffs and hem to create a sense of unity across the three even as their destinies diverged. The costumes helped convey important information about the characters to the audience and demonstrate Bunzaburō's full attention to the puppet body.

The prominence of puppetry prompted theaters that adapted the plays to integrate the movements, staging, and costumes already developed by puppeteers into their productions, rather than relying on imitating the chanters' performances. For instance, when a puppet theater based in in Edo, the Toyotake Hizen Theater, decided to perform *Sugawara*, they sent a puppeteer and a chanter to Osaka to learn the piece. The Edo artists watched the performances and received instruction from the chanter and puppeteers before returning to Edo to open their production.[27] Likewise, when *Yoshitsune* was adapted to kabuki, the theater invited a chanter, a shamisen player, and six puppeteers from Takemoto Theater to guide rehearsals.[28] One commentator noted that in Osaka "puppet theatre had become so popular, it is as though kabuki no longer existed."[29]

Within the productions of *Summer Festival*, *Sugawara*, and *Yoshitsune*, Bunzaburō developed new techniques to enhance the expressive potential of the puppet and create a realism of the everyday. In *Summer Festival*, Bunzaburō utilized the intricacy of the three-operator puppet to conjure a theatricality that reveled in the ordinary body and everyday movements. In *Sugawara* and *Yoshitsune* he refined the long rod for the left hand that enabled the expressivity of the left hand to match the right. As the playwrights and chanters worked to fit the speech patterns and rhythms to the characters, Bunzaburō aligned the costumes to the characters. In the move toward representations of the everyday, the balance between the chanters and puppeteers began to shift as well. The slimmer scripts with more dialogue and exchange between characters gave the staging and movements of the puppets more centrality in the storytelling. With the production of *Chūshingura* (*Kanadehon Chūshingura*) in 1748, the puppeteer became the premier artist of the puppet theater.

The Ascendancy of the Puppeteer

Chūshingura was a particularly pivotal production in the shift toward the primacy of the puppeteer. The play tells of a group of loyal retainers led by the protagonist, Yuranosuke, who seek revenge on Kō no Moronao, the man who wronged their master, Enya Hangan. After their lord is compelled to commit ritual suicide and they become masterless samurai, the retainers plot a lengthy revenge in secret while outwardly feigning disinterest. The play ends with their successful assault of Kō no Moronao's mansion and his death. The Takemoto Theater production achieved enormous success and was quickly adapted to kabuki. In *Chūshingura*, Bunzaburō continued his work toward a realism of the everyday and staging became an increasingly critical element of the storytelling.

Staging was used to particularly strong effect in the brothel scene in which Yuranosuke, the role performed by Bunzaburō, reads a letter from a partner in the revenge plot. Yuranosuke has taken to frequenting the brothels to convince Kō no Moronao's men that he has given up on revenge and instead lives a life of sensual pleasure and indulgence. In this scene, Kudayū has come to spy on Yuranosuke to see if the rumors of his dissipation are true. Also present in the brothel is Okaru, a woman who entered prostitution to secure the funds necessary for her husband, a disgraced former retainer to Enya Hangan, to participate in the revenge plot. The scene incorporates what is known as a "silent scene," a technique adapted from kabuki that depicts the relationships between characters, as well as the characters in their separate worlds, through gestures and poses alone.[30] The tableau places Yuranosuke stage center within the brothel, reading a letter. Okaru perches above him in a separate room of the brothel, leaning over the banister to read the letter in the reflection of her hand mirror. Kudayū hides underneath the veranda below Yuranosuke and reads the letter as it spills over the edge. Both the tension between the characters and the inner life of the characters are conveyed not through text or voice but through the visual arrangement of the characters on stage.

In addition to incorporating the silent scene from kabuki, the performers imitated kabuki actors in their rendering of the characters. For the brothel scene described above, the chanter, Takemoto Konotayū (1700–1768), and Bunzaburō both drew inspiration from kabuki actor Sawamura Sōjūrō (1685–1756). Konotayū captured his vocal rhythms and facial expressions, and Bunzaburō's puppetry portrayed the actor's physicality and movement.[31] The choice to copy Sōjūrō in voice and movement has been taken by some scholars to point to the profound influence of kabuki on the puppet theater of the period. But does this deliberate imitation not also demonstrate the advancements of puppetry? Bunzaburō could replicate Sōjūrō's movements through his animation of the puppet closely enough that audiences found his puppetry to not only be humanlike but to represent a very specific human in a way that was recognizable to all.

After two months of acclaimed performances, Bunzaburō requested a change in the recitation that caused a rift between puppeteer and chanter. For the scene in which Yuranosuke meets Honzō, who brings the plans for Kō no Moronao's complex, Bunzaburō asked Konotayū to change the rhythm of his performance to draw out a specific set of lines and to add a pause between certain phrases. Bunzaburō wanted time to allow Yuranosuke to enact three specific actions: rising from a seated position, putting on his wooden clogs, and crossing the stage to the bamboo grove.[32] Yokoyama Tadashi has suggested that this alteration would show Yuranosuke processing valuable new information.[33] Or perhaps Bunzaburō intended to draw attention to these everyday movements of rising, donning clogs, and walking. Either way, the proposed stage actions depict a moment of the everyday rather than an explosive, theatrical moment. Konotayū refused the request, which left the two lead artists of the Takemoto Theater at an impasse. Since they were unable to compromise, the theater manager, Takeda Izumo II (1691–1756), was forced to conclude the matter and sided with Bunzaburō. This unprecedented privileging of the puppeteer's expressivity over the chanter resulted in Konotayū and his disciples quitting the Takemoto Theater and moving to the Toyotake Theater, which blended Takemoto and Toyotake styles of chanting and ended the distinction in styles for which the theaters had been known. It also marked the clear ascendancy of the puppeteer as the main artist of the puppet theater.

Conclusion

Over the eighteenth century, the puppet theater shifted from an emotional realism generated through the dramatic situation as crafted by the playwright and the expressiveness of the chanter's voice, to a realism of the everyday produced through the articulation of the puppet body by the puppeteer. This development was made possible by technical advancements in the art of puppetry, including the incorporation of mechanisms from *karakuri ningyō*, techniques that enabled three operators to manipulate one puppet, and Bunzaburō's invention of the long rod to articulate the fingers of the left hand. Puppeteers first used these new abilities to create characters with extraordinary bodies and superhuman strength, such as the two porters in *The Courtly Mirror*. But as Bunzaburō developed the ability to add nuance to these large puppet bodies through smaller movements of the hands, he used the puppet to cultivate a realism of the everyday that mimicked human bodies and human movements in everyday life as closely as possible.

In productions from the 1740s, Bunzaburō perfected his realism of the everyday and brought great acclaim to the art of puppetry. With *Summer Festival*, *Sugawara*, and *Yoshitsune*, Bunzaburō advanced new techniques for more precise movements of individual body parts and carefully crafted the costumes to highlight the body and convey character. These advances in the realization of puppetry and design elements led to puppetry having a larger impact on adaptations of these plays by rival theaters. In *Chūshingura*, attention to the visual arrangement of characters, the imitation of kabuki actors' voices and movements, and the lengthening of a moment to reveal everyday movements all indicate the shift in puppetry toward a realism of the everyday that expresses character. Bunzaburō made use of external elements, such as costumes, the positioning of puppets on stage, and the physicality and gestures of the puppets to convey details of characters as they might have appeared in everyday life.

By the golden age of puppetry in the 1740s, the three-operator puppet was being used for key characters and to realize crucial theatrical moments in plays, although single-operator puppets continued to be used for the majority of characters. The three-operator puppet did not become the norm in theaters until sometime in the 1750s or 1760s, shortly before the major puppet theaters closed in the late 1760s, eclipsed by the popularity of kabuki and suddenly lacking their star talent due the demise of a number of great artists around the same time. Even when the three-operator puppet became the main puppet used in performances, single-operator puppets continued to be used for isolated scenes, particularly travel scenes (*michiyuki*), and in performances at private residences through the early nineteenth century.[34] The persistence of the single-operator puppet demonstrates that there was still an audience for the virtuosic puppetry of a single puppeteer. The three-operator puppet's most salient attribute was its ability to achieve higher degrees of realism.[35]

Puppetry's move toward realism that emphasized fidelity to the everyday movements of the human body—and away from emotional realism that revealed inner feelings not usually expressed in everyday life—has been cited as one reason for its decline. Perhaps by narrowing the margin between the real and unreal so completely, puppetry no longer stood apart from kabuki.[36] Yet even today, audiences delight in seeing a puppet recreate the everyday, whether smoking a pipe, playing the koto, or drawing water from a well. The current repertoire mixes plays from across the eighteenth century, so that audiences witness virtuosic puppetry feats alongside emotionally sweeping recitation from the chanters and moments of meticulously rendered everyday movement, so these separate strands of realism intertwine and offer access to the characters' interiority as well as representing an illusion of the external reality of the everyday.

Notes

1. The precise number of theaters shifted over the century as some theaters temporarily closed.
2. Donald Keene, trans., "Chikamatsu on the Art of the Puppet Stage," in *Anthology of Japanese Literature*, ed. Donald Keene (New York: Grove Press, 1955), 389.
3. Keene, "Chikamatsu on the Art of the Puppet Stage," 388.

4. Mori Shū, *Chikamatsu Monzaemon* (Kyoto: San'ichi Shobō, 1959), 149.

5. Translated in C. Andrew Gerstle, *Circles of Fantasy: Convention in the Plays of Chikamatsu* (Cambridge, MA: Harvard University Press, 1986), 193.

6. Gerstle, *Circles of Fantasy*, 16.

7. Mori, *Chikamatsu Monzaemon*, 93.

8. Gerstle, *Circles of Fantasy*, 132.

9. Donald Keene, *Major Plays of Chikamatsu* (New York: Columbia University Press, 1990), 150.

10. Keene, *Major Plays of Chikamatsu*, 51.

11. Chikamatsu Monzaemon, *Sonezaki shinjū* (*Love Suicides at Sonezaki*), in *Chikamatsu Monzaemon shū* 2, ed. Torigoe Bunzō, Yamane Tameo, Nagatomo Chiyoji, Ōhashi Tadayoshi, and Sakuguchi Hiroyuki, *Shinpen Nihon koten bungaku zenshū* (Tokyo: Shōgakukan, 2003), 75: 35–36.

12. Quoted in Gidayū Nenpyō Kinseihen Kankōkai, ed., *Gidayū nenpyō* (*Chronology of Gidayū*) (Tokyo: Yagi Shoten, 1979), 1: 27.

13. Shinoda Jun'ichi, *Chikamatsu Monzaemon, Shinpojiumu Nihon bungaku 7* (*Japanese Literature Symposium 7, Chikamatsu Monzaemon*) (Tokyo: Gakuseisha, 1976), 120–21.

14. Tsunoda Ichirō, "Jōruri ayatsuri sanninzukai no sōshi to fukyū ni tsuite" ("On the Creation and Spread of the Three-Operator Method in Jōruri Puppetry"), *Bungakuin zasshi* 85, no. 11 (1984): 169.

15. Tsunoda, "Jōruri ayatsuri sanninzukai no sōshi to fukyū ni tsuite," 165.

16. Tsunoda, "Jōruri ayatsuri sanninzukai no sōshi to fukyū ni tsuite," 164.

17. Tsunoda, "Jōruri ayatsuri sanninzukai no sōshi to fukyū ni tsuite," 168–69.

18. For a thorough discussion of the evidence and various hypotheses regarding the identity of the lead puppeteer in this scene, see Kanō Katsumi, *Nihon ayatsuri ningyhi: Keitai hensen, sōhō gijutsushi* (*A History of Puppets in Japanese Puppetry: The Development of the Form and a History of Puppetry Techniques and Mechanisms*) (Tokyo: Yagi Shoten, 2018), 612–13.

19. Kawatake Shigetoshi, *Nihon engeki zenshi* (*The Complete History of Japanese Theater*) (Tokyo: Iwanami Shoten, 1968), 478.

20. James R. Brandon, "The Theft of Chūshingura: or The Great Kabuki Caper," in *Chūshingura: Studies in Kabuki and the Puppet Theater*, ed. James R. Brandon (Honolulu: University of Hawaii Press, 1982), 118. These costuming and staging choices were included in the kabuki production that premiered shortly after the puppet theater version.

21. Kawatake, *Nihon engeki zenshi*, 478.

22. "Jōrurifu" ("Chronology of Jōruri"), in *Jōruri kenkyū bunken shūsei* (*Collection of Documents for Research on Jōruri*), ed. Kawatake Shigetori (Tokyo: Hokkō Shobō, 1944), 348.

23. Yokoyama Tadashi, *Jōruri ayatsuri shibai no kenkyū* (*Research on Jōruri Puppet Plays*) (Tokyo: Kazama Shobō, 1964), 618–19.

24. Tsunoda, "Jōruri ayatsuri sanninzukai no sōshi to fukyū ni tsuite," 170.

25. Tsunoda, "Jōruri ayatsuri sanninzukai no sōshi to fukyū ni tsuite," 171.

26. Tsurumi Makoto, "Sakuhin no kaisetsu" ("Commentary on the Plays"), in *Takeda Izumo shū* (*The Works of Takeda Izumo*), ed. Tsurumi Makoto, *Nihon koten zensho* (Tokyo: Asahi Shinbunsha, 1956), 40. Sugawara Michizane (845–903)

was a scholar and statesman in the Heian period. A political rival orchestrated his exile to Dazaifu in Kyushu, where he later died. After his death, natural disasters and disease struck the capital, which many interpreted to be the wrath of Michizane's spirit. To pacify his spirit, he was deified as a god of scholarship and learning.

27. Tsurumi, "Sakuhin no kaisetsu," 34.
28. Brandon, "The Theft of Chūshingura," 145.
29. Quoted in Gotō Shizuo and Alan Cummings, trans., "Bunraku Puppet Theatre," in *A History of Japanese Theatre*, ed. Jonah Salz (Cambridge, UK: Cambridge University Press, 2016), 171.
30. Yokoyama, *Jōruri ayatsuri shibai no kenkyū*, 619.
31. Yokoyama, *Jōruri ayatsuri shibai no kenkyū*, 619.
32. Kawatake, *Nihon engeki zenshi*, 479.
33. Yokoyama, *Jōruri ayatsuri shibai no kenkyū*, 619.
34. Tsunoda, "Jōruri ayatsuri sanninzukai no sōshi to fukyū ni tsuite," 173.
35. Tsunoda, "Jōruri ayatsuri sanninzukai no sōshi to fukyū ni tsuite," 173.
36. Odanaka Akihiro and Iwai Masami, *Japanese Political Theatre in the 18th Century: Bunraku Puppet Plays in Social Context* (Oxon, UK: Routledge, 2021), 189.

10 | Costumes of the Present

Clothing and Realism in Traditional Chinese Theater

GUOJUN WANG

Qi Rushan (1877–1962), an aficionado of Beijing opera, once summarized the essence of the art in four lines: "Every sound should be song; every movement should be dance; no real objects should be used; and no action should imitate reality."[1] Qi's characterization represents a still-common understanding that traditional Chinese theater is antirealistic, and that it exhibits at best limited concern about staying true to how events transpire in real society. Joshua Goldstein's thorough investigation of Beijing opera history contextualizes Qi's statement; as he notes, it was only during the May Fourth era, especially the 1920s, that realist conventions of mimeticism became a universal code of representation, which led Qi to regard Chinese drama as realism's Other.[2] This paper is not concerned with the introduction of Western realist drama or theater to China. If we follow Jean Benedetti's proposition that "realism is a question of belief, of the actor's conviction that what he is doing is genuine," and that in contrast, naturalism "depends on the exactness of externals—decor and costume and props," then we can speak of a broad definition of realism predicated on a strong sense of the association between theater and (perceived) social reality.[3] Following that understanding, we can ask whether and how theatrical practitioners in premodern China used certain theatrical tropes to help the audience perceive the ties between stage and society.

One way to explore the question is to examine the relationship between theater costumes and clothing in wider society, and inquire whether Chinese theater ever used costumes to produce realistic representations of social events.⁴ This paper scrutinizes the relationship between theatrical costuming, sartorial styles in society, and ideas about verisimilitude. In particular, it focuses on a group of terms that integrate clothing and current society by adding the word *shi* 時 (current) as an adjectival prefix to sartorial terms, as in, for example, *shifu* 時服, contemporary-style costumes or costumes of the present. It explores whether and how costumes fashioned in contemporary styles helped create a sense of realism for the audiences of traditional Chinese theater.

This paper considers both theater costumes as material objects and written descriptions of clothing in play scripts. In his seminal study of fashion, Roland Barthes chose to focus on written or described fashion rather than fashion as actual clothing as worn or photographed. He explained, therefore, that his "study actually addresses neither clothing nor language but the 'translation,' so to speak, of one into the other."⁵ Using a similar method, this paper focuses on a particular discourse on clothing—the dress or costume in contemporary styles. It is not my intention to trace how theater costumes as material artifacts resonated with everyday clothing in style or material. Rather, I would like to outline, in broad strokes, the changing meanings of contemporary-style costumes in Chinese theater, with a focus on the seventeenth through nineteenth centuries, when contemporary-style costumes increasingly became an indicator of real events in the current society.

Contemporary-Style Costumes as Fashion

Conventional wisdom suggests that costumes in traditional Chinese theater are highly stylized and far removed from historical reality. The received saying of "three types of indistinction and six types of distinction" (*san bufen liu youbie* 三不分六有別) summarizes the basic principles in the design and use of costumes in traditional Chinese theater, namely, that though theater costumes reflect different characters' social and ethnic identities, there's little distinction between the costumes of characters from different dynasties, from different geographical areas, or in various seasons. Based on the costume design and usage in modern-day Beijing opera, Alexandra Bonds points out both the "absence of time" in the stage use of opera costumes and the fact that "very little of what appears onstage replicates reality."⁶

Recent studies have presented us with a comprehensive history of theater costumes in premodern China. Song Junhua's study demonstrates that throughout imperial China, theater costumes were modeled after the clothing of everyday life, and constantly incorporated new apparel from society.[7] Surviving evidence indicates that theater performances in the Song-Yuan period (tenth to fourteenth centuries) used costumes based on clothing styles of the current and preceding dynasties, including those from different ethnic cultures. After toppling the Yuan dynasty, the Ming founders initiated a campaign to purge Mongolian elements and restore the "Chinese" sartorial tradition.[8] Over time, the costumes in Ming-dynasty (1368–1644) theater adopted the clothing styles of Ming society, providing the foundation for costumes in various performance genres in the following centuries. This brief review indicates that new additions to the repertoire of theatrical costumes at different points in China's theater history probably reflect current clothing trends in those historical contexts.

When the onstage costumes resembled the styles of clothing seen in everyday life, it is conceivable that the use of those costumes in early Chinese theater imparted a sense of the real to the audiences attending those performances. However, material that might shed light on audience perception of the costumes of that time is sparse.[9] In surviving drama texts and performance records from before the Ming dynasty, I have not found explicit discussions of contemporary-style costumes.[10] In other words, despite their stage use, contemporary-style costumes in early Chinese theater do not appear to have been a prominent subject in theater criticism.

Surviving drama scripts from the Ming dynasty include a large number of terms using the prefix *shi* to indicate seasonal time or fashion within the context of those dramatic stories. Such terms include "contemporary fashion" (*shixing* 時興), "contemporary mode" (*shiyang* 時樣), "contemporary style" (*shikuan* 時款 or *shishi* 時式), "contemporary headgear" (*shijin* 時巾), "contemporary makeup" (*shizhuang* 時妝), and more generally, "contemporary dress" (*shifu* 時服). In *Explaining Simple Graphs and Analyzing Compound Characters* (*Shuowen jiezi* 說文解字), a first-century dictionary, the editor Xu Shen (ca. 30–124) explained, "*Shi* means the four seasons" (時, 四時也).[11] Whereas Xu defined the word based on natural time, another interpretation situates the word within the social milieu of the speaker. When annotating the *shi* entry in *Explaining Simple Graphs*, the Qing-dynasty scholar Duan Yucai (1735–1815) explained that "*shi* refers to this and here" (時是也).[12] In the latter explication, *shi* entails the sense of here and now from the perspective of the person making the utterance. As a result, different phrases referring to contemporary-style costumes signify the time-space compound in which the corresponding character is located.

These terms appear in two types of textual spaces—the characters' dialogues and monologues, and stage instructions. When appearing in dramatic dialogues, current-style clothing usually indicates the present in the story's time. An example can be found in *Yulun pao* 郁輪袍, a sixteenth-century drama that tells the story of the Tang-dynasty poet Wang Wei (692–761), whose musical score "Yulun pao" wins him the patronage of members of the royal family. While traveling on the road, Wang talks about a shirt (*danshan* 單衫) he earlier received as a gift from a lady, saying, "In the current weather of the early fall, this is exactly the dress for the time" (當此新秋天氣，正是時衣).[13] The phrase "dress for the time" (*shiyi* 時衣) refers to the time of the story, specifically, one fall during the Tang dynasty, and not the Ming era in which the play was composed. In other examples from the Ming dynasty, the stories are set in different time periods in Chinese history, and the phrases about current-style clothing share the same meaning, namely, styles that were contemporary and in vogue in the society depicted in the drama. In that sense, different variants of the expression "dress of the present" in Ming drama all convey an effort to capture the fleeting moment the characters perceive as now.

However, the perceived "present" in most of those historical dramas does not readily translate into the real present of the Ming society in which those dramas were produced—at least not through theatrical costuming. During the Ming dynasty, ideas of historical accuracy in the use of costumes had not yet appeared in drama performances. Although historical dramas were set in various time periods, the same set of costumes based on the everyday clothing of the Ming dynasty would be employed in the performances of those dramas. The disparity between Ming-style costumes and the dramatic setting in previous dynasties would certainly not contribute to a sense of realism among the watching audience members.

Since costumes in Ming theater were modeled after clothing in Ming society, would those contemporary-style costumes create a sense of realism in dramas set in the current Ming dynasty? The late-Ming drama *The Pavilion Overlooking the Lake* (*Wanghu ting ji* 望湖亭記), written by Shen Zijin (1583–1665), serves as a salient example for addressing this question. Set in the Ming dynasty, the play tells a story of romance and deception in which Yan Xiu, an ugly-looking and untalented young man, tries to secure a marriage with a noble lady by having his handsome and talented cousin impersonate him in the first half of the wedding ceremony. In this drama, sartorial descriptions frequently appear in stage instructions, either upon the appearance of a character or through monologues or conversations between the characters. The stage instructions at the beginning of one scene read: "Enter *jing* [the painted-face role] wearing fashionable headgear and colored dress" (淨時巾色衣上).[14] The fashionable headgear (*shijin*) mentioned in the costume instruction indicates Yan's family wealth. To illustrate Yan's ignorance despite his family's wealth, the drama has Yan comment on his own looks and clothing in his opening monologue:

> Flowing sleeves of fine Wu silk, a thin-bordered pleated hat of the newest fashion, boots with inch-and-a-half toes on both feet.
> I can dress in the latest mode, but what can I do about my homely face?
> 兩袖吳綾飄大幅,新興摺帽薄沿邊,寸半靴頭雙纏足。
> 雖然打扮能在行,怎奈龐兒忒齷齪。[15]

The phrase "fashionable headgear" in the costume instructions corresponds to the phrase *xinxing* (new fashion) in Yan's monologue. Whereas the former refers to a piece of costume that could, potentially, be used in performances of that drama during the Ming era, the latter refers to a piece of apparel in the story of the drama itself.

The Pavilion Overlooking the Lake was purportedly based on a real event during the Wanli era (ca. 1572–1620), and the drama itself was composed sometime between 1627 and 1644.[16] Since the play represented a perceived recent event, costumes modeled after fashionable apparel in late Ming society could possibly have been employed in actual performances of the drama. Discussing Chinese theater in the sixteenth and seventeenth centuries, Sophie Volpp writes: "As in the West, the figure of the theater helped articulate the sense that the increasing permeability of status hierarchies and the fluidity of emblems of status had made possible a new degree of social imposture. The self-fashioning of actors provided a metaphor for the self-fashioning of individuals."[17] In line with Volpp's analysis of the theater-society correlation, the costumes described in *The Pavilion Overlooking the Lake* would have helped audiences perceive the play as reflecting realistic issues of the time, such as class difference and imposture.

Although current-style costumes could serve as a commentary on contemporaneous social issues, theatrical practitioners in the Ming dynasty did not intentionally use different sartorial styles out of concern for historical accuracy. As scholars have argued, Ming theater furthered the tradition of a highly stylized use of stage costumes, which was followed in different performance genres in the ensuing centuries.[18] Whether appearing in dramas set in the current or previous dynasties, current-style costumes in Ming drama did not serve as markers of periodization: they simply referred to the current season or current fashionable style without associating clothing with a certain dynasty. Even in dramas based on Ming-dynasty events, the expression of current-style costumes was not predicated on a distinction between Ming clothing and the clothing of other dynasties or cultures.

Contemporary-Style Costumes as Political Metaphors

The sartorial changes during the Ming-Qing transition in the mid-seventeenth century fostered a stronger association between clothing and ethnic politics in society. As the Manchus toppled the Ming government ruled by Han Chinese, they forced Han Chinese males to adopt the Manchu hairstyle and clothing as a gesture of submission.[19] Those policies significantly shaped the sartorial landscape of the following centuries. Qing theater largely followed Ming theater in costume design, rendering Ming-dynasty clothing the basis of the theater costumes used in the Qing era. Given the by-then-established tradition of stage performances employing current-style costumes, we must ask whether the conception of current-style costumes was associated with the nascent Manchu-style apparel, and whether current-style costumes were used to represent current social events in the Qing dynasty (1644–1912).

Due to the Qing government's explicit and implicit censorship, only a limited number of dramas based on events during the Ming-Qing transition have survived. The well-known drama *Peach Blossom Fan* (*Taohua shan* 桃花扇, 1699) by Kong Shangren (1648–1718) succinctly demonstrates the shifting meanings of current-style clothing during these transitional years. *Peach Blossom Fan* revolves around the love story of Hou Fangyu and Li Xiangjun while also providing a panoramic view of the dynastic change. In the drama, which is set in the late Ming dynasty, the first reference to current styles of fashion appears in scene 7, "The Rejected Trousseau" ("Quelian" 卻奩). The couple have just been married. When the corrupt official Ruan Dacheng delivers wedding gifts to Li Xiangjun in an effort to befriend Hou Fangyu, Li Xiangjun forcefully rejects the gifts. The scene ends with the following lines:

MALE LEAD: Only Xiangjun has the wisdom to untie the jade pendant;
FEMALE LEAD: My demeanor is free from the styles of the current world.

(生) 只有湘君能解佩,(旦) 風標不學世时粧[20]

Since the scene is set in the year of 1643, the phrase "styles of the current world" (*shishi zhuang*) specifically refers to fashion in southern China during the late Ming era. Here, the sartorial styles are not connected with the ethnic tensions that resulted from the Qing government's clothing regulations.

The second instance involving current-style clothing appears toward the end of the drama in a scene set in 1648. The capital of the Southern Ming dynasty, Nanjing, has been captured by the Qing army. A few remnant subjects of the Ming live as recluses in the mountains near the city. At one of their gatherings, a government runner secretly joins them and tries to recruit them to serve the Manchu regime. The stage instructions describe the runner as wearing "the dress of the time" (*shifu*).[21] The prop list at the end of one of the drama's early Qing print editions includes a red runner's hat corresponding to "the dress of the time" in the main script.[22] Figure 10.1, a Qing-dynasty painting based on that scene, shows the runner supposedly dressed in a Qing-government uniform watching three Ming loyalists, garbed in Ming-style clothes, singing a song at a mountain retreat.[23] Whereas the prior example in the drama uses *shi* to indicate fashion in the late Ming society, here the word *shi* indicates a Qing government uniform, which signifies the political power of the Manchu regime.

Lovebirds Reversal (*Dao yuanyang* 倒鴛鴦), written by Zhu Ying (b. ca. 1621), is another drama set during the years of dynastic change. Here the expression *shifu* is more closely tied to the shifting political regimes. In this play, the hero exchanges clothes with the heroine, so that he can avoid shaving his head as required by the Manchu government and so the heroine can avoid sexual assault. Later, the heroine, cross-dressed as a man, becomes a successful examination candidate in the city of Nanjing during the early Qing. The second half of the drama focuses on life in Nanjing during this time. Describing the clothing of Nanjing residents, one character mentions "white headgear and narrow sleeves in pursuit of the current fashion" (白巾小袖趁時興).[24] It again references fashion as seen in Ming drama while

Figure 10.1: The scene "Remaining Trace" ("Yuyun" 餘韻) in *Peach Blossom Fan*. Source: Kong Shangren 孔尚任, *Qing caihuiben Taohua shan* 清彩繪本桃花扇 (*Peach Blossom Fan with Colored Illustrations from the Qing Dynasty*), illustrated by Jianbai Daoren 堅白 道人, preface dated 1810 (Beijing: Zuojia chubanshe, 2009), 181.

also introducing Manchu ethnic elements, such as narrow sleeves, as fashionable styles.

In addition to civilian dress, the drama also associates the word *shi* with political uniforms. After the cross-dressed heroine succeeds at the imperial examination, she changes her clothing from a Han-style student uniform of the Ming dynasty to a Manchu-style one for Qing-dynasty degree holders. At this point, her foster father congratulates her, saying "I am happy that today you have donned the apparel of the time" (喜今朝身掛時袗).[25] "Apparel of the time" (*shizhen* 時袗) here refers to the Manchu-style uniform mentioned in the drama. In these examples from *Lovebirds Reversal*, *shi* refers to the time of the Qing dynasty. When used to describe clothing, the sartorial terms refer to official uniforms and everyday clothing in the Manchu style of the Qing dynasty.

Although costumes following the styles of different dynasties had already appeared before the Qing dynasty, surviving theatrical works from that period do not explicitly contrast different sartorial styles as representative of different cultures or political regimes. Early Qing dramas such as *Peach Blossom Fan* and *Lovebirds Reversal* are among the first Chinese dramas that explicitly juxtapose clothing of the current dynasty with that of the previous dynasty. Current-style costumes started to indicate the political affairs of the current dynasty.

Despite the use of words such as *shifu* in theatrical scripts, theater performances did not extensively use Manchu-style costumes in the early Qing era. As I have discussed at length elsewhere, the Manchu regime of the Qing dynasty, especially during its early decades, was antitheatrical in the sense that it regarded theater as a depraved Han Chinese practice and prohibited bannermen, especially Manchu people, from visiting theaters or participating in performances onstage; they went even further and prohibited the composition of any theatrical work based on real events that transpired during the Qing dynasty.[26] Those regulations reflected the regime's understanding of theater's relation to social reality: they considered the stage as an inferior space reserved for the unreal, the historical past, and the defunct Ming dynasty. Those antitheatrical sentiments influenced the development of theater costumes in the early Qing: except for occasional court performances, it was widely perceived as taboo to use Manchu-style costumes for popular drama performances.[27] The realistic descriptions of Manchu clothing in early Qing drama scripts did not immediately translate into corresponding stage practices.

However, by the eighteenth century, Manchu-style costumes appeared more frequently in popular drama performances. During the Qianlong emperor's (r. 1735–1796) purge of drama in south China around the late eighteenth century, officials in the Manchu government reported cases in which theater practitioners used Manchu-style costumes for male and female characters, which was considered a violation of the costume regulations. Some of those official reports used the phrase "attire of the current dynasty" (*benchao fuse* 本朝服色) to refer to the Manchu-style clothing of the Qing dynasty, especially political uniforms, which were expected to be guarded against stage appropriation.[28]

Here, we see a nascent connection among theatrical costumes, time, and realism: the stage was regarded as a space to represent the historical and the unreal, not a place to represent real social events of the Qing dynasty; as a result, costumes onstage could only be modeled after Ming-dynasty clothing, reserving Qing-dynasty clothing for the audience located in the realm of spectatorship, a sector of the real society. During much of the Qing dynasty, the Manchu regime explicitly separated theater costumes from the fashion of the time.

The preceding discussion demonstrates that, alongside the establishment of the Qing dynasty and the concomitant enforcement of the Manchu government's sartorial policies in the mid-seventeenth century, current-style costumes, as a literary trope, appeared in drama scripts to signify the Manchu government's control of China. Similar use of Manchu-style costumes apparently appeared in the early Qing period. However, because they considered theater a depraved Han Chinese practice, the Manchu government prohibited the theatrical representation of current affairs and the use of current-style costumes onstage. The fact that current-style costumes onstage remained taboo throughout much of the Qing dynasty nonetheless proves the perceived connection between those costumes and contemporary ethnic politics.

Contemporary-Style Costumes for Dramas on Current Affairs

During the early decades of the Qing dynasty, playwrights largely refrained from composing dramas about the Ming-Qing transition or other events during the Qing dynasty due to the Manchu court's censorship of these kinds of literary works.[29] Toward the late eighteenth century, some playwrights composed dramas based on stories in Qing society to celebrate Qing loyalism. Following their fleeting appearance in dramatic works in the wake of the Manchu conquest in the 1640s to 1650s, Manchu-style clothing and costumes resurfaced in drama scripts. In the following centuries, current-style costumes, as a literary theme and stage props, increasingly appeared in Chinese drama and theater to connect stage and society in different ways.

Possibly due to the theme of Qing loyalism, some playwrights around the turn of the nineteenth century used the Manchu-style clothing of the Qing dynasty to represent historical figures from the time. *The Frost of Guilin* (*Guilin shuang* 桂林霜, 1771), by Jiang Shiquan (1725–1785), tells the story of the Ma family, who died as martyrs for the Qing government during the Wu Sangui (1612–1678) rebellion in the late seventeenth century. It dresses some characters who are loyal to the government in the official uniforms of the Qing dynasty (*guochao guanfu* 國朝官服).[30]

If the confrontation between Manchus and Han Chinese during the dynastic change gradually became historical memory, ongoing rebellions by ethnic groups in the Qing empire still posed serious challenges to Manchu rule. During the early nineteenth century, several theatrical works emerged featuring the Qing government's pacification of rebellions, mostly in south and southwest China.[31] The drama *A Pavilion of Frost* (*Yiting shuang* 一亭霜) represents the Qing government's crackdown on the Miao rebellion (1795–1806) in southwest China. In the drama, after quelling the rebellion, the Qing government commends and promotes a group of Qing officials who fought valiantly during the military campaign. One official explicitly sings about the new official uniform he receives, using phrases such as "red tassels on the hat, crystal finial gleaming like water, and a flying bear on the embroidered badge" (簇簇紅纓, 晶球注水, 繡補飛熊).[32] As salient elements of the Qing uniform, the hat with a crystal top and the bear badge correspond to the fifth-rank position the character now enjoys. Those current-style costumes contribute to a strong sense of historical authenticity regarding the characters and their remarkable deeds. However, most of these works were composed as literature for reading instead of stage performance.

Around the mid-nineteenth century, the use of Manchu clothing onstage gradually ceased to be taboo. As a result, Manchu-style costumes, including some based on Qing government uniforms, were directly used in drama performances. One particular case regarding the drama *The Temple of the Red Gate* (*Hongmen si* 紅門寺), which features a Qing-dynasty official called Yu Chenglong (1617–1684), illustrates the shift in the Manchu government's regulations on stage costumes. Performances of the drama were banned during the Qianlong era (1780s) due to its use of "attire of the current dynasty." In 1855, however, the Xianfeng emperor (r. 1850–1861) explicitly instructed that, in court performances, the character Yu Chenglong should wear the Manchu-style official uniform previously banned.[33] The Xianfeng emperor's lifting of the ban on Manchu-style costumes indicates that the stage was no longer considered a profane space from which sacred Manchu cultural elements must be kept away. Some theatrical works composed and performed during the early decades of the Qing dynasty might have already used Manchu-style costumes, but it was not until the mid-nineteenth century that such usage started to be encouraged by the Manchu court.

The late nineteenth and early twentieth centuries saw the appearance of a variety of new terms that connected clothing and theater in more complicated ways, including new dramas using ancient-style costumes (*guzhuang xinxi* 古裝新戲) and dramas using Manchu-style costumes (*qizhuang xi* 旗裝戲).³⁴ But it wasn't until the advent of a new theater movement which utilized contemporary-style costumes (*shizhuang xinxi* 時裝新戲) that both the ideas of the present and the real were tied to clothing. In this movement of theatrical experimentation, *shizhuang* refers to costumes based on the current styles of clothing, and *xinxi* indicates that the dramas were composed based on current social issues, and not rehashed from old stories in China's theatrical tradition.³⁵

The trend of dramatizing the political events of late Qing society had already started around the 1840s.³⁶ Some of these dramas featured events in the Qing and Republican societies and accordingly used costumes that reflected the shifting sartorial styles in China. One of the earliest plays in this category is *Lament of an Opium Addict* (*Yangui tan* 煙鬼嘆), which first appeared in 1845, only a few years after the First Opium War (1839–1842).³⁷ During the following decades, at least a dozen versions of the play in Han Chinese as well as Manchu languages were performed in different parts of China.³⁸ The short play features the remorseful account of an opium addict's ghost, who tries to educate the general public about the harms of opium addiction, which had started to plague Chinese society around the time of the drama's circulation. It is generally considered one of the earliest dramas addressing a current social issue and using costumes in contemporary styles.³⁹ Other dramas in this movement were based on events in foreign countries and used costumes in foreign styles.⁴⁰ Adamant as he was against the pursuit of realism in Beijing opera, Qi Rushan, at the bidding of his collaborator, the renowned female impersonator Mei Lanfang (1894–1961), "helped write five of the most successful contemporary-costume plays of the decade" that were performed by Mei between 1913 and 1918.⁴¹

Figure 10.2 shows Mei Lanfang in the role of Lin Renfen in *A Strand of Hemp*, a drama set in early twentieth-century China and adapted by Qi Rushan based on a contemporary work of fiction. The story features a young lady who suffers from an arranged marriage and eventually commits suicide.⁴² It was the first play in which Mei wore current-style costumes. The photo shows Mei dressed in the realistic style, not adopting a typical pose of the Beijing opera, but instead appearing as a lady in real life. These theatrical productions indicate that concerns about social reality had simultaneously become a defining motive for and a feature of drama composition and costume design.

In sum, then, in the mid-seventeenth century, playwrights began experimenting with the nascent trend of using Manchu clothing as

Figure 10.2: Mei Lanfang costumed as the female protagonist of *A Strand of Hemp* (*Yilü ma* 一縷麻). Source: Zi Yu 子與, ed., *Jingju lao zhaopian* 京劇老照片 (*Historical Photos of Beijing Opera*) (Beijing: Xueyuan chubanshe, 2014), 16.

current-style costumes in theatrical scripts. However, the literary and stage appropriation of Manchu-style costumes was forestalled by the Manchu government's regulations on clothing and costumes. Around the eighteenth and nineteenth centuries, theatrical practitioners resumed their attempts to utilize Manchu clothing in drama and theater. This, in turn, led to the full-scale embrace of dramatizing current affairs with contemporary-style costumes at the turn of the twentieth century. By that time, theatrical practitioners openly employed contemporary-style costumes with the clear purpose of addressing contemporary social problems. Those works resurrected the aborted tradition of dramatizing current affairs and upended the Manchu government's initial animosity toward the theatrical appropriation of current-style clothing. The realistic use of everyday clothing continued throughout the recurrent theater reforms of the Republican (1912–1949) and early PRC decades, leading to the "true to life" approach to stagecraft and costume design in the "revolutionary Peking opera" during the Cultural Revolution (1966–1976).[43]

Conclusion

As this paper demonstrates, in China's theater history, stage costumes evolved based on changing sartorial styles in society. Contemporary-style costumes as a literary theme frequently appeared in Ming-dynasty drama, usually referring to fashion in the different historical contexts of those dramatic works. In plays set in the Ming dynasty, current-style costumes for contemporary characters would serve as references to current social issues, such as status imposture. In spite of this, costumes in Ming drama did not serve as markers of dynastic periodization, nor were costumes used to distinguish between different political entities or ethnic groups. It was during the Qing dynasty that the concept of contemporary-style costumes was associated with Manchu ethnic clothing and Manchu political rule. During the nineteenth and early twentieth centuries, especially through the new theater's use of contemporary-style costumes, theater practitioners consciously used contemporary-style costumes to address pressing social issues of the time.

The specific lens of contemporary-style costumes reveals that the seventeenth century was an important period for the development of realism in the history of Chinese theater. Sophie Volpp's examination of the relationship between the theatrical and the social shows a significant change in the understanding of theatricality before and after the Ming-

Qing transition. She writes: "The actor's plasticity of identity earlier provided a metaphor for social imposture. . . . After the fall of the Ming, however, the actor's privileged understanding of the illusory nature of the world of forms also came to be viewed as exemplary, a means of coming to terms with dynastic transition, as we see in Kong's *Taohua shan*."[44] In line with Volpp's analysis, contemporary-style costumes in Ming and Qing theater also signified different connections between stage and society: in Ming theater, current-style costumes indicated fashion embedded in those theatrical stories, whereas in early Qing theater, current-style costumes reminded the audience of the poignant political and ethnic conflicts during the dynastic change.

Materials discussed in this paper suggest the strong role political control played in shaping ideas about theatricality and realism, especially during the seventeenth century. By prohibiting the theatrical representation of Qing-dynasty events and the use of Manchu-style costumes during the seventeen and eighteenth centuries, the Manchu government strengthened the understanding that theater could obscure the boundaries between the real and the unreal, and that theater costumes in particular frequently served as realistic signifiers of the current society. With authors, performers, and the censoring state all participating in drama composition and production, the ethnic tensions in seventeenth-century China engendered a heightened sense of the ties between theater and reality, particularly through theatrical costuming.

The case of Chinese theater costumes also resonates with developments in world theater history. Although it is commonly held that realistic theater as an artistic movement appeared in nineteenth-century Europe first and foremost through staging and costuming, pursuit of the realistic use of theater costumes started much earlier. In her seminal work examining the connections between clothing in art and clothing in life through 2,500 years of Western history, Anne Hollander points out that the neoclassic ideals in Western theater introduced the principle of historical accuracy for stage costume for the first time around the seventeenth century.[45] Diana de Marly's study shows in more detail that Roman attire dominated the theater stage of Renaissance Europe, and that costumes in contemporary styles gradually appeared onstage in the seventeenth and eighteenth centuries.[46] It is perhaps coincidental that strong connections between theater costumes and social reality started to emerge during the seventeenth century in both the Chinese and European contexts. The lens of theatrical costuming can thus help reveal shared features and trajectories among different theatrical traditions despite their apparent disparity. The phenomena discussed in this paper warrant a reconsideration of realism in theater, especially its emergence in various historical contexts worldwide.

Notes

1. Cited from Wilt Idema, "Traditional Dramatic Literature," in *The Columbia History of Chinese Literature*, ed. Victor H. Mair (New York: Columbia University Press, 2010), 845. Qi's reservation about realistic theater in China resonates with T. S. Eliot's critique of realism in drama as the "desert of absolute likeness to reality." For a quotation and discussion of Eliot, see Jovan Hristić, "The Problem of Realism in Modern Drama," *New Literary History* 8, no. 2 (Winter 1977): 315.

2. Joshua Goldstein, *Drama Kings: Players and Publics in the Re-creation of Peking Opera, 1870–1937* (Berkeley: University of California Press, 2007), chapter 4.

3. Jean Benedetti, *The Art of the Actor: The Essential History of Acting from Classical Times to the Present Day* (New York: Routledge, 2007), 102.

4. For an introduction to the shifting sartorial styles in late imperial and modern China, see Antonia Finnane, *Changing Clothes in China: Fashion, History, Nation* (New York: Columbia University Press, 2008), especially chapter 2.

5. Roland Barthes, *The Fashion System*, trans. Matthew Ward and Richard Howard (Berkeley: University of California Press, 1983), x.

6. Alexandra B. Bonds, *Beijing Opera Costumes: The Visual Communication of Character and Culture* (Honolulu: University of Hawaii Press, 2008), 265.

7. Song Junhua 宋俊華, *A Study of Costumes in Traditional Chinese Theater* (中國古代戲劇服飾研究 *Zhongguo gudai xiju fushi yanjiu*) (Guangzhou: Guangdong gaodeng jiaoyu chubanshe, 2011).

8. For a discussion of this movement, see Zhang Jia 張佳, "Restoring Chinese Costume: The Reform of the Clothing System during the Reign of Hongwu" (重整冠裳: 洪武時期的服飾改革 "Chongzheng guanshang: Hongwu shiqi de fushi gaige"), *Zhongguo wenhua yanjiusuo xuebao* 58 (2014): 116–17.

9. One such example is the widely discussed song-suite "Country Cousin Knows Nothing about the Stage" (莊家不識勾欄 "Zhuangjia bushi goulan," ca. mid-thirteenth century), which depicts a country bumpkin's theater-going experience. In it, the costumes and makeup of a clown character only surprise him as being unnatural and unrealistic. For a translation and discussion of the song-suite, see Stephen H. West and Wilt L. Idema, ed. and trans., *Monks, Bandits, Lovers, and Immortals: Eleven Early Chinese Plays* (Indianapolis, IN: Hackett Publishing Company, 2010), xii–xv.

10. Most of the drama scripts and theater-related documents from the Yuan dynasty have been lost. My judgment here is based on the surviving materials.

11. See Xu Shen 許慎, *Notes on Explaining Simple Graphs and Analyzing Compound Characters* (說文解字注 *Shuowen jiezi zhu*), ed. Duan Yucai 段玉裁 (Shanghai: Shanghai guji chubanshe, 1988), 302.

12. Xu Shen, *Notes on Explaining Simple Graphs*, 302. Duan designated the interpretation of "this and here" as the "original meaning" (本義 *benyi*) of the word.

13. Zhang Qi 張琦, *Yulun pao* (郁輪袍), in *Collectanea of Ancient Editions of Chinese Drama* (古本戲曲叢刊 *Guben xiqu congkan*), series 2 (Beijing: Shangwu yinshuguan, 1955), *juan* b, 21b.

14. Shen Zijin 沈自晉, *The Pavilion Overlooking the Lake* (望湖亭記 *Wanghu ting ji*), in *Collectanea of Ancient Editions*, series 2, *juan* a, 7b.

15. Shen Zijin, *The Pavilion Overlooking the Lake*, *juan* a, 8a.

16. For a brief introduction to the drama, see Guo Yingde 郭英德, *Comprehensive Narratives of Ming-Qing Chuanqi Dramas* (明清傳奇綜錄 *Ming Qing chuanqi zonglu*) (Shijiazhuang: Hebei jiaoyu chubanshe, 1997), 381. Guo explains that the drama was based on a work of fiction featuring the real event.

17. Sophie Volpp, *Worldly Stage: Theatricality in Seventeenth-Century China* (Cambridge, MA: Harvard University Asia Center, 2011), 19.

18. For one discussion, see Song Junhua, *A Study of Costumes*, 164.

19. For an English introduction to the sartorial disputes during the Qing dynasty, see Weikun Cheng, "Politics of the Queue: Agitation and Resistance in the Beginning and End of Qing China," in *Hair: Its Power and Meaning in Asian Cultures*, ed. Alf Hiltebeitel and Barbara D. Miller (Albany: State University of New York Press, 1998), 123–42.

20. Kong Shangren 孔尚任, *Peach Blossom Fan* (桃花扇 *Taohua shan*), Kangxi print edition, in *Collectanea of Ancient Editions of Chinese Drama*, series 5 (Shanghai: Shanghai guji chubanshe, 1986), *juan* a, 55a.

21. Kong Shangren, *Peach Blossom Fan*, *juan* b, 133a.

22. Kong Shangren, *Peach Blossom Fan*, *juan* b, 141a.

23. It must be pointed out that the clothes depicted in the illustration are not strictly modeled after stage costumes, nor can they be treated as authentic records of actual clothing worn during the dynastic change.

24. Zhu Ying 朱英, *Lovebirds Reversal* (倒鴛鴦傳奇 *Dao yuanyang chuanqi*), preface dated 1650, in *Collectanea of Ancient Editions of Chinese Drama*, series 3 (Shanghai: Wenxue guji kanxingshe, 1957), *juan* b, 2b.

25. Zhu Ying, *Lovebirds Reversal*, *juan* b, 19b.

26. See Guojun Wang, *Staging Personhood: Costuming in Early Qing Drama* (New York: Columbia University Press, 2020), chapter 1.

27. In occasional court performances, Manchu-style costumes were probably employed, but they were not referred to as *shifu*. See Wang, *Staging Personhood*, chapter 1.

28. For a discussion of this purge of theater, including the ban on Manchu-style costumes, see Ding Shumei 丁淑梅, *A Chronicle History of the Censorship and Destruction of Ancient Chinese Drama* (中國古代禁毀戲劇編年史 *Zhongguo gudai jinhui xiju biannian shi*) (Chongqing: Chongqing daxue chubanshe, 2014), 413–19.

29. Scholars have noticed a hiatus in the composition of dramas on current affairs during the eighteenth and early nineteenth centuries. See Li Jiangjie 李江傑, *A Study of Dramas on Current Affairs in the Ming and Qing Dynasties* (明清時事劇研究 *Ming Qing shishiju yanjiu*) (Jinan: Qilu shushe, 2014), 31–34.

30. Jiang Shiquan 蔣士銓, *The Frost of Guilin* (桂林霜 *Guilin shuang*), in *Collection of Dramas by Jiang Shiquan* (蔣士銓戲曲集 *Jiang Shiquan xiqu ji*), ed. Zhou Miaozhong 周妙中 (Beijing: Zhonghua shuju, 1993), scene 1.

31. For a list of those plays, see Li Jiangjie, *A Study of Dramas on Current Affairs*, 33.

32. Liu Yongan 劉永安, *A Pavilion of Frost* (一亭霜 *Yiting shuang*), manuscript edition, in *Collectanea of Ancient Editions of Chinese Drama*, series 8 (Beijing: Guojia tushuguan chubanshe, 2019), end of scene 24 "Guanbang" 觀榜 (no pagination).

33. See discussion in Zhu Jiajin 朱家溍 and Ding Ruqin 丁汝芹, *An Examination of the Beginning and the End of Drama Performance in the Inner Court of the Qing Dynasty* (清代內廷演劇始末考 *Qingdai neiting yanju shimo kao*) (Beijing: Zhongguo shudian, 2007), 267.

34. For a general discussion of dramas using Manchu-style costumes, see Li Desheng 李德生, *An Anecdotal History of Manchu-Costume Dramas* (梨花一支春帶雨—說不盡的旗裝戲 *Lihua yizhi chundaiyu—shuobujin de qizhuangxi*) (Beijing: Renmin ribao chubanshe, 2012).

35. The term "current-style clothing" (*shizhuang* 時裝) had already appeared in written records of the Qing dynasty. For one example, see He Bang'e 和邦額 (b. 1736), *Random Notes from Night-time Chat* (夜譚隨錄 *Yetan suilu*), ed. Wang Yigong 王一工 and Fang Zhengyao 方正耀 (Shanghai: Shanghai guji chubanshe, 1988), *juan* 10, entry "Wu Zhe" 吳哲, 290. By the late Qing and early Republic eras, *shizhuang* had become a term with two meanings: first, fashion, and second, real clothing of the contemporary period.

36. Li Jiangjie, *A Study of Dramas on Current Affairs*, 34–40.

37. For a thorough study of the group of plays, see You Fukai 游富凱, "The Influence of Popular Tunes and Role Performance on the Script Form—A Case Study of the New Play *Yan Gui Tan* in the Late Qing Dynasty" (試論俗曲(時調)與行當表演對文本流變的影響—以晚清新編戲《煙鬼嘆》為例 "Shilun suqu shidiao yu hangdang biaoyan dui wenben liubian de yingxiang—yi wan Qing xinbian xi *Yangui tan* weili"), *Xiju xuekan* 25 (2017): 79–104.

38. For a study of the bilingual Manchu-Chinese edition of the play, see Zhao Zhan 趙展, "Preliminary Discussions on the Manchu-Han Bilingual Drama *Yangui tan*" (滿漢合璧劇本煙嘆芻議 "Man Han hebi juben *Yangui tan* chuyi"), *Manyu yanjiu* 2 (2000): 99–105.

39. For one example, editors of the *Annals of Traditional Chinese Theater* regarded the drama as a contemporary-costume play (*shizhuang xi* 時裝戲) in Beijing opera. See *Annals of Traditional Chinese Theater: Tianjin* (中國戲曲志天津卷 *Zhongguo xiqu zhi Tianjin juan*) (Beijing: Wenhua yishu chubanshe, 1990), 125.

40. For a study of late-Qing dramas featuring foreign themes or using foreign-style costumes, see Zuo Pengjun 左鵬軍, *A Study of Chuanqi and Zaju Dramas in Modern China* (近代傳奇雜劇研究 *Jindai chuanqi zaju yanjiu*) (Guangzhou: Guangdong gaodeng jiaoyu chubanshe, 2011), chapters 4 and 8.

41. For a discussion of Qi's participation in composing contemporary-costume plays, see Goldstein, *Drama Kings*, 119.

42. For a discussion of the tragic female characters in Beijing opera during the 1910s and 1920s, including those performed by Mei Lanfang, see Catherine V. Yeh, "National Pastime as Political Reform: Staging Peking Opera's New Tragic Heroines," in *Testing the Margins of Leisure: Case Studies on China, Japan, and Indonesia*, ed. R. G. Wagner et al. (Heidelberg, DE: Heidelberg University Publishing, 2019), 43–85.

43. See Colin Mackerras, "Chinese Opera After the Cultural Revolution (1970–1972)," *China Quarterly* 55 (1973): 478–510. For a study of the relationship between theater and political changes in modern China, see Hsiao-t'i Li, *Opera, Society, and Politics in Modern China* (Cambridge, MA: Harvard University Asia Center, 2019).

44. Volpp, *Worldly Stage*, 16.

45. Anne Hollander, *Seeing Through Clothes* (Berkeley: University of California Press, 1993), 276.

46. Diana de Marly, *Costume on the Stage 1600–1940* (London: B. T. Batsford, 1982), chapters 1 and 3.

PART IV | Evolving Realisms

11 | Colonial Temporality, Diasporic Displacement, and Korean Realism in Yun Baek-nam's *Destiny*

MISEONG WOO

The colonial legacy and cultural import of the Japanese understanding of nineteenth-century European realism as a new mode of representation mediated the earliest formation of Korean realism. Unlike in Japan, where traditional theater forms coexisted with newly imported European drama, the transition from the traditional performance arts to the new modern theater in Korea did not occur gradually, because Japanese colonization in 1910 forced Korean society to abruptly drop all Korean traditions, including those related to language and the theatrical arts. Prior to the Korean nationalist movement of March 1, 1919, Korean theater practitioners had eagerly tried to implant the theater imported from Japan as a way of bringing Western enlightenment to colonial Korea. Since the grassroots uprising of the March First Movement, however, Korean theater practitioners and audiences had begun to share the idea of Korea as a separate nation, and the early stage of Korean realism drama manifested a newly awakened sense of national identity and cultural subjectivity. Any critical depiction of colonial social reality and political exploitation had to be muted and veiled by the topics of the autonomy of female protagonists and the self-liberation of male characters. My discussion in this chapter focuses on the Korean theater scene of the 1910s in order to clarify the significance of the transitional period, highlighting *Destiny* (*Unmyung*, 1920) as the first play that ushered Japanese theater from the replica period of *shinpaguk* into the decade of Korean-style realism drama in the 1920s.

Realism and Premodern Korean Theater

Theatrical realism has been defined in terms of capturing contemporary life and social issues and staging temporality through theatrical forms. Scholarly discussions of realism, however, have never reached a broad scope beyond a Western context, and have not explicitly considered intercultural differences to assess how different cultures and societies conceptualize time and space, the two key components of understanding a surrounding temporality. In Asian philosophical frameworks, time and temporality occupy only a derivative status; thus, from a phenomenal point of view, time and space are illusions.[1] Even Aristotle emphasized the subjective and speculative nature of time and temporality, writing, "time only seems to exist when perceived by a soul, or at least, when it is perceived by a soul capable of noting motion or change."[2] The different myths, religions, and historical contexts of Asian cultures affected how its people and arts conceptualized time and space.

In premodern East Asian traditions, art's purpose was to cultivate morality, and its primary value highlighted an understanding of the timeless metaphysical structures and moral principles that operate the world.[3] Space and time in visual arts were approached as both concepts and practices, the simultaneous realm of spirituality and materiality, not as merely physical places or present conditions. East Asian paintings that fascinated European artists at the end of the nineteenth century depicted flat space and simple, natural landscapes accompanied at times by calligraphy, inviting the active interpretation of viewers to complete the space and time. In that sense, arts in East Asian philosophies tended to avoid direct representation of reality, asking spectators to look beyond current lived experience, and suggesting that staged temporality may have different meanings and layers.

Theater as a form of performing art also aimed at presenting aesthetics and ethics as philosophical practices. In traditional theater forms in Korea, such as *talchum* (masked dance)[4] and *pansori* (staging voice; a single-person opera accompanied by a sole drummer),[5] presenting stories emphasizing moral sensibilities occupied a principal place; theatrical conventions therefore required a heightened awareness of the audience's dynamic association of current conditions with the metaphoric or symbolic realm of the staged works. Korean masked-dance dramas lack formal structure in an Aristotelian sense; thus, there is often no main plot running from the beginning to the end of the play, and most available scripts consist of a series of episodes or acts that can be disjoined, rearranged, and even deleted. The patrons of *pansori* are quite familiar with the stories unfolding in the performance, because *pansori* delivers several repertories based on orally transmitted Korean fables that many Korean adults already know, such as *The Tale of Chunhyang* and *The Song of the Underwater Palace*.[6] *Talchum* attracted spectators with the genre's dynamic, improvised movement, and the text of this masked-dance performance was transmitted orally, as in all forms of Korean traditional drama. The popular repertoires of traditional Korean theater were well known to the public, and the focus of the entertainment therefore was not the storytelling itself, but how well the performers sang and delivered narrative passages with convincing emotions and gusto. Traditional Korean theater delivered sharp social commentaries critiquing the shallow and hypocritical ruling class, often told from the perspective of social minorities allowing the expression of a festive revolutionary spirit. Despite the rigid social hierarchy and the unfair, harsh reality of life for the working classes and serfs during the Joseon dynasty (1392–1897), theater offered a more dynamic, democratic, and improvisational entertainment to Koreans than any of the other genres of art, including music, dance, paintings, or literature. The audience's level of satisfaction and their expectations for traditional Korean theater genres depended on affective experience, release of collective social anxiety, and acquiring a harmonious awareness of temporality.

Revisioning Colonial Korean Theater

When Korea was going through national turmoil at the turn of the nineteenth century, *changguk* (a drama sung by multiple cast members) emerged as a transitional modern popular genre for the public, a form that again gave more emphasis to song and dance than to storytelling. Subsequently, a new trend of theater called *shinpa* (new wave) gradually became popular in Seoul.[7] By 1910, when Japan formally annexed Korea through the Japan-Korea Treaty, more than 170,000 Japanese civilians had poured into Korea, with the largest number residing in Seoul.[8] Soon Japanese entrepreneurs and settlers had opened theaters, mostly in the Japanese commercial districts in Seoul, and particularly on the streets of Myongdong and Chungmuro, to bring more itinerant theater troupes to Korea.[9] According to one account, by 1910 at least five theaters in Seoul were owned by Japanese, and in these theaters Japanese *shinpaguk* (new wave drama), consisting of military plays, detective drama, and domestic tragedy, was performed, probably by third-rate traveling companies.[10]

Most of the Korean *shinpaguk* productions presented storytelling-focused drama influenced by Western theater, and attending *shinpaguk* performances was therefore considered fashionable. Japanese settlers made up the majority of the audience at these performances, but some Korean viewers were also drawn to this new trend. Approximately twenty *shinpaguk* groups were formed, mostly in Seoul,[11] but some Korean intellectuals who had studied in Japan and had firsthand experience of Japanese *shinpa* theater denounced the commercially motivated poor quality of *shinpaguk* productions in Korea. One of these few privileged intellectuals was Yun Baek-nam (1888–1954), who launched a theater group, Literary Star (Munsusong), in Seoul. Yun had seen performances in Japan between 1905 and 1910, including Japanese *shinpa* drama. He wanted to use theater to educate the Korean public and to improve their awareness, and he and Literary Star mounted productions focusing on issues relevant to contemporary Korean society. Just before Yun launched his theater company, some Korean *shinpa* theater companies were trying several different styles of presenting popular stories. Military plays, mostly stories of patriotic Japanese soldiers and Korean freedom fighters who had defeated the Russian and Chinese armies, initially became popular in the early 1910s, reflecting the unstable political situation surrounding the Korean peninsula.

When the Japanese military began to detect veiled political meanings in these military dramas, however, *shinpaguk* companies shifted play selection from military plays to domestic tragicomedies. The March First Movement in 1919, when Korean leaders announced their Declaration of Independence and students and civilians staged street demonstrations across the country, became another pivotal point in the Japanese military oppression of Korean political resistance. The Japanese military used force to stop any Korean political uprising, using interrogation, imprisonment, torture, and execution; cultural surveillance became harsher than ever. To avoid accusations and punishment from the Japanese military, *shinpa* theater companies staged domestic tragicomedies, which became the most popular genre among *shinpaguk* productions.[12] Focusing mostly on dramatic relationships between men and women, the domestic tragicomedies could bring an audience to tears; they were the safest political topic, avoiding censorship trouble for theater companies, and the audience could easily identify with the characters.

To compensate for the lack of spectacle in domestic tragedies, *shinpa* adopted an exaggerated acting style, a common trademark of this genre of extremely dramatic stories. These productions had the bare minimum scenic background, often with two-dimensional props and poor-quality makeup and costuming, mostly because budgets were low and understanding of clear aesthetic directions was lacking.[13] After Korean independence in 1945, the definition of *shinpa* eventually drifted away from its original meaning of "new wave," and in Korean popular culture it now indicates excessive emotional expression, along the lines of the traditional Western concept of "melodrama." Lee Young-mee, a South Korean popular-culture historian, correctly perceives that *shinpa* is still part of Korean popular culture today, in films, TV dramas, songs, novels, and comic books; the term itself has come to signify a mode of expression. She defines the Korean notion of *shinpa* as an aesthetic trait centering on a feeling of sorrow, when an individual's basic desires have to be suppressed in a repressive environment, and one therefore has to succumb to a powerful world.[14] Although the artistic value of these tear-jerking *shinpaguk* has been underestimated in the past, Korean studies scholars since the 1990s have reevaluated the social and cultural function of *shinpa* as a major part of popular culture. The predictable domestic tragicomedies or ill-fated sentimental romance stories staged or screened in theaters during the colonial period of Korea provided a means of coping with the harsh reality of the oppressive colonial conditions. As a part of popular culture, theater provided a site of compassion and catharsis, healing the collective sadness and grief over losing the country, and channeling the oppressed anxiety of the audience into the perseverance needed to go on with their everyday lives.

Highlighting the female protagonist's sense of loss and grief, these domestic tragicomedies appealed to Korean audiences through touching their raw feelings of sorrow and giving people a chance to open up their emotions. The Korean theater scholar Oh-kon Cho insightfully observes that the tears the audience shed for characters' misfortunes in domestic tragicomedies were actually shed for their ill-fated nation. The plights of characters, often victims of an oppressor who demanded unconditional submission and absolute loyalty, seemed to personify the national situation to Korean audience members—the ruthless husband symbolized the atrocious Japanese military, while the downtrodden yet golden-hearted wife embodied the suffering Koreans.[15] The audiences identified with the heroine enduring misfortune, and related her woes to the grievous state of their country.

The problem of arranged marriage was one topic that Yun's theater company frequently focused on during the 1910s and 1920s. *Fidelity* (*Bulyeogwi*, 1912) was a domestic tragedy about a young girl engaged to an army captain who is sent to war in Germany; *Youth* (*Cheongchun*, 1914) was a sentimental domestic drama about family conflict caused by an arranged marriage. Yun himself had to go through an arranged marriage: he married a sixteen-year-old girl when he was fifteen years old. His attempt to study in Japan the following year was prompted by his desire to escape from his unwanted early marriage. Many other Korean intellectuals who crossed borders to Japan to study were similarly escaping arranged marriages. Such marriages often resulted in abandonment, infidelity, and affairs; parents who wanted to prevent these problems and ensure that their sons did not engage in sexually promiscuous lifestyles by getting involved with prostitutes, forced their sons to consummate their marriages before they left for foreign countries for study. Many Korean intellectuals and social reformers of the time perceived arranged marriages as the epitome of an unreasonable tradition, a pressing problem that needed to be addressed.

Previous studies about *Destiny* (*Unmyung*, 1920) have focused on whether this work can be viewed as a modern realist play or if it should be considered as a typical premodern *shinpa* work. Min-young Yoo and Seung-guk Yang, two Korean theater scholars, evaluate *Destiny* as the earliest modern Korean drama that highlights the problems of arranged marriages—so-called "photo marriages"—as a social issue; they find that the heroine, Mary Park, expresses her will to pioneer her own destiny after having a moral conflict regarding the confines of her arranged marriage.[16] On the other hand, scholars Bang-ok Kim and Soo-jin Woo contend that, despite the timely theme of photo marriages, the binary opposition between good and evil characters and the melodramatic structure are not characteristic of modern realism, and thus the drama does not reach the level of modernity.[17] Although Soo-jin Woo offers a meaningful analysis in that she reads Hawaii as a geopolitical space of coloniality, her discussion, like those of other scholars, revolves around the rigid notion of modern drama, excluding the affective function of theater as a newly emerging popular culture during the colonial period.

Destiny, a Transitional Play by Yun Baek-nam

Aspiring to plant culture in the colonial Joseon period, Yun led the theater movement by creating a modern theater company in the 1910s, and he made the first Joseon film in the 1920s, *The Vow Made Below the Moon* (*Weolhaui mangseo*, 1923). He also wrote popular novels and newspaper articles and made radio broadcasts. Yun's cultural activities parallel the popular cultural history of colonial Joseon in the early days. Ironically, however, for the very reason that Yun's activities were diverse and entailed a wide range of practices, his artistic endeavors have been underestimated. His passionate efforts to speed up the intellectual awakening and social development of Korea led him toward his pioneering cultural activities. In the 1920s, he developed social dramas and the folk drama movement, and in the 1930s he opened a new field of popular art as a storytelling artist through the *Yadam* (popular storytelling) movement. As Baek Doo-san, the editor of an anthology of Yun's dramatic works, points out, as with most theater productions of the 1910s and 1920s, many of Yun's activities were not fully completed or documented, but he pioneered theater, film, theater criticism, and popular storytelling based on the Korean context, providing a foundation for the next generation. Ahead of his time, he prioritized popular-culture content as a significant part of the lived experience of the Korean public, and many of his performative works catered to contemporary Korean audiences.

Yun's *Destiny* portrays a triangular love affair involving a well-educated Korean picture bride in Hawaii, Mary; her illiterate husband, Gil-sam; and her former lover, Su-ok. The play's events take place in Gil-sam's house and at the public cemetery on a summer evening in Honolulu, Hawaii. Through representing the Korean diasporic experience in a foreign land, the play boldly attempts to depart from the tear-jerking *shinpaguk*, although this topic was born out of that genre's domestic tragedies and the theme of the problems of arranged marriages—popular topics of the early 1920s. Yun referred to the play as "a social drama in one act and two scenes,"[18] clearly emphasizing the social concerns he presented in the play. Yun clarified that the creative motivation for this work was "to reveal the harmful effects of photo marriages that were popular between Korean migrants in Hawaii and people in their home country, and to depict the tragic process that they cause."[19] The play was clearly intended to generate public discussion by dramatizing the social issues of a specific era. Compared to Yun's previous plays dealing with the problems of arranged marriages, *Destiny* manifests a liberal attitude toward love, and the narrative ends with the protagonists overcoming obstacles—albeit reluctantly—that prevent their reunion.

The first Korean diasporic experiences in the Western world were mediated by Christian missionaries from the United States. Presbyterian and Methodist missionaries such as Horace Allen and George Herbert Jones converted many Koreans to Christianity, and also provided avenues for Koreans to immigrate to North America. In fact, almost half of the first group of Korean immigrants to the US were Christians who Presbyterian missionary Allen recruited from Korean churches.[20] Some Korean people had high expectations about the possibilities for a new life in the US after Joseon opened up the nation's doors to foreign countries in the late nineteenth century. In 1882, the United States (represented by Commodore Robert W. Shufeldt of the US Navy) and Korea negotiated and approved the Treaty of Peace, Amity, Commerce and Navigation in response to the possibility of foreign attack. In international trade with Joseon, the US maintained most-favored-nation status until Japan annexed Joseon in 1910.[21]

In fact, Mary's father in *Destiny* is a Christian pastor who worships Western values and culture and considers the American people to be honorable, knowledgeable, and generous. Initially Mary tried to object to her father's idea of sending her off to Hawaii as a picture bride; soon, however, Mary herself is also tempted by the idea of experiencing a new life in the "land of opportunity." Although Mary is a "new woman" who graduated from Ewha-dang (the origin of today's Ewha Womans University, the most prestigious women's educational institution in Korea), when she learns of her father's unilateral decision about her marriage and visa application, she lacks the courage to confess to her father her romantic relationship with Su-ok, and her father almost coercively takes her to board the ship to Hawaii.

However, the reality Mary faces in Hawaii is that her husband, who was said to be wealthy and educated, turns out to be an unsuccessful shoe repairman who is a gambler, a drunk, and ten years older than he claimed. The playwright Yun successfully maintains balance in his theatrical representation of Hawaii, introducing the faraway region as a new land of opportunity, but at the same time expressing disillusionment about the land of freedom. In addition to portraying the harsh realities of picture-based marriages, the play shows extreme poverty as a major issue. The first scene shows a room in Mary's husband Gil-sam Yang's house in a Hawaiian slum where poor immigrant workers live. There is a shabby wooden bed, a table with peeling paint and three small fishing chairs, a few simple cooking utensils, and a shoe-repair box and oil barrel in the left corner of the stage. Yun writes in the stage description, "all of this represents poverty."[22] This extreme poverty is associated with a primal realm of humanity.

A neighboring woman brings a rat's tail with her when she comes to chat with Mary. The rat's tail symbolizes the extremely poor life of the immigrants. Mary's disgusted reaction to the rat's tail indicates her unconscious horror and abjection regarding her own miserable everyday life. The reality of Korean immigrants in Hawaii, mostly indentured laborers and their dependents, was staged for the first time in Korean theater as depressingly unstable and associated with the constant threat of danger and death. The neighboring wife tells Mary about a picture bride whose husband continually and wrongfully accused his wife of cheating; the wife secretly planned to escape from Hawaii, but ended up being stabbed to death on a ship about to depart to Panama. To Mary, the story seems to foreshadow her own situation, and fear and despair creep into her mind. To make matters worse, her husband's friend, Han-gu Jang, repeatedly attempts to sexually assault her whenever she is alone.

Mary is doubly marginalized even among the photo brides on the island. Unlike other wives, Mary is educated, and as her neighbor woman assumes, has the ability to "make more money than most men if [she is]determined." Although Mary is terrified by her alcoholic husband's abuse and the sexual harassment by her husband's friend, she does not share her burden with other women, because that might create a scandal and further her isolation. The mentally, emotionally, and financially distressed Mary receives a visit from her former lover, Su-ok, when he comes to Hawaii on his way to New York to study. Although he says he will stay another two or three days on the island while his ship is being repaired and fueled, his actual intention in visiting Mary seems to be based on his desire to know why Mary left him. When Mary laments how miserable her married life with her husband is, Su-ok asserts:

> It is the harm of the photo marriage contract. It is the poisonous consequence of rotten Confucianism. It is an abuse of patriarchy. Until we get rid of the wrong morals and useless rigidity from Joseon, our society has nothing but foolish stumps. It is life's fearful anesthetic. It takes away all vitality and freedom. But Mary, why didn't you refuse the marriage after coming to Hawaii? Isn't it a kind of fraudulent marriage?[23]

Through Su-ok's dialogue, the play criticizes the evil of the photo marriage. Mary hopes that Su-ok will save her from her miserable, loveless marriage by taking her with him. Interestingly, however, because of his rigid morality and perhaps his hurt ego, Su-ok emphasizes that marriage is holy, so she should not break the contract:

MARY: No matter how hard I try, will there be a day when I will be emancipated from suffering?

SU-OK: Emancipation? Impossible, don't even think about it. Live as a spirit. Seek redemption through your soul.

MARY: Spirit? Is that even possible? My body is dying but just holding on to my soul? I am disabled.... I need to seek a new space where I can healthily maintain my mind and body.... The endless anguish and pain I've suffered have changed me so I'm now completely different from myself in the past and my regret and realization have reached the point of cursing myself....

SU-OK: Too late, too late, Mary! Why didn't you find the strength even on the last day of departure from our homeland? All has passed. It's destiny, let's take everything as fate.[24]

Mary honestly expresses her feeling that her body and soul are suffering. Su-ok, however, coldly asserts that Mary should accept the unfortunate marriage as her destiny. When he says to Mary, "you must reap the seeds you sow.... You're the guilty one who drew the dangerous lottery,"[25] he sounds as though he is condemning Mary for not choosing him. Although Su-ok is an intellectual who studied at the Hokkaido Agricultural College in Japan, the country that colonized Joseon, and is now pursuing further study in the United States, his ethical and emotional stance is unclear and variable. When Mary suffers, is in trouble, and desperately asks for help, Su-ok feels conflicted and indecisive about finding a solution, and dwells on the emotional burden of feeling defeated in his relationship with Mary.

The rhetoric of "emancipation," "redemption," and "disabled" in the dialogue between the two characters regarding Mary's trapped situation resonates with the colonial condition of Korea. Su-ok symbolizes the Korean intellectual classes who feel defeated, powerless, and cynical about any potential solution to the depressing colonial condition of their nation. He constantly departs from his homeland, criticizing the old traditions and systems as evil, but, oppressed and tormented, he resists being transparent and vulnerable toward his past lover, let alone admitting his own shortcomings such as his rigid morality and emotional passivity. While Mary represents a newly emerging type of woman who actively makes life choices, the pessimistic Su-ok detaches himself from the reality of his homeland. As a divided and conflicted colonial subject, he resembles Frantz Fanon in *Black Skin, White Masks*, who characterizes his Black identity as denying his native historical origin and embracing the culture of the imperial powers. Su-ok tries to appropriate and imitate the culture of the colonizer, but this process may have left him with an inferiority complex that hinders his ability to take decisive action.

Yun's characterization of Su-ok seems intended as a critical portrayal of rigid patriarchal morality, inspired by Torvald Helmer in Ibsen's *A Doll's House*. In Yun's article "Congratulations to the Emergence of Nora" on Ibsen's playwriting, which he contributed to the monthly magazine *Sisapyeongnon* in July 1922, he asserts the importance of expressing genuine human desire based on faith and courage over oppressive morality:

> What is the most fearful obstacle for us who have tried to escape all the masks of hypocrisy and go out to seek the truth? Because there is no firm faith. It is only through faith that courage will be created, and only after courage will there be a practice that does not bend. After there is a human, there is morality and only after becoming a perfect human will you be able to realize perfect morality. If we always go through all the discomfort, dissatisfaction, and pain under the name of morality and goodness, it will be a person who is not faithful to the self, a person who deceives the self, and a person who kills the self. How can a person who is not faithful to himself be faithful to others, and how can a person who deceives himself be right to others?[26]

Without the supportive partnership of Su-ok, Mary's diasporic sense of displacement deepens as she is confined to the isolated and depressing space of the island. The ending of the play further highlights Su-ok's ambivalent attitude as a bystander. On her way to church, Mary accidentally encounters Su-ok running to shelter near the public cemetery to avoid the severe rain, and the two share a passionate embrace; scholars criticized this scene as the most melodramatic moment of the play. Seeing her only hope of salvation in Su-ok, Mary wants him to take her to the mainland. However, Su-ok emphasizes resignation, saying that the circumstances are their destiny, so they have no choice but to each go their own ways. Mary's jealous drunken husband Gil-sam finds the two and tries to stab Mary, but Mary picks up the knife. As they struggle, Gil-sam is stabbed by the weapon, collapses, and dies. When Mary runs to Su-ok in shock, he says, "Mary, we can't help it. It's destiny. Gil-sam who tried to possess you has now passed away, and I who didn't mean to, finally have you. . . . Oh God! Please guide poor Gil-sam's soul to his Father's dwelling place and direct the sinful us where to go."[27] After this final dialogue, Mary's husband's friend Han-gu takes off his hat and kneels on his knees, and the sound of hymns and church bells is heard in the distance as the curtain falls.

It is interesting to note that Christianity dominates the dramatic background of this play. The two main characters, Mary and Su-ok, are represented as Christians, whereas the other characters are uneducated nonbelievers who need salvation. As Soo-jin Woo insightfully observes, the play begins with a scene of Mary washing dishes "with the sound of a church bell from the distance," and ends with "a song of hymns and bells . . . heard in the distance."[28] Su-ok's last dialogue sounds like a prayer, evoking a sublime feeling and expanding the meaning of "destiny" to include providence and the poetic justice of the universe. American civilization is associated with Christianity, and the play's religious undertone reveals the collective desire of Korean intellectuals for an alternative imperial power as a potential salvation for their nation.

Diasporic Displacement

Destiny tells a fascinating story of the experience of displacement among the earliest Korean migrants in Hawaii. It is set in Honolulu, an imaginary space that most contemporary Korean audiences had never seen portrayed anywhere before, including in the theater.[29] The introduction of an imaginary place on stage as a shared space is one of the theater's most vital and important elements. Jerzy Grotowski believed that the spatial relationships created between the actors and spectators contribute to meaning in theatrical productions, and that the theater is a quasimystical ritualistic experience of intense presence.[30] In that sense, the stage space serves as a third protagonist who performs, and the imaginary faraway place takes the audience on a journey into the unknown as well.

Yun's *Destiny* marks the beginning of theatrical representations of the Korean diaspora that began in the early twentieth century, along with colonialism. Hawaii, the spatial background of this work, can be said to be a symbolic space of colonial history. Discovered by Captain Cook in 1778, Hawaii had been the target of imperialist aggression from the early nineteenth century due to its geographical features and location in the Pacific Ocean; it finally became the fiftieth US State in 1959. As the cultivation of sugarcane and pineapple flourished in Hawaii in the late nineteenth century, physical laborers were needed, and many Filipino, Chinese, and Japanese workers migrated to the islands. In the United States, the Chinese Immigration Restriction Act of 1882 reduced Chinese immigration and led to a labor shortage, so manpower companies turned to other countries in Asia. Japanese immigration companies that used to export Japanese workers to Hawaii set up a company in Seoul, and recruited Korean workers after the US annexation of Hawaii in 1898. The fates of Hawaii and Korea were parallel in that Hawaii was a colony of the United States, and Korean migrant workers were colonial Koreans who the Japanese government forced to enter Hawaii with Japanese passports after Japan annexed Korea.

On December 22, 1902, the first 121 migrant workers departed from the port of Incheon, arriving at Honolulu on January 13, 1903. After the Japan-Korea Treaty of 1905 was signed, 7,226 Korean immigrants (including 465 children) boarded ships bound for Hawaii. The first immigrants were mainly employed on sugarcane plantations. They worked ten hours a day from Monday to Saturday, making about $16 or $17 a month, one-tenth of what an average worker would receive in Hawaii.[31] Overseas migration of Koreans increased even more after Japanese annexation of the Korean peninsula in 1910; many political refugees had no choice but to leave. During Japanese colonial rule, Koreans overseas suffered further political, economic, and social alienation in foreign countries because of the loss of their national sovereignty. The extreme gender imbalance between men and women made Korean Hawaiian workers a bachelor society, and the photo bride business, in which brokers received money to bring brides from Korea to marry the workers, became prevalent.

From 1915 to 1920, as the economy expanded due to World War I and labor wages rose to several dollars more, many Koreans migrated from farms to Honolulu, and photo marriages contributed to the settlement process of immigrants during this period. Because many men who went to Hawaii were addicted to alcohol, gambling, and opium, and because fighting in the migrant communities was incessant, the Sugar Cane Farm Association encouraged any type of marriage.[32] From November 1910 to October 1924, 951 Korean women entered Hawaii as picture brides, and 115 Korean women later moved on to the US mainland.[33] To successfully find brides, some grooms sent photos of younger and better-looking men, and when brides met their grooms, they found that some were old men the age of their fathers. Some brides tried to commit suicide or ran away, as in the case dramatized in *Destiny*.[34] Around the time *Destiny* was staged between 1920 and 1924, about 700 Korean picture brides were living in Hawaii.

Korean Theater as *Allusion* to Reality

Destiny premiered at Galdophoe, a student theater association, on December 13, 1920. According to the preface to *Destiny*, Yun claims that

Destiny was his first work and the first play written by a Korean performed on the stage of a Joseon theater at that time.[35] Prior to *Destiny*, *Three Patients* (*Byungja Samin*) was published in *Maeil Shinbo* in 1912, but there is no historical record that the play was actually staged, which suggests that more research is needed to gather historical facts about Yun's work. In his article "Theater and Society," Yun wrote, "theater should provide an *allusion* to reality."[36] His article proves his deep understanding of contemporary Western theater's trend of focusing on social reality and the cultural function of theater. His emphasis on allusion over the illusion of reality reveals his keen awareness of the colonial condition of Korea, and how theater can deliver a national allegory to a contemporary audience.

Destiny reminded the audience about Korean diasporic conditions that mirrored the gloomy colonial reality Koreans were facing at home. When Yun describes the relationship between the aesthetic characteristics of a play and its social utility, he emphasizes how the emotions operate suggestively and unconsciously on the audience. He believed that theater is ultimately the most suitable institution for producing social change, because a play works implicitly, through the dynamic relationship between the audience's comprehension and the artistic representation, rather than through direct delivery or presentation.[37] In addition, he emphasized *minjung* (ordinary people) and Joseon-ness as the two key words that contemporary drama should pursue. Through *Destiny*'s diasporic setting, Yun captured and represented the temporality and peculiarity of Koreans' colonial condition.

From the very beginning of the modern history of Korean theater, political circumstances hindered the realistic depiction of society; Korean theater practitioners and audiences had to exchange their mutual concerns, sadness, and the collective feeling about the nation's defeat in hidden metaphors and allusions. The tragic domestic situations in these productions provided veiled allusions to national suffering. They gave many Korean audiences a proper excuse to cry openly about the female protagonist's predicaments, which connoted the miserable situation of their motherland. Homi Bhabha's notion of the "third space" can help explain Korean cultural identity in the colonial period.[38] The new imaginary space in *Destiny* gave the audience colliding cultures, a liminal space offering something different, a new area for negotiation of meaning and representation. In that regard, the Korean realism that emerged during colonial modernity was a translated modernity, based on an understanding of Western realism, adapted and informed through Japan, but also taking into consideration Korean particularity and the

Korean colonial condition. Under colonial censorship, the isolated, depressing space of the confined islands, along with the female protagonist's diasporic sense of displacement and her emotional struggle in the play, may have resonated with the audience given the colonial temporality of the times, alluding to and mediating the country's disjointed past, present, and future.

Set in Hawaii, *Destiny* reflects the imaginary space of the faraway island and the experiences of Korean immigrants who were not part of the mainland United States. Metaphorically, the geographical location of the island and its history mark the colonial status of Korean immigrants; the presence of the sugarcane plantation is ironic, since the Korean experience was far from sweet. The diasporic sense of displacement and of being sojourners was much stronger among the diaspora community on the islands.[39] Victimized by the colonial conditions in Korea, the Korean migrants could not quite make it to mainland America, nor could they emotionally leave behind memories of their homeland. The islands represent isolation, in-betweenness, and longing for the mainland; they act as a cultural marker of the diasporic condition. Although Hawaii has always had a hybrid population and its society includes many ethnic minority groups, colonial Koreans were people from an orphaned state. Korean immigrants who had sought their own American dream with new opportunities and a better life on the new continent were forced to become indentured laborers or picture brides. The islands also occupy a poignant geographical location representing colonial Koreans' dual, paradoxical state of mind: they were free from their troubled motherland, yet trapped on an island in a vulnerable state, without proper citizenship or a sense of economic and social stability.

Yun Baek-nam may have projected his own diasporic sense of displacement, experienced while traveling between Japan and Korea, onto Mary, with her sense of loss and isolation, and Su-ok, with his feelings of defeat and emotional detachment. Redefining diaspora through a phenomenology of postmemory,[40] Sandra So Hee Chi Kim argues that diaspora is a phenomenon that "emerges when displaced subjects who experience the loss of an 'origin' (whether literal or symbolic) perpetuate identifications associated with those places of origin in subsequent generations."[41] As Kim suggests, focusing on the social and political formation of the diasporic consciousness of a particular ethnic group can help us better understand the lived experience of diasporic subjects, and each ethnic group's collective desire. The Korean diaspora can be characterized as an abrupt, forced, and traumatic dispersion in space; historically, colonial conditions often spur diasporic movement both within a nation and across national borders. Phenomenologically, diasporic consciousness, formulated among the shifting interstices and negotiations of homeland and host land, generates a sense of loss and trauma similar to that caused by the colonial condition; it forces the subject to accommodate multiple spatial and social identities. Under colonial censorship, the gendered struggles of the two educated protagonists Mary and Su-ok in *Destiny*, written by the diasporic colonial intellectual Yun Baek-nam, may have reflected to the Korean audience the colonial temporality of the time and space, and functioned as a concealed commentary on the country's history and destiny.

Notes

1. Hari Shankar Prasad, "Time in Buddhism and Leibnizian Intercultural Perspective," in *Time and Temporality in Intercultural Perspective: Studies in Intercultural Philosophy*, ed. Douwe Tiemersma and Henk Oosterling (Amsterdam, NL: Rodopi, 1996), 53.

2. Aristotle, *Physics*, Book IV, 218b–219a; 223a.

3. For further discussion of Asian aesthetics and philosophies in art, please refer to Hannah Kim, "Art beyond Morality and Metaphysics: Late Joseon Korean Aesthetics," *Journal of Aesthetics and Art Criticism* 77, no. 4 (Fall 2019); and Pyong-mo Chong, "Korean Folk Painting and Chinese Nianhua: A Comparison of the Formative Processes," *Korea Journal* 40, no. 4 (2000): 113–66.

4. *Talchum* is a traditional Korean masked performance that emerged in the Goryeo period (918–1392), originating from shamanic rituals. Kim Chae-Cheol, *The History of Korean Theater* (*Joseon yonguksa*) (Seoul: Minhaksa, 1974), 56. It became a part of royal events during the Joseon dynasty (1392–1897), and in the late Joseon dynasty, it became part of popular culture, satirizing the upper social classes or humorously portraying the hard lives of the people.

5. *Pansori* is a compound of the word *pan*, meaning play area, and *sori*, chanting. Scholars agree that the genre was derived from shamanic rituals in southwestern Korea in the seventeenth century; the earliest writing containing this word is the 1754 version of *The Tale of Chunhyang* by an unknown author. Oh-kon Cho, *Korean Theatre: From Rituals to the Avant-Garde* (Fremont, CA: Jain Publishing, 2015), 87.

6. Cho, *Korean Theatre*, 104.

7. Seoul was called *Kyungsung* during the Japanese colonial period, 1910–1945.

8. Woo-keun Han, *The History of Korea* (Honolulu: University Press of Hawaii, 1974), 451–52.

9. Park Jin, "A History of Modern Korean Theater" ("Hanguk shinguksa"), in *A Collection of Art Papers* (*Yaesulnonmunjip*) (Seoul: Yaesulwon, 1975), 309.

10. Yi Du-hyon, *A Study of Modern Korean Theater* (*Hanguk shinguksa yongu*) (Seoul: Seoul National University Press, 1981), 49–50.

11. So Yon-ho, *A Study of Modern Korean Drama* (*Hanguk kundae higoksa yongu*) (Seoul: Korea University Minjok Munhwa Yonguso, 1982), 53–54.

12. The 1913 production of the Reform Group, *Tears* (*Nunmul*), is a good example of a tear-jerking narrative, adapted from a newspaper serial novel of the same title by Yi Sang-hyop. *Tears* tells a story of a middle-class woman expelled from her home by her husband after he starts having an affair with a professional entertainer. After an unsuccessful attempt at suicide, she spends some time with her parents, and finally, with the help of her faithful servant, saves her husband, who ends up in a debtor's prison. The golden-hearted wife forgives her husband, and the family, including their little son and loyal servant, have a happy reunion. Cho writes that "the production of this play appealed to many audiences since it provided them an excuse to weep over the defeat and ruin of the nation," *Korean Theatre*, 138–39.

13. Cho, *Korean Theatre*, 135.

14. Lee Young-mee, *Reading History of Korean Popular Culture through Shinpa* (*Hanguk daejoongyesulsa, shinpasungeuiro ikda*) (Seoul: Pooreun yuksa, 2016), 38.

15. Cho, *Korean Theatre*, 138–39.

16. Yoo Min-young, *History of Korean Modern Drama* (*Hanguk hyundae higoksa*) (Seoul: Hongsungsa, 1982); Yang Seung-guk, "Study of Yun Baek-nam's Plays" ("Yun Baek-nam higok yungu"), *Study of Korean Theater Arts* (*Hanguk geukyesul yongu*) 16 (October 2002): 97–143.

17. Kim Bang-ok, *Study of Korean Realism Drama* (*Hanguk sasiljueui higok yongu*) (Seoul: Dongyang Gongyun Yesuk Yeonguso, 1988); Woo Soo-jin, "Yun Baek-nam's *Destiny*, Colonial Consciousness and Melodrama of Desire" ("Yun Baek-nameui unmyung, sikminjijeok mueuisikgwa yokmangui melodrama"), *Journal of Korean Drama and Theater* 17 (April 2003): 51–77.

18. Yun Baek-nam, *Destiny*, in *Selected Works of Yun Baek-nam* (*Yun Baek-nam sunjip*), ed. Baek Doo-san (Seoul: Hyundae Munhak, 2013), 36. All translations in this chapter, including the dialogues from *Destiny*, are mine.

19. Baek Doo-san, ed., *Selected Works of Yun Baek-nam* (*Yun Baek-nam sunjip*) (Seoul: Hyundae Munhak, 2013), 474.

20. Yong-ho Choe, "A Brief History of Christ United Methodist Church, 1903–2003," in *Christ United Methodist Church, 1903–2003: A Pictorial History* (Honolulu, HI: Christ United Methodist Church, 2003).

21. Yong-ho Choe et al., "Korean Mission to the Conference on Limitation of Armament, Washington DC, 1921–1922" (Washington, DC: US Government Printing Office, 2000), 29.

22. Yun, *Destiny*, 37.

23. Yun, *Destiny*, 50.

24. Yun, *Destiny*, 61.

25. Yun, *Destiny*, 51.

26. Yun Baek-nam, "Congratulations to the Emergence of Nora," *Sisapyeongnon* 3 (July 1922); Baek, *Selected Works of Yun Baek-nam*, 426.

27. Yun, *Destiny*, 67–68.

28. Yun, *Destiny*, 68; Soo-jin Woo, "Yun Baek-nam's *Destiny*, Colonial Consciousness and Melodrama of Desire," 70.

29. Many of Yun's modern plays written in the 1920s are set in foreign spaces. *The Wife of Eternity* (1922) is an adaptation play set in Madrid, Spain; *Heemoojung* (1924) is an adaptation of Victor Hugo's *Les Miserables*; *Louis XVI* (1924) is set in France at the end of the eighteenth century; and *My Lady's Dress* (1923) is an adaptation of the British writer Edward Knocklock's 1914 play.

30. Jerzy Grotowski, *Towards a Poor Theatre*, ed. Eugenio Barba (New York: Routledge, 2002).

31. Lee Eun-joo, "Migrant Laborers and Their Picture Brides," *Korea JoongAng Daily* (*JoongAng Ilbo*), November 20, 2008, https://koreajoongangdaily.joins.com/2008/11/20/features/Migrant-laborers-and-their-picture-brides/2897559.html

32. Woo, "Yun Baek-nam's *Destiny*," 11.

33. Kim Won-yong, *50 Years of History of Korean Americans* (*Jaemi Hanin 50nyeonsa*) (Seoul: Hyean, 1959), 27–29.

34. *Dong-A Ilbo* [a daily newspaper], January 9, 1973.

35. For a detailed discussion of the Galdophoe performance, see Doo-Hyun Lee, *A Study on the History of Korean New Theater* (Seoul: Seoul National University Press, 1966), 62.

36. Yun contributed his articles between May 4 and May 16, 1920, to *Dong-A Ilbo*, the daily newspaper. Emphasis is mine.

37. Yun Baek-nam, "Theatre and Society: Discussing Modern Theatre of Joseon," in Baek, *Selected Works of Yun Baek-nam*, 394–95.

38. Homi K. Bhabha, *The Location of Culture* (Abingdon, UK: Routledge, 2004).

39. Miseong Woo, "Diaspora and Geographies of Identity," *Journal of Modern English Drama* 17, no. 1 (April 2004): 177–200.

40. Marianne Hirsch, an American Holocaust scholar, coined this term to describe "the relationship of the second generation to powerful, often traumatic, experiences that preceded their births but were nevertheless transmitted to them so deeply as to seem to constitute memories in their own right," in *Family Frames: Photography, Narrative, and Postmemory* (Cambridge, MA: Harvard University Press, 1997), 103.

41. Sandra So Hee Chi Kim, "Redefining Diaspora through a Phenomenology of Postmemory," *Diaspora: A Journal of Transnational Studies* 16, no. 3 (Winter 2007): 337–52.

12 | The "Deep Realism" of Style

From Michel Saint-Denis to Huang Zuolin

SIYUAN LIU

When assessing the most influential directors of China's modern spoken drama *huaju* in the twentieth century, the phrase "Bei Jiao nan Huang" (Jiao of the north, Huang of the south) is a common refrain, referring to Jiao Juyin (1905–1975) of the Beijing People's Art Theatre and Huang Zuolin (1906–1994) of the Shanghai People's Art Theatre. Notably, they were also the only two *huaju* directors with postgraduate degrees in theater from Europe in the 1930s, with a PhD for Jiao from the Sorbonne and an MLitt for Huang from Cambridge. Such solid foundations in European theatrical history, and in the contemporaneous clashes of theatrical realism and antirealism, gave them the capability to transcend the dominant Stanislavsky System in post-1949 *huaju* with productions that embraced both Chinese and Western theater. Jiao sought to establish a Chinese school of directing by borrowing from traditional performance, especially *jingju* (Beijing opera), while Huang proposed the *xieyi* ("writing meaning") view of theater (*xiju guan*) that sought to encompass the representational System, the dialectics of Brecht, and the theatricality of Chinese theater. Having discussed Jiao's relations with Stanislavsky elsewhere,[1] in this chapter I focus on the impact of Huang's English education on his *xieyi* theory and practice, especially the significance of his two-year study at the London Theatre Studio under the French antirealist director Michel Saint-Denis (1897–1971).

Impact of Saint-Denis's Evolving Assessment of Stanislavsky

China's modern, Western-oriented spoken theater started at the turn of the twentieth century, in part as a corrective to traditional song-and-dance theater's supposed entertainment-only deficiencies, by utilizing speech to propagate enlightenment and national salvation. This approach was evident in the 1907 Tokyo production of *Heinu yutian lu* (*Black Slave's Cry to Heaven*), an adaptation of *Uncle Tom's Cabin*, generally considered to be the beginning of modern Chinese theater. Known as *wenmingxi* (civilized drama), this first iteration of modern theater thrived for the next decade in Shanghai as a hybrid form in both ideological and formal terms. It was commercial while also acutely attuned to national crises; it was speech-based but included singing and dancing; it relied largely on scenarios and improvisation while also using scripts; and it included emerging actresses competing with the predominant female impersonators.[2] In the late 1910s, the New Cultural Movement introduced Ibsen's social critical realism, and by the early 1920s the term *huaju* (spoken drama) was adopted to denote a more evolutionarily advanced form that was speech-only and socially conscious.

Yet the debate between realism and antirealism in *huaju* was never settled. The first skirmish started as early as 1926, when a group of Western-educated scholars and artists initiated the *guoju yundong* (national theater movement) by advocating for reintegrating indigenous theatricality in *huaju*, and denouncing the introduction of Ibsen as "the wrong track for theater."[3] The group's leader, Yu Shangyuan (1897–1970), first adopted the concept of *xieyi* in a 1924 article written while studying theater in the US, to discuss the presentational style of performance and design in Max Reinhardt's New York production of *Miracle*. He borrowed the term *xieyi* from Chinese painting, to denote an interpretive and freely expressive style, the opposite of the carefully realistic technique of *gongbi* ("meticulous brush"). By 1926, when Yu had returned to Beijing, he further positioned *xieyi* opposite the representational and realist *xieshi* ("drawing from nature") style. However, Yu's national theater movement turned out to be shorted-lived due to fierce opposition from a younger generation, including his students at the National Arts School, who were already entrenched in the social efficacy of Ibsenian realism.[4]

By the late 1930s, after the English publication of *An Actor Prepares*, the Stanislavsky System began to be introduced to *huaju*, although it was not until the 1950s, when Soviet experts came to China to teach the System, that it became the official method of *huaju* production. By 1956, however, the problem of blindly following the System was already manifest during that year's national *huaju* festival, prompting a brief period of interest in surviving productions of *wenmingxi*—by then known as *tongsu huaju* (popular spoken drama) in Shanghai—as a possible nationalized alternative to the purely realist *huaju*. Such enthusiasm, however, soon came to a halt with the advent in late 1957 of the Anti-Rightist Movement, which ended a year-long period of liberal arts policies.[5]

Yet this debate between realism and antirealism continued in 1962 during yet another brief era of liberalization, when Huang Zuolin gave a speech in a national theater conference entitled "Mantan 'xiju guan'" ("On 'Theatrical Views'") that reiterated the *xieyi* concept and employed Brecht to reintroduce *xiqu* (traditional Chinese theater) to the Stanislavsky-dominated *huaju*. In proposing the concept of theatrical views, Huang positioned it as deriving from worldviews (*shijie guan*) and artistic views (*yishu guan*): "We all know that art workers use artistic means to influence and change life with a certain worldview; and theatrical workers use theatrical means to bring a certain worldview and a certain artistic view to achieve this goal. While worldviews and artistic views have certain limitations in each historical period and each class society, theatrical methods are diverse."[6] This connection of theatrical views to worldviews and artistic views put Huang on safe ideological grounds while also allowing him to separate from historically diverse theatrical views, from Greek tragedy to Gordon Craig, on methodological grounds. This separation of form from ideology allowed him to view Brecht and Stanislavsky as "generally consistent in artistic views, but opposite in theatrical views."[7] Furthermore, it gave him permission to bring in Chinese theater—represented by Mei Lanfang—to contrast the three styles' stances on the illusionist fourth wall: "Stanislavsky believed in the fourth wall; Brecht wanted to topple the fourth wall; and for Mei Lanfang, this wall did not exist at all."[8] Such a contrast, consequently, allowed him to declare the fourth wall—and by implication the Stanislavsky System—as "just one of the many expressive methods in *huaju*."[9] While the subsequent ideological tightening the following year did not allow Huang to put his theory into measurable practice, the speech's discussion of *xieyi* and the three systems garnered enough attention to merit publication in the *People's Daily* that April. Furthermore, soon after the Cultural Revolution (1966–1976) ended, it triggered a national theatrical debate around *xieyi* that became the starting point of dazzling theatrical experimentations in the 1980s, with Huang's productions as prominent examples.

What, then, gave Huang the insight to challenge the predominant

System in 1962 and to implement *xieyi* theater in the 1980s? The answer lies in the formative two-year theatrical education Huang and his actress wife Jin Yunzhi (stage name Danni, 1912–1995) received in England (1935–1937). During those two years, Huang wrote his 263-page thesis at Cambridge on the three-and-a-half-century history of Shakespearean productions, while he and Jin also enrolled in Saint-Denis's London Theatre Studio as part of its inaugural group of students, with Jin in acting and Huang in directing (and auditing in acting). In a couple of two-week occasions, they also observed the acting course of Michael Chekhov (1891–1955), Stanislavsky's disciple and rebel from the Moscow Art Theatre and influential acting teacher, at Chekhov's school in Darlington Hall in Devon, southwest England. While there, they also studied dance with the German avant-garde choreographer Kurt Jooss (1901–1979), especially his movement system, called eukinetics, to increase body expressiveness. They also read Stanislavsky's *An Actor Prepares* and *My Life in Art* as well as Brecht's "Alienation Effect in Chinese Acting." Finally, on their way back to China after the Japanese invasion in the fall of 1937, they spent September in Moscow observing the Moscow Theatre Festival, which included two productions each by the Moscow Art Theatre and the Vakhtangov Theatre; the latter was known for the theatricality of its productions.

Given this eclectic education in European theatrical realism and antirealism, it is important to note that at the core of Huang's post-1949 refusal to follow the *huaju* orthodoxy in the Stanislavsky System was his belief, following Saint-Denis, that modern realism was only one of many styles in the more than 2000-year history of world theater. Saint-Denis discussed the difference between "deep" and "superficial" realisms:

> On the one hand we have the deep realism, which studies and expresses the nature of things, the meaning of human life, what happens behind and below appearances; and on the other, we have the realism that is satisfied with the representation of the external, the superficial realism which was called at the beginning of the present century "naturalism." If you will allow me, I would like to make a distinction between "realism," which applies to the art of all times, and "naturalism" which is an ephemeral form of art, belonging to the period of Zola, Ibsen, Strindberg, Antoine, Stanislavsky, etc.[10]

As the nephew of French antirealist director Jacques Copeau (1879–1949), Saint-Denis distilled his belief in the importance of style that "by taking us away from the external forms of reality, from appearances, has itself become a reality, representative of a deeper world."[11] This was the vision he implemented through six acting schools he created, starting with the London Theatre Studio in 1936 and ending in the Juilliard Drama Division in 1968.

Notably, while Saint-Denis relegated Stanislavsky to the naturalist camp of superficial realism in a 1950s lecture delivered in the United States that specifically targeted American Method acting, his assessment of the System's efficacy in actor training had undergone an evolution that is significant to our understanding of Huang Zuolin's view of the System. According to Saint-Denis, he was initially enthralled with Stanislavsky when the Moscow Art Theatre toured Paris in 1922, especially with their production of *The Cherry Orchard*, which "filled me with admiration, almost against my will. Nothing had prepared me for the discovery that a banal story about the sale of a country estate could be so moving. . . . The deftness of the company's acting was absolutely incredible. . . . What struck me most was the lightness of their acting: these performers seemed constantly to improvise their movements and their text. . . . The words, so clearly enunciated, expressed the mood musically. . . ."[12]

Huang quoted this paragraph—with the ellipses matching his Chinese citation—in a 1991 article about Saint-Denis's writings and pedagogy, but attributed it to a class discussion at the London Theatre Studio: "1936 happened to be [the year] when the English version of *An Actor Prepares* was published and we each had a copy. During discussion, Saint-Denis remembered one incident," which turned out to be the quote above.[13] Notably, Huang did not seem to keep his contact with Saint-Denis after returning to China. Consequently, he did not discuss the significant influence Saint-Denis had on him until the late 1970s, after the Cultural Revolution. In fact, he only started attributing his indebtedness to his teacher in great detail after receiving "some relatively systematic materials about Saint-Denis" from the latter's widow, Suria Saint-Denis (née Magito), a movement teacher at the London Theatre Studio and their later training programs.[14] Judging from Huang's subsequent discussion, the materials possibly included the two published books by Saint-Denis and praises of his training programs and philosophy. One of the books was the 1960 *Theatre: The Rediscovery of Style*, which includes a series of lectures delivered in the United States in the late 1950s, including the aforementioned piece on realism and style. The other book was *Training for the Theatre: Premises & Promises*, published posthumously in 1982 and edited by Suria Saint-Denis. It focused mostly on his training philosophy and practice, with detailed examples from Juilliard's four-year curriculum. These two books formed the foundation of an article by Huang that was written in 1991 but published in 2008, which sought to introduce Saint-Denis's training system to China.[15]

Perhaps as a testimony to his initial impression of Saint-Denis's admiration of Stanislavsky, Huang, in this article, never touches on his teacher's later denunciation of the System, instead choosing to follow Saint-Denis's first impression of *The Cherry Orchard* with two more examples—Stanislavsky's portrayal of Gaev, and a detail in act 1 that crystalized the *grummelotage*—the music of meaning—of the scene:

> One of the most astonishing moments was in the first act: the travelers enter, home after a long journey from Paris. Although visibly tired, one feels how moved they all are to find themselves back in the old nursery. Anya, the youngest, a frail creature, runs in, throws herself on the sofa and snuggles into a corner like a little bird. She starts to laugh! That laugh expresses happiness, exhaustion, youth and tenderness. It is a laugh so crystalline, so wonderfully free, with such an emotional impact, that the audience of two thousand people [in the Grand Théâtre des Champs Elysées] burst into applause, without a word having been uttered from the stage.[16]

Based on these observations from Saint-Denis, Huang declares: "In short, Saint-Denis absolutely admired the Moscow Art Theatre and was even more devoted to Stanislavsky. . . . From Saint-Denis's teaching and practice, I realized that none of Antoine, Copeau, and Stanislavsky were naturalists; they were all pursuers of meaning and substance."[17]

How do we assess Huang's declaration of the affinity between Saint-Denis and Stanislavsky? To start with, it should be noted that as China's most vocal advocate of *xieyi* theater, Huang was always careful to point out how much he admired Stanislavsky, and in the 1950s he tried mightily to follow the System in his productions, with mixed results. One such example can be found in his methodical, frank, and at times painful to read postmortem of the 1955 production of a Soviet play titled *Yangguang zhaoyao zhe Mosike* (*The Sun Shines over Moscow*, orig. *Rassvet nad Moskvoi* [*Dawn over Moscow*]) by Anatoli Aleksandr Surov, including failures in creating characters by veteran actors such as Danni.[18] He always claimed to believe in the System, even though in his 1962 speech he clearly aligned himself with Saint-Denis by recognizing two fundamentally different theatrical views in the 2,500-year history of world theater, the illusionist *xieshi* and the anti-illusionist *xieyi* views, plus a hybrid one. He argues: "the purely *xieshi* view of theater only has a history of seventy-five years, and the naturalistic drama that produced this view of theater has already completed its historical mission, dead, but our Chinese *huaju* creation seems to be still constrained by the remnants of this view of theater, believing this is the only expressive method for *huaju*."[19]

It is worth noting, however, that Huang recalls in a 1978 article that when he proposed abandoning the fourth wall and the unities or the total adoption of *xiqu* conventions in *huaju*, it was Chen Yi (1901–1972), liberal-minded and highly respected former Shanghai mayor and then foreign minister, who admonished him: "Western realist theater, the fourth wall, is also a weapon, indeed a very powerful weapon. Why do you want to abandon it? . . . Wouldn't one more weapon be better for your battle?"[20] Chen's admonition may have added yet another layer, apart from Saint-Denis's initial infatuation with the Moscow Art Theatre, to Huang's careful triangulation among the three systems of Stanislavsky, Brecht, and *xiqu*, and to the seeming contradiction between his professed devotion to the System and, when possible, his practical adoption of antirealist *xieyi* methodologies in production. Indeed, while most of his productions from 1949 to the late 1970s, when he was finally free to experiment with *xieyi* staging, remained in the realistic mode, he was able to stage four epic-style productions that, while propagandistic in content, were *xieyi* in style: they were episodic in structure, stylized in performance and design, and they largely dispensed with the fourth wall. They were *Kang Mei yuan Chao da huobao* (*Resist the US and Assist Korea: A Great Live Report*, 1951), *Bamian hongqi yingfeng piao* (*Eight Red Flags Fluttering in the Wind*, 1958), *Jiliu yongjin* (*Surging Ahead*, 1963), and *Xin changzheng jiaoxiangshi* (*New Long March: A Symphonic Poem*, 1978).

Furthermore, even in the 1980s and early 1990s Huang's stance on realism and the System might have been a self-preservation mechanism to make his *xieyi* advocacy more palatable, as the debate between the two views remained heated. But Saint-Denis's evolving assessment of the System might have also played an important role in Huang's disregard for his teacher's eventual disillusionment with the System, let alone Saint-Denis's ardent denunciation of the American Method.

In terms of his evolution in assessing the System's efficacy, Saint-Denis conceded in a 1964 article comparing Shakespeare and Stanislavsky that "in fact, the example of the [Moscow Art Theatre] had gotten under our skin."[21] In part this was due to the fact that *An Actor Prepares*, the first of three books delineating the System, was not published until 1936, and it would take another decade for the second book, *Building a Character* (1948), to emerge.²² Once the books came out, Saint-Denis's devotion to Stanislavsky based on Moscow Art Theatre's 1922 Paris tour obviously shifted toward doubt about the System, which was confirmed after reading *Building a Character* and *Stanislavski Produces Othello*, also published in 1948: "In facing Shakespeare we were forced to make a rigorous choice among the training methods Stanislavski suggested. We had at this time no precise information about the fate of Stanislavski's Shakespearean productions, although later the publication of his *Othello* book threw light on the matter."²³

At the core of Saint-Denis's rejection of Stanislavsky was the belief that while the System was perfect for Chekhov's psychological realism, it was woefully lacking for teaching the rich tradition of physical performance techniques required for period pieces, particularly Shakespeare, as was evident in Stanislavsky's awkward attempt to ascertain a naturalist mise-en-scène of Venice in his preparation for *Othello*. Saint-Denis argues, "in Europe these traditions were there—the Comédie Française, Moliére, Goldoni, Schiller, and above all, Shakespeare. Men like Appia, Barker, Copeau, Craig, and Reinhardt had already tried to renovate these traditions."²⁴ Pointing out that even Stanislavsky admitted in *My Life in Art* and *Building a Character* that the System was only good for Chekhov, particularly his strength in depicting the inner truth, but not for Shakespeare, thus admitting defeat, Saint-Denis casts doubt on the ability of "naturalistic sets, psychological preoccupation in the acting . . . to bring us closer to Shakespeare's essence."²⁵

Such a realization, of course, came too late for Huang and Jin, who left England in 1937 and, on their way home by train, spent a month watching plays at the Moscow Theatre Festival.²⁶ The festival staged fourteen productions in September, including *Anna Karenina* by Nikolai Dmitrievich Volkov and *Lyubov Yarovaya* by Constantin Trenyev at the Moscow Art Theatre, and *Much Ado about Nothing* and Maxim Gorky's *Yegor Bulychov and Others* at the Vakhtangov Theatre.²⁷ Before leaving England, they had also twice observed Michael Chekhov's classes, each time for two weeks during the summer and spring breaks, probably in 1936 and 1937.²⁸ Notably, these short spurts did not seem to allow Huang to discern much difference between the younger Chekhov and Stanislavsky, for he discussed the experience with Chekhov as part of his "initial contact with Stanislavsky."²⁹ It was through these observations, together with the experience at the Moscow Theatre Festival, that he eventually "gained some understanding of Stanislavsky's theater," after initial persistent "bafflement" at *An Actor Prepares*, despite repeated reading.³⁰

Impact of the London Theatre Studio Training on Huang's Practice and Theorization

Huang's two-year training at the London Theatre Studio, together with his understanding of English theatrical history through his thesis on Shakespearean productions, aligned him and Jin squarely with the Saint-Denis camp of theatrical performance and actor training; Jin Yunzhi even adopted "Danni," after Saint-Denis, as her stage name for the rest of her career. What, then, did they learn in those two years that made them such devoted disciples of Saint-Denis and pioneering forces in *huaju* for the following half century? The story necessarily starts with Saint-Denis's philosophy and practice of actor training, told in his posthumous book *Training for Theatre*, although the book's reliance on Juilliard's four-year curriculum makes it necessary for the purpose of this chapter to balance this account with archival materials of the two-year London Theatre Studio program found in the British Library and the National Theatre Archive. Saint-Denis later admitted that the original program's length was inadequate and eventually necessitated expansion, first to three years in 1954 when he opened L'École Supérieure d'Art Dramatique in Strasbourg, and then to four years.³¹

In a way, the difference between Stanislavsky and Saint-Denis in actor training boils down to style, which, "by taking us away from the external forms of reality, from appearances, has itself become a reality, representative of a deeper world."³² This sense that "reality is a style" was such a cornerstone for Saint-Denis's training program that he warns against "pushing realism too far too early," before solid work in style; the fear, he wrote, is that "it restrains, it hinders the work of interpreting the great classics, and, therefore, impoverishes the craft of the actor, rather than enriching it."³³ Consequently, his programs were based on foundational trainings in the three pillars of movement, improvisation, and speech. Huang Zuolin followed this regime in his two training programs in Shanghai People's Art Theatre in 1950 and 1960, adopted it in his nonrealist, *xieyi* productions at the theater, and advocated for it in 1978 as an alternative to "the Stanislavsky System in learning, teaching, and practice."³⁴

As Jane Baldwin contends in her introduction to Saint-Denis's lecture on his training program at the postwar Old Vic School, also a two-year program:

In Saint-Denis's training, the key to depicting character was the transformation of the self. For example, classes in voice, speech, and movement gave the students the technical tools to expand themselves in the creation of a range of characters. Improvisation classes took them ever further away from their everyday lives into different worlds. Mask work added another layer of complexity and strangeness. Through these and their interpretation classes, students became aware that the development of the imagination was crucial to characterization.[35]

According to a 1937 handwritten, table-form curriculum found in the National Theatre Archive, during the six terms over two years that started in fall—or five terms for Jin Yunzhi's inaugural class starting in spring 1936 and ending in summer 1937—the first two terms of each year generally included about thirty-three weekly hours of teaching divided into sections on dramatic work, movement, voice, lectures, and manual work. Dramatic work included mime, improvisation, and texts; movement involved gym, acrobatics, dance, and fencing (for men); voice was divided into voice work, singing, and choral speaking; lectures covered topics from "origins," through periods including commedia dell'arte, to "art"; and manual work taught makeup, masks, and props. A substantial amount of time in the final spring term of each year was devoted to rehearsing for the end-of-year performance, especially for the second-year group, although at least for Jin's inaugural group, there was also a winter show in 1937 that was the first for the Studio.[36]

According to Angelica Garnett (1918–2012), a writer and artist who was Jin's classmate and friend who first met her at the London Theatre Studio audition, Jin's spoken English was "not very good."[37] This would be unsurprising given that she had just arrived in England, and that audition pieces for female students were generally scenes for well-known Shakespearean heroines such as Beatrice, Juliet, her Nurse, Portia, and Helena.[38] This might in part explain Jin's minor roles in the Studio's first and second shows at the end of the spring and summer 1937 terms, in her group's second year. For the first show, which ran between April 1 and April 7, she played one of five Syrian women in *Judith*, which was "adapted from the Apocrypha," and Moth, one of four servants of the fairy Queen Titania in the woods scene in *A Midsummer Night's Dream*. She was also part of "The Fair," a "musical and acrobatic finale with all the students of the Studio." Another piece of the show, in which Jin was not involved, was a scene from *The Three Sisters*, although for some reason it was unlisted in the program, and was only available in the show's photo album. For the second show, from July 14 to July 25, Jin played Belinda, one of five servants in *A Woman Killed with Kindness*, a tragedy written in 1603 by Thomas Haywood. She was also a member of the chorus in the "Programme of Songs," singing Bach's "Brightest and Best" and Mandel's "The Foolish Lover Squanders." The show also included Noel Coward's 1925 comedy *Hay Fever* and a dance titled *The Possessed Woman*, produced by Suria Magito, Saint-Denis's future wife.[39] Two photo albums at the British Library also include shots of training and performances from 1936 in addition to the two shows in 1937, revealing more comedy, commedia, and movement-heavy pieces.

These shows clearly demonstrate the realization of Saint-Denis's philosophy of training the student with a variety of styles through movement, improvisation, and speech, from classical tragedy and comedy to modern realist and comic plays, plus abundant singing and dance.

In the 1978 article discussed above regarding why he kept the System as another weapon in his toolkit, Huang provided the first open defense of the Saint-Denis method of training and performance in answer to the question of "how to conduct learning, teaching, and practice without the Stanislavsky System."[40] He summarized Saint-Denis's method as including three elements: mime (*yaju*), improvisation (*jixing biaoyan*), and poetic recitation (*shi langsong*), roughly corresponding to the dramatic work, movement, and voice sections of the 1937 London Theatre Studio curriculum. This is also close to Saint-Denis's summary of the three interrelated departments of his two English training programs: movement, language, and improvisation and interpretation.[41] As I mentioned earlier, in that 1937 curriculum, the core training, in addition to lectures and manual work, comprised dramatic work (divided into mime, improvisation, and text work); movement (gym, acrobatics, dance, and fencing); and voice (voice work [marked by the teacher's name, Iris Warren], singing [by Herbert Scott], and choral speaking).[42] In the eventual four-year Juilliard curriculum, the main areas were bifurcated into technique and imagination, with the former encompassing body, voice/diction, and speech/language, and the latter including improvisation, interpretation (rehearsal and performance), and imagination/background/miscellaneous (lectures and manual work).[43] Most likely from his and Danni's class notes and from memory, without access to the London Theatre Studio or Juilliard curricula before receiving Saint-Denis's books, Huang essentially deployed "mime" to mean movement and "choral speaking" to mean voice work, in addition to improvisation. Indeed, he was rather specific in singling out these elements as the core of the London Theatre

Studio training, especially in contrast to the text-centric and character-based System.

Together, these three elements were key to Huang's *xieyi* theory, starting with mime as "using the whole body to talk, to express, i.e. to use movement for expression."[44] Apart from movement training at the London Theatre Studio, Huang also relied on the eukinetics he and Jin had studied with German choreographer Kurt Jooss in the summer of 1936 at Dartington Hall, where Jooss had moved his dance school in defiance of Nazi pressure to dismiss his Jewish staff. Hailed as "one of the significant artistic achievements of this century in the European Theatre—the creation of a completely new method of theatrical dance," Jooss's dance system, according to A. V. Coton in his elaborately illustrated book on the system, "is closer to the idiom and the ideology of the earliest sorts of theatrical dancing, than is the traditional system as expounded through the mechanism of the Classical Ballet."[45] Based on his teacher Rudolf Laban's principle of movement analysis, Jooss's system comprises choreutics (the laws of space) and eukinetics (the laws of dynamics). Choreutics focuses on choreographic composition on the principle that a "specific emotion will always favour a certain direction or directional path in space," thus underscoring "the psychological content of movement and [making it] one of the keys to dramatic dance."[46] Eukinetics, on the other hand, analyzes movement dynamics through eight "Eukinetic Qualities," combining elements of time (quick or slow), intensity (strong or weak), and modus (i.e., space: central or peripheral, at the start of movement, or subsequently). It is also notable that "the study of Eukinetics begins with experimental improvisation."[47]

Translating the eukinetics as *youdong xue*, literally "the study of beautiful movement," Huang called it a way "to make every part of the body speak, not just relying on the mouth," and adopted it half a century after learning it from Jooss, in the production of *Zhongguo meng* (*China Dream*, 1987), arguably his most representative *xieyi* production. He deemed the movement in it "neither conventionalized as in *xiqu* nor abstracted as in ballet; it had to emerge from life but must also be endowed with a sense of beauty."[48] The use of this technique may have been the only way to sustain a full-length play with two young academy-trained *huaju* actors on a bare stage, portraying multiple characters in China and the United States, through both the Cultural Revolution and at the present time.

The second aspect of Huang's adherence to Saint-Denis's training and practice was improvisation, which was of the utmost importance in the London Theatre Studio and subsequent training programs, so much so that Saint-Denis differentiated actor/improvisers from actor/interpreters. He even posed the rhetorical question that, given this distinction, "should we not stimulate the initiative and invention of the future interpreter by making him pass through the experiences of the actor/creator?"[49] This is recommended because "the process the latter follows is more complex, as he must bring to life from a text a character with the same reality as the characters an improviser creates with no text. The interpreter begins with a text, the improviser begins with himself. It might be said that a memorised text should be assimilated by the actor/interpreter in such a way that it finally comes out of him with a spontaneity comparable to that which is achieved by an actor/improviser."[50] In addition, improvisation is also key to training in imagination and body awareness. The former point is evident in the fact that the subject is part of the "imagination" section of his four-year program, while the latter point is reinforced when the first year is devoted completely to silent improvisation without using any written text.[51] Furthermore, with part of the curriculum involving commedia dell'arte, another function of improvisation training is creating group-devised scenarios that can be developed into written scripts; this took place with Saint-Denis's play *Noah* (1935), which emerged as a result of his collaboration with the playwright André Obey in his Compagnie des Quinze, before the London Theatre Studio adventure.[52] This production thrilled Huang and Jin to such a degree when they saw it that they felt compelled to join the London Theatre Studio program.[53] As I have argued elsewhere, such an improvisation-based creative process was also key to both traditional Chinese theater and China's first hybrid modern spoken theater, *wenmingxi*.[54] Indeed, like many of his fellow avant-garde directors in the early twentieth century, Saint-Denis was also a lover of Asian theater. He asked Huang to arrange a lecture at the Studio by professor Zhang Pengchun, Mei Lanfang's advisor for his 1935 Soviet tour, and even planned to have him invite a *jingju* movement teacher to join the Studio staff, which was unfortunately made impossible by the Japanese invasion in 1937.[55]

In a way, then, Huang's training with Saint-Denis, through both improvisation/scenarios and witnessing his teacher's passion for *jingju*, gave Huang the license to appreciate and adopt indigenous aesthetics and processes unimaginable by virtually all other *huaju* directors of his time. The only possible exception was Jiao Juyin, who was in Paris during roughly the same period, after serving as principal of a *jingju* training school in Beijing; he later became Huang's counterpart in Beijing in the use of innovations through hybridization with indigenous theater. In this regard, it is notable that soon after arriving in Shanghai in 1940 Huang praised the work of the Lübao (Green Treasure) Theatre Company, a *wenmingxi*-style group that still used scenarios and improvisation, noting that they were astute at feeding on audience response and highly skillful in performance, movement transitions, and control of rhythm. More significantly, Huang refused to accept that there was an artistic gulf between the Green Treasure and *huaju* companies, which most other *huaju* practitioners firmly believed.[56] In fact, the two sides were able to coexist only after Green Treasure agreed to lower its stature by calling its practice *tongsu huaju* (popular spoken drama), with the added "popular" signifying an evolutionarily lower status due to the use of scenarios and improvisation instead of fully scripted plays.[57] The fact that Huang refused to be bothered by such literary centrism provides yet more evidence of his belief in Saint-Denis's prioritizing of improvisation over the text.

A related aspect of improvisation as a training tool, as Huang implemented it in his two acting classes in 1950 and 1960 in Shanghai, was the power of self-discovery as the first stage in his three-step process of "performing myself," "performing you" (someone familiar), and "performing him" (a stranger). Intriguingly, his training programs ended up producing more playwrights than actors, which Huang attributed to the curtailed schedule of the first class, which was only able to finish the first half, mime and improvisation training. While this is certainly plausible, another factor could be the potential of the scenario-to-play process to unlock creativity and imagination in playwriting, which Saint-Denis maintained as an integral part of improvisation, again as evidenced by the success of his play *Noah*, which was created through the improvisation-to-play process.

Yet another notable manifestation of Huang's adoption and promotion of improvisation in China was a talk he gave on commedia dell'arte in 1961 to Shanghai's *huajixi* (farce) actors. This talk was triggered by an inquiry from Zhou Yang, literature and art theorist and vice minister of both the Chinese Communist Party Propaganda Department and the Cultural Ministry, about the training of comic actors in the West. In the talk, Huang discussed commedia dell'arte's form, *lazzi* (scenarios), masks, and six representative masters.[58] Furthermore, his suggestion that Xu Pingyu, director of the Shanghai Cultural Bureau, pay attention to *huajixi* as Shanghai's local farce form even resulted in the merger of the city's *huajixi* theater into Huang's Shanghai People's Art Theatre. While he later insisted that the merger had resulted from a misunderstanding of his suggestion, which he only meant to encourage the authorities to pay attention to the form,[59] this example testifies to his decades-long attentiveness to improvisational forms, which had continued since his return from London.

The final aspect of Huang's Saint-Denis-inspired training and directorial philosophy was *shi langsong*, which I earlier rendered as "poetic recitation" and aligned with choral speaking in the London Theatre Studio's curriculum. Yet another, probably more suitable, rendition of the term is *l'expression parlée*, a French phrase Saint-Denis adopted for the Juilliard curriculum and translated as "the speaking aloud of verse": "In it we strive to find a way of acting without *doing*. In rehearsals of a play our principal interest is in 'doing,' but in these specialised exercises on poetic texts we are more concerned at first with obtaining a complete expression of meaning through the use of the voice alone; with finding a way of acting which is based, almost entirely, on the use of the voice—on tone, phrasing, pace and rhythm."[60] Stage shots of performances by Jin's class show the result of such training; in their performance of classic plays, such as *Judith*, student actors are endowed with a special force of gravity and intensity without body movement.[61] Huang also noted that unlike mime and improvisation, *l'expression parlée* was not unique to Saint-Denis; it was fundamental training in all theater schools in England, although, as he also pointed out, "currently we are not paying enough attention to it."[62]

What is notable, however, is the role this technique performed in Huang's innovative formal escapes from the strictures of fourth-wall realism—if still rather propagandist in content, as he readily admitted—in the aforementioned four productions from the 1950s to the late 1970s, including the 1978 *New Long March: A Symphonic Poem*. During the play's rehearsal, Huang used *l'expression parlée* to help the production's 250 actors rid themselves of the habit of shouting on stage, which was still highly prevalent at the time. Using the contrast in performances between the flamboyant Laurence Olivier and the restrained John Gielgud as an example, he further explained that the rivalry between the "shouting" (*hou*) and "humming" (*heng*) schools of actors, and among the audience, had existed in theater since at least Shakespeare's time, as he had discovered while working on his thesis. Furthermore, while he personally favored the latter "humming" style, both had enjoyed audience support, with the shouting style often being more popular. Nonetheless, Huang made his allegiance with Gielgud clear to his actors because Gielgud "expressed the delicate tones and qualities of the sound through highly subtle emotions, a testament that *l'expression parlée* is a very important art."[63] He also distributed to his actors Hamlet's speech on acting in act 3, scene 2 of *Hamlet*, where Hamlet instructs the actors to refrain from shouting.

In the same 1978 article, Huang summarized his *xieyi* view as encompassing four areas of theatrical creation: refined and elevated depiction of life, in contrast to the realistic *xieshi* style; movement evocative of the artistry of *jingju* or ballet; refined language, approaching the level of poetry; and stage design. Together, these four elements—(depiction of) life, language, movement, and design—formed Huang's "outlook for the development of *huaju*."[64] What followed in the next dozen years until his retirement was a burst of creativity, which started with the Brechtian *Life of Galileo* (1979) and the intercultural *kunqu* (Kun opera) *Macbeth* (renamed *Xieshou ji* [*Blood-Stained Hands*], 1983), and culminated in the quintessential *xieyi* piece *China Dream* (1987) and his last directorial work, *Naozhong* (*Alarm Clock*, 1991), in which he borrowed *jingju* techniques, including movement routines, from a well-known pre-1949 play *Da piguan* (*Breaking Open the Coffin*).[65]

These productions attest that Huang was a highly eclectic director whose European experience was critical to his opposition to the dictatorship of the Stanislavsky System after 1949. While his influences included Shakespeare, Bertolt Brecht, Michael Chekhov, and Kurt Jooss, among others, this chapter demonstrates that it was his two-year study with Michel Saint-Denis at the London Theatre School that largely solidified his convictions and practices regarding the primacy of style in theater, which he later crystalized as the *xieyi* view of theater.

More broadly, the significance of this concept became highly visible in the early 1980s; the speech Huang had made in 1962 served as the starting point of the far-reaching "theatrical views" debate that dislodged the centrality of Stanislavsky and ushered in a decade-long new wave of experimental theater. Critics credited Huang with introducing the *xieyi* view of theater, which "reached the root problem of *huaju*,"[66] specifically by "making 'the fourth wall' the touchstone of judging a view of theater."[67] *Huaju* artists touted *xieyi* as a method they would utilize "to break through the constraints of relying mainly on realistic techniques to create the illusion of life on the stage . . . [and] to reach the other side of non-illusionist art."[68] Through Huang's *xieyi* view of theater, Saint-Denis's teachings on style as the core of "deep realism" finally played a pivotal role in *huaju*'s liberation from the strictures of the illusionist Stanislavsky System in China.

Notes

1. Siyuan Liu, "Towards a Chinese School of Performance and Directing: Jiao Juyin," in *Stanislavsky in the World: The System and Its Transformations Across Continents*, ed. Jonathan Pitches and Stefan Aquilina (London: Methuen, 2017), 149–65.
2. See Siyuan Liu, *Performing Hybridity in Colonial-Modern China* (New York: Palgrave Macmillan, 2013).
3. Xixi (Wen Yiduo), "The Wrong Track of Theatre" ("Xiju de qitu"), *The Morning Post Supplement: Theater (Chenbao fukan: jukan)*, June 24, 1926.
4. Siyuan Liu, "The Cross Currents of Modern Theatre and China's National Theatre Movement of 1926," *Asian Theatre Journal* 33, no. 1 (2016): 1–35.
5. Siyuan Liu, "'Spoken Drama (*Huaju*) with a Strong Chinese Flavor': The Resurrection and Demise of Popular Spoken Drama (*Tongsu Huaju*) in Shanghai in the 1950s and Early 1960s," *Theatre Research International* 42, no. 3 (2017): 265–85.
6. Huang Zuolin, "On 'Theatrical Views'—Speech at the National Symposium on the Creation of Spoken Drama, Opera and Children's Plays" ("Mantan 'xiju guan'—zai quanguo huaju, geju, ertongju chuangzuo zuotanhui shang de fayan"), *People's Daily (Renmin ribao)*, April 25, 1962.
7. Huang, "On 'Theatrical Views.'"
8. Huang, "On 'Theatrical Views.'"
9. Huang, "On 'Theatrical Views.'"
10. Michel Saint-Denis, *Theatre: The Rediscovery of Style and Other Writings* (London: Routledge, 2009), 51.
11. Saint-Denis, *Theatre: The Rediscovery of Style*, 52.
12. Michel Saint-Denis, *Training for the Theatre: Premises & Promises* (London: Theatre Arts Books, 1982), 35.
13. Huang Zuolin, "Introducing My Teacher Saint-Denis" ("Jieshao wode enshi Sheng Danni"), *Dramatic Art (Xiju yishu)* 3 (2008): 7.
14. Huang, "Introducing My Teacher Saint-Denis," 5.
15. Huang, "Introducing My Teacher Saint-Denis." According to an editor's note, while the article was published in 2008, Huang wrote it in January 1991 for a national conference on performance training.
16. Saint-Denis, *Training for the Theatre*, 36; Huang, "Introducing My Teacher Saint-Denis," 7. Huang omitted the theater's name in his Chinese retelling.
17. Huang, "Introducing My Teacher Saint-Denis," 8.
18. Huang Zuolin, *The Xieyi View of Theater and I (Wo yu xieyi xiju guan)* (Beijing: Zhongguo xiju chubanshe, 1990), 114–38.
19. Huang, "On 'Theatrical Views.'"
20. Huang Zuolin, "Review, Reference, Outlook" ("Zongjie, jiejian, zhanwang"), *Dramatic Art (Xiju yishu)* 4 (1978): 42.
21. Michel Saint-Denis, "Stanislavski and Shakespeare," trans. Simone Sanzenbach, *Tulane Drama Review* 9, no. 1 (1964): 78.
22. Saint-Denis writes: "But until 1937 we did not know the System" (1964: 78), which should obviously be 1936 because of both the official publication

date of Elizabeth Reynolds Hapgood's English translation, and Huang's reminiscence of his London Theatre Studio quoted above.

23. Saint-Denis, "Stanislavski," 78–79.

24. Saint-Denis, "Stanislavski," 78.

25. Saint-Denis, "Stanislavski," 83.

26. Ke Ling, "An Overview of Dramatic Literature during Shanghai's Occupation Era" ("Shanghai lunxian qijian xiju wenxue guankui"), *Journal of Shanghai Normal University (Philosophy and Social Sciences Edition)* (*Shanghai Shifan Daxue xuebao [zhexue shehui kexue ban]*) 1 (1982): 11.

27. Michael Leonard Kersey Morris, *The Socialist Construction of the Moscow Theater Festival 1933–1937* (MA thesis, Tufts University, 2012), 223. Coincidentally, in 1956, Boris Grigorievich Kulnyov (1896–1959), a Soviet expert from the Vakhtangov Theatre who was teaching the Stanislavsky System at China's Central Academy of Drama, directed *Egor Bulychov and Others* at the Beijing People's Art Theatre, introducing what he called "script and character analysis through action" that prioritized improvisation over character analysis. His approach may have inspired Jiao Juyin's experiments with Chinese theatrical techniques in his subsequent productions. See Siyuan Liu, "Towards a Chinese School of Performance," 154–55; Hanyang (Harry) Jiang, "By Means of Études: Boris Kulnev in an Advanced Actor Training Class in Beijing, 1955–1956," *Stanislavski Studies* 8, no. 1 (2020): 33–50.

28. Huang, "Review, Reference, Outlook," 31; Huang, "Introducing My Teacher Saint-Denis," 4–5.

29. Huang, "Review, Reference, Outlook," 31.

30. Huang Zuolin, "How to Judge Performance" ("Biaoyan de haohuai zenyang qu pingding"), *Theatrical Art (Juchang yishu)* 3, no. 1–2 (1941): 4–8.

31. Saint-Denis, *Theatre: The Rediscovery of Style*, 85.

32. Saint-Denis, *Theatre: The Rediscovery of Style*, 52.

33. Saint-Denis, *Training for the Theatre*, 195.

34. Huang, "Review, Reference, Outlook," 26.

35. Saint-Denis, *Theatre: The Rediscovery of Style*, 83.

36. Jocelyn Herbert Archive, London Theatre Studio, 1936–1956 (JH/2/64), National Theatre Archive, London, UK; Jocelyn Herbert Archive, LTS (London Theatre Studio) Programmes, etc., 1937–1949 (JH/1/67), National Theatre Archive, London, UK.

37. Angelica Garnett interviewed by Wendy Hitchmough, 2003 (C466/167/01–13), British Library, London, UK.

38. Jocelyn Herbert Archive, London Theatre Studio, 1936–1956.

39. Jocelyn Herbert Archive, LTS (London Theatre Studio) Programmes, etc., 1937–1949.

40. Huang, "Review, Reference, Outlook," 26.

41. Saint-Denis, *Theatre: The Rediscovery of Style*, 89–90.

42. Jocelyn Herbert Archive, London Theatre Studio, 1936–1956.

43. Saint-Denis, *Training for the Theatre*, 88–99.

44. Huang, "Review, Reference, Outlook," 26.

45. A. V. Coton, *The New Ballet: Kurt Jooss and His Work* (London: Dobson, 1946), 9.

46. Anna Markard, "Jooss the Teacher: His Pedagogical Aims and the Development of the Choreographic Principles of Harmony," *Choreography and Dance* 3, no. 2 (1993): 47.

47. Markard, "Jooss the Teacher," 47.

48. Huang Zuolin, "*Chinese Dream*—Words from the Director" ("'Zhongguo meng'—daoyan dehua"), *Theatre Gazette* (*Xiju bao*) 6 (1987): 8.

49. Saint-Denis, *Theatre: The Rediscovery of Style*, 114.

50. Saint-Denis, *Training for the Theatre*, 179.

51. Saint-Denis, *Theatre: The Rediscovery of Style*, 91.

52. Saint-Denis, *Training for the Theatre*, 168.

53. Huang, "Introducing My Teacher Saint-Denis," 5.

54. Siyuan Liu, *Transforming Tradition: The Reform of Chinese Theatre in the 1950s and Early 1960s* (Ann Arbor: University of Michigan Press, 2021), chapter 5; Siyuan Liu, *Performing Hybridity*.

55. Huang, *The Xieyi View of Theater and I*, 3.

56. Ye Mingzhu, "Interview of Mr. Zuolin, Director of *Small Town Story*" ("'Xiaocheng gushi' daoyan Zuolin xiansheng fangwen ji"), *Theatre News* (*Juchang xinwen*) 3/4 (1940): 5.

57. Xu Banmei, *Memoir of Spoken Drama's Founding Era* (*Huaju chuangshiqi huiyilu*) (Beijing: Zhongguo xiju chubanshe, 1957), 125–26.

58. Huang Zuolin, "Italian Commedia Dell'Arte" ("Yidali jixing xiju"), *Dramatic Art* (*Xiju yishu*) 3 (1981): 34–44.

59. Li Jiayao and Huang Zuolin, "Talking about Farce" ("Pingshuo huaji"), *Shanghai Theater* (*Shanghai xiju*) 2 (1990): 11.

60. Saint-Denis, *Training for the Theatre*, 124.

61. Michel Saint-Denis Archive, London Theatre School Photograph Albums 1936–1937 (Add MS 81251), British Library, London, UK.

62. Huang, "Review, Reference, Outlook," 27.

63. Huang, "Review, Reference, Outlook," 28.

64. Huang, "Review, Reference, Outlook," 31.

65. For more on *Breaking Open the Coffin*'s pre-1949 popularity and its censorship before and after 1949, see Siyuan Liu, "'Ruined by Several Actresses Who Added Pornographic Elements': The Popularity of Emerging Actresses in Chinese *Jingju* (Beijing Opera) and the Censorship of Two Plays," in *Women in Asian Performance: Aesthetics and Politics*, ed. Arya Madhavan (London: Routledge, 2017), 97–109.

66. Chen Gongmin, "The Issue of Theatrical Views" ("Xiju guannian wenti"), *Play Script* (*Juben*) 5 (1981): 82.

67. Tong Daoming, "Also on Theatrical Views" ("Ye tan xiju guan"), in *Collected Essays from the Theatrical Views Debate* (*Xiju guan zhengming ji*), ed. Yu Qingyuan (Beijing: Zhongguo xiju chubanshe, 1986), 1: 66.

68. Hu Weimin, "The Essence of the Wave of Innovations in the Art of Spoken Drama" ("Huaju yishu gexin langchao de shizhi"), *People's Theatre* (*Renmin xiju*) 7 (1982): 36.

13 | After the Colloquial

Legacies of Realistic Expression in Contemporary Japan

JESSICA NAKAMURA

The final scene of Okada Toshiki's (b. 1973) seminal play *Sangatsu no itsukakan* (*Five Days in March*, 2004) stages a seemingly banal exchange between a man and a woman.¹ The man, having just taken money out of an ATM, gives the woman 20,000 yen (approximately $185 in the year *Sangatsu no itsukakan* premiered). The money repays her for fronting the cost of their stay at a love hotel and meals for the past five days. Set against the backdrop of the start of the second Iraq War, the play is about their brief affair, retold separately by the man and the woman to friends. On its surface, this final scene—a few lines of mundane dialogue played in a quotidian naturalism—feels out of place. It is drastically different from the preceding ninety minutes, where characters recount the last five days in monologues in a style that can be described as stream of consciousness, unfolding characters' experiences at length through starts, stops, and repetitions. At the same time, actors' bodies mirror their verbal flow in repeated motions that resemble but do not replicate everyday gestures.²

Instead of as a departure, another way to understand *Sangatsu no itsukakan*'s final scene is as a reflection of the influence of playwright-director Hirata Oriza (b. 1962) and his style *gendai kōgo engeki*. In the early 1990s, Hirata developed *gendai kōgo engeki* (contemporary colloquial theater), which can be understood as realistic expression based in the structure and emotional tenor of the Japanese language.³ His plays work through dialogue built on quotidian expressions, and his productions attempt to look like a slice of life: actors speak in hushed tones, turn their backs to the audience, and sometimes carry out simultaneous conversations. Audience interest in and critical acclaim for *gendai kōgo engeki* made Hirata one of the key figures in 1990s theater, creating work that, as M. Cody Poulton notes, theater critics described as a "new realism" and Poulton himself characterizes as Japan's "return of realism."[4]

Hirata's influence on Japanese theater continues today. He regularly produces work, frequently remounting his signature *gendai kōgo engeki* productions from the early to mid-1990s, and his company Seinendan (the Youth Group) supports emerging artists by providing mentorship and rehearsal and performance space. Okada, approximately ten years younger than Hirata, has acknowledged the ways in which Hirata's writings and theatrical style have influenced him. Okada's early style, described as "super-real" Japanese, both points to connections to Hirata and calls attention to how notions of realistic expression may develop from Hirata's quotidian dialogue to Okada's extra-daily gestures.[5]

In this chapter, I consider the life of *gendai kōgo engeki* beyond Hirata's own theatrical productions. I focus on how artists of the next generation stage and revise a central idea of Hirata's *gendai kōgo engeki*, the attempt to "directly portray the world." Given Okada's expressed influence by Hirata, if I consider *Sangatsu no itsukakan* as a direct portrayal of the world, the mundane qualities of the play's final scene undo the verbal and embodied expressiveness of earlier parts of the play. In this short scene, the minimal dialogue, movement, and lack of overt emotion illustrate that the moments of connection we see earlier between the man and the woman are displaced by the impersonal attributes of a financial transaction. The ending of *Sangatsu no itsukakan* suggests that the effects of the play's world—a contemporary Japan in which flexible labor practices prevent financial stability—alter the everyday lives of young people, disallowing the potential for emotional connection. In other words, as a direct portrayal of the world, *Sangatsu no itsukakan* exposes how contemporary Japan's economic conditions limit personal relationships and affective attachments.

By exploring artists influenced by Hirata, I think about the ways in which realistic styles evolve with changes in the world they portray. Much has been written about Hirata's own *gendai kōgo engeki* productions, focused on his dramaturgy and staging conventions, but little attention has been devoted to how others may transform *gendai kōgo engeki*. To be clear, none of the artists discussed in this chapter have stated directly that they are taking up and revising *gendai kōgo engeki*, but considering

Hirata's significance in contemporary Japanese theater, I explore their work as potential new developments of that style that push its manifestation in performance outside the boundaries of what we might consider realistic expression. I ask: if *gendai kōgo engeki* aims at a direct portrayal of the world, what happens when the world transforms? In so doing, I tap into questions about theatrical realism more broadly: if realism serves as a mirror of society, how does it evolve to reflect it, what might it look like, and how do these changes affect how we think about realism?

To explore the evolution of a realistic expression that starts with Hirata, I examine representative productions of two artists who worked directly with him, Iwai Hideto (b. 1974) and Matsui Shū (b. 1972), who went on to establish their own theater companies. Despite their plays premiering less than fifteen years after Hirata's early productions of *gendai kōgo engeki*, Iwai's and Matsui's work is both inspired by and diverges from what appears on Hirata's stage. To trace their work as potential legacies of *gendai kōgo engeki*, I move beyond Hirata's specific performance style, looking instead to his writings to identify *gendai kōgo engeki*'s main philosophical underpinnings. In so doing, I define this style as an approach, a mode of engaging with the world, that can result in multiple aesthetics, including ones better suited to the contemporary Japan of Iwai and Matsui after the bursting of the economic bubble and the resultant neoliberal structural reforms. In opposition to the individualism fashioned by these reforms, Iwai's and Matsui's performances reflect their worlds by portraying multiple and often conflicting perspectives to undo any notion of perceived stability. Instead, the emotional lives of their characters become key in determining the realities portrayed onstage. By reading Iwai's and Matsui's plays as evolutions of *gendai kōgo engeki* adjusting to a changing Japan, we can consider it as more than a theatrical style: instead, it—and by extension realistic expression—becomes a malleable mode of response to the contemporary world.

Gendai kōgo engeki as Approach

To consider *gendai kōgo engeki* after Hirata, it is important to uncouple it from Hirata's signature performance style. While English-language scholarship has typically discussed *gendai kōgo engeki* in terms of how it appears in Hirata's performances, in this chapter I turn to Hirata's writings to understand this style as an approach to theatrical expression.[6] Hirata himself considers it this way in his aptly titled 1995 treatise, *Gendai kōgo engeki no tame ni* (*For the Purposes of Contemporary Colloquial Theater*).

Early in the text, Hirata explains that his *gendai kōgo engeki* theory is "not simply acting theory or theater theory," but rather a way of "showing a viewpoint on humanity and the world."[7] Hirata thus asks us to think of *gendai kōgo engeki* more broadly, moving beyond the mechanisms of the stage to an approach to viewing people and their environments.

Hirata's *gendai kōgo engeki* is particularly generative for a discussion of realism in East Asia because it clearly diverges from the meaning-making practices of Western-realism-inspired *shingeki*. Developed after Western realistic dramas were imported in the early twentieth century, *shingeki* became popular in the postwar period and remains a major theater form today.[8] Japanese theater critics developed the term *shizukana engeki* (quiet theater) to position the understated, slice-of-life performances of Hirata and his contemporaries against the frenetic, highly spectacular theatrical work of the 1980s. In contrast, Hirata called his own style *gendai kōgo engeki*, which according to Poulton "eschews such terms as 'realism' or 'quiet theatre,'" focusing on language and how it is spoken.[9]

In his treatise, Hirata characterizes the style as a departure from *shingeki*. Central to *gendai kōgo engeki*'s divergence is Hirata's critique of the association between *shingeki* (and realism more broadly) and ideas of truth. Hirata makes clear that such an association is a construct when he describes how modern thought (近代思想) gravitates toward an idea of realism based in truth (真理).[10] Interested in the objective (as opposed to the subjective, which Hirata considers to be premodern), modern thought connects objectivity to ideas of the real and truth, resulting in the "pitting of truth against artifice."[11] Accordingly, notions of the "theatrical" take on negative connotations as being fake or untruthful, and, as Hirata laments, result in a move to entrust representations of reality to film instead of theater.[12] Yet, as Hirata explains, while realism may present ideas of objectivity, at the same time it aims to transmit arguments about society and politics. For Hirata, the particular genre of socialist realism, a style highly influential in the development of *shingeki*, manifests the constructed links between objectivity, reality, and truth, a theater form he critiques as being art "in service of spreading ideology."[13]

In contrast, Hirata aims for his *gendai kōgo engeki* to "directly portray the world." The word "directly" (直接的に) is important to Hirata; he brings it up several times—for instance, when explaining that theater and art more broadly should be separate from ideas of value and morals, instead "directly grasping the actual world." Key to this representation is Hirata's expressed desire to work from "how I understand the world." His focus on his individual perspective acknowledges that it is one of many, aiming to reflect the "essence of an event" without conveying any sense of right or wrong.[14] Because Hirata separates *gendai kōgo engeki* from expressions of truth, his staging avoids past critiques of realism's reaffirmations of the status quo, what scholars such as Elin Diamond have described as realism's work of performatively reproducing norms: "Realism is more than an interpretation of reality passing as reality; it *produces* 'reality' by positioning its spectator to recognize and verify its truths."[15] In contrast, following Hirata's language, *gendai kōgo engeki* insists on being a reflection of reality and not a reproduction; it does not produce the "truths" of reality, but rather aims to portray such reality from Hirata's own point of view.

Hirata's focus on individual perception and the role of the individual in Iwai's and Matsui's works must be further contextualized by the enduring economic crisis in late-twentieth- and early twenty-first-century Japan. Hirata was developing *gendai kōgo engeki* in the early 1990s, immediately after the economic bubble burst in 1991. Hirata's company Seinendan staged early productions in the style of *gendai kōgo engeki* before the resultant ongoing economic recession and stagnation undermined the narrative of postwar economic progress and brought uncertainty to youth entering the job market. By the first decade of the twenty-first century, when Iwai and Matsui were launching their careers, the lingering economic stagnation ensured that postwar progress, both national and personal, were not only distant memories but also goals completely foreclosed on by the economic downturn. As David Leheny explains, in recessionary Japan, the sense of the future had changed, resulting in an "absence of hope."[16]

The political response to Japan's dismal economic state brought neoliberal structural reforms that shifted attention from social networks to individual responsibility. First with Koizumi Jun'ichirō's government (2001–2006) and then with Abe Shinzō's governments (2006–2007; 2012–2020), economic reforms, affecting multiple levels of Japanese society, from business and labor to the postal service and the makeup of the home, were driven by a notion of self-responsibility (*jiko sekinin*). As Hiroko Takeda describes, these reforms are "profoundly intertwined with the updating of individual subjectivity through the recalibration of everyday family life."[17] Along with changing conceptions of the subject, according to Takeda, these reforms work beyond the realm of economics, as a "set of discourses" that "presen[t] a normative framework for its people in a changing socio-political environment."[18] This line anticipates Wendy Brown's argument that "neoliberal rationality disseminates the *model of the market* to all domains and activities—even where money is not an issue—and configures human beings exhaustively as market actors, always, only, and everywhere as *homo oeconomicus*."[19] In Japan, shaping normative ideas of the neoliberal subject resulted in increased economic precarity for those in flexible labor situations and in the privatization of once-public programs, dismantling social safety nets and widening the income gap between permanent regular employees and temporary contract workers.[20]

This conception of the individual, with its establishment of norms or standards for everyday life, reflects a world that had changed between Hirata's early productions with Seinendan in the 1990s and the mid-2000s, when Iwai and Matsui began to stage their work. Thinking of Iwai's and Matsui's productions as further developments of *gendai kōgo engeki*, I contemplate how they may comment on neoliberal notions of the individual and self-responsibility, and in turn on how realistic expression may shift to reflect these major changes to contemporary Japan. I look to *gendai kōgo engeki*'s emphasis on direct portrayal based on perception as a vehicle to comment on this neoliberal conception of the individual. For Hirata, *gendai kōgo engeki* works from the playwright's expression of his point of view. This point of view is singular, unfolding in public and semipublic spaces, including the art-museum lobby of Hirata's landmark play *Tokyo Notes* (1994). As I will explore, the work of the next generation of theater makers develops the notion of individual perspective to introduce multiple and at times competing points of view that reflect the ongoing lack of stability in contemporary Japan. In turn, these productions exhibit staging choices that move beyond the quotidian expression of Hirata's performance style.

Iwai's Multiple Perspectives and Unraveling Reality in *Te*

As an iteration of *gendai kōgo engeki*, Iwai Hideto's *Te* crafts its direct portrayal from individual perspectives.[21] At first, *Te* appears to be the most "realistic" play discussed in this chapter, seeming to show a family get-together through quotidian expressions. Yet as it unfolds, *Te* switches perspectives from one character to another, not only revealing more of the drama it portrays, but calling attention to the inability of a single perspective to fully reflect the world. Premiering in 2008, *Te* tells the story of a family gathering twice: first from the perspective of the family's youngest son, Jirō, and then from the perspective of his mother, Michiko.[22] After opening with the funeral of the family grandmother, Kikue, most of the action of the play takes place three days earlier on the night Kikue passes away, when the entire family gathers at her house. As Iwai himself has discussed, the multiple perspectives reflect the effects of domestic violence—as the events of the evening develop, it becomes clear that the father has been abusive for years, deeply affecting the family. Iwai has explained that the structure of *Te* came from his own experiences of domestic violence shaping how he remembered his family past, where an event that he recalled varied drastically from his mother's memories of it.[23] By presenting two points of view deeply altered by family trauma, *Te* challenges how we comprehend and retain events. Accordingly, *Te*'s individualized perspectives highlight how the inner emotional lives of its characters influence how they see and relate to the world around them and how that world is depicted on the stage.

Iwai's career intersected with and was influenced by Hirata and *gendai kōgo engeki* in several ways. As a teenager, Iwai was inspired by viewing rehearsals and performances by Hirata and his contemporaries, including a performance of Hirata's *Tokyo Notes*.[24] Iwai formed his own company, hi-bye, in 2003, staging plays he wrote, many of them based on his own experiences and many featuring Iwai as a central actor.[25] In 2007, the year before *Te* premiered, he joined the directing department at Hirata's company, Seinendan.[26] There, Iwai planned and executed Seinendan's "Classics in Vernacular" series, in which he worked to adapt Western and Asian classics into a colloquial theater style.

Based on this history, it is possible to identify Hirata's influence on *Te*'s performance aesthetics. *Te* initially resembles the kind of staging found in work directed by Hirata. In the scenes from Jirō's point of view, actors engage in everyday behaviors, including eating and drinking. Most of the stage action unfolds in real time, centering on one night when the family gathers to drink and sing karaoke. The audience on two sides of the stage, as seen in the 2013 performance video, ensured that actors turned their backs to the audience multiple times. Iwai primarily constructs the play out of quotidian dialogue, but it notably diverges from Hirata's everyday expressions in key ways. For one, the dialogue reflects Iwai's scatological humor: early on, Jirō picks his nose and threatens to wipe his snot on his friend Maeda, and when Michiko first enters after the funeral scene, she is covered in bird droppings. *Te* also foregrounds family conflict more than do Hirata's plays, with the final scene in Michiko's version portraying an argument between her and her husband.

In part, *Te* echoes the ways in which Hirata's plays often present multiple perspectives of characters. For instance, some of the characters who cross through the art museum lobby of Hirata's *Tokyo Notes* are grown siblings meeting in the museum's restaurant to discuss what to do about their aging parents; the youngest son is in the process of separating from his wife, and we hear about the family's situation from multiple members without the play providing any resolution. Similarly, Iwai lets his two versions land without commentary or any attempt to resolve them.

What distinguishes Iwai's dramaturgy from Hirata's is the way the play narrowly focuses in on two characters' perspectives, showing a single point of view before moving on to another. Whereas *Tokyo Notes* expresses multiple characters' perspectives, *Te* distinguishes one character's from the other's to highlight that the play's depicted world is defined by individuals who understand events differently. The play begins with Jirō's version, but it does not make clear that the scenes are from Jirō's perspective, so it seems as if they are *the* events as they are happening, unfiltered. Jirō's point of view begins immediately after the prologue scene at Kikue's funeral. While this scene is unassigned to a particular character, *Te* begins to align the audience with Jirō's perspective when throughout the priest's strange eulogy, Jirō complains to Maeda about the priest excessively revealing his personal interest in Kikue's hometown of Otaru, including that the town was visited by Helen Keller, a name the priest mispronounces.[27] From Jirō's asides, when the play subsequently transitions to the scenes that take his perspective, it does so seamlessly.

When *Te* shifts to Michiko's perspective, the play disrupts our understandings of the events as they occurred in Jirō's scenes. Having so closely followed Jirō's perspective in *Te*'s realistic staging, Michiko's scenes add information and sometimes contradict Jirō's to undo any assumptions about the reality we thought we knew. As Michiko's scenes unfold, *Te* reveals the complexity of family dynamics, including that Kikue's dementia is much more severe than Jirō understands, and that Tarō, Jirō's older brother, is less emotionally distant and gruff than what we know from Jirō's perspective. In Jirō's scenes, he complains that Tarō has collected a number of car parts in the foyer of his grandmother's home; when Jirō confronts him about it, Tarō seems cold and easily prone to anger, while Jirō seems reasonable. In contrast, Michiko's scenes reveal that Tarō regularly takes care of his grandmother and is resentful that Jirō seldom visits her—Tarō interacts with Kikue with an ease that makes Jirō's exchanges with her seem awkward. These revelations about the family develop the ways in which *Te*'s *gendai kōgo engeki* unfolds individual perspectives: in Iwai's conception, a direct portrayal of the world means conflicting impressions of it that undo any sense of a shared or unified reality.

In Michiko's scenes, *Te* shows that the emotional experiences of characters shape their perception of the world. Michiko's scenes depart from the realistic staging conventions in Jirō's, integrating more spectacular elements to portray her emotional state. One of the more striking contrasts in staging occurs partway through the family gathering when Michiko takes a phone call. In Jirō's scene, she simply leaves the stage, but in Michiko's perspective, she wanders around the darkened stage while the rest of her family is frozen in place. After she hangs up, the family rearranges themselves on one side of the stage, singing karaoke together in unison—they appear joyous, lifting a seated Kikue up and dancing around her. The father, seated on the ground in front of them, points the rest of the family out to Michiko, alone on the other side of the stage. To her, it appears that they are all on his side in their troubled marriage. The staging drastically contrasts the same events we witnessed earlier through Jirō's perspective, where the staging was fairly mundane, portraying the family as continuing with their party.[28]

Considered as a development of *gendai kōgo engeki*, this scene, instead of as an unrealistic representation of the world, introduces a portrayal of reality based on emotional interiority. Michiko's emotions determine how her reality is depicted, and *Te*'s staging reveals the mother's isolated emotional state. In response to seeing this karaoke vision, Michiko starts crying, and when her family continues to sing, *Te* further reflects the ways in which Michiko feels ostracized from her own family. In so doing, *Te* foregrounds emotional experience as a valid part of one's perspective; moreover, the play suggests that emotions are a factor in determining how we understand the world. Significantly, the play manifests Michiko's emotional realities in physical staging choices, some of which depart from realistic theatrical conventions, expanding *gendai kōgo engeki*'s portrayal as determined more by emotions than through a unified performance style.

The emotional intensity of Michiko's scenes also alters how we remember Jirō's staged reality. Jirō's scenes are more understated emotionally, his feelings seeming not to affect the staging, contributing to the early impression that Jirō's scenes are a general point of view and not a single character's perspective. However, after watching Michiko's emotions shape *Te*'s unfolding of her reality, Jirō's scenes begin to feel emotionally repressed, the play asking whether his muted emotional engagement may be part of his strategy for coping with ongoing domestic violence. Prompting us to reconsider the emotional tenor of Jirō's scenes, *Te* undoes the possibility of emotional neutrality and highlights the centrality of emotional engagement in reflections of the world.

In its direct portrayal of contemporary Japan, *Te* stresses the importance of individual experiences in determining reality. Given the new norms of individual responsibility after Japanese neoliberal structural reforms, under which the daily lives and experiences of individuals are situated within the market, *Te* presents a reflection of the world based in a different kind of individualism. It is not the market that contributes to either Jirō's or Michiko's perspectives, but rather their emotions, derived from their relationships with their family members. *Te* not only makes room for such individual experiences, but also suggests that our very understandings of our realities are built on them.

Matsui's Dark Interior World in *Jiman no musuko*

If *Te* foregrounds individual perspectives and emotional engagement in its direct portrayal of its world, Matsui Shū's *Jiman no musuko* (*Prideful Son*) questions the qualities of the world to be perceived and the role of theater in engaging with it. Similar to *Te*, *Jiman no musuko* explores how reality is determined by an individual's perspective. By separating its reality from Japanese society, however, *Jiman no musuko* takes up questions of normalcy and belonging to make its social critique. The play is about Tadashi, a *hikikomori* (shut-in) who creates his own kingdom in his apartment. He invites others, including a brother and sister who are in love with each other, to join him, and it soon becomes clear that Tadashi's efforts to create a new society are simply an effort to rule over his own domain. Like *Te*, the play portrays a reality that is specific to an individual and driven by affective experience, but *Jiman no musuko* physicalizes this reality as Tadashi's apartment kingdom. Taking us into an alternatively imagined world, *Jiman no musuko* integrates theatrical elements to challenge how we understand events portrayed onstage, while insisting that characters' emotions may be more real than the stories represented.

Of the three artists discussed in this chapter, Matsui has worked the most with Hirata: he began his career as an actor for Seinendan before leaving the company to start Sample Theater in 2007. During Sample's early days, Matsui cast Seinendan actors in his productions and benefited from being able to use Seinendan rehearsal space and small theater in the Komaba neighborhood in Tokyo. *Jiman no musuko*, as one of Sample's early productions that brought Matsui notoriety by winning the Kishida Drama Award in 2010, displays stylistic elements of Hirata's *gendai kōgo engeki*: dialogue in the play tends toward quotidian expression; characters do not openly discuss social issues; and there is a clear emphasis on the world of the play.[29] In performance, the acting at times appears similar to that of Hirata's productions, in part because several Seinendan company members appeared in the 2010 premiere production.[30]

At the same time, Matsui's staging of *Jiman no musuko* could be described as exceeding Hirata's quotidian expression with elements of the fantastical. When the sister and brother travel to Tadashi's kingdom, along with Tadashi's mother who seeks to reunite with her son, and a deliveryman who serves as a guide (and sometimes narrator for the play), they all embark on a stylized journey that involves a sea voyage—their bodies sway and bend to indicate a boat that encounters rough waters (see figure 13.1). In this instance, stylized movements become the vehicle through which the characters enter Tadashi's kingdom. We could describe the setting of more spectacular staging choices into quotidian dialogue as Matsui's spin on *gendai kōgo engeki*, one suited to the play's distinction between the reality of Japanese society and that of Tadashi's apartment.

With Tadashi's apartment, *Jiman no musuko* makes a clear transition to a place that exists outside of society. When the brother and sister characters prepare to travel to Tadashi's kingdom, they describe their journey as ending their connections to their work and social lives: the sister throws away the flowers the brother received from his job's farewell party, telling him that he needs to leave the world behind, to "sever" his attachments.[31] Later in the scene, the sister claims they "cannot return," and the two imaginatively bid their parents farewell.[32] That Tadashi's kingdom is a removal from both society and reality becomes more apparent later in the play when the sister tells Tadashi she will follow him because, as she claims, they are alike in that they both do not accept reality (even though, as she adds, her heart belongs to her brother).[33]

Jiman no musuko thus uses Tadashi's apartment to call into question the norms of everyday Japan. In light of Takeda's making a connection between neoliberal reforms and the construction of social norms in other areas of life, including the home, when the characters enter Tadashi's apartment, they reject neoliberal values of economic productivity. To move to Tadashi's kingdom, the sister and brother leave the workforce and their earning potential; Tadashi, too, does not hold a stable job. The characters' residence in Tadashi's apartment also works to remove them from the expectations of Japanese social norms. The brother and sister are in love with each other, and their entrance into Tadashi's kingdom allows them to be together. The incestuous relationship between brother and sister is an extreme example, but this rejection of normalcy can

Figure 13.1: A promotional photograph from *Jiman no musuko* of the scene in which characters travel to Tadashi's kingdom-apartment. The deliveryman character, who leads the others on this journey, is at the top left. © Tsukasa Aoki. Image courtesy of Sample Theater Company.

be found in Tadashi, who appears to be a *hikikomori*, rarely leaving his apartment-kingdom. That *Jiman no musuko* features characters outside of society is significant—it shows people who long to leave social norms behind, and it implies that Japanese society holds no place for those who do not choose to follow those norms.

Jiman no musuko does not simply move characters outside of society, but, like *Te*, questions the possibility of understanding a singular reality. By casting doubt on what the play shows, the play puts the very idea of understanding the world in question. After Tadashi welcomes the brother and sister to his kingdom, the deliveryman stops the action of the play. All other characters freeze, and the deliveryman tells two conflicting stories while referencing Tadashi and his mother: in the first story, he explains, a man (indicating Tadashi) murders five people on the subway, a person for each of the five strokes in the *kanji* character in his name; in the second story, a woman (indicating the mother) murders her son.[34] In this moment, the deliveryman introduces multiple stories that call into question what we are seeing and what the characters express to us. It is unclear: Did Tadashi or his mother commit these crimes? Will they in the future? Instead, are these alternative stories to the play performed, and if so, what, exactly, is the story we are seeing now?

Knit up in this moment that troubles the relationship between theatrical representation and perceived reality is the photograph, an art form tied to realistic expression. What prompts the deliveryman's conflicting tales is the mother asking him to take a photo of her and Tadashi. When the deliveryman snaps the photograph, everyone else freezes, and a slide projector downstage turns on. Unlike earlier, when the play projects an image of Hawaii's Diamondhead landmark while the mother describes her love for Hawaii, in this moment there is no photograph. Instead, a harsh light illuminates Tadashi and his mother, positioning the live figures as the photograph. In part, this moment is a challenge to the photograph that follows Hirata's argument in *Gendai kōgo engeki no tame ni*, where he points out that while photographs and then film have been associated with "reality," the theater, unlike the "reality" cast onto a two-dimensional page or screen, presents actual objects and people.[35] When *Jiman no musuko* uses this moment to present a theatrical 3D rendering of the photograph, the scene also reminds us that underneath this seemingly realistic art form lies an undercurrent of multiple stories. The scene undoes the photograph's projection of happy mother and son, while the conflicting tales make it impossible to know what goes on underneath that image. In this way, *Jiman no musuko* not only breaks what Hirata describes as the false link between realism and the impression of truth, it positions the theater as the very site to disrupt the guise of portraying a truthful reality.

Instead of suggesting that we can comprehend the truth of a story, *Jiman no musuko* insists that the reality of what we perceive onstage resides in the emotions experienced by characters. In performance, *Jiman no musuko* may separate Japanese society from Tadashi's kingdom and the wishes of those who inhabit it, but the emotional lives of characters play out as lived realities to be believed. For instance, although the sister claims that she and Tadashi share a desire to reject reality, she characterizes her emotions—the love that she feels for her brother—as real. At other times, characters feel for people or situations that may not be grounded in the reality we see. For instance, *Jiman no musuko* casts doubt on the existence of the neighbor woman's son, even though she seems to have real feelings for him. We are first introduced to the neighbor woman hanging up laundry while listening to metal music. In a later conversation with Tadashi's mother, she claims she has a son who suffers from severe light sensitivity. After that scene, we see the neighbor woman in a moment of emotional intensity, when she hangs up a child's pajamas and caresses them, her action expressing longing and sadness, presumably for her son. As the play goes on, however, it becomes unclear whether her son actually exists; her emotions feel real even though it is unclear whether or not their conditions are true. We never see him onstage, and the brother character eventually moves into her apartment to become her son. By the end of the play, it seems as if the neighbor woman never had a son in the first place—another instance of the ways in which *Jiman no musuko* suggests we create our own realities.

As *Jiman no musuko* highlights the emotional realities of characters, it further builds doubt about the world it displays onstage. Toward the end of the play, the deliveryman reminds us of the contingency of the stories we have seen. After providing another story of mother and son—this time, of a double suicide—he explains that it could be "anyone's story."[36] The moment resituates the idea of a "direct portrayal" as defined and constructed, in which theatrical representation includes replicating familiar tales. When metatheatrical references end the play, *Jiman no musuko* turns us to contemplating the theater itself: all of the actors pause on stage and repeat a gesture over and over, like "machines."[37] At this point, the deliveryman re-enters and describes the scene as an expression of a display. In these moments, *Jiman no musuko* not only suggests that emotions can be more real than the conditions that people live in, but as a "direct portrayal," *Jiman no musuko* also makes clear where it stands in relationship to representing the world—it stages *the portraying of* reality. In other words, part of *Jiman no musuko*'s representation of the world is its dismantling of the world's depiction. Matsui's *gendai kōgo engeki* affirms the role of theater in engaging with and undoing realistic expression to understand its very constructedness.

Theater, Reality, and Critique

In this chapter, I have considered how artists in the generation after Hirata create work that can be considered developments of Hirata's *gendai kōgo engeki* realistic expression. Instead of replicating Hirata's staging aesthetic, productions by Okada, Iwai, and Matsui feature stylistic changes to account for changing conditions of contemporary Japan. As Okada's, Iwai's, and Matsui's productions all show, direct portrayal can vary greatly depending on context, and Iwai's and Matsui's productions in particular emphasize how individual perception changes understanding of and reflection about a staged reality. These plays suggest that there are multiple realities, specific to individual people, highlighting that individual emotions may alter the realities perceived. Thus, these three plays further the uncoupling of realistic expression and any notion of truth that Hirata calls for in *Gendai kōgo engeki no tame ni*.

Based on the work of Okada, Iwai, and Matsui, *gendai kōgo engeki* can be considered to be responsive, a realistic approach that artists can use to contemplate and comment on their surroundings. Accordingly, the style can become a means of critique and more politically inflected than scholars initially imagined Hirata's work to be.[38] As *Sangatsu no itsukakan*, *Te*, and *Jiman no musuko* reflect, the world in contemporary Japan is fragmented, foregrounding financial transactions and pushing out those who do not conform. In these works, direct portrayal focuses intensely on individual perspectives, insisting on the relevancy of our own individual realities, and undermining the normalcy expected of the individual subject after neoliberal structural reforms. In the plays' portrayals, thus, individual perspectives become the mode for unravelling ideas of conformity, suggesting that multiple experiences reside outside the neoliberal norms based on economic conditions.

More broadly, all three celebrate theater as the medium through which to engage with a critique of contemporary life. In the stylized and theatrical elements of Okada's, Iwai's, and Matsui's plays, theater is the site not only to reflect reality but to comment on it. While *Te* is less overt about the role of the theatrical, it still uses stylized elements to portray Michiko's sense of ostracism. *Jiman no musuko* goes even further to make the theatrical the means of its critical engagement, calling attention to the multiple stories that can ensue. Such faith in the role of theater returns us again to Hirata, who insists on its expressive potential in his treatise. As these artists demonstrate, despite the changes to how their versions of *gendai kōgo engeki* look, one of the enduring legacies of *gendai kōgo engeki* is the reaffirmation of theater's power in understanding the world.

Notes

1. A major milestone in Okada's career, *Sangatsu no itsukakan* won him major awards in Japan, including the Kishida Kunio Award in 2005. Touring to multiple countries, it also garnered him international recognition as *the* new rising star of Japanese performance.

2. For a discussion of embodiment in Okada's work, see Holger Hartung's

"Ruptures, Gravity, Dwelling: Reflections on Okada Toshiki's Movement Aesthetic," in *Okada Toshiki and Japanese Theatre*, ed. Peter Eckersall, Barbara Geilhorn, Andreas Regelsberger, and M. Cody Poulton (Aberystwyth, UK: Performance Research Books, 2021), 73–81.

3. See M. Cody Poulton's "Hirata Oriza on the Rise and Fall of Japanese Literature . . . and Theatre Too," *Asian Theatre Journal* 38, no. 1 (2021): 35–53, for a discussion of Hirata's thoughts on the Japanese language and their influence on his theater style.

4. M. Cody Poulton, "The Rhetoric of the Real," in *Modern Japanese Theatre and Performance*, ed. David Jortner, Keiko McDonald, and Kevin J. Wetmore Jr. (Lanham, MD: Lexington Books, 2006), 17. In keeping with the aims of this volume, Poulton is quick to point out that among critics, "no one is quite sure what 'realism' is or whether the 'new realism' is in fact a return of the 'old' kind" (17).

5. See Okada's 2005 interview with Performing Arts Network Japan for the ways in which he was exposed to Hirata's style, first in a two-day workshop and then through Hirata's treatise *Gendai kōgo engeki no tame ni* (*For the Purposes of Contemporary Colloquial Theater*). Notably, Okada "was very much inspired by [Hirata's] method of diverting the actor's consciousness of the script by intentionally placing some kind of physical burden on the actor." Also see this interview for discussion of "super-real" Japanese, https://performingarts.jp/E/art_interview/0510/1.html

6. For discussions that center on performance, see, for example, Poulton's essay, "The Rhetoric of the Real"; Peter Eckersall's "Towards a Dramaturgy of Robots and Object-Figures," *TDR: The Drama Review* 59, no. 3 (2015): 123–31; and my "Reflecting on the Unknowns of History: Theatrical Ghosting, Transgenerational Remembrance, and Japanese Imperialism in the *Seoul Shimin* Play Series," *Modern Drama* 61, no. 2 (2018): 149–70. An exception is Poulton's essay, "Hirata Oriza on the Rise and Fall of Japanese Literature," where he discusses a 2019 public lecture by Hirata in Vancouver. In this volume, Poulton furthers his analysis of Hirata's dramaturgy by reading it through the theories of Siegfried Kracauer.

7. Hirata Oriza, *Gendai kōgo engeki no tame ni* (Tokyo: Banseisha, 1995), 5. The translations of Hirata's treatise and Iwai's and Matsui's plays are mine.

8. See chapters 6 and 7 of Brian Powell's *Japan Modern Theatre: A Century of Change and Continuity* (London: Japan Library, 2002) for a history of *shingeki* in the postwar period.

9. In "Rhetoric of the Real," Poulton explains that Hirata preferred the expression "'contemporary colloquial theater'" (29).

10. Hirata, *Gendai kōgo engeki no tame ni*, 23–24.

11. Hirata, *Gendai kōgo engeki no tame ni*, 24. He describes the tendency of modernism/modern theater/modern thinking and its "inclination towards the real," where we have the development of an idea of "objectivity" (*kyakkanteki*) (23).

12. Hirata, *Gendai kōgo engeki no tame ni*, 30–31.

13. Hirata, *Gendai kōgo engeki no tame ni*, 25

14. Hirata, *Gendai kōgo engeki no tame ni*, 25–26.

15. Elin Diamond, "Mimesis, Mimicry, and the 'True-Real,'" *Modern Drama* 32, no. 1 (1989): 60.

16. David Leheny, *Empire of Hope: The Sentimental Politics of Japanese Decline* (Ithaca, NY: Cornell University Press, 2018), 17. Leheny elaborates: "it was not simply that conditions were bad . . . but rather the sense that the Japan that had emerged in the 1990s and 2000s was not the future Japan imagined back in the 1960s, 1970s, and 1980s, when people were encouraged to believe that Japan's future would be better, richer, and more successful than its past" (12).

17. Takeda Hiroko, "Structural Reform of the Family and the Neoliberalisation of Everyday Life in Japan," *New Political Economy* 13, no 2 (2008): 168. For Anne Allison, "under this new regime of labor . . . what is productive of and for capitalism is no longer the family or the long-term employment of company workers. Rather, it is the detached, adaptable, and self-responsible individual—a deterritorialized, decentered, de-collectivized subject." *Precarious Japan* (Durham, NC: Duke University Press, 2013), 29–30.

18. Takeda, "Structural Reform," 156.

19. Wendy Brown, *Undoing the Demos: Neoliberalism's Stealth Revolution* (New York: Zone Books, 2015), 31. Emphasis in original.

20. See Allison, *Precarious Japan*, 30–34.

21. *Te*'s title appears in hiragana (て), though it has sometimes been translated as "hand." See, for instance, Nobuko Tanaka's "Dramatist Hideto Iwai connects with his audiences in ways he never could have imagined by being honest about his own life experiences," *Japan Times*, August 15, 2018, https://www.japantimes.co.jp/culture/2018/08/15/stage/dramatist-hideto-iwai-connects-audiences-ways-never-imagined-honest-life-experiences

22. *Te* was staged by hi-bye in 2008 (premiere), 2009, 2013, and 2018. See hi-bye's website for its production history (http://hi-bye.net/past). The performance I reference is of a DVD recording from 2013. Iwai restaged *Te* multiple times since its premiere, serving as the director and appearing as an actor in several productions. In the production I viewed, Iwai played the role of the mother character.

23. He describes his writing process for *Te* in his interview with Performing Arts Network Japan, https://performingarts.jpf.go.jp/E/art_interview/1108/1.html

24. For Iwai's explanation of his early inspirations, see the interview cited in the previous note.

25. Iwai's company's first production *Hikky Cancun Tornado* (2003) is about his experiences as a *hikikomori*, and despite their serious subject matter, many of his works integrate humor, what Iwai has described as "funny traumas." Iwaki Kyōko, "Interview with Iwai Hideto," in *Tokyo Theatre Today: Conversations with Eight Emerging Theatre Artists* (London: Hublet Publishing, 2011), 139.

26. Iwai also discusses how former Seinendan members, including Matsui Shū, were influential to him; see interview cited in note 23.

27. Iwai Hideto, *Te/Fūfu (Te/Husband and Wife)* (Tokyo: Hakuinsha, 2018), 8.

28. Photographs of *Te* were not available to publish. However, much of the action in Jirō's scenes is quotidian, resulting in a staging that is most evocative in its pacing and delivery, which cannot be conveyed through still images alone.

29. In *Gendai kōgo engeki no tame ni*, Hirata discusses what the actor does in terms of existing (*sonzai*)—that he should exist in the world of the play (66).

30. Like Iwai, Matsui has restaged *Jiman no musuko* multiple times with Sample Theater Company. See Sample's website for its production history, http://samplenet.info/play/

31. Matsui Shū, *Jiman no musuko* (*Prideful Son*) (Tokyo: Hakuinsha, 2011), 17.

32. Matsui, *Jiman no musuko*, 19–20.

33. Matsui, *Jiman no musuko*, 68.

34. Matsui, *Jiman no musuko*, 36. The deliveryman adds that this mother and child are "not special," and describes himself as a "channel" that delivers items and words (36).

35. Hirata, *Gendai kōgo engeki no tame ni*, 30–31.

36. Matsui, *Jiman no musuko*, 72.

37. Matsui, *Jiman no musuko*, 77 (stage directions).

38. For instance, Japanese performance studies scholar Uchino Tadashi has described Hirata's work as part of the "politically conservative and artistically innovative" *shizukana engeki* (quiet theater) movement. *Crucible Bodies: Postwar Japanese Performance from Brecht to the New Millennium* (Greenford, UK: Seagull Books, 2008), 54. In contrast, Peter Eckersall, M. Cody Poulton, and I have explored the political potential of Hirata. See, for example, Eckersall's (with Denise Varney, Chris Hudson, and Barbara Hatley) *Theatre and Performance in the Asia-Pacific* (New York: Palgrave Macmillan, 2013); Poulton's "The Rhetoric of the Real"; and my "Reflecting on the Unknowns of History."

Contributors

Jyana S. Browne is assistant professor of premodern Japanese literary and cultural studies at the University of Maryland. Her areas of research include early modern Japanese performance, Japanese puppetry, and the intersections of performance, sexuality, and embodiment. Her writing has appeared in *Puppetry International* and the edited volume *Troubling Traditions: Canonicity, Theatre, and Performance in the US* (Routledge, 2022).

Xing Fan is associate professor in the Centre for Drama, Theatre, and Performance Studies at the University of Toronto. Her research interests include art and politics in the People's Republic of China, practice and aesthetics in Asian performance, historiography, gender and performance, sound studies and theater, and theater pedagogy. She is the author of *Staging Revolution: Artistry and Aesthetics in Model Beijing Opera during the Cultural Revolution* (Hong Kong University Press, 2018).

Rossella Ferrari is University Professor of Chinese Studies at the University of Vienna, Austria, and a specialist in the contemporary performance cultures of the Chinese-speaking world. Her publications include *Pop Goes the Avant-Garde: Experimental Theatre in Contemporary China* (Seagull Books, 2013), *Transnational Chinese Theatres: Intercultural Performance Networks in East Asia* (Palgrave Macmillan, 2020), and *Asian City Crossings: Pathways of Performance Through Hong Kong and Singapore* (co-editor, Routledge, 2021).

Siyuan Liu is professor of theatre at the University of British Columbia and editor of *Asian Theatre Journal*. His recent published books include *Xin Fengxia and the Transformation of China's Ping Opera* (Cambridge University Press, 2022), *Transforming Tradition: The Reform of Chinese Theatre in the 1950s and Early 1960s* (University of Michigan Press, 2021), and *Rethinking Chinese Socialist Theaters of Reform: Performance Practice and Debate in the Mao Era* (co-editor, University of Michigan Press, 2021).

Kee-Yoon Nahm, DFA, is assistant professor in theatre at Illinois State University. He has published articles in *Theater, Performance Research, Situations: Cultural Studies in the Asian Context,* and the *Journal of American Drama and Theatre,* as well as the anthologies *Performing Objects and Theatrical Things* (Palgrave Macmillan, 2014) and *Migration and Stereotypes in Performance and Culture* (Palgrave Macmillan, 2020), among other academic journals and essay collections. He also works professionally as a dramaturg and theater translator in the US and South Korea.

Jessica Nakamura is associate professor in the Department of Theater and Dance at the University of California, Santa Barbara. Her research on contemporary Japanese performance has appeared in journals including *Modern Drama, Journal of Dramatic Theory and Criticism,* and *Performance Research,* and in the monograph *Transgenerational Remembrance: Performance and the Asia-Pacific War in Contemporary Japan* (Northwestern University Press, 2020). Her current research project explores representations of the domestic in twentieth-century Japanese theater from the end of the Asia-Pacific War until the present.

M. Cody Poulton is professor emeritus at the University of Victoria, Canada, and author of numerous studies on and translations of Japanese theater. He is a co-editor of *The Columbia Anthology of Modern Japanese Drama* (Columbia University Press, 2014) and of *Okada Toshiki and Japanese Theatre* (Performance Research Books, 2021), and editor of *Citizens of Tokyo: Six Plays by Oriza Hirata* (Seagull Press, 2019).

Aragorn Quinn is associate professor at the University of Wisconsin–Milwaukee. His work focuses on modern Japanese theater and has appeared in journals including *Asian Theater Journal* and *Proceedings of the Association for Japanese Literary Studies.* His most recent monograph is *Staging the Resistance: Performing the Politics of Translation in Modern Japan* (Routledge, 2020).

Katherine Saltzman-Li is associate professor of premodern Japanese performing arts and literature at the University of California, Santa Barbara. She is the author of *Creating Kabuki Plays* (Brill, 2010), co-editor of

Cultural Imprints: War and Memory in the Samurai Age (Cornell University Press, 2022), and has published numerous articles and chapters on early modern kabuki plays and professional and commercial materials related to kabuki. She is a director of the Japanese Performing Arts Research Consortium, an international group of scholars devoted to the development of online resources on Japanese performing arts.

Guojun Wang is associate professor in the Department of East Asian Studies at McGill University. He specializes in early modern Chinese literature and culture, especially the intersections between writing, performance, materiality, and gender. He is the author of *Staging Personhood: Costuming in Early Qing Drama* (Columbia University Press, 2020) and currently studies the forensic literature of early modern China.

Miseong Woo is professor of theater studies, Asian diaspora, and East Asian cultural studies in the Department of English at Yonsei University. Her book *Representation of Asian Women in the West* (Sam & Parkers, 2014) won the 2014 Korea Research Foundation Achievement Award. She has served as the director of the Institute of East and West Studies and the director of the Institute of Media Arts at Yonsei University.

Min-Hyung Yoo is currently an instructor at Korea University and Jeonbuk National University. His research focuses on *pansori* and Joseon dynasty Korean novels. He teaches in the fields of Korean folklore and oral tradition, and his interests also encompass comparative literature and cross-cultural studies. In 2022, he received his PhD with a dissertation entitled "The Source and the Stature of Shin Jae-hyo's *Jeokbyeokga*."

Soo Ryon Yoon is a performance researcher specializing in racial politics and contemporary performance in Korea. She is the co-editor (with Emily Wilcox) of the special issue of *Inter-Asia Cultural Studies* titled "Inter-Asia in Motion: Dance as Method." Her other writings appear in *positions: asia critique*, *Performance Research*, *GPS: Global Performance Studies*, as well as edited volumes *Corporeal Politics: Dancing East Asia* (University of Michigan Press, 2020), the 58th Venice Biennale Korean Pavilion catalogue, *Cambridge Guide to Mixed Methods Research in Theatre and Performance* (Cambridge University Press, forthcoming 2023), and *Routledge Companion to Feminist Performance* (Routledge, forthcoming). She has taught at Northwestern University, Yale University, Lingnan University, and Ewha Womans University.

Ji Hyon (Kayla) Yuh received her PhD in theatre and performance from CUNY Graduate Center and teaches theater courses in NYC and New Jersey, currently as adjunct professor at Montclair State University. Her research interests focus on the sociopolitical implications of the growth of musical theater in South Korea, especially with regard to the genre's relationship with the development of racial awareness and understanding in Korea. She is a contributing author to the *Routledge Handbook of Asian Theatre* (Routledge, 2016) and the *Palgrave Handbook of Musical Theatre Producers* (Palgrave Macmillan, 2017).

Index

Aristotle, 164, 173, 216

Baudrillard, Jean, 81, 145–46, 156–58, 171
Beijing opera, *see jingju*
Beijing People's Art Theatre (Beijing renmin yishu juyuan; BPAT), 104–7, 109, 233
Berlant, Lauren, 9, 80, 84–85, 87
bunraku, *see* puppet theater

Cha Bumseok, 9, 56–74; *Yeoldaeeo (Tropical Fish)*, 9, 56–74
Chekhov, Anton, 2, 89, 237–38, 240
Chekhov, Michael, 236, 240, 248
chengshi (conventions), 38–42, 46, 50–51, 54n39
Chikamatsu Monzaemon, 29–30, 176–81
Chinese Communist Party (CCP), 101–2, 104, 246
Christianity, 63, 65, 70–72, 221–22, 226
Chūshingura (Kanadehon Chūshingura), 188–91
clothing, *see* costume
commedia dell'arte, 242, 243, 245, 246–47
costume, 12, 153, 194–209; in puppet theater, 184–87, 190–91
The Courtly Mirror of Ashiya Dōman (Ashiya dōman ōuchi kagami), 182–83, 190

COVID-19, 160, 169, 171–73
critique booklets, *see yakusha hyōbanki*
Cultural Revolution, 101–2, 108, 207, 235, 237, 244

Danni, *see* Jin Yunzhi
de Certeau, Michel, 96–97
Destiny (Unmyung), *see* Yun Baek-nam
Don't Be Too Surprised, *see* Park Kun-hyung

eukinetics, 236, 244
l'expression parlée, 247–48

film, 11, 69–73, 102–4, 108, 113, 116, 143–58, 160–66, 220
Frog Experimental Drama Troupe (Wa shiyan jutuan), 105–6

geidan (actors' treatises), 20, 22, 25
gekisho (theater treatises and encyclopedias), 20, 22
gendai kōgo engeki (contemporary colloquial theater), *Gendai kōgo engeki no tame ni (For the Purposes of Contemporary Colloquial Theater)*, *see* Hirata Oriza
Genroku era, 20–32
Geomchalgwan, 58–60, 62
Gidayū, *see* Takemoto Gidayū
Grass Stage (Caotaiban), 111–13, 116

Hirata Oriza 11, 13, 83, 160–73, 252–66, 269n38; *gendai kōgo engeki* (contemporary colloquial theater), 13, 166, 252–66; *Gendai kōgo engeki no tame ni* (*For the Purposes of Contemporary Colloquial Theater*), 254–55, 264, 266, 269n29; Seinendan (the Youth Group), 253, 256–58, 261–62; *Tokyo Notes*, 164–66, 257–59
Hu Shi, 37, 52n6, 104
huadan (type of female role), 46–50
huajixi (farce), 246–47
huaju (spoken drama), 5–6, 12–13, 40, 53n18, 104–5, 107–8, 113–14, 233–48
Huang Jisu, 100–101, 121n2
Huang Zuolin, 12–13, 53n18, 105, 233–48

Ibsen, Henrik, 2, 37–38, 104, 225, 234, 236
Ichikawa Danjūrō: Ichikawa Danjūrō I, 22; Ichikawa Danjūrō II, 22; Ichikawa Danjūrō IX, 30–31, 157
ilsanggeuk, see theater of the everyday
In Praise of Youth, see Park Kunhyung
Ishiguro Hiroshi, 167
Iwai Hideto, 13, 254, 256–61, 265–66; *Te*, 257–61, 265–66
I Want to Be in Your Arms Again (*Geudae gaseume dasi hanbeon*), 69–73
Izumo no Okuni, 20–21, 32

Jang Sung-hee, 80–83
Jeokbyeokga, 6, 10, 126–38
Jiao Juyin, 105, 233, 245–46, 250n27
jidaimono (period pieces), 21, 34n6
jigei (early kabuki acting style), 24–25
jikyōgen (plays requiring *jigei*), 24
Jiman no musuko (*Prideful Son*), see Matsui Shū
Jin Yunzhi (Danni), 236, 238, 241, 243
jingju (Beijing opera), 1, 8–9, 37–51, 194–95, 205, 211n42, 233, 245–46, 248
jishizhuyi ("on-the-spot realism"), 116
jiuju (old theater), 37, 39, 51n3
Jooss, Kurt, 236, 244

juchang (twenty-first-century Chinese theater practice), 108, 113–17, 121
Juilliard, 237–38, 243, 247

kabuki, 8, 19–33, 146–47, 162, 175–78, 187–89
karakuri (puppet mechanisms), 175–76, 180, 190
kata (forms or patterns), 29, 31, 146, 166–67
katsureki mono (late nineteenth-century genre of kabuki plays), 30–31
Kawatake Mokuami, 30–31, 36n44, 36n45
Kim Sa-gyeom, 69–70
Kim Sung-hee, 80–86, 88–91, 96–97
kinodrama, 1, 11, 143–58
Kinogusa Teinosuke, 143, 149–51, 154, 156
kizewamono (late nineteenth-century genre of kabuki plays), 30–31
Kracauer, Siegfried, 11, 161–63

Lao She, 104–5, 106, 108, 109–10
The Laughing Letter, 1, 11, 143–58
Lee Kyung-mi, 81–82
Li Jianjun, 112, 114–20
Li Ning, 112, 115, 117–18
Li Yinan, 112, 114–15
Li Yuru, 44–50
Lin Zhaohua, 105, 107
London Theatre Studio, 233, 236–37, 241–45, 248
Lovebirds Reversal, 200–202

Manchu, 199–200, 202–4, 207–8; Manchu-style clothing, 199–208
Martin, Carol, 3, 111, 163
Matsui Shū, 13, 254, 256–57, 261–66; *Jiman no musuko* (*Prideful Son*), 261–66
Mei Lanfang, 39, 53n18, 205, 206, 235
Meng Jinghui, 100–101, 103–7, 116, 122n3
Method Acting, 166, 237, 239
Mokuami, see Kawatake Mokuami

monomane, 22–24, 34n14; *monomane kyōgen*, 23–24; *monomane kyōgen zukushi*, 23
Moscow Art Theatre, 236–41
Mou Sen, 105–6, 107, 116
Murayama Tomoyoshi, 149, 153–54, 156

New Youth (*Xin qingnian*) magazine, 104, 117
New Youth Group (Xin qingnian jutuan; NYG), 117–21
noh, 20–21, 23, 33n5

Okada Toshiki, 171–73, 252–53, 265–66; *Sangatsu no itsukakan* (*Five Days in March*), 252–53, 266
onnagata (female role specialist), 24, 26–28, 146–47
Osanai Kaoru, 146, 148
Ozu Yasujirō, 164–66, 168

pansori, 6, 10, 126–38, 139n2, 216–17, 230n5; *see also Jeokbyeokga*
Park Kunhyung, 1, 9, 79–97; *Don't Be Too Surprised*, 1, 80, 85, 91–97; *In Praise of Youth*, 80, 85–91
The Pavilion Overlooking the Lake, 197–98
Peach Blossom Fan (*Taohua shan*), 199–200, *201*, 202
photo marriage, *see* picture bride
Picking up a Jade Bracelet, 1, 8–9, 37–51
picture bride, 221–24, 227, 229
powell, john a., 57, 61
puppet theater, 11–12, 20, 175–91; *see also* costume

Qi Rushan, 39–40, 45, 194, 205

realism theater (*sasiljuuigeuk*), 6, 9, 56–74
rensageki, 144, 149, 155–56
Revizor, 58, 59–60
Richie, Donald, 160–61
The Romance of the Three Kingdoms, 6, 10, 126–38

Saint-Denis, Michel, 12–13, 233–48
Sakata Tōjūrō, 25–26, 29, 33, 178
Sangatsu no itsukakan (*Five Days in March*), *see* Okada Toshiki
Sanha Theater Company, 57, 63–64, 66, 67
sasiljuuigeuk, *see* realism theater
Seinendan (the Youth Group), *see* Hirata Oriza
Senda Koreya, 143, 149, 156
sewamono (plays depicting current life), 21, 34n6, 178, 184
Shanghai People's Art Theatre (Shanghai renmin yishu juyuan), 105, 233, 241, 246
shi (prefix meaning current), 195–98, 200–202
shifu (contemporary-style costumes), 195, 196, 200, 202
shingeki (New Theater), 5, 146–48, 162–63, 166, 255
shinpa (New Wave), 6, 12, 217–20
shinpaguk (New Wave Drama), 215, 217–21; *sinpageuk* 58, 74n7
sinpageuk, *see shinpaguk*
Stanislavsky (Stanislavski), Konstantin, 2, 53n18, 104–6, 146, 166–67, 235, 238, 240–41; Stanislavsky System, 233–41, 243–44, 248

tachiyaku (male-role actors), 22, 24, 26, 28
Takeda Izumo I, 176
Takeda Izumo II, 190
Takemoto Gidayū, 176–81
Takemoto Theater, 175–91
talchum (masked dance), 216–17, 230n4
Te, *see* Iwai Hideto
theater of the everyday (*ilsanggeuk*), 6, 9, 79–97
Théâtre du Rêve Expérimental (Xinchuan shiyan jutuan), 108–11
Tiananmen Square, 101–2
Tokyo Notes, *see* Hirata Oriza
Tokyo Performing Arts Meeting (TPAM), 169, 174n20

Tsai Ming-Liang, 169–71
Tsukiji Little Theater, 60, 146, 148

virtual reality, 161, 169–71
Vocaloid, 168, 169

Wang Chong, 108–11
Wang Mengfan, 112, 115,
wenmingxi (civilized drama), 234–35, 245, 246
Western realism, 2–9, 12–13, 32–33, 37–38, 41–42, 50–51, 56–59, 215, 228–29, 239, 255

xianchang (concept of presence), 116–17
Xiao Cuihua, 43–48, 50
xieshi (drawing from nature), 5–6, 39, 41, 104, 234, 238–39, 248
xieyi (writing meaning), 5–6, 39–41, 53n18, 233–39, 241, 244, 248
xiju (late twentieth-century avant-garde theater forms), 113–14, 116

xiqu (traditional Chinese theater), 38–41, 51n3, 53n18, 235, 239, 244; see also *jingju*
xuni (pretense), 38–46, 51

yakusha hyōbanki (actor critique booklets), 20, 22–25, 27
Yeoldaeeo (*Tropical Fish*), see Cha Bumseok
Yoshida Bunzaburō, 176, 182–91
Yoshizawa Ayame, 24, 26–28
Yu Shangyuan, 39, 234
Yun Baek-nam, 12, 215–30; *Destiny* (*Unmyung*), 12, 215, 220–30

zangiri mono (late nineteenth-century genre of kabuki plays), 31
Zeami, 22–23, 25
Zhang Houzai, 38–39, 52n6
Zhang Xian, 107, 116
Zhao Chuan, 111, 116